"I think I've landed in Bedlam."

Alex could hear laughter on the other side of the door. "You're Lord Vikar? No offense, honey, but you look more like a silly Viking than a vampire."

"Silly Viking?" he hissed suddenly and flashed a pair of impressive fangs at her.

"Spare me the hokey act. I've seen more than enough fangs in town today. Lots more authentic than yours, too."

"You are not afraid of me?" He seemed confused.

"Not a bit. You wouldn't believe how many . . . Whoa, what are you doing?"

He'd opened the door with one hand and grabbed her by the upper arm with the other, yanking her inside with him. The door closed loudly behind them.

All around them, strange-looking men and a few women stared at her. They all had pale blue eyes. Almost all of them showed fangs.

She glanced toward Lord Vikar.

He smiled at her through white, straight teeth . . . no fangs in sight now. "Welcome to Hotel Transylvania, my dear. I need to taste you . . ."

SANDRA HILL

KISS OF PRIDE

A DEADLY ANGELS BOOK

AVON

An Imprint of HarperCollins*Publishers*

This is a work of fiction. Names, characters, places, and incidents are products of the author's imagination or are used fictitiously and are not to be construed as real. Any resemblance to actual events, locales, organizations, or persons, living or dead, is entirely coincidental.

AVON BOOKS
An Imprint of HarperCollins*Publishers*
10 East 53rd Street
New York, New York 10022-5299

Copyright © 2012 by Sandra Hill
Excerpt from *Kiss of Surrender* copyright © 2012 by Sandra Hill
ISBN 978-0-06-206461-5
www.avonromance.com

First Avon Books mass market printing: May 2012

Avon Trademark Reg. U.S. Pat. Off. and in Other Countries, Marca Registrada, Hecho en U.S.A.
HarperCollins® is a registered trademark of HarperCollins Publishers.

Printed in the U.S.A.

10 9 8 7 6 5 4 3 2 1

This book is dedicated to my three critique partners who have been with me from the beginning of this book. The hallmark of a good critique group is differing talents, and, boy, do we have those in abundance!

Author Trish Jensen, whose sense of humor and brainstorming ideas add zest to my books. Remind me some time to tell you about the clicker in the bedroom incident.

Trish almost died a few years back, but you can bet she kept her doctors in stitches. However, Trish never met a love scene she didn't hate, and I write hot love scenes.

Cindy Harding, on the other hand, loves a good love scene. The hotter the better. Cindy has the most marvelous, earthy gift for sensory detail; maybe it comes from living on a farm. She's always asking, but how did it smell? How did it taste? How did it feel?

And Eve Homan, who is an editor extraordinaire, when she is not writing her incredible books. Eve thinks she has no voice for humor, but any writer who can create a hero covered with green grust and make him sexy has to have a well-honed funny bone.

Thanks, ladies, for all your help. The combination of all three of you makes my books better.

Abou Ben Adhem

Abou Ben Adhem (may his tribe increase!)
Awoke one night from a deep dream of peace,
And saw, within the moonlight in his room,
Making it rich, and like a lily in bloom,
An Angel writing in a book of gold:

Exceeding peace had made Ben Adhem bold,
And to the Presence in the room he said,
"What writest thou?"
The Vision raised its head,
And with a look made of all sweet accord
Answered, "The names of those who love the Lord."

"And is mine one?" said Abou.
"Nay, not so," replied the Angel.
Abou spoke more low, but cheerily still; and said,
"I pray thee, then,
Write me as one who loves his fellow men."

The Angel wrote, and vanished.
The next night it came again with a great wakening light,
And showed the names whom love of God had blessed,
And, lo! Ben Adhem's name led all the rest!

Leigh Hunt (1784-1859)

KISS OF PRIDE

Prologue

Long ago in the icy North . . .

Out of the barren glaciers and snowcapped mountains, fjords emerged like shimmering snakes, and a god-like race was created.

Tall men with glorious features. Strength to survive the harsh climate. Wicked smiles to lure women to their frigid lairs. Superb lovemaking talents perfected over long winter nights. Brave fighting skills to defend their homeland.

These seafaring warriors came to be called Vikings.

And God was pleased. Some said these Men of the North were like angels on earth (which really annoyed some angels Up There).

For three hundred years they reigned, until God realized how arrogant and bloodthirsty they had become, not to mention their worshipping false gods, like Odin and Thor. Then, one Viking family displeased Him mightily. The Sigurdssons. Not only did Sigurd the Vicious participate in the infamous raid on Lindisfarne, a Saxon monastery, but his seven sons offended God by each committing one of the seven deadly sins in a most heinous manner.

Lust. Gluttony. Greed. Sloth. Wrath. Envy. Pride.

"I am deeply disappointed in the Vikings. I made them proud examples of a favored race." Lightning bolts shot from God's hands, which He raised on high, and the clouds wept.

"Michael!" God called out, and immediately appeared the Archangel Michael, feathers flying as he rushed to His side.

Without words, Michael could see down below to what had so offended his Lord. "Tsk, tsk!" was the best he could come up with.

"Let it be known henceforth that the Viking race, male and female, will fade into extinction. Furthermore, for their wickedness, these seven sinners are condemned to Hell for all eternity. Take care of it for me."

St. Michael, who was the patron of warriors everywhere, decided to intercede on their behalf, despite his having no liking for the full-of-themselves Norsemen. "I agree that these Sigurdsson men have gone too far, but maybe they would change if given a second chance. On the other hand . . ." Already he was wishing he had bitten his angelic tongue.

Still, he reminded God that Sigurd was the seventh son of a seventh son and that Sigurd in turn begat seven sons of his own. Ivak, Trond, Vikar, Harek, Sigurd, Cnut, and Mordr. Seven was a number of import in holy circles, sacred and magical.

"I am touched by your plea, Michael, but this family has to be punished. After all, I banished Adam from the Garden of Eden for a much lesser sin."

Michael bowed his head, waiting for his orders.

After much thought, God proclaimed, "This I say unto you, the Viking race will dwindle off into non-existence, but not by death. No, they will blend into other cultures, losing their identity. Their pride is too great to stand alone. Hereafter, no one will worship Norse gods ever again."

"As you say, Lord." Michael paused before asking, "And the seven Sigurdsson sons?"

"These seven sinners must prove themselves sevenfold. By sins they were judged, by grace they will be saved. For seven hundred years, they must roam the earth doing good works. If they fail, Satan may have them for his unholy domain."

"Shall they be priests, or missionaries?"

"No, that would be too obvious. And too easy."

And then Michael knew.

Satan had recently delegated his comrade-in-rebellion Jasper to unleash on the earth creatures of the most evil nature. Lucipires . . . Lucifer's vampires. These vultures fed on human souls, no longer allowing free will to play itself out. Instead, they swooped in before a sinner had a chance to repent, thus ensuring a hellish eternity. Why couldn't good vampires be created to save those prey to the dark legions before they did their unholy work?

God loved Michael's idea. "You will head this enterprise. Viking vampire angels. Well, not really angels. More like angels-in-training."

The archangel gasped with horror at his mistake. "Oh, not me, Lord. I have to help St. Peter repair the Pearly Gates. And Noah is building another ark. We have no room to put another ark. And those hippos! Phew!"

God frowned.

Michael sank to his knees and nodded his head in assent.

God's frown was a frightful thing, like a lash to the soul. Besides, Michael was the one who had cast Lucifer, the fallen angel now known as Satan, from Heaven. But then God's expression softened. After all, Michael was one of His favorites. "Who better than you to lead these angelic vampire soldiers?" God asked softly.

Angelic? Vampires being angelic? Hah! And Vikings? Really, Vikings being angelic? Hah!

Michael rolled his eyes and wished he had kept his mouth shut.

Thy will be done . . .

Thus was born in the year 850 a band of Viking vampires, a mere two hundred or so years from the time when the Northmen would begin to disappear from the earth. These vampires, known as the VIK, were different from any other vampires because they were made by God.

Some said they were fallen angels . . . the darkest of all God's angels.

Others said they were God's sign of hope for all mankind. Redemption.

The Sigurdsson brothers, who were thereafter

referred to as The Seven, or the VIK, thought they were God's joke on the world.

They were all right.

And then he saw the light . . .

Vikar awoke, as if from a deep sleep. The air was still around him, and he was alone on a vast plain with not a tree or fjord in sight. The skies were dark as pitch.

It felt as if every bone in his body was shattered when he slowly sat up. Glancing downward, he realized that he was naked.

Not even his trusted sword Death Flame was at hand.

With what must be hysterical irrelevance, he noted that Death Flame was a highly prized damascened sword made by the pattern-welded process with two different colored metals twisted and refired over and over until the final blade had a design on it. In his case, flames.

What *was* relevant was that the sword was worth a fortune. He never went anywhere without it.

But wait. There was a light approaching. A light so bright he was blinded for a moment. Then the blaze of light faded to a shimmering glow, especially about the head of the most glorious-looking creature. A man, about his height, but beauteous of features. He wore a long, white, belted robe, but even so Vikar could see he was built like a warrior . . . a warrior with the face of an angel.

That should have been a clue, but betimes Vikar was thickheaded.

"Who are you? Declare yourself," he demanded, though he felt foolish giving orders when he was naked and weaponless.

The man did not answer, but there was a flutter near his back.

Oh my gods! Wings. Massive white wings. Now that he looked closer, he could see that the shimmery light had settled about the man's head like a halo.

It really was an angel.

"I must be dead, then," he murmured, accompanied by a few Norse expletives.

"Not quite," the angel replied, "and if I were you, I would watch thy mouth."

"Chastened by an angel? Ha, ha, ha! Where are my seventy virgin Valkyries to welcome me to Valhalla?"

"I told you, Viking. You are not dead yet. And besides, there will be no virgins where you are headed."

Uh-oh! "Who *are* you?" He deliberately toned down his belligerence. A good soldier knew when to pick his battles.

"St. Michael."

Although he worshipped Viking gods when it suited his purposes, Vikar had been baptized in the Christian church . . . a convenience practiced by many Norsemen traveling to far lands. As a result, he knew a little about the One-God and His followers. "The archangel?"

The angel nodded. "Some call me St. Michael the Archangel."

"Slay any dragons lately?" Vikar quipped.

The angel did not smile. "St. George does all the dragon slaying these days."

"Oops! So what are you slaying? Toads?"

"Best you ponder your fate, Viking, instead of making jests."

No sense of humor. If Vikar could laugh at this horrible situation, why couldn't the angel? But then he had no idea what his situation was. Frowning, he tried to imagine what had happened.

"Think, Viking," Michael said, as if he could read his mind.

Hmm. I better not insult him in my thoughts. "Last I recall, I was in the midst of a *holmganga*. That is a form of duel fought on a cloak. Whoever steps off the garment is considered a coward. Whoever wins such a fight to death gets all of the loser's property, including his women."

Michael made a snorting sound of disgust. "You cared only about Jarl Gaut's comely wife, whom you wanted to add to your many concubines."

Vikar shifted uneasily from hip to hip. In truth, he had realized just before the duel began that Bera was newly wed to Gaut and fancied herself in love, but by then his pride was great. He could not withdraw the challenge. Besides, a little tupping never hurt any woman, even if she was marriage-bound to another.

"Can you hear yourself? Do you honestly dare to justify your actions thus?" Then more softly, Michael added, "You were not always so black-hearted."

Suddenly, into Vikar's mind came an image of his first wife, Vendela. It was their wedding ceremony. She had been fifteen to his seventeen. Sixteen years back, it had been. And what a joyous occasion! He a smitten, newly blooded warrior, and she with adoration in her clear blue, virginal eyes as they stood under the bridal canopy.

"Your heart was pure then, Viking." With a wave of the angel's hand, a new image came into Vikar's mind. Vendela again, but now she was twenty-five, as he'd seen her last. With eyes closed, her face and body lay battered on the rocks below Lodi's Leap, the salt cliff.

Horror filled him, even now after five years. "Why would she take her own life?"

"Can you possibly be that thickheaded? You put Vendela aside for your viperous new wife, Princess Halldora."

The daughter of King Ormsson from Norsemandy was indeed aspish on occasion, but seductive beyond compare. She had insisted that no other wives be in his keep afore speaking her vows, and he had been obsessed with her at the time. Even so . . . "I would have given Vendela her own steading at the far reaches of my estate. There was no shame in that," he defended himself. "She should have seen the esteem such an alliance would give my name."

"Thoughtless man!" the angel said with a shake of his head.

Tears burned his eyes and almost overflowed. He could not remember the last time he had wept, if ever. *Oh, Vendela! I am so sorry.* But immediately he shook such weak thoughts away.

The angel waved his hand again, and a new mind picture came to Vikar.

His grand home at Wolfstead. A palace, many said with awe. No wood fortress had been good enough for him. No, with the wealth amassed from his amber trading, along with a-Viking for plunder, he'd insisted on a stone edifice, three floors high, with tapestries and finely carved furniture from far lands. All a monument to his success.

"A monument to your vanity," Michael scoffed.

The picture in his mind changed. The stone castle dripped with blood, and he saw clearly the ten men who had died in the two years it had taken to build the structure.

He sensed where this was going. The angel meant to guilt him. "They were mere thralls. Slaves' lives do not matter."

"Can you hear yourself, Viking?" Michael repeated, gazing at him with sadness. "I do not know what I was thinking when I pleaded your case. You are a lost cause."

"I am not," he argued, though for what he was not sure.

As if by magic, that Wolfstead vision was replaced with his most recent memory. Was it only this morn? A blood-soaked cloak and a screaming female voice just before the heavens opened with raging thunder and lightning as he'd never witnessed before.

Had he offended Thor, god of thunder? He glanced up at the frowning angel.

"There is only one God," the angel roared.

He flinched, but then he straightened. If death was his fate, he would face it boldly.

"I went to God, fool that I am, asking that He give you another chance," the angel told him.

Vikar brightened. Not death, then? "What would you . . . He have me do?"

"For your sins . . . and they are grievous . . . you will do penance sevenfold. For seven hundred years, you will do my bidding against the armies of Jasper."

"Jasper? Never heard of him. Is he a Saxon?"

Ignoring his question, the angel went on, "I will be the *hersir* of your soul."

The chieftain of my soul? Pfff! "Seven hundred years!" he exclaimed with outrage, but then an idea came to him of a sudden. "I would live for seven hundred years?"

"Sort of."

That sounded like a trap to Vikar. "And the alternative would be . . . ?"

"The fires of Hell for all eternity."

Well, that was certainly blunt. And he did so hate the thought of burning flesh, especially his own. "I agree," he said without hesitation, especially when a brief image flicked in his brain of a fiery pit with screaming creatures that must once have been humans.

The angel almost smiled. It was not a nice almost-smile. "Do you not want to know in what capacity you shall serve?"

Vikar waved a hand blithely. Seven hundred years was a very long time, but eternity in that fiery pit was unimaginable. "It matters not." He assumed he would be a warrior in some land of the angel's choosing. Perchance even a warrior angel.

"So be it!" Michael raised both hands on high, causing his wings to flutter and feathers to fly on a sudden breeze.

Then the most ungodly pain hit Vikar's face. It felt as if his jaw was breaking and all his teeth were being yanked out, one at a time. And on his back, a sharp object appeared to be hacking at his shoulder blades. When it was over, he found himself lying on the ground, felled with agony. As he rose to his knees, he glanced up at the angel with a mixture of anger and inquiry, but the angel said nothing.

Vikar reached over his shoulders where he discovered raised bumps, like healed scars, over his shoulder blades. His mouth felt odd, too, and was filled with the not unpleasant taste of blood. He ran his tongue under his teeth, which were . . . "Oh no! It cannot be so." He put fingertips to his teeth, which were uncommonly even and white . . . leastways, they had been in the past. Now two of the incisors on either side of his front teeth seemed to have elongated and grown pointy.

The angel had turned and was about to fly off.

With all these questions hanging in the air? "Wait! Fangs? You gave me fangs? Like a wolf?"

"No. Not a wolf." The angel did smile then . . . with glee. "A vampire."

On those ominous words, the angel disappeared.

And all Vikar could think was, *What is a vampire?*

Too soon, he found out.

Club Med for the undead . . .

In a cold, cold, miles-long cave known as Horror, far below the surface of the earth, Jasper paced. It was not Hell, of course, but that place where Lucipires brought their victims before eventually sending them off to Satan's fiery pits, or to become vampire demons in Jasper's personal army.

"It is too much!" he railed at his assistant Sabeam, who raced to keep up with him. Being a mung demon, a species of full demon, unlike former Seraphim angels like Jasper or even prestigious haakai demons, Sabeam had limited status and authority, even with his massive seven-foot height. Then, too, there was the slimy, poisonous mung that covered every surface of its body.

"What shall we do, master?" Sabeam asked, puffing for breath.

The boy, who was only three hundred years old, didn't get enough exercise these days. Maybe Jasper should order him a treadmill.

"Satan demands his due," Sabeam told Jasper, as if he didn't already know that. "We must send the souls to him as prescribed by demon law."

Unlike most mungs, Sabeam was not mute. Sometimes Jasper wished he were.

Still, Jasper nodded, knowing that he had no choice but to give up his collection soon. The last time had been two hundred years ago. This latest delivery was long overdue. "Grieves me, it does, to release my 'babies,' only to start all over. It will take us twice . . . no, thrice as long . . . to replenish the supply, what with the vangels hindering our efforts." Vangels were vampire angels that Michael the Archangel had created specifically to fight Jasper's legions.

He could not think at the moment of Michael, who had once been his friend. If he did, he would fall into the pit of despair that had held him the first hundred years of his exile.

Instead, Jasper gazed fondly around him at the life-size killing jars that held the newly dead human souls who fought wildly against the glass sides, to no avail. Once subdued, they were placed on display slabs with a two-foot pin through the heart holding them down. Like butterflies, they were, especially when they flailed their arms and legs in a wing fashion. Undead human butterflies that fought their confinement, eyes wide with horror at their fate. Jasper's own personal human butterfly collection. Playthings, really, that he liked to take out from time to time and torture. Thousands of them.

Most special of all was one of the few vampire angels they'd been able to capture, and that only a lowly ceorl, David, who was stretched out on the rack at the moment whilst imps and hordlings, Jasper's foot soldiers of grotesque appearance characterized by oozing pustules, danced about the body, piercing the skin with white-hot spears, wrapping barbed wire around the always erect phallus, jamming odious objects up the anus, stuffing imp offal in the mouth. "Good work, Fiendal," he said, patting one of the hordlings on the head as he passed. "Do not go too far, though, lest the vangel get accustomed to the pain."

Fiendal nodded, his excessively long tongue lolling out with dripping drool.

Jasper continued his pacing, trying to think. As he walked, fury turned his face into icy shards that flaked off like scales. His eyes glowed bloodred, his fangs hung down almost to his chin, and his tail dragged behind him on the stone floor. He hated that his once-renowned beauty could be turned into this travesty of ugliness. Oh, he could transform himself into the most beauteous of humans, male or female, when prowling the earth. But this monstrous carcass was his true self now. And he blamed Michael for this most odious fate.

Long ago, before the world was created, he had been one of the chosen archangels until he'd been expelled from Heaven, along with Lucifer and all the rest of his rebellious followers. And it had been Michael, a fellow archangel, who had been the one to kick their unholy butts out of the celestial presence of God. Forevermore.

Now Michael was after him again.

For centuries Jasper had been sending out his special creations, demon vampires, to the earth to bring in more doomed human souls in a faster, more efficient fashion than just waiting—*ho-hum*— for bad people to die. Horror was just a way station on the journey to Hell, but it was Jasper's own special playground, and now Michael threatened to take even that away from him by creating vampire angels to fight him. At the same time, Satan was demanding his due.

"We cannot continue at our present pace, one soul at a time. We must needs speed up the process. Bring in hundreds, no, thousands of doomed souls at one time."

"Like 9/11?"

"Holy Hades, no! God sent legions of His angels to Manhattan afore we could even arrive. Instead of Satan or I or any of the Lucipires being able to grab them, angels led them right and left to that holy place of which we do not speak. There were so many feathers flying about that day, it was a wonder the news media did not notice."

"Smoke," Sabeam remarked.

"Huh?"

"The feathers were hidden by the smoke," Sabeam said.

I was kidding. Can a demon not even tease anymore? I am surrounded by idiots.

"So, there is no event where you could harvest souls in large numbers?" Sabeam concluded.

"I did not say that." Jasper thought for a long moment as he continued to pace. Then he stopped abruptly. "I have the perfect idea. Did Satan not invent the Internet to blacken the souls of mankind?"

"I thought Al Gore invented the Internet."

Jasper rolled his burning eyes. *Can anyone spell idiot?* "It matters not who invented what, but how Satan uses human obsessions for his own ends."

"Okay," Sabeam said, though he clearly did not understand. No matter!

"We will prowl the Internet superhighway 'til we find the perfect venue for mass harvest of sinners all in one place at one time." Jasper would have licked his lips with anticipation if his frickin' fangs were not in the way.

One

There's Transylvania, and then there's
TRANSYLVANIA...

Vikar Sigurdsson hadn't had sex in a hundred years, and he was not in the greatest of moods. The last time had resulted in two hundred years being added to his penance, and it hadn't even been good sex.

Add to that hated celibacy the fact that he was on Seven Mountains in podunk Transylvania, Pennsylvania. He was presumably trying to turn a hundred-and-twenty-year-old crumbling castle, built by an obviously demented lumber baron Joseph Waxmonsky, into a five-star hotel. Hotel Transylvania. *Presumably* being the key word. And oh, by the way, in his spare time he was expected to fight off Satan's vampires.

Then the doorbell rang, loud enough to be heard in every corner of this seventy-five-room monstrosity. That's all he needed . . . company. That, in addition to the twenty-seven various annoying, troublesome, needy members of his personal troop of vangels. Who ever heard of a needy Viking?

In the middle of the ringing, he yelled out, "Go away!" as if anyone could hear him about two dozen rooms away from the kitchen, which he had been contemplating for the past half hour. It needed a major cleaning now that new appliances had been delivered and the floor retiled. *Where should I start?* he wondered, staring with dismay at the mess that surrounded him. Enough dirty dishes and pots and pans to feed a Viking army—*who knew twenty-eight people could eat so much?* Greasy countertops—*no one ever mentioned cutting boards to him afore.* Groceries to be ordered—*his list was now two feet long, and growing.* He sighed. *I can kill a dozen Saxons in the blink of an eye. I can guide a longship across the ocean. But command a kitchen? It's demeaning, that's what it is.* Immediately, he chastised himself. Pride was e'er his downfall.

Gong! Gong! Gong! Gong! Gong! Gong! Gong!

The fact that it was seven rings told him loud and clear that it was not one of the cuckoo bird wannabe vampires from the village, or one of the Lucipires, who would hardly knock, but one of the vangels, God's vampires. Another brand of cuckoo bird, for the love of . . . well, God. Yep, almost immediately his brother Trond materialized before him.

"Your doorbell is loud enough to wake the dead," Trond remarked.

"Good thing we're dead."

They looked at each other, burst out laughing, then drew each other into a bear hug worthy of six-foot-four Vikings.

"You're early," Vikar said when they drew apart. "The Reckoning isn't for another month." The Reckoning was the centennial meeting of all the vangels. Hundreds of them would be in attendance, in addition to The Seven, or the VIK, the designation given to him and his six brothers.

The high mucky-muck at the Reckoning would, of course, be their heavenly mentor, St. Michael the Archangel, whom they rudely referred to as Mike.

Mike just called them Viking, each and every one of them, and he did not say it like a compliment. Usually, it was something like, "Viking, God is not pleased."

Uh, I'm kinda aware of that fact since I've been sporting these fangs for more than a thousand years.

Or "Viking, I saw what you did on that yacht."

That wasn't me. I swear, it was Mordr.

Or "Viking, you are not here for a vacation."

No shit!

And, by the runes, was Mike hard to please! At the last Reckoning in 1912 Vikar had another four hundred years smacked on to his "penance" for a few teeny tiny sins, including the bad sex. The angel jury of one had obviously not been of the same opinion on the "teeny tiny" evaluation.

His brother Harek, once a highly skilled battle strategist, now a computer geek, of all things, was teaching Mike how to organize a software spreadsheet for every blasted member of vangeldom. Mike was inputting every single sin or grace each of them had committed. It was enough to give a Viking warrior hives. When Harek asked Vikar if he wanted to learn how to set up his own computer chart, Vikar told him what he could do with his mouse. Vikar did make use of Harek's talents in ordering supplies for the castle, and clothing for all the vangels. It wasn't that they couldn't shop in stores themselves, but the less notice they garnered, the better.

Mike might bring Gabe and Rafe with him this time. He hoped so; those two tended to act as a counterbalance to Mike's testiness. That would be Gabriel and Raphael, in angel circles.

"You better feed," he advised Trond now. "Your skin is getting transparent, almost like Saran wrap. I can see your veins."

Back in the old days, like the Roman empire where Trond had spent the past twenty years, there were no SPF 1000 sunscreens or tanning products. Contrary to popular opinion, vampires could go out in sunlight, providing they'd blood-fed properly, except that their skin got whiter and whiter, eventually translucent, broadcasting to one and all, *Hey, look at me. I'm a vampire. Wanna get sucked?*

On the other hand, demon vampire skin got red when overexposed to the sun. Really, really red.

Trond walked over to the commercial-size fridge and took out three pint bottles of Fake-O, invented by their very own ceorl chemist, who worked with his brother Sigurd, a physician. Not as good as real blood, but it would do in a bind. Trond's fangs slid out, and he punctured the thin plastic lids. He bowed his head and said grace in a low murmur. When he'd sucked the pints dry and wiped the back of his hand over his mouth, his skin tone was already changing. Not the good, healthy color obtained by drinking real blood, but satisfactory.

With a soft belch, he said, "I thought you might need some help. That's why I came early."

"Hmpfh! I hope you brought an army."

"I did. Well, about fifty karls and ceorls. Half of them will be here this evening." Like ancient Viking society, the VIK was organized below The Seven into jarls, comparable to earls; karls, high but not necessarily of noble standing; ceorls, who were apprentices; and thralls, or slaves. "Where are yours, by the way?"

"Hiding."

"Hiding?" Trond folded his arms over his massive chest and leaned back against the stone wall.

"I have twenty-seven karls and ceorls here already. I might have snarled at them one or two or a hundred times. Rollo is afraid of bats, and, whooboy, do we have a *hird* of them here. Any idea what I should do with a truckload of guano? That's bat shit, in case you didn't know."

"I know what guano is. Just because I'm lazy does not make me a halfbrain."

That was debatable, in Vikar's opinion. Trond really was lazy—big-time, as modern folks would say. He had been condemned for sloth, which was one of the seven deadly sins. Vikar's biggest sin had, of course, been pride.

Vikar continued his tirade. "Thrain fell off a shaky balcony." Everyone knew that Thrain had to be the clumsiest Viking, or vampire angel, who ever lived . . . or died.

"Good thing he has a hard head."

"Tell me about it. Then there is Armod, the teenage ceorl from Iceland. He keeps scaring the clerk at

Uni-Mart, deliberately. The youthling is fascinated with his new set of fangs and hasn't got past the lisping stage yet."

"A lisping rock star?" Trond laughed. "I heard about him. The kid is only sixteen years old, right?"

"In years, yes, but considering how many people he killed before being saved, well, he's an old fellow. And now Armod fashions himself the new Michael Jackson. You ever seen a vampire moonwalk? Not a pretty sight. I had to buy him an iPod because he kept blasting out 'Thriller' on that music box he carries everywhere."

"Jacksson? Hmm . . . that is a fine Viking name."

Vikar rolled his eyes. "Trond! Michael Jackson was a pop music star. He was as far from a Norseman in appearance as a cat from a tiger."

Trond's chest shook with suppressed mirth. Then he punched Vikar in the arm. "I know who Michael Jackson was, lackwit."

He shook his head at Trond's mirth making, oddly touched at this simple expression of closeness betwixt them. It was lonely living for all these years, isolated from the rest of society . . . living but not really living. At least they had each other.

He coughed to get his emotions under control. Time to change the subject. "And then Hoder is making pets of the rats in the dungeon. Yes, this place has a friggin' dungeon. I'm thinking about locking myself in there for a decade or two." He tried to continue frowning, but it was hard when Trond was laughing his arse off.

"Where were you assigned before this?" Trond asked him.

"Sodom and Gomorrah." Vikar grimaced. Enough said! At least Vikar hadn't been turned into a salt shaker. "I thought you were in Rome playing Spartacus with a bunch of lions."

"I was, but Mike said I was killing too many lions. Too conspicuous. Besides, lion blood tastes like curdled piss."

"You get all the good assignments, and you get to dress cool," Vikar teased. Actually, Trond got jobs that required work, lots of demanding exercise that forced him off his lazy arse. "Lion fighting, that's what I'd like to do," Vikar said. *What is it with my teasing? Have I suddenly developed a sense of humor after all these centuries? Or more likely my brain is melting. Sucking blood does that to a man, I warrant.*

Trond did in fact look like a gladiator in his thigh-length, pleated leather tunic, with a wide leather belt, and cross-gartered sandals, exposing his big feet and bare, hairy legs. He might be lazy, but he was one good-looking lazy man.

"Wait 'til you hear what my next assignment is. I'm gonna be a SEAL," Trond revealed.

"Holy crap! Mike's gonna turn you into an animal? That's a first for us VIK. My luck he'll turn me into a maggot."

"Not an animal, lackwit. A Navy SEAL."

"That's just great. If I asked to be in the military, he'd probably plop me into the middle of Genghis Khan's army with no weapon except for my teeth."

Trond smiled.

Vikar wondered if Trond realized how much hard work was involved in SEAL training. Well, he would find out soon enough.

"Actually, I've got some news for you," Vikar said. "We're no longer going to be traveling through time on our assignments. We're going to stay in this time period. While we'll still work around the world, the headquarters is going to be here. Our heavenly bosses believe this modern world is as sinful and depraved as Sodom and Gomorrah ever were. So we'll concentrate all our efforts in the twenty-first century."

"My SEAL assignment makes sense then." Trond tapped his closed lips with a forefinger thoughtfully, then asked, "How do you know all this?"

"Mike told me. Called me in for a special one-on-one last month." He sighed deeply. "He's given me until the Reckoning to have this pile of rocks at least minimally suitable to house all the resident and visiting vangels."

Trond snorted his opinion. "For two hundred and sixty-seven VIK members? That was the number last count I heard."

Vikar nodded.

"Is that even possible in four weeks?"

"It will have to be. You know the alternative."

Trond cringed. "What did you do to piss Mike off?"

"I mocked his molting wings."

"Oh, I remember now. Anyhow, you wouldn't have wanted to be a gladiator. Lions stink, in case you didn't know. Speaking of stink, what is that smell? Have you been eating hard-boiled eggs again?"

Vikar flashed Trond a dirty look. 'Twould seem his brother's brain must be melting, too. Either that or he was changing the subject to make him feel better.

Fat chance! "Very funny! You know damn well what that smell is. Lucies." Long ago, the vangels had invented that nickname for Lucipires. "I killed one of Satan's pals who snuck in here last night."

"And it still reeks?"

"Molly Maids were supposed to start working here today. Yeah, I know we're supposed to avoid outside help, but . . ." He shrugged. "Anyhow, the two ladies who showed up took one look at my bloody broadsword over there on the counter and the pile of slime left behind on the floor and took off faster than a Saxon with an arrow in his arse."

Any time one of Satan's vampires was killed by the vangels, either with a bullet containing a tiny shard of wood representing slivers of the True Cross or metal weapons "quenched" or hardened in the symbolic blood of Christ, they melted into a puddle of smelly, sulfurous slime. Holy water was a great deterrent, too, but it only burned their skin off, didn't kill them. And you did not want to see a skinless Lucipire. Eew!

"Aren't you worried about them going to the police?"

"No. I told them we have a theatrical group rehearsing one of those mystery weekend skits for when the hotel opens."

"And what happens when the hotel never opens?"

He shrugged. "By then, I hope they'll have forgotten, or chalk it up to eccentric pretend-vampires up at the castle."

"Still. Lucies in our private domain is nothing to disregard." Trond drew his broadsword out of its scabbard and began prowling about the huge kitchen, sniffing at the windows and doorways. The presence of Lucipires in the area was serious business.

"It's safe for now. This castle is a mess, but I've armed all the karls and ceorls. Even the thralls. We've secured the castle itself. As soon as Cnut arrives, we'll have high-tech equipment out the yin-yang. Not only in and around the structure, but within a mile perimeter, all the way around. There are a hundred acres with the property to be patrolled." His brother Cnut was a highly skilled security expert, when he was not being a soldier in William the Conqueror's army or a Regency gentleman. He and his team of ceorls would get the job done within one day, at least for the immediate vicinity.

"Nice hair, by the by," Trond remarked. "You better cut it before the Reckoning, though."

Vikar did have good hair. Really good hair. Shoulder-length. Blond. Like silk, thanks to modern hair products. A source of pride that would be frowned upon by Mike.

"How about a tour of this dump?" Trond looped an arm over his shoulders. As they began to walk through the rooms where karls and ceorls were busy carrying out old furniture, carpets, and bath fixtures to a commercial Dumpster parked out back, Trond asked, "By the way, Vikar, how many years do you have left?"

Hard to believe but their seven hundred years had been up more than five hundred years ago, but, being Vikings, none of them had been able to maintain a saintly life. As a result, years kept being added. At this rate, they would be vampires until the Apocalypse, and that wasn't coming any century soon.

"Two hundred and seven, last count," Vikar replied. "You?"

"One seventy-eight, but I've been bad this year. I expect the tally to go up. Big-time."

Vikar glanced at his brother with curiosity, but he didn't ask, not wanting to be intrusive. But then he had to make at least one inquiry. "Sex?"

"Near-sex."

Do not ask. It is a trap. But curiosity got the better of him. "What in blue blazes is near-sex?"

"Blue blazes?" Trond homed in on that one phrase, and laughed.

That did sound silly. "I'm trying not to swear so much."

Trond laughed some more. Expletives—using God's name in vain—were a problem they all fought. Hard to believe, but a good "What the fuck!" was not nearly so bad on the sin scale.

"Near-sex?" he repeated.

Trond explained, in detail.

Holy lutefisk! "And we're permitted to do *that*?"

"I'll soon find out."

"Let me know, for fang's sake! There may be hope for me yet."

You want to send me *where*? . . .

Alexandra Kelly walked into the office of her boss at the national D.C. headquarters of *World Gazette* magazine, braced for yet another argument.

"I have a new assignment for you," Ben Claussen, managing editor, said right off.

"Let me guess. It's one that will take me out of the city, right?"

"Damn straight it will." Ben's ruddy face grew ruddier. With his balding head and pudgy build, he looked like a fortysomething version of Ed Asner from that old *Mary Tyler Moore Show.* "You *are* going to take the assignment."

"I just can't—" she started to protest.

"Alex, you've wallowed long enough. No, no," he said, raising a halting hand, "listen for a change. You're a good reporter . . . one of the best feature writers I have . . . and it's time you get back in the game. Enough with this extended 'vacation' of yours. I know you want to be around when the trial starts, but that's not for another six weeks. You'll be back by then."

Alex's husband, Brian, a DEA lawyer, and her five-year-old daughter, Linda, had been kidnapped and killed by a Mexican drug cartel two years ago. And, yes, she had been wallowing ever since then in alternating bouts of fury and self-pity, which she felt she was entitled to. Two of the cartel members, the Mercado brothers, had been caught and were to go on trial shortly, if they didn't get off on technicalities, which might very well happen, according to her informants.

"You're going in some dark directions, Alex, and it has to stop."

"What do you mean?" Alex thought she'd been hiding her secret plans very well.

"Do you think I'm unaware that you've been

taking target lessons over at that Bethesda shooting range?"

She could feel her face bloom with color. "Everyone's entitled to protection in this country."

"As long as that's all it is."

"What? You think I'm going to kill myself or something," she teased.

Ben's doleful expression said that's exactly what he feared. She breathed a sigh of relief. "I did not buy a pistol for suicide purposes, Ben. All that mess."

He did not laugh. "I mean it, Alex. You want to keep your job, you have to get back in the game."

Alex didn't need the money, but she did need the work. Otherwise, she really would go insane. "Maybe you're right."

"I *am* right. Dammit, you were nominated for a Pulitzer five years ago for that piece you did on Bin Laden's daughter. You can't rest on your laurels forever, honey."

With any other employer, Alex would be bristling at what had come to be called a sexual harassment term in the workplace, but this was Ben, her best friend, a father figure, her daughter's godfather.

"Laurels be damned," she said. "Okay, what's the assignment? Where do you want to send me?"

"Transylvania."

"*What?* You're crazy if you think I'll go to Romania. That Count Dracula story has been done to death."

"Not Transylvania, Romania. Transylvania, Pennsylvania."

She looked at him and burst out laughing.

He shoved a folder across the desk, which she quickly flicked through.

"A vampire town?"

"A town full of wannabe vampires. *Twilight* fever to the max! The whole place goes to unbelievable extremes to promote itself as a vampire haven. And there's some dude who recently bought the town castle. He's allegedly a real-life vampire. Royalty, no less. Lord Vikar."

"Give me a break!"

He shrugged. "In any case, go and check it out. I've always said you could find a story in a load of sand. I've set up an appointment with this Lord Vikar. At the very least, you should come back with a color feature."

"Hmm," she said, still skimming through the material. "I went to a writers' conference years ago where Anne Rice was a speaker. This was in the days she was still writing vampire novels. Anyhow, she had this entourage with her, a bunch of crazies dressed up like vampires, right down to the actual filing of teeth into fangs. Sounds like the same thing here."

"Except on a much larger scale. Did you see in that one article"—he pointed to the open folder—"how they turned this depressed community around with dozens of thriving businesses related to vampires? They even changed the name of the town to Transylvania, which was no mean feat with all the legal mumbo jumbo that must have entailed."

"Sounds ridiculous, but I'll do it if it'll get you off my back. A few days should be sufficient." She smiled as she spoke, then tried for a lighter note. "Aren't you worried about the danger, sending me into a nest of Draculas?"

"Hah! Anyone who would tweak Bin Laden's tail

should have no fear of a few vampire groupies. Besides, you might just hit it off with this Lord Vikar."

The last few months Ben and his wife, Gloria, had tried to fix her up with dates, which she'd declined. But this was ludicrous.

"You want me to make a love connection with a vampire?"

"Stranger things have happened."

Little did she know then how prophetic that statement was to be.

Two

**One flew over the cuckoo's . . .
uh, vampire's nest . . .**

Midway between Penn State University and Harrisburg lies a sleepy small town that can only be described as *Twilight* meets Bram Stoker's *Dracula*, with a little Monty Python satire tossed in for special effect. Transylvania, Pennsylvania, is not for the faint of heart . . .

Alex had been in Transylvania only one day, and already she was amazed. In fact, incredulous.

First of all, because the town was swamped with tourists at this time in July, the only hotel accommodation she'd been able to find was at Bed & Blood, a bed-and-breakfast two miles out of Transylvania. She shouldn't be surprised at the B&B's vampire connection. As soon as she'd entered the valley this morning, she was jolted by a bulletin board in front of St. Vladimir Catholic Church that read: "Vampires Welcome."

The woman who rented her the room was warm in her welcome to the pristine farm, with its fields of lush green, knee-high corn and neat vegetable and flower gardens.

"Welcome, welcome," Sarah Yoder greeted her in a heavy Pennsylvania Dutch accent at the front door of the black-shuttered white farmhouse. Sarah then proceeded to talk a mile a minute, most of the time not even waiting for a response.

The woman, who had to be in her late thirties, and her husband, Samuel, had apparently been Old Order Amish at one time. The journalist in Alex recognized that there was probably a story there, but not one she would probe. Although they had left that community years ago, Sarah still dressed "plain." Her gray-streaked blonde hair was parted down the middle and raked back off her face into a bun and tucked under a white mesh cap. The loose ties of the cap dangled onto a long blue cape dress with a black apron.

"This is the south bedroom," Sarah said after leading her upstairs, where there were three other guest rooms, all occupied. And one shared bathroom! "Wonderful good sunshine you get in this room, but you daresent open the windows. Ach, but the smells from the pigsty!"

The room was almost austere, with white walls and no pictures, but there was a pretty blue and white quilt on the iron bed, which Sarah explained was a Double Wedding Ring pattern and that it had been made by Grossmanni Yoder, her grandmother-in-law, for her wedding twenty years ago. Alex considered buying an Amish quilt while she was in this area. She could use it for her summer cottage at Barnegat, not that she'd been there in the past two years. In fact, she'd been considering selling it.

An antique Bible sat on the dresser along with a pile of brochures highlighting all the tourist attractions around Transylvania. Not just the vampire stuff, but the giant flea market at the Amish sale barn in Belleville every Wednesday morning, fishing in Colyer Lake, estate auctions every weekend in the area, the Arts Festival in State College, even Penn State football. And guided tours around the Amish communities, though visitors were warned not to take photographs or annoy the plain people, who cherished their privacy.

Alex set the brochures down and sniffed. Yes, she could smell pig poop, even with the windows closed. She was about to say that the odor didn't matter, that she would be here for only a day or two, and that she had grown up on a horse farm in Virginia, but Sarah was already off on another tangent.

"Did you have lunch yet? I got a pot of chicken 'n' dumplings on the stove and shoofly pie just out of the oven."

"That sounds wonderful, but I've already eaten."

"Well, we eat dinner here about six, if you're interested. We're having ham, mashed potatoes, green beans, creamed cucumbers, pickled beets, coleslaw, sliced tomatoes, biscuits, and peach cobbler."

Good Lord!

"Oh, and I have some leftover rhubarb pie, too. Plus, I always got whoopie pies. Wonderful *gut*, they are!"

And super sweet. From what I've heard, about a thousand calories each.

"Englishers love to take some of my whoopie pies home with them."

Englishers? It would seem you could take the woman away from the Amish, but you couldn't take the Amish out of the woman. Not totally, anyhow.

"So, you're a writer, are you? I write. Letters. Lotsa letters to all my cousins, and then there's the chain letters. Do you ever write letters? What a *dummkopp* I am! Of course you don't write letters. You write important things. That's your work."

"Well, I don't know about—"

"Oh, look, here comes my Samuel." A sweet look came over Sarah's face as she glanced out the window.

A familiar pain clenched Alex's heart. She recognized Sarah's look. It was how she used to look at her husband. All he would have to do is walk into a room, and she would light up.

In the early days, anyhow. Not later. Definitely not later. She visibly shook her head to rid herself of the memories.

"Your husband?" Alex asked.

"*Jah*, and a good husband is he, too. A hard worker. Me, I just sell my eggs and stinking roses . . . that's what we call garlic . . . at my vegetable stand out at the end of the lane. Some of my heads of garlic are big as baseballs. Restaurants in town buy them to roast for their customers, and, of course, others buy them to ward off the vampires." Sarah grinned unabashedly at that last comment.

"Do you mind if I ask how you're able to reconcile

being Amish, or former Amish, with all this vampire stuff?"

Sarah tidied the bed, even though it looked perfect to Alex. "It's all in fun, you know. As long as nobody gets hurt, or nobody really believes all the nonsense, me and Samuel decided it would be all right for us. No worse than scarecrows and spooks at Halloween."

That was a stretch, but Alex wasn't about to argue the point. "Do you have children?"

A profound sadness came over Sarah's plain features, and Alex wished she could take the question back. "I'm sorry. That's none of my business."

Sarah waved a hand dismissively. "I lost four children. Three of them were miscarriages, and one . . . a baby girl"—Sarah's voice choked up—"she died after two weeks."

"I am so sorry."

"Sad it was, but it was a long time ago." Dabbing at her eyes with a pristine white handkerchief, Sarah asked, "Do you have little ones of your own?"

Alex shook her head. "I had a little girl but she died."

Before Alex could back away, her usual reaction when people got all sympathetic on her, Sarah took both of her hands in hers and squeezed. "For sure and for certain, losing a child is the worst thing in the world. I can only think God has a special place in Heaven for us mothers left behind."

Alex had strong feelings to the contrary, but Sarah would not appreciate her jaded opinion. "Does your husband help you run the B&B?"

"Goodness' sakes, no! Samuel works all day on

the farm, and then he stays up nights in his workshop making specially carved caskets."

"Caskets?" she squeaked out.

Sarah nodded with an impish grin. "He sells them to that fancy Englisher funeral home down the highway. And on his Internet website, Deluxe Death."

Alex grinned. An Amishman . . . or rather, former Amishman on the Internet! Actually, that might not be as much of a stretch as she'd once thought. Yesterday she'd noticed a group of Amish men in a rented van; they might not believe in owning cars, but they had nothing against riding in them. The irony was, each had a cell phone to his ear.

The next day, as she killed time before her appointment with Lord Vikar, Alex strolled through the small, picturesque community near Colyer Lake, doing constant double takes. She rubbed every so often at her neck. Having failed to heed Sarah's warning about not opening the window last night, she was now suffering from the world's worst mosquito bite.

And oddly, Alex found herself fixating on the upcoming trial of the Mercado brothers and what she'd like to do if they somehow managed to get out. She'd never had a Suzy Sunshine personality before, but there was so much hate bubbling up in her now that it felt as if she was being eaten alive.

Ah, well, she had an assignment to complete. Maybe that would take her mind off all these dark thoughts. She continued walking and noticed right away that Sarah wasn't the only one profiting from garlic. The whole town reeked of it, the smelly cloves being a necessary item in every home garden. At the same time, dentists advertised filing teeth into fangs. All the clothing stores featured black capes. One store even sold wooden stakes, which could also be used to hold down camping tents.

"T-shirts. Get your T-shirts," one street vendor hawked. And Alex could only smile at the usual "Fangbanger," à la Sookie Stackhouse, as well as "Bite Me!," "Got Blood!," "Bitten," and "Vampires Suck." She bought one of the "Bite Me!" ones in an XL size for Ben.

Throughout the town, she'd seen signs and banners announcing the upcoming Labor Day Monster Mash. Live bands. Blood-drinking contests. Barbecued vampire ribs. Stake-throwing events. The usual.

She still had more than an hour to kill before her appointment; so she walked into a small cafe with the least kitschy name on the street, Good Bites. It was dark inside, even though it was only two p.m., and cool, a blessing since the temperature outside was in the high eighties. But because it was past the lunch hour, there were few customers; in fact, only a pair of young vampire lovebirds in the corner, alternating whispers and little kisses. She wondered idly how they kissed with those fangs. Carefully, she would guess. And, good Lord, that guy better guard his "precious jewels" with the fingernails on that babe. At least two inches long, pointy, and painted black, of course.

It took a few moments for her eyes to become acclimated to the shadowy interior, but then she couldn't help but release a hoot of laughter. It could only be described as gloomy chic. Instead of tables, there were small coffins with gothic-looking candles dripping red wax. Huge cobwebs decorated the corners. The walls were stone, like a dungeon. A slate board near the entrance announced the drink of the day, "Scotch and Bloody Soda."

Since there didn't appear to be a hostess at the moment, she sat down at a nearby table and pulled a small netbook out of her purse. She wanted to jot down a few observations about what she'd seen this morning while they were fresh in her mind. She'd already started a first draft on her laptop last night.

"Whath can I do fer you?" someone slurred out.

Alex had heard a lot of slurring today as people tried to speak through their fake vampire teeth. So it was no surprise when she glanced up to see her waitress wore fangs.

The woman stood, shifting wearily from hip to hip, anxious to end her workday, Alex guessed. Alex had seen a bus pulling away from the curb moments ago with the logo "Punxsutawney Senior Citizens Club" on the side. Alex recalled her college restaurant jobs. The waitress's feet were probably killing her.

But then she had to smile. This had to be the only vampire in history wearing orthopedic shoes with her black cape, over which there was a badge that read, "Hi! I'm Glenda." She was short, slightly plump, with black curly hair and freckles that were obvious, even with the white pancake makeup she wore. She resembled a goth Rosie O'Donnell.

"Uh, just a drink."

Glenda handed her a beverage menu.

Quickly scanning the list of vampire-themed drinks, she said, "Just a Bloody Mary, without the vodka."

"A Bloody Shame?"

She referred to what was commonly called a Virgin Mary, but Bloody Shame worked just as well. "Right."

When the waitress returned with the drink, she seemed to be in a little better mood, especially since she'd removed her fangs. Pointing to Alex's netbook, she asked, "You a reporter or something?"

"Yes. *World Gazette* magazine."

"We get lots of reporters here. The *Philadelphia Inquirer* comes every other month."

Alex nodded as she sipped at her drink. "This is very good, Glenda."

"We use fresh tomatoes. My husband, Bob, usta be a farmer before we bought this place."

"Oh, you're the owner."

"Yep. Me and Bob. I kin tell you right now. It's a helluva lot harder than farming."

Alex smiled. "I have an appointment this afternoon with Lord Vikar."

"That lord up at the castle?" she asked, not in a kindly way. "I'm surprised he agreed to meet with you. He ain't given interviews with any other reporters that I know of."

"Have you met him?"

"Nah! They're an unsociable bunch. I've seen him in passing, though."

"And?"

"He's hot, if you're into vampires."

"I would think that the hotel renovation would provide a lot of new jobs for the area."

"You'd think so, wouldn't you? But no, they're bringing in their own workers, I hear. Oh, they do shop in our stores sometimes, but they get most stuff from the Internet or over the mountain in State College."

"Well, once the hotel opens, your local economy should flourish, even more than it is now."

"I s'pose, as long as they don't modernize it too much. It's that creepy old castle, and all the rumors of vampires, that started all this Dracula crap here."

"You don't approve of the . . . uh, Dracula crap?"

"Sure I do. Half the town was on welfare before that, and— Oops, Bob is calling me from the kitchen. You kin pay on your way out. Stop by again, honey."

When it was about a half hour before her appointment, she left the cafe and drove out of town, then up a narrow dirt road heading toward 777 Colyer Lane. Then she came to a set of closed wrought-iron gates that were half hanging on their hinges. A big, pale-skinned man dressed in a black T-shirt and jeans put up a hand when she was about to get out of her car and try to open the gate herself.

"Sorry. No entrance to the public." The guy, who was really spooky-looking, with pale blue eyes and albino-ish skin, was staring at her in an intimidating fashion. He even licked his bloodred lips, between which fangs were slightly exposed.

"I have an appointment."

"That's what they all say. Sorry."

"Really, I have an appointment."

"With whom?"

"Lord Vikar."

"So you say. And your name is . . . ?"

"Alexandra Kelly from *World Gazette* magazine."

He ran a forefinger down a list on his clipboard. "Nope. No Alexandra Kelly. Sorry." He turned and walked away from her.

Now what? She pulled out her cell phone and saw that she had no bars. Swearing beneath her breath, she decided that she'd have to go back to town and call Ben, see if he could clear up the misunderstanding. Turning her car around, she was halfway down the dirt road to the highway when she saw a big-wheeled pickup truck headed in her direction. Thinking quickly, she pulled over to the side of the road and got out, waving the pickup to a stop.

"Hey, buddy, can you give me a lift? I ran out of gas."

The guy, who could be no more than sixteen, had the same fangs, pale skin, and pale blue eyes as the gate guard, except his black hair was combed like Michael Jackson in that "Thriller" video and he was, in fact, dressed in a similar red jacket and one white glove. She would bet her BlackBerry that inside she'd see slim black pants with white socks exposed . . . the whole nine Michael Jackson yards. "Uh, I'm not thaposed to give anybody a ride."

"It's okay. I'm the interior designer here to meet with Lord Vikar."

"Oh, I guess ith all right then."

She crawled up onto the passenger seat, not an easy feat with it being about four feet off the ground. "Thanks," she said. "Have you been here long?"

"I justh got here lath week," she thought he said, but his lisping voice could barely be heard or understood over the loud music blaring from the speakers. "Beat It," of course. He was seat dancing and singing along as he drove.

Uh-oh, they were approaching the gate. So, again thinking quickly, Alex tipped her purse over, dumping the contents onto the floor. With her hunkered down and with the truck up so high, the guard just waved the truck through after her driver called out, "Hey, Svein," and the guard called back, "How's it going, Armod?"

They drove another quarter mile or so until the castle came into view.

"Holy moley!" she exclaimed.

"Yeah, ain't it greath?" Armod said, pulling up front to drop her off. "I need to go around back to unload," he explained.

It was a huge stone castle. Probably four or five stories high, with turrets and gargoyles. Oddly, all the shutters were closed over what must be leaded windows. She'd already done her research on the lumber baron with aspirations to royalty who'd built the place more than a hundred years ago. It had been unoccupied for more than fifty years . . . and it showed. Creepy would be an understatement with the grounds overgrown with monster weeds and wild bushes.

At least a dozen workmen's trucks and vans were parked nearby, and scaffolding was already erected around the exterior where work had started on repointing the stonework and repairing broken shutters.

"Thanks for the lift, Armod," she said, jumping down.

She smiled as "Billie Jean" could be heard in his wake.

Walking carefully up the broken sidewalk, she noticed how interested some of the workers were in her appearance. Hard to tell whether they were outside contractors or resident dilly bars. She approached the enormous iron-studded, double front doors with a brass knocker big enough for Godzilla. There was a half-installed high-tech security plate on the right side of the threshold, where tools were lying on the steps and wiring hung out of the metal plate.

She knocked a few times.

No answer. In fact, despite all the workmen and vehicles outside, the house . . . rather, castle . . . seemed oddly silent.

Just then, she noticed a doorbell. She pressed the button and could hear a gonging noise inside. How cornily appropriate, she thought with a smile. If Herman Munster answered the door, she was going to puke.

Still no answer.

After the rebuff by the gate guard, and now this, she was getting more than frustrated. Plus, when she'd dressed this morning in a black silk pants suit, it had been a little chilly. Now it was hot. She took off the jacket, fanned herself with her notebook, then leaned on the doorbell. Really leaned on it. It should be heard all the way to Hell and back.

"Go away!" she thought she heard someone shout from some distant place inside.

No way! She gave the doorbell a good press this time and didn't let up. *Gong, gong, gong, gong, gong* . . .

"WHAT?" a belligerent voice yelled at her, yanking the door open suddenly.

She would have liked to say, *Well, hello to you, too,* but she was stunned, at a loss for words.

Standing before her was the most gorgeous man she'd ever seen, and the oddest. Early thirties, she would guess. He had long, dirty blond hair down to his shoulder blades, with pencil thin braids framing each side of his face. The braids were intertwined with turquoise beads. He had beautiful blue eyes and almost perfect facial features. She was tall, five-nine, but he had to be six-foot-four. And what a body! The odd thing, though, was his attire. He wore a Grateful Dead T-shirt, drab green cargo shorts, and flip-flops, like some overage surfer dude. Not your average vampire. He had a nice deep tan, unlike the others she'd seen so far. She'd probably just caught him out of costume. In one hand, he carried a long-handled net.

"Butterflies?" she asked.

"Bats."

Okaaay!

"Who in bloody hell are you?" the man asked rudely.

"I'm Alexandra Kelly. From *World Gazette* magazine. I have an appointment with Lord Vikar."

"Is that a fact?" he said, leaning lazily against his bat catcher pole, giving her an insolent once-over, with a pause over her ivory-colored camisole top.

"Are you the pool boy, or something?"

"Or something."

"Are you going to invite me in?"

"No."

No? "Listen, whoever you are, I'm hot. I'm tired. My feet hurt in these new heels. I've driven all the way from D.C. I'm staying with Donald and Ivana Trump Yoder in a farmhouse out of the nineteenth century with the ambience of eau de pig poop. And I'm starting to get annoyed. Move aside. I'll wait inside for your boss."

"I do not think so, wench." He spread his arms and legs, barring her way.

"Wench? How juvenile!"

They were at a stalemate. Her glaring at him. Him not budging.

"I have a gun in my purse," she blurted out before she could bite her tongue.

He laughed. The jerk had the nerve to laugh.

Just then another man came up behind the jerk. "Who is it?"

"Nobody."

Nobody? She'd like to give him *nobody*, right in his insolent six-pack abs.

The second guy pushed the jerk to the side. And, whoa, another good-looking stud muffin, this one in a gladiator outfit. Of the same height as blondie but different as night and day. He had shorter black hair, barely reaching his shoulders, and wore a belted, leather tunic thingee that only reached midthigh, exposing bare, hairy legs down to heavy sandals. *Gerard Butler in the flesh!* she decided. *But no, Gerard Butler played a Spartan, not a Roman, didn't he? Whatever!*

"I think I've landed in Bedlam," she remarked.

"I often have the same thought," Spartacus said before extending a hand to her. "Greetings, m'lady. I am Trond Sigurdsson. And you are . . . ?"

She shook hands with him and said, "Alexandra Kelly."

"You've met my brother Vikar Sigurdsson?"

Her eyes went wide.

"Vikar! Have you been surly again? Tsk, tsk!"

Vikar shoved his brother inside with a sharp hip slam and closed the door behind him, leaving them both on the doorstep. She could hear laughter on the other side of the door.

"You're Vikar?"

"In the flesh," he said on a long sigh.

"Lord Vikar?"

He nodded.

"Ha, ha, ha! You? Some kind of Lord of the Vampire Dance?"

"Surely you jest, m'lady. I do not dance."

"No offense, honey, but you look more like a silly Viking than a vampire."

"Silly Viking?" he hissed suddenly and flashed a pair of impressive fangs at her.

"Spare me the hokey act. I've seen more than enough fangs in town today. Lots more authentic than yours, too."

"You are not afraid of me?" He seemed confused.

"Not a bit."

He shook his head as if to clear it, then seemed to come to a decision. "Listen, I'm sorry for the inconvenience, but I agreed to no interview with your magazine. There were several phone calls asking for an interview with a man named"—his eyebrows raised with sudden understanding—"Alex Kelly."

"Obviously not a man."

"Obviously," he agreed, his eyes regarding her with deliberate sexual interest.

Oh jeesh, this guy must really be Lord Vikar. Hope I haven't killed my chances for an interview.

"But I did not agree to an interview. So, male or female, it is a moot point." He put his hand on the doorknob and was about to go back inside.

"Your agent arranged it," she said quickly.

"My what?" He half turned back to her.

"Agent. A guy named Mike Archer."

"Mike Arch-her," he said slowly, facing her directly again. Then understanding seemed to hit him. He was not pleased with whatever that understanding was. "That figures. No matter! I am not doing an interview. Send me a bill for your expenses, and I'll send a check. In the meantime—" He stopped suddenly and put a hand to her chin, turning it so that her neck was exposed. Sparks erupted where he touched her skin, and they slingshotted throughout her body. She was immediately aroused. "You have two marks on your neck."

At first she was bewildered, but then she put a hand to her neck. "Oh, those are just mosquito bites. Did I tell you I'm staying on a farm? The Bed & Blood. You wouldn't believe how many— Whoa, what are you doing?"

He'd opened the door with one hand and grabbed her by the upper arm with the other, yanking her inside with him. The door closed loudly behind them.

At first she was disoriented because of the poor lighting, which was not helped by the closed shutters. All around them, on the wide stairway, in the corridors, and in what must have once been salons, standing on high ladders with feather dusters and paint rollers, and on hands and knees on marble floors with scrub brushes, strange-looking men and a few women stared at her. Big half-opened boxes of furniture and accessories—recently delivered, she presumed—towered in piles up to the ceiling, including what must be at least a dozen wide-screen TVs. In the background, on what must be a castle-wide sound system, hymns played. *Hymns?*

The strange people silently gawked at her, as if she were the oddball. Or the next item on their menu, if those licking their lips were any indication.

They all had pale blue eyes. Many had very light skin, although there appeared to be something resembling a tanning bed on the other side of the hall in the old dining room, where two men paused in the midst of a fencing match using huge swords. A set of free weights lay along the edge, along with boxing gloves and a yet to be installed punching bag.

Some of the people wore regular T-shirts and jeans. Others wore historical attire totally out of place in this time period. A Mississippi riverboat gambler. More Vikings. A Regency lady. And, of course, Spartacus, who was grinning, as if he were in on the joke of the century. Which would be her.

Almost all of them showed fangs.

She glanced toward Lord Vikar.

He smiled at her through white, straight teeth . . . no fangs in sight now. "Welcome to Hotel Transylvania, my dear."

And thus her nightmare began.

Three

Welcome to *my* world, sweetling . . .

I need to taste you," Vikar said and almost immediately wished he'd bitten his tongue, except his fool fangs had come out in anticipation of—what else?—a taste.

Son of a troll! How he hated these fangs! They were embarrassing, really. And inconvenient. In fact, they seemed to have a mind of their own. Like another part of his body.

But wait. Something strange was happening here. The air fair crackled, and he could swear his skin tingled. Tingled, for the love of a cloud! Every hair on his body was standing at attention, like bloody antennae.

The woman backed up a bit, but he was between her and the door to his office where he'd yanked her after seeing her alarm on first viewing his fellow vangels. There was a telling silence on the other side of the door now, as if all twenty-seven vangels in residence so far were attempting to listen in on how he would handle this latest disaster.

He wasn't sure if she sensed the same chemistry in the air, or if it was his rude behavior that frightened her. Probably both.

"Taste . . . taste . . . ?" she sputtered, her green eyes sparking anger at him. "In your dreams, buster. I'm here for an interview, and nothing else. I don't appreciate your manhandling me, either."

"I 'manhandled' you for your own safety. The tasting must be done, for your own safety."

"That's a new line, right up there with 'I have to have sex or my blue balls will fall off.'"

She has a mouth like a drukkinn *sailor. I like it.* "You have a coarse tongue, m'lady."

"Yeah, well, *m'lord*, you put *your* tongue, coarse or otherwise, anywhere near my private parts, and you will be very sorry."

"What? That is not what I meant by tasting." *But now that you've planted the picture in my mind, I wonder if it fits in with Trond's "near-sex"?* "You missay me. 'Tis your blood I must sample in order to—"

"Whoa! The only taste you're going to get is of the mace I'm going to blow your way."

"A gun and mace? What are you, some kind of bounty hunter?" He was fairly certain she referred to the eye-blinding substance, not the medieval ball and chain weapon. So he put both hands up in mock fear.

She made a snarling sound and was already digging into a briefcase-style purse the size of a boar's behind. As she bent forward, he relished the sight of her reddish-blonde hair falling forward out of the knot at her nape. He also relished the sight of the cleavage exposed under her flimsy upper garment, a wisp of flesh-toned silk and lace. "Ah, here it is." She held up a pocket-size canister that might fell a dwarf, but not a man his size, and certainly not one with his supernatural makeup.

He tried but failed to hide his grin. "Blow away, but the only effect it will have is to make me sneeze. You do not want to see a vampire angel in a sneezing fit. Last time my fangs turned my lower lip into bloody pulp, and feathers flew everywhere." That was not quite true, his not being winged yet, but exaggeration was a God-given Viking prerogative, in his opinion.

"Angel?" she scoffed. "First you're a vampire. Now an angel. I can't wait to hear what else you claim to be."

"Viking."

"Huh?"

"I'm a Viking vampire angel. A vangel. My six brothers and I, Norsemen to the bone, are called The Seven, or the VIK. I am the oldest, but not by much. We seven are leaders of the vangels."

She rolled her eyes.

"Are journalists usually so cynical . . . and rude."

She blushed. "No. I apologize. Let's start over here. I'm Alexandra Kelly, *World Gazette* magazine." She extended her hand toward him.

"And I am Vikar Sigurdsson." He shook her hand, but only lightly, fearing a recurrence of the erotic current that flowed betwixt them. "I mean you no harm, that I do swear." He placed a hand over his heart for emphasis.

She studied him for a moment, then set her canister on the desk that was piled high with bills and account books and wallpaper samples, a Bible, and two empty bottles of Fake-O. Cobwebs hung from every corner. Apparently, she'd decided he was no longer a threat. "How come you're being so open now, when a few minutes ago you were refusing my interview?"

I have no idea. "Because I saw the fang marks on your neck." *Maybe Mike has put a motor on my tongue now.*

"I beg your pardon."

Enough! There was no way to convince this woman that he needed to suck out a bit of her blood to test for a demon infection. No quick way, leastways. And time was of the essence.

So, with a speed faster than any human could comprehend, he grasped both her wrists and held them behind her back with one of his hands, his hips propelled her back against the floor-to-ceiling bookshelves, and his other hand grasped her chin, forcing it to the side so that her neck lay open to him. With a reflexive hiss of anticipation, his fangs came out and he sank his teeth into her skin where she'd already been bitten.

He'd done this hundreds of times before. He could do it in his sleep. He could do it and recite the Poetic Edda in his head. He could be cool, calm, and as collected as any Viking vampire angel in the midst of a fanging. But this was different, he recognized instantly.

The taste of her washed over him like a tidal wave. His cock shot up without warning and he went lance hard without any forewarning. It was a thickening so exquisitely orgasmic that he felt his knees begin to buckle.

Jerking backward, he released his hold on her and put the back of his hand to his mouth, rubbing. Staggering to the other side of the desk, he plopped down to the swivel chair to hide the continuing erection that tented his shorts, the thigh-length braies men wore here in the summer months.

At the same time, she appeared more stunned than angry, although the anger was sure to come. Gingerly picking up a dirty tunic from another chair, she dropped it to the floor before sitting down to stare across the desk at him.

"Who *are* you?" they both asked at the same time.

Was that arousal hazing her green eyes? Was she feeling as shocked as he was? And why, after being dead for one thousand, one hundred and sixty-two years, was he being sucker-punched with this kind of temptation?

Mike, he immediately thought. Again.

On the other hand, what if the fiendish Jasper, head of all the demon vampires, had a hand in this? What if this reddish-blonde vision was actually a Lucipire? Hmm. He would have to tread carefully. At least the pole between his legs was unthickening.

"I am Vikar Sigurdsson," he repeated. *I sound like a dumb dolt.* "You ask who I am. I am the owner . . . um, developer of this property." Well, that was true. To a point.

"And a vampire?"

The smirk on her face was not pleasing to him. Not at all.

Still, he advised himself, *tread carefully.* "Not precisely. The word *vampire* implies dark. Evil. I am neither of those."

She arched her pretty reddish-blonde brows in question.

"I am a Viking vampire angel. A vangel, to be precise." Betimes honesty was the best policy. She'd never believe him anyhow.

"I notice you've put your fangs away."

Vikar felt himself blush. "I only go fangy on occasion. We Vikings are vain about our appearance." He shrugged as if he could not help himself.

"Do you ever turn into a bat?"

He shivered with distaste. He hated the ugly buggers.

"Do you even have wings?"

"Not yet." *Probably never.*

"And you drink blood."

"Anything red will do," he joked.

"So, a vampire and a Viking. I guess instead of going a-Viking, you go a-vamping." The snide tone to her voice betrayed her disbelief. She must have realized how impolite she sounded for a person requesting a favor . . . an interview. "Sorry. Sometimes I have trouble suspending disbelief. Seriously, though, what's going on here?"

"Seriously, you wouldn't believe me if I told you."

"Try me."

"Are you a Lucipire?" he blurted out.

"Huh? No. I already told you my name is Alex."

"Lucipire is the name for one of Satan's vampires. You know, fires of Hell, burn and sizzle, and all that."

"Sizzle? Hah! Don't blame me for the sizzle between us. I didn't create this fire. That's your magic crap." She slapped a hand over her mouth, realizing how once again she'd failed to rein in her tongue.

But sizzle? She feels the sizzle, too. Her blood is on fire for me. Oh, I am in big trouble. "Lucipire. L. U. C. I. P. I. R. E."

Her face turned a lovely shade of beet.

"A demon vampire."

She rolled her eyes. "You people in this town really do take this whole vampire charade a bit too far. I understand why. The tourist attraction and all that. But I'm not writing a promo piece for you in my magazine. If you're not going to be straight with me, you're wasting both our time. And, frankly, I don't appreciate your biting me, either." She put a hand to the bite mark on her neck, but the way she rubbed it was almost a caress.

Which caused the air to crackle again and ripples of electricity to shoot right to . . .

Down, thickening! Down!

All right, so maybe she wasn't in league with the devil. But how much information could he trust her with? On the other hand, she said Mike had sent her. Besides, there wasn't any way he could let her leave after having tasted her blood. She'd definitely been infected. He had work to do on her if she was to be saved.

"You've been bitten by a Lucipire, not a mosquito. That's why I had to sample your blood, to evaluate the extent of your infection."

"Oh please . . ." she started to say.

He held up a halting hand. "The Lucipire must have been interrupted in the midst of feeding on you." He tilted his head in question at her.

"The Yoders' dog did start barking wildly, now that you mention it. I slapped a hand at my neck at the same time I heard Mr. Yoder walking down the hall to call the dog in. But it was a mosquito," she insisted, "not some devil bloodsucker."

"Are you sure?"

"Of course I'm sure."

The warrior in him recognized that it was best to surprise the enemy with a sudden attack. Not that she was his enemy. So he launched his big question point-blank: "What big sin have you committed?"

"What?" That question certainly got her attention and caught her unawares, as he'd planned. She stared at him like a deer in the headlights, poleaxed.

"You are clearly in a state of mortal sin."

No longer poleaxed, she was now pole-stiff. "How dare you make such a personal statement about me, a perfect stranger?"

"The Lucipires only attack those who have committed some grave sin, or are contemplating such." Plus the scent of it teased his enhanced sense of smell, as well.

"Oh." That one word said it all, guilt personified, along with another beet blush.

So the sin has not yet been committed. That is good. Although even the small amount of demon infection is heightening her already heightened inclination to evil. He tented his fingers in front of his face, his two forefingers resting on his forehead. Finally, he came to a conclusion.

"You have to tell me everything so that I can save you," he said.

"Save me?" she sputtered. "Like you're my guardian angel?"

"So to speak," he agreed. Time enough to explain later.

"That's it. I'm out of here." She stood and walked

to the door. When she tried the doorknob, it was, of course, locked. "Unlock. This. Door." She glared at him over her shoulder.

"Sorry, m'lady, but you are going nowhere."

She gasped. "You'd force me to stay?"

He shrugged. "I prefer to say you are the first guest of the Hotel Transylvania."

"Are you people escapees from a mental hospital? Is this the vampire version of *One Flew over the Cuckoo's Nest*? Am I going to see Jack Nicholson popping out of the woodwork with an axe in hand like he did in *The Shining*?"

She was going to see an axe or two, that was certain. Battle-axes. Lots of them. Along with swords. Lances. And any number of modern weapons, including his favorite Sig pistol. But he did not need to inform her of that just yet.

"Aren't you a little old for these kinds of silly games? How old are you, anyway?"

"You do not want to know."

"Which means you're older than you look. Let me guess. That's a weave you're wearing to hide your receding hairline. And they say women are vain about their appearance!"

He hated that she'd hit his sin right on its unruly head. Vanity, ever his downfall! Still, he attempted to defend himself. "I shaved my head one time so I could avoid the sin of pride. Mike made it grow back even better. He said cloistered virtue was no virtue at all."

"The poet John Milton was the one who said that."

"He did? Wait 'til I tell Mike about stealing someone else's quote."

"Who's Mike?"

"Saint . . . I mean, Mike Archer. My . . . uh, agent."

"And he told you not to shave your head?"

"I have a thing about hair." He shrugged.

She went on to discuss just about everything that was wrong with the male gender, from plagiarism, to comb-overs, to infidelity, to sex obsessions, to self-ishness. On and on she went, lumping him in with the worst.

He let her vent for a while longer, then asked politely, "I don't suppose you know how to cook? We have a side of beef in the kitchen that we got from a local Amish farmer, and our cook has not yet arrived. No one knows how to prepare it without building a fire, and that would surely ruin the new floor tile." He was teasing, of course, just wanting to stop her tirade.

She told him to do something to himself that he knew for a fact was physically impossible.

The woman was going to have to do something about her language before Mike got here. "I take that for a no."

"Correction. That would be hell, no!"

"We don't mention that place here."

She gave him a look, the one women have perfected through the ages that essentially said of their menfolk, *Dumb dolt!*

He widened his eyes with innocence, pretending not to understand.

"I need a drink. A Dirty Martini would go over great about now. Even a Bloody Mary, minus the blood. I don't suppose you vampires have any alcohol?"

"M'lady! We are Vikings. We practically invented beer."

"Angels who drink beer," she muttered as she followed him out of the office.

"We prefer to think of ourselves as beer-drinking Vikings. We Northmen do love our mead, but a Rolling Rock or Bud will do in a pinch. Of course in our day cold beer was an unknown. Now I cannot imagine drinking warm ale."

She ignored his attempt at humor. "And vampires, besides. I suppose you only suck on beer-sodden alcoholics."

"Ha, ha, ha!" he said. "You have much to learn, wench. Much!"

He wondered if her obvious sense of humor would be intact after a day or two in VIK land.

**It was a castle, all right,
but he was no Prince Charming . . .**

Alex didn't for one minute think she would be prevented from leaving Land of the Lost Idiots, in other words, Hotel Transylvania. It was an empty threat tossed her way by Prince Not-So-Charming, meant to frighten her, she was sure. Well, fairly sure.

In the meantime, she would do what she did best. Snoop around for the story behind the story. Her journalistic instincts were on red alert. Besides, she needed a bit of space to evaluate what had just happened to her when Vikar had put his mouth to her neck . . . and sucked. She hadn't been turned on like that since . . . well, forever.

"So, are you going to show me around?" she asked.

He rose from behind the desk, eyeing her suspiciously. "You're not going to fight your stay here with us?"

"Depends on how long of a stay," she answered truthfully.

Then, to avoid an argument, she said, "Tell me about this place. Oh, not its history. I already know that. How long have you owned it? What did you pay for it? What are your plans? When will the hotel open? What attractions or amenities do you plan? And who are all those weird people out there?"

"C'mon," he said, opening the door and holding a hand out to her. "I'll give you the tour. Afterward, we'll talk."

Then began the most bizarre trip Alex had ever taken, and she'd been in some bizarre places in her journalistic history, not least of which was interviewing Bin Laden's daughter in a desert harem while both of them were in full purdah. As they walked back toward the front door, Vikar pointed out the various rooms, telling her what they had been originally—in some cases, there were old sepia photographs taped to the wall—and how they would be used after the renovations. Built on the side of a mountain, some of the rooms had a cavelike appearance.

None of Vikar's descriptions sounded like a hotel to her.

A game room contained billiards, dartboards, and every kind of video game imaginable. A TV and movie screening room held theater-type seats as well as numerous cushy sofas. A weight room already had StairMasters, stationary bikes, and Nautilus equipment. A tanning salon drew raised eyebrows on her part, but Vikar said he would ex-

plain later. A weapon room he allowed her only a
brief glimpse into, but she'd seen enough to know
they could supply a small army. A chapel was already complete with stained glass windows, a life-
size crucifix, and pews with kneelers. And this was
only half the rooms on the first floor.

As they entered the kitchen, which was incidentally the size of her whole D.C. apartment, she burst
out with laughter. There was indeed a side of beef
lying on one of the counters. An alarming prospect
occurred to her. Did these pseudo vampires feed on
raw meat?

She turned to Vikar. "Isn't this taking steak tar-
tare to a new level?"

There were several beats of silence in which he
just stared at her, but she could see his displeasure
in the tic at the side of his mouth. She'd become very
cynical and sarcastic lately . . . in the past two years,
specifically. Not a very attractive trait, she had to
admit. Maybe she'd gone too far this time.

"Yes, a dinner bell rings, and all us vangels come
running to feed on the carcass. Saves on dinner-
ware. And no clean-up."

Well, he'd matched her sarcasm tit for tat that
time. At least she assumed he was being sarcastic.
The alternative didn't bear imagining. And what
was that he called himself? A vangel. That was a
new one.

"Ulf! Floki!" Vikar yelled suddenly, causing Alex
to jump back with surprise. "Get your arses in here
and put this carcass in the freezer."

Immediately two young men rushed in. Twentysomething, wearing jeans and T-shirts and the latest
in athletic footwear, they were Nordic in appear-

ance, with differing shades of blond hair and blue eyes. More Vikings?

"Sorry, Lord Vikar," one said. "We were helping Trond carry mattresses down to the dungeon."

Alex arched her brows and mouthed, *Dungeon?* at Vikar.

"We are going to use it for dormitories for the time being," he explained. "A big . . . um, convention is coming up, and not enough rooms to house all the attendees."

Alex knew from her research that there were twenty-five bedrooms in this mansion. How many attendees were there going to be? And a convention of what? Vampires? Angels? Vikings? Escapees from mental asylums? This story was getting more and more bizarre. And compelling. Alex had learned over the years that the most hyped story idea often petered out in the interview, and a gold mine of an exclusive could emerge in the oddest places.

Just then a heavyset, older woman bustled in from the back door. She wore Victorian upper-class attire, a fringed, black silk shawl over a white, high-necked, lace-trimmed, mutton-sleeved blouse that was tucked into a full-length black skirt.

"Miss Borden, thank God!" Vikar said, going over to give her a hug. "We expected you two days ago."

"Stuck in Portland. A male prostitute there was a bugger to save." She grinned at her pun as she handed the shawl to Armod, the Michael Jackson wannabe, who was in the process of unloading groceries. Armod got a strange look on his face at the woman's words, but then the woman noticed his expression, and said, "Sorry, Armod." She gave the boy a quick hug, then began to roll up the sleeves of her blouse.

"Miss Borden, you know Armod, obviously, and Ulf, and Floki. This is Alexandra Kelly. She's a . . . uh, visitor."

Miss Borden eyed her warily as she hiked an obviously heavy canvas carryall up onto the counter and pulled out a meat cleaver. "Just call me Lizzie." On those ominous words—*Lizzie Borden*—she began to expertly carve the side of beef into steaks and ribs, calling out orders as she worked. "Floki, get me some freezer paper. Ulf, do we have a roasting pan big enough for a twenty-pound rump? Armod, what in bloody mud are you doing with all those cans?"

Armod's pale face turned pink. "No one wanted to cook, so we've been living out of cans," he lisped as he pointed to industrial-size cans of stew, Spa-ghettiOs, SPAM, fruit cocktail, soup, pudding, tuna, and sardines. "Mostly we been having pizza delivered. Domino's loves us." He grinned sheepishly, exposing his two fangs.

"Well, put it all away," the cook said. "Vikar, you could go out and help my assistants bring in bags of potatoes and some sweet corn I bought at a roadside stand."

Vikar groaned and told Alex in a whispered aside, "You think lisps are bad? You do not want to see vampires eating corn on the cob."

She laughed, but then had to ask, "Lizzie Borden? *The* Lizzie Borden?"

"One and the same."

"And she was a vampire?" Alex had noticed that

the woman's upper lip protruded a bit, as if fangs were there, though not extended.

"Not until she died."

"And she was a Viking?"

"She has a bit of Viking in her family history. Bordenssons from way back."

He chucked her under her hanging jaw and went out to do the lady's bidding.

While he was gone, Alex walked around the kitchen, examining things. All the appliances appeared new, including one whole wall of stainless-steel refrigerator and walk-in freezer units. She opened one and saw dozens of different kinds of beer. She laughed and took out a Sierra Nevada, one of her husband Brian's favorites. Amazingly, that remembrance, and the image of them sitting on the back deck of their Barnegat Bay cottage drinking beer and eating late-night snacks, didn't squeeze her heart as it might have months ago. Of course, that had been in the early years of their marriage. Before his betrayal.

The next unit held a pigload of pint- and quart-size glass containers, like old-fashioned milk bottles, holding a red beverage. They were marked Fake-O. She didn't need to ask what they were, and, really, whatever was going on in this wacky castle, they knew how to get the special effects right. Creepy, that's what it was.

She was opening the next unit where she discovered about fifty different gallon pails of ice cream when Vikar's brother Trond walked into the kitchen. He picked up an apple from a basket on a side table and began to chomp on it as he approached her. His fangs were recessed, or in his pocket more likely, so he had no trouble eating.

"Vampires with a sweet tooth?" she inquired, pointing with her long neck toward the open freezer.

"More like Vikings with a sweet tooth. Back in our day, sugar was rare," he replied, tossing his apple core in a high arc that slam-dunked into a waste can on the other side of the room.

When he saw her amusement over his dubious talent, he winked at her. "We have lots of time on our hands to perfect life's important skills."

"Why are you dressed like that?"

He glanced down at his gladiator costume. "Just got back from Rome."

"The Vatican?"

"*No,* the Colosseum."

She raised a hand to halt what she knew would be a bunch of baloney. "Tell me no more."

"Are you married?" he asked, glancing at the platinum band on her left hand.

Vikar came up to join them just as Trond had asked his question. "I, too, am interested. For some reason, I assumed you were unwed."

Probably because of the sizzle they generated, but she wasn't about to say that aloud. Besides, it was none of their business whether she was married or not, and Alex really didn't want to discuss her personal life. On the other hand, it was a common question. "I *was* married. My husband died."

Both men nodded, their faces reflecting sympathy.

"How long ago?" Trond wanted to know.

"Two years." *And it wasn't just Brian who died. It*

was Linda, too. My precious Linda. Oh God! She gritted her teeth to calm herself.

Vikar's eyes narrowed oddly with suspicion. "How did he die?"

Okay, this interrogation had gone on long enough. She took a long swallow of her beer, then carefully set the half-empty bottle on the counter. Turning slowly, she addressed Vikar, "Let's get one thing straight right now. I'm here to interview you. While I'm willing to be polite, I have no intention of discussing my personal life." She hated the shakiness of her voice that betrayed how emotional she'd become, and she hated that these two men witnessed her veneer cracking.

Trond reached forward and squeezed her arm before walking away, but Vikar remained, staring at her intently, as if trying to fathom some deep mystery. "I might be able to help you," he said finally.

She put both hands to her head and tugged at her hair. "Have you heard a word I've said? My privacy is important to me, and you have to respect—"

"Would you feel better knowing where he is?"

"Who?" She was not a violent person, but she was seriously thinking about clunking Vikar over the head with a heavy object. Good thing Lizzie had a firm grip on her cleaver on the other side of the room.

"Your husband."

He has a death wish. This idiot has a death wish. "My husband is dead."

"So you said."

Her heart kick-started into warp speed as she began to comprehend what Vikar was implying.

"You can bring a dead person back to life?" *I can't believe I actually asked that.*

"*No!* Oh, sorry I am if I led you to believe that. But I might be able to tell you whether he is in a good place. Or not. Would you want to know that about your husband?"

"Not Brian. Someone else. Well, yes, I would want to know that Brian was all right, but, more important, I would want to know about . . ." She gulped. ". . . my daughter. Linda."

"Ah. You lost your husband *and* a daughter."

"This is an intrusive, pointless conversation, and, frankly, I'm offended that you would even—"

"My leader . . . the man I work for . . . is the Mike Archer you mentioned as my agent when you arrived. He has influence Up There," he explained, gazing upward, as if that were any explanation at all. "Up *There*," he repeated.

The strangest, most outlandish idea occurred to her then. "Are you saying your boss is St. Michael the Archangel?"

"Precisely," Vikar said.

And Alex, who'd never fainted a day in her life, even at the horrific moment when she'd been notified of the death of the most important person in her life, felt the blood drain from her head, and she was falling, falling, falling.

Eyes closed, she sensed a number of people looking down at her, and she recognized Trond's voice as he said, "Well done, Vikar! You always did have a knack for having women fall at your feet."

Four

Even vampire angels benefit from a good Excel chart . . .

ikar was sitting at the kitchen table later that evening with Trond, two laptops and a printer in front of them, following a meeting they'd just completed with some of their jarls and karls. As a result, he now had a very detailed plan complete with computer printouts of how to transform the castle into a VIK fortress and comfy home headquarters. Not that Michael would care about the latter; he would probably prefer that they sleep on concrete slabs and twiddle their thumbs between assignments. Or pray. Constantly.

Before going abroad, his brother Harek, still in Germany—1943 Germany—had given him a list of every existing vangel member and their specialties so that Vikar could come up with a chart of duties. In order to prepare for Michael's arrival here next month, they all had to help.

Harek wouldn't arrive for another few days, and

Vikar knew from past experience that it would take a week or more for his brother to overcome the depression that enveloped him after having been in the Holocaust death camps. They'd all been there, done their jobs, and wept afterward. Yes, Vikings did weep when the atrocity was great. Needless to say, Hitler occupied a special suite in Hell.

Vikar took the organization chart of duties and tacked it on the wall for all to see in the morning. There was everything from housekeeping to security. Equipment, furniture, plumbing, food, landscaping, painting, accounting, computers, laundry, linens, clothing.

"I feel much better having all this spelled out," Vikar told Trond, who'd just opened two bottles of dark ale and handed one to him.

For a long moment, they both just swallowed and enjoyed. That was one good thing modern times had to offer. A wide variety of beers. Vikings had long appreciated a good brew, whether it be honeyed mead or a hearty malt ale, but there had been no choices between light, dark, sweet, bitter, hearty, even where they had been made.

"Wait until Regina finds out that you've put her in charge of the household cleaning." Trond chuckled. "I plan to be in town with Armod buying groceries, or something."

Regina had been a witch back in the Norselands of the 1200s. A real spell-casting, cauldron-boiling, spooky witch. Spookier than vampires, truth to tell. And she had delusions about her importance in the vangel world. "She'll have a dozen ceorls working under her. I do not imagine Regina will ever pick up a toilet brush herself, or mop a floor."

"Unless Michael wishes to humble her," Trond pointed out.

"True. True."

"I've been thinking . . ." Trond said, pausing until he had his attention, "there are some big jobs here that would be better done by outside people. Like plumbing and electricity. Remember the time I tried to fix that light socket and about electrocuted myself? Wait. Hear me out. How about you send us all out of here for a week? If only you and a handful of others stay behind, you can stay out of view while the workers are here."

"You're right that some of these things are beyond our expertise. In fact, we could bring in wall framers, plasterers, floor refinishers, and bathroom tilers at the same time. Give them a deadline of one week or they don't get paid."

"You'd have to toss out a lot of cash to get those kinds of results."

"Money talks in these bad economic times."

Trond nodded. "I'll take care of all your people as well as mine." Trond's half hird of about twenty vangels had arrived the night before; the others were still out in the field on assignments. Vangels were stepping on vangels at every turn here inside the castle. "Mayhap we could go to that mountain retreat we rented years ago."

Vikar had to laugh. Retreat was a glorification of what had been ten excruciating days in tents, eating over open fires, in the forests of Upper Mongolia.

"We could leave behind a blood ceorl in case you need her services. And mayhap Armod. He still needs constant watching during this transition period, not to mention speech lessons to get rid of that lisp. Plus you better keep a few warriors here in case more Lucies show up."

The idea was becoming more and more appealing to Vikar.

"What about your 'guest'? Have you started the cleansing yet?"

"*No.* I'm going up now." He'd placed Alex in a tower room where there was a single bed and not much more. Thankfully, he'd had the foresight to put a tranquilizer in the water she'd been offered when she'd first awakened from her faint. As a result, she'd been sleeping these past four hours.

"If we all vacate the premises, you would have time to cleanse her thoroughly," Trond said with a grin that implied the cleansing might involve something other than the ritual de-demonizing. "Speaking of cleansing, while you have the plumbers here, how about a few Jacuzzi tubs, and I'd personally like one of those rainforest showers that hit you from a dozen different directions."

"What would Mike say about that?"

"Does he have to know everything?" Trond stood and stretched, prepared to leave the room. "Is the cable hooked up? There's a Three Stooges marathon on AMC."

Vikar smiled as he straightened out some of their papers and put the empty beer bottles in the recycling bin. Yes, Vikings who recycled! "Keep the volume down. There are probably ceorls sleeping on the couches."

After Trond left, a cold six-pack under his arm, Vikar prepared a tray for Alex since she hadn't been awake for dinner.

Sliced roast beef, whipped potatoes, a thick-sliced

tomato, an ear of buttered corn on the cob, and a piece of garlic bread, along with a bottled water and a can of diet soda.

With trepidation, he then climbed the four flights of stairs to the tower room, wondering what reception he would get. He was weary, both physically and mentally. So it was with a sigh of relief that he opened the door that had been locked from the outside and found that Alex was still asleep, lying on her side, facing the wall.

He put the tray on a side table where a fat beeswax candle burned brightly. Armod had gone to the bed-and-breakfast and brought back Alex's luggage and other belongings, which he'd placed on a window seat, opened but unpacked. A pint of vodka, nestled among her clothing, caught his attention.

He stood at the end of the bed and watched Alex for several long moments. She looked so peaceful. Mayhap she wasn't really hungry. Mayhap he could put off the cleansing until morning to avoid her inevitable distress. Mayhap she wouldn't mind if he lay down with her, just to rest, just to soak in some of her peace. Mayhap he was an idiot.

So, with a cluelessness ingrained in men through the ages, he kicked off his flip-flops and arranged himself carefully against her back, spoon-style.

There was still that crackle in the air, as earlier today when he'd fanged her, and his cock appreciated being nestled against the crease of her backside, but it was more than that. In truth, he felt as if a warm cocoon was enveloping them, like the wings of a giant bird. *Please, God, let it be a bird, and not an angel.*

This was almost better than sex. Almost.

Just before he closed his eyes for a short rest, his nose tickled and he barely suppressed a sneeze. Putting a hand to his face, he found—*surprise, surprise*—a white feather.

Blood of my blood . . .

Alex awakened groggily in the middle of the night.

For a long time, since Brian and Linda's deaths to be precise, she'd had trouble sleeping. Vodka had become her nighttime friend. She wondered idly how much she'd drunk to reach this state of baby-like slumber.

She wriggled her butt and burrowed deeper into the soft mattress. Against her back she felt something hard. The wall? But over her was the softest, cuddliest blanket she could ever imagine. Like a cloud, it was, especially when it kind of fluttered over her. Forget Amish quilts. She wanted one of these blankets. She would have to ask Vikar in the morning where she could buy one.

But then, her nose twitched. Was it a feather from the pillow that tickled her? Or the scent? The scent of a man.

She rolled over suddenly, causing a large object to jerk backward and fall off the single bed.

It was Vikar.

"What the hell are you doing in my bed?" she demanded, sitting up. At the same time, she glanced downward to see a common fleece blanket about her waist, nothing like what she'd been imagining.

He stood in one fluid motion, rubbing his behind

as if he'd been hurt when he landed on the stone floor. He probably had with that tight butt sans fat padding. Well, it served him right.

"I brought a tray of food up for you"—he glanced at a wristwatch and seemed surprised—"five hours ago. You were sleeping so soundly I thought I would lie down for a moment to rest, and . . ." He shrugged. "What can I say? You are snuggly."

"Snuggly? A Viking who snuggles?"

He shrugged again. "Must be the angel in me."

"Or the vampire?" she scoffed.

"Vampires do not snuggle." She noticed something odd then. Vikar was wrapping a rubber tube around his arm, just above the elbow, the kind labs used as a tourniquet before taking blood samples. "What are you doing?"

"Making sure that the blood down to my wrist remains pure."

"Why wouldn't it?" she asked, suspecting that she was somehow not going to like his answer.

She didn't.

"Because I must suck some of the demon-tainted blood out of you, and then replace it with some of my pure blood."

"Oh no! No, no, no!" She had no idea how he intended to complete such a process, and she didn't want to know.

"It's essential for the cleansing ritual."

"Sorry. I decline. I'll keep my blood just the way it is, thank you very much."

"Not an option." He was also setting a glass on the table next to the bed, into which he poured two inches or so of vodka. Her vodka, by the way. When had her luggage been brought here? He had a helluva nerve going through her things. "Drink this," he said. "It will relax you."

"No!" She squirmed away until her back was against the wall.

Undaunted, he leaned over, pinched her nose with two fingers of one hand, and forced her to drink the vodka with the other, even as she sputtered and flailed.

Most of the booze went down, and she felt an immediate buzz.

"You are in so much trouble. The magazine has a boatload of lawyers on retainer. We are going to sue your ass off."

Ignoring her threats, Vikar tugged on her legs, forcing her to lie on her back. Putting a hand under her back, he arched her up, exposing her neck. Before she could kick out at him or scratch his eyes out, he laid himself gently over her and bit into her neck.

The shock of his action immobilized her. That and the sweet, sweet euphoria that overcame her. His big hands held her face gently to the side, and he made a humming sound of satisfaction as he drank from her. She could tell that he was aroused by the hard ridge pressing into her thigh, but she didn't feel threatened. Truthfully, she was also aroused. But unlike earlier when his touch and fanging had brought her almost to climax, this was a slow titillation of her senses. More sensual than overtly sexual.

It seemed like forever that he drank from her, and it must have been a lot because she started to feel light-headed. With a growl of frustration, he pulled out, then licked her neck over and over, as if unwilling to pull away totally yet.

"Are we done?" she asked groggily, no longer angry. More confused than anything else.

"No. This part will be hardest for you. The first time, anyway." Without warning, he rose and sat on the side of the bed, pulling her up and onto his lap. She almost fainted at the fuzziness of her senses, due to the blood loss, no doubt.

While she watched, he used a penknife to slash his wrist, first one way, then another in an X, or was it a cross? Then he put his wrist to her mouth and forced her to swallow. At first, she gagged at the unpleasant taste, but he would not relent. He held her tightly in his embrace and kept making soothing sounds, "Shh. Don't struggle. It will be over soon. Relax, sweetling. Relax. That's the way. Suck. More. Good girl. Good girl."

When he finally took his wrist away, she tried to pull it back, which confused her further. Her mind said this was repulsive, but her body said, *Give me more.*

"That's it for now," he said, laying her down on the bed again. "Sleep for a while longer."

He pulled the fleece over her and kissed her forehead. Meanwhile *his* forehead was furrowed with what appeared to be confusion. Was he as affected by this strange ritual as she was?

"I don't understand," she murmured as her body succumbed to an unnatural lethargy.

"I will explain all in the morning," he said as he approached the door. At the last minute, he turned and told her, "You are not to worry. Everything will be back to normal soon."

But Alex knew—she just knew—nothing would ever be normal for her again. Especially when she awakened after dawn and heard the most incredible music. Truly, it was like angels singing.

Had she died and gone to Heaven?

Day One in La-La Land . . .

Vikar was in the chapel with Trond, on his knees, singing the "In Paradisum" hymn, their way of marking the end of morning services. It was the way the vangels started every new day.

They and all the other karls, ceorls, and thralls had already been given the bread and wine of Communion by the elderly priest, Father Peter, as in Peter Jorgensson, a seventeenth-century cardinal from Denmark who'd failed to take his celibacy vows seriously enough. He had sired fifteen children. Enough said! You could say he'd earned his fangs the enjoyable way, and his name as well. Drinking the symbolic blood of Christ was an important daily activity for the VIK and their underlings, with many parallels to their vampire blood activity.

Vikar and Trond, and his other five brothers when they were together, sang out the Latin "In Paradisum" chant, *"In paradisum deductant te Angeli,"* translated, "May Angels lead you into paradise."

The rest of the vangels answered with their own chant, *"Chorus Angelorum te suscipiat et cum Lazaro quondam pamere aeternam habeas requiem,"* or "May a choir of Angels receive you and may we have eternal rest."

It was amazing to Vikar, even after all these years, how good they sounded. Vikings loved to sing, of course, but usually ribald lyrics after consuming vast amounts of beer, but now they were like frickin' angels.

If they weren't vampires and if they didn't already have other jobs, they could probably make it big in the Christian music business. Imagining his motley crew on *The 700 Club* boggled the mind.

It was then that he turned slightly and saw Alex standing in the hallway outside the chapel. A stunned Alex.

He whispered to Trond that they had company.

Trond, the idiot, turned and gave her a little wave.

He told Trond to get the "gang" on its way ASAP, as they'd discussed the night before.

"What? We haven't had breakfast yet."

"If you wait for Miss Borden to cook a meal, it'll be noon before you're out of here. Stop at McDonald's."

Even though vangels partook of normal human food and drink, they needed blood to survive, in particular the blood of the sinners they saved. For example, when Vikar was done cleansing Alex, his body would be greatly rejuvenated, a nice side benefit of a good deed. Fake-O was a poor substitute. Vangels, unlike the traditional view of vampires, did not attack humans for blood.

"Make sure you take a good supply of Fake-O with you, just in case," he advised Trond.

Father Peter shh-ed at them.

He and Trond shrugged in apology, but then Trond grinned and added in an aside, "I can't wait to see the look on the clerks' faces at Mickey D's when more than fifty vampire angels show up en force, swords in hand."

"You *could* leave the swords hidden."

"What would be the fun in that?"

Vikar stood then, and after bowing his head and genuflecting, made his way back to Alex. "You could have come in," he told her.

"I don't do religion."

He arched his brows at her, even as he led her down the corridor toward the kitchen.

"I was born Catholic, and was a churchgoing pick-and-choose Catholic as an adult, but then . . . well, I got clobbered with enlightenment."

He assumed she referred to the death of her husband and child.

"Are you all Catholic? I noticed a priest in there."

He shook his head. "We are no precise religion. A bit of this and a bit of that."

"Like Unitarians?"

"Hardly. We are way more conservative than that."

"I don't believe in God."

He flinched at her words. Apparently, she was farther along than he'd thought. All it would have taken was a bit longer of a demon fanging, and she would have reached her tipping point. He still didn't know what mortal sin she was contemplating. That was a subject he would address later. For now, he needed to get the vangels out of the house so he could launch his one-week makeover project with an empty castle.

"Your voice is incredible," she remarked. "All of you. I don't think I've ever heard such magnificent hymns. Are you famous singers I've never heard of?"

"Hardly."

"You sounded like angels."

"Exactly."

She cast him a scoffing frown. "Not the vampire angels again!"

Now wasn't the time for this argument. "Why don't you go up and shower? Then we'll break fast. And talk."

"Is there a working bathroom in this place? The one attached to my tower prison has only a trickle of water, and the toilet appears to be circa 1900."

"It probably is that old," he said. "Use the bathroom next to my bedroom on the second floor. You can take the servants' staircase here off the kitchen. It'll be the first room on the right."

She hesitated. "What you did to me last night . . ."

"Everything will be all right, I promise." *I hope.* "Just give me a half hour to get some things taken care of with my brothers in the VIK, and—"

"The VIK? You mentioned that before. What is it?"

"Later." He steered her up the first step. "There are plenty of towels, soap, hair products, even a robe, I think." He and Trond had showered earlier using that bathroom. He hoped there was still hot water left. He'd soon find out if he heard a shriek from above.

She went up several steps as he watched, then turned. "If I don't get some satisfactory answers, I'm out of here," she warned.

"Absolutely," he said. *Not until you are purified.*

An hour later, he sat on a stool at the counter in the kitchen, a laptop in front of him and a cordless phone at his ear; cell phones didn't get any reception through all this rock. Thankfully, the old landlines still worked here, although he would eventually upgrade them, and he'd been able to get DSL service.

Vangels today depended on the Internet for many of their supplies.

He was on the phone with a Harrisburg contractor he'd found online. J.D. Donovan & Sons had recently lost a big job at Penn State due to decreased public funding, so their schedule had a sudden hole. He was speaking to J.D. Sr. himself.

"Is this a joke? You have a seventy-five-room house you want renovated in seven days?"

"No joke. I don't need everything done right away, but the specialized stuff has to be completed. Construction of some rooms with new walls"—he was thinking of the dungeon/dormitory—"plumbing, heating, electricity, tile work, some floor finishing and plastering or sheet rock, if there's enough time."

"There's no way that—"

"I will pay three times the going rate. Cash."

There was a long sigh. Vikar could tell he'd caught the contractor's interest. "Buddy, you could be talking a half mil or more."

"That I am." Vikar took his black American Express card out of his pocket and read the numbers over the phone.

While he was waiting for a response, the contractor no doubt checking out his credit rating, Alex walked into the kitchen. Her hair was still wet and combed off her face and down her back. She wore tight, calf-length white pants and a lime-green T-shirt that proclaimed, "D.C. Marathon." On her bare feet, he noticed pale peach enameled toenails.

Immediately his cock did a happy dance. Aroused by toes? What next?

"You have an American Express Centurion

card?" he heard in the phone still pressed to his ear.

"Yes, I do."

"How 'bout I come up there in say, two hours, no later than noon, and we can talk?"

"I will be here." Vikar gave the man the address and directions.

Before the contractor hung up, he added, "Do me a favor, pal? Don't call anyone else. I might be able to handle it all with subcontracting. Unemployment is high in Pennsylvania at the moment."

"Agreed! But a seven-day completion schedule is a deal breaker for me. Ten days in a crunch, but that's it."

After he ended the call, he turned and saw Alex standing in front of the open cooling box . . . refrigerator. She'd already turned on the coffeemaker and it was bubbling away. He would have done it himself but last time he'd tried, he'd ended up with hot water and nothing else.

"I'm starved," she said.

"Me too."

She arched her brows at him. "Where's Lizzie?" She cocked her head to the side, listening. "And everyone else?"

"They're all gone, except for you, me, Armod, two warrior karls, and one blood ceorl."

She opened her mouth to ask more questions about where everyone had gone, why they'd gone, and what were a warrior karl and a blood ceorl, no doubt, but instead asked, "Has anyone eaten yet?"

He shook his head slowly.

"How does a mushroom and cheese omelet sound?"

"Wonderful," he started to say, but his stomach

growled first, giving her a better answer. They both laughed.

"Go see if anyone else wants to share breakfast with us," she ordered.

He did, and soon he, Alex, Armod, Svein, Jogeir, and Dagmar were seated on stools along the counter, devouring cheese-oozing omelets, toasted and buttered French bread—*turned out Armod knew how to work a toaster oven*—along with cold orange juice, warm Fake-O, and hot coffee. Everyone talked amiably, except for Alex, who was soaking up all the information she could from their conversation, and Dagmar. Blood ceorls were unable to talk.

While Svein and Jogeir went off to their guard stations, and Armod and Dagmar were cleaning up the dishes and countertops, Vikar booted up his laptop and pulled out a legal pad and pen from a box of supplies he'd brought from the office.

"What are you doing?" Alex asked, sipping at her second cup of coffee. He could only handle one. Caffeine affected vampires like a sugar high for kids. His nerves were already jangling.

"I've sent everyone . . . almost everyone . . . away for one week. Maybe ten days. I need to have this heap of rocks renovated by then, or at least habitable."

"You're joking."

"That's what the contractor said on the phone a little while ago. He'll be here soon to assess the situation."

"It would take a miracle."

"Money creates miracles betimes. If you throw enough cash at the right person, it might be doable."

"So, what's on your list?" she asked, pulling

her stool closer so that she could see his computer screen.

For a moment, he was disconcerted by the scent of her apple-scented shampoo. First peaches, now apples. He was becoming a fruit connoisseur. He stupidly said the first thing that came to mind. "Your hair doesn't look so red when it's wet."

"I do not have red hair," she said indignantly. "I have strawberry-blonde hair, I'll have you know."

He smiled. *Peaches, apples, and strawberries. Can anyone say fruitcake?* "Having red hair is a bad thing?"

"Hah! Try having red—rather, strawberry-blonde hair—as a kid and being teased all the time. 'Red head, peed the bed!' Or 'Red head, never wed!'"

"Huh?"

She ignored him and studied his list, reading aloud, "'Reframe dungeon into dormitory with flat-screen TVs and game room. One large bathing room with six shower stalls, six toilet stalls, and sinks.

"'Rewire entire castle, indoors and out, including security lighting. Refit the other eleven bathing rooms with fixtures: toilets, sinks, showers, tubs.

"'Refinish floors, tile bathrooms, painting.'"

"How about furnishings?"

He groaned.

"Won't you at least have to provide beds and mattresses for all those rooms? A dining room table and chairs? Living room furniture? Lamps and ceiling lights? Bed linens and towels?"

He groaned again. "'Tis impossible!"

"Hey, you're the one who believes in miracles."

"What are you saying?"

"Honey, you have just met Ms. Super Shopper. I

can spot a bargain at one hundred paces. With an unlimited budget? Be still my heart! Plus I have great taste."

He smiled. "You would be willing to help me?"

She nodded. "You should smile more often. You're handsome when you smile."

And I am not handsome all the time? he wondered with consternation, foolish pride rearing its head, then immediately chastised himself, *Look where my appearance has got me thus far.*

Her face turned a light shade of pink, a wonderful complement to her red . . . uh, strawberry-blonde . . . hair, which was incidentally now forming unruly waves.

Oh crap! First, fruit gets my sap running. Now colors. What next? "Why would you help me?"

"Tit for tat."

He didn't like the sound of that. "Explain yourself, wench."

"You mentioned something about St. Michael the Archangel and perhaps being able to tell where my daughter is."

Uh-oh!

With much reluctance, he conceded, "I did."

"Great!"

Great for whom? So that's why she was being so amiable.

Mike is going to kill me. Again!

Five

Have credit card, will travel . . .

With the world spinning out of control, crime rampant, jobs disappearing, and the economy tanking, angels sent to the rescue would be a boon to mankind. But angels don't really exist. Do they?

The residents of a castle in Transylvania, Pennsylvania, known more for vampires than angels, would beg to differ . . .

"Hey, Ben," Alex said into the cordless phone she held to her ear in Vikar's office while he was off giving the contractor a tour and signing contracts. It appeared that money did truly talk. The job would be done in one week, or the guy wouldn't be paid.

"Alex! Where the hell have you been? I've been trying to call you."

"Sorry. Here's the landline telephone number in

case my cell isn't working." She gave him the number because, even when she'd plugged her phone into a kitchen outlet this morning, she still didn't get any bars.

"I thought you were staying at some bed-and-breakfast."

"I was, but when Lord Vikar invited me to stay here at the castle, I decided to go with the flow."

"Are you sure that's wise?"

Probably not. "What could go wrong?" *More than already has.*

"Is there a story there?"

"Oh yes! Definitely." *The question is what.*

"Tell me."

"First of all, Transylvania itself has got to be the nutcase capital of the world. It could make a fun feature."

"And? I can tell there's more."

She hesitated, not sure how much to tell him. Oh hell! He wouldn't believe her, anyway. "The castle is a monstrosity which Lord Vikar is going to renovate in one week."

Ben laughed. "Obviously, he's never worked on a renovation before." Ben and his wife, Gloria, had been renovating a Virginia farmhouse for twenty years now, and they still weren't done.

"But that's not the real story. You are going to think I'm crazy, Ben, but the folks here at the castle claim to be Viking vampire angels. Vangels."

"Have you been bitten yet?" He was teasing, of course, and never expected her answer.

"Actually, yes."

"What?" he roared. "You get yourself out of there right now. Do you want a police escort?"

"No. It wasn't one of the vangels who bit me," she said quickly, although that wasn't quite true. With selective honesty, she explained, "It was a demon vampire, a Lucipire, and it happened back at the B&B which is incidentally called Bed & Blood." She had to suppress a giggle every time she said that name for the B&B. "It's run by a couple who sell stinking roses, garlic bulbs the size of baseballs, at a roadside stand, to ward off vampires, and spiffy hand-carved caskets on the Internet."

"You're shittin' me."

"No shit!"

"You don't believe this vampire/angel/demon crap, do you?"

"No, of course not." *Maybe.*

"And there's a story there?"

"Definitely a story. I'm just not sure what it will be yet." *Should I tell him about the imminent arrival of St. Michael the Archangel? Nah. He's having a hard enough time with vangels and Lucipires. So am I.*

"How long will you be there?"

"I'm not sure. Today we're going shopping for towels. Me and Lord Vikar." She grinned at the domestic picture. A vampire trolling the aisles of Bed Bath & Beyond.

Ben knew how much she liked to shop. Or used to. She could hear the smile in his voice when he said, "Go to town, sweetheart. And have a little fun."

Surprisingly, Alex *was* having fun, she realized after saying good-bye and promising to keep in touch every day. Since Vikar wasn't back yet . . . she could hear talking through the open doorway, coming from the kitchen area . . . she browsed the office. Once the library, it could be restored to a handsome room with its walnut paneling and floor-to-ceiling bookshelves that were mostly empty.

She did see one box-type filing container, the kind that held folders for folks who didn't want to bother with actual filing cabinets. Taking it down, she had to dust it off with someone's T-shirt lying on the floor. The box looked old.

And it was. Turned out, these were papers the original owners had used when buying supplies and furniture. A gold mine for a restorer. Her heart started to beat wildly when she found one particular document.

"Vikar!" she squealed, and went running down the hall.

He and the contractor, a fortyish man wearing khakis and a golf shirt with the logo "J.D. Donovan & Sons," came running toward her.

"What?" Vikar asked with concern, grabbing her by the shoulders. "Are you hurt? Did something fall on you? Oh, clouds! Did Armod accidentally bite you?"

"No, no, no!" She handed him the folder and did a little boogie dance step toward the kitchen.

J.D. stared at her as if she'd flipped her lid. Vikar was more interested in ogling her behind as she danced. They both followed after her.

"I think I found all your furniture," she announced, flopping the open folder on the counter in a ta-da fashion. "The original owner, before he was forced to go into a hospital for a long stay, had everything removed and taken to an Amish barn in Belleville that he'd rented. He'd planned on having the whole interior painted before he returned, which he never did."

"After all these years, do you think it would all still be there with no additional rent having been paid?" Vikar asked skeptically. His eyebrows rose as he perused the list: parlor chairs and settees, Tiffany-style lamps, carpets, a dining room table and chairs, a baby grand piano, for heaven's sake! Beds, armoires, dressers. Even fireplace accessories. Who knew what kind of taste a guy who built this castle would have, but, hey, it would give them a start.

Odd, how she'd referred to *them* and not just *him*, she pondered for a moment.

"Hey, you never know with the Amish," J.D. remarked. "They're a very moral people. And their farms stay in the family."

"It's worth checking, right?" Alex asked Vikar.

Thus it was that Alex found herself riding in a black Lexus SUV with shaded windows next to a vampire angel with a ponytail, wearing aviator sunglasses and what he swore was his normal attire: black jeans, black Gucci loafers without socks, a black silk T-shirt, *and* a full-length black cloak with a raised collar and epaulettes on the shoulders in the form of silver wings, which hid his WTF sword in a belt sheath and an equally WTF Sig Sauer pistol in a shoulder holster.

She glanced over at Vikar and smiled.

He smiled back at her.

Forget about Beavis and Butthead. She was having the best Great Adventure.

A vampire needs a sense of humor, too . . .

Vikar was treading a high wire with no net. He knew it, sure as sin, and that's just what he was tempting. Sin.

He was knee-deep in the near occasion of sin and had never been happier. Like a pig wallowing in quicksand, pretending it was mud, that's how foolish he'd become. The risks he was taking defied explanation. Was it because betimes the anticipation of sin was as delicious as the sin itself? Or was it something more? Not that lure of sex wasn't enough.

"Why are you grinning?" Alex asked him. She was sitting across the table from him at a booth in the Blood Bath, a tavern just outside Transylvania known for its red beer on tap. *Ugh!* At least he didn't draw any attention here, as the staff and some of the customers looked more like vampires than he did. Besides, the restaurant was mostly empty, it being past the lunch hour and too early for the dinner crowd.

"I'm pleased with all we accomplished today at the farmer's," he replied, which was not really a lie, just not what he'd been thinking, "thanks mostly to your help."

He couldn't stop staring at all the bare skin exposed by the short-sleeved, scoop-necked, mint-green sweater she wore over a short white skirt, the green just a shade lighter than her clear emerald eyes. While her face and neck were creamy white, her arms and chest had freckles, lots of them, which made him think she must use some cosmetic product to cover up her face. She shouldn't bother because, really, her freckles were attractive, to him leastways.

"Thank you, kind sir, for the compliment." She did a little seated curtsy for emphasis.

For a moment, he forgot what he'd said and had to shake his head to clear it of carnal musings. "I called the contractor when you went to the ladies' powdering room, and he already has a dozen men tearing out the old plumbing pipes, some of which are lead and might cause someone to die of lead poisoning." He waggled his eyebrows at her as if to say, *Ha, ha, dead people dying of lead poisoning.*

She didn't laugh, but then she was still not convinced she'd landed in a den of dead people.

"Will there be running water while they're working?"

He nodded. "J.D. promised to renovate the bathing room next to my bedchamber last, along with the kitchen and nearby half bathroom, all of which are workable at the moment. Those should suffice for the six of us."

"Good thinking. I'm glad you went with my suggestion about keeping some of the old fixtures."

He nodded. In many ways, they were a good match. Certainly it had been her good thinking that led them to the Amish farmer today. *And, yes, I fear other ways in which we match, too, and it has naught to do with furniture, except mayhap tongue and groove. By thunder! My brain is a melting puddle of running sex-sap.* "At least we have some furniture to start with now," he said, trying his best to sound calm and not so lustsome, "because, truth to tell, I consider shopping as painful an experience as plucking nose hairs."

"Nice image there!"

He shrugged. He was a Viking, not a girlie man.

"It's truly amazing that I found that file and then just as amazing to find out that the lump sum the lumber baron gave the farmer all those years ago literally saved the farm."

To him, it was also amazing that this amazing woman had walked into his life just yesterday and made him feel . . . well, amazing. *I wonder . . . do those amazing freckles cover her amazing bosom as well?* Her breasts were not all that big, but they appeared so because of her slim frame. He knew a lot about women's breasts. Past history, of course.

"The farmer and his family couldn't have been more thankful," she continued, oblivious to his wandering mind, "and they always thought one of the family would come for the contents eventually. Unfortunately, there was no family. It makes you wonder about the man who built the castle, Mr. Waxmonsky. What his dreams were, why such an edifice, did he have a woman in mind who would share it with him, so many questions."

He smiled at her. "You see stories everywhere, don't you?"

"I do. Printer's ink in my blood, as the old saying goes." She smiled back at him.

A companionable silence followed until he exclaimed, "But fifty years!" Though fifty years should seem like a week to a man like him who had more years on him than Methuselah. "I cannot believe that the farmer's descendants held everything for fifty years."

"And he couldn't believe you were willing to pay him twenty thousand dollars in past rent. Do you always carry that much cash around in the well of your SUV?"

He shrugged. Money meant little to him. Harek, whose sin had been greed, had a flair for finances. In fact, he'd bought Apple stock when folks probably thought it was a seed company. To say they had a hefty bank account, spread across the world to avoid attention, was a vast understatement. "You're right, Alex. I swear, the farmer practically had a orgasm when I started peeling off those hundreds." *Oh, clouds! Did I have to say that word? Now I will be having more lustsome thoughts. Forget tongue and groove. I will be thinking about rolling waves and longboats and tight channels. I swear, this woman has put a spell on me. Or else I am falling apart due to overlong celibacy.*

"Do Amish have orgasms?"

Oh, this is just wonderful. Now she is saying that word, too. I am doomed.

"Isn't it against their religion or something?" she inquired with an irrelevance he found fascinating. Conversations with her always meandered in the oddest directions.

"Sweetling, there isn't a religion in the world, in any age, that can stop a man from spilling his seed with great joy." *Hopefully inside a willing woman.* "Besides, how do you think they beget all those children?"

"You have a point there."

Of course I do, and if you are not careful, I might decide to elaborate. Or demonstrate. "Do you think the stored items are worth that much?" he asked, bringing the subject back to safer territory.

"Absolutely. Oh, some of the carpets and paintings might be damaged beyond repair. Even though the barn was water-tight, and everything was covered, there were temperature changes, and mice. Lots of mice. Did you see how much mice dirt was on that big mirror? Yuck!"

He grinned. "If you think mice dirt is bad, you should have seen how many barrels of guano we had to remove from the castle."

"Actually, guano makes a good fertilizer. You probably could have sold it to some local farmers."

"Hah! 'Twas bad enough shoveling the crap out of a window to land in a Dumpster. I cannot imagine the protests if I'd asked my ceorls to put it into neat little bags."

"You have a great sense of humor," she remarked after wiping tears of mirth from her eyes.

"Me? You think I am funny?" That was not the way he wanted to appear, especially to a beautiful woman.

"Not funny. Appreciative of the humor in life. Being able to laugh at yourself."

Well, that wasn't so bad, he supposed, and whacked himself mentally for caring. Foolish pride, again!

The waitress, a young girl who wore a low-cut blouse that exposed her neck and painted-on fang marks dripping blood, brought their order. Juicy bacon cheeseburgers, French fries, and iced tea for her and a bottle of beer for him.

At first they just ate in silence, enjoying the meal. He especially enjoyed watching her enjoy eating French fries. First she dipped the long fried potato sticks in catsup, then sucked the red matter off the end before taking precisely three sharp bites out of each and every one. But then Alex pulled out a little black box and set it on the table between them. A mini tape recorder.

Uh-oh!

"Do you mind?" she asked. "It helps for accuracy when I get down to writing my article."

He hesitated, then shrugged. There was going to be no article, but she did not need to know that yet.

"I noticed that your fangs were not out at all today? So, they're fake, right?"

He finished swallowing from his long-necked bottle. "For a certainty, my fangs are real, but I can control them. Most times. That comes with age."

"How old are you?"

"I was born in 817 and died when I was thirty and three."

She choked on her hamburger and had to take a long drink of iced tea before scoffing, "More than a thousand years old?"

"Yes. As for the fangs. Mostly I can keep them recessed, but when I am angry, about to engage in a fight to the death with a Lucie, or excited . . . in other ways . . . I cannot control them."

"What in blazes is a Lucie?"

"Lucies are a short name for Lucipires. I told you about them before."

She still looked skeptical.

Oh, now you have done it, wench! You will regret your hasty disbelief when I show you. "For example, if I picture you lying on my bed, naked, with black satin sheets framing your white skin, your red hair spread out like flames, your nether hair a nest of red dandelion fluff, and your freckles standing out like gold dust—"

"That is enough!" she squeaked out. "And I do not have red hair. And it doesn't look like dandelion fluff down there."

He shrugged and licked his bottom lip, then showed her his extended fangs. "You excite me," he explained, pointing to his teeth.

"It must be a trick. Some kind of marvel you've perfected."

It was a good thing a table separated them and hid him from waist down or he would show her other marvels. "Accept it, m'lady. For my sins, I am a Viking vampire angel. If you believe naught else, believe that."

"Okay, let's assume that I do believe, tell me how it happened. When did it start?"

"Is this going to be *Interview with the Vampire*?" he teased, avoiding the inevitable, knowing how revolted she would be by him afterward.

"I'm no Anne Rice, Vikar."

"And I'm no vampire Louis."

She gave him a sharp touché! look of approval at his quick retort. "I'm just a reporter. A good one. Be honest with me, and I'll do an honest story. Now, start at the beginning."

He took a deep breath, then started, "God was angry with the Vikings for our arrogance and bloodthirstiness and mostly because we worshipped other gods. Odin, Thor, and the like. He decided to destroy our entire race."

"Whoa, whoa, whoa! You don't pull any punches."

"If you want the truth, you are going to have to let me tell the story, my way. And if you think about it, you will realize there is no Viking society today.

Why is that, do you suppose? How could such a powerful class of people just disappear and meld into other cultures?"

She shook her head slowly, having no answer for him. You didn't have to be a Norse historian to realize he spoke the truth. There was no Viking country today. Certainly not Norway or Denmark. The closest to the old society was Iceland, whose language was similar to Old Norse.

"In any case, God was also angry with my family in particular. My father Sigurd the Vicious—"

"Sid Vicious? Holy cow! The rocker from the Sex Pistols?"

"Huh? *No*, Sigurd . . . the . . . Vicious," he enunciated. "A ninth-century warrior jarl."

"Sounds like a WWE wrestler," she scoffed, but motioned for him to continue when he frowned at her interruption.

"My father was the seventh son of a seventh son, and he begat seven sons, including myself. Seven is an important number in the Bible, you know, but we can discuss that later."

"Okay, so God was angry with Vikings in general, and your family in particular. And?"

"He was going to destroy us all, but St. Michael the Archangel intervened on our behalf."

She rolled her eyes. "What did your family do that was so grievous?"

He sighed. "So much! But I will speak only of myself. I was a prideful man. So vain and full of myself, though I did not see myself that way at the time."

"Pride doesn't seem so bad."

He arched his brows at her. *You have no idea!* "Because I was so blind with pride, my first wife, Vendela, pregnant at the time, killed herself by jumping off a cliff. I built a castle to glorify my name and never cared that numerous slaves died in the process. I killed indiscriminately in battle, taking the innocent along with the enemy."

Her face went pale. He'd only just started and already she was horrified, but he was wrong in his assessment of why.

"Did you have other children, Vikar?"

Ah, he saw where this was going now. "I did."

"How many?"

"I honestly do not know. Two daughters with Princess Halldora, though they may or may not have been of my blood. She had the morals of a feral cat. But I do know that I had at least a half-dozen illegitimate boys and girls on my concubines. And there were the thralls, of course. I misdoubt there were any less than twelve."

The expression on her face was so cold, he swore he could feel the temperature around them drop to freezing. "What were their names? What happened to them?"

"I have no idea. I mean, I could name a few, but not all of them." He had asked, but Mike didn't think he deserved to know. There could very well be a child of his blood walking the earth today, but he would never know.

She gave him a look of such loathing, he recoiled. "Men like you make me sick." On those harsh words, she stood and ran from the restaurant.

With a sigh of regret, he paid their bill, picked up her tape recorder and purse, and walked out into the parking lot.

That's when all hell broke loose. Literally.

Alex had walked to the far side of the lot near a wooded area and was leaning her forehead against a tree. At the same instant Vikar opened the SUV and tossed her purse inside, he heard two motorcycles enter the area, screech up almost to Alex, rev their motors in place, then jump off.

A man and a woman leisurely removed their helmets and glanced around, as if they were here to enjoy the scenery . . . or a victim. *Lucipires!* Alex's sin scent must have attracted them.

Whoosh! Faster than thought, faster than any human could run, he was in front of Alex, barring her from the Lucipires.

"What? Oh my God! What . . . who are they?" She had moved slightly and was staring around him.

Before their eyes, the man and woman in leathers transformed from beautiful twentysomething bikers to gnarled, giant, red-skinned creatures with open, oozing sores, claw-like hands, and fangs that kept snapping with anticipation. Their eyes were red as well, and pure evil.

"Run to the car and lock the door," he told her as he pulled out his sword and the Sig with its special bullets. He would need both if he and Alex were to survive, not that he doubted his ability to overtake a mere two Lucipires.

Frozen in shock, Alex didn't move.

"Alex!" he shouted, and shoved her away from him as he stepped forward. Finally, she heeded his warning. Only when he saw that she was safely inside the vehicle did he engage the two mungs. In the Lucipire hierarchy, these were full demons. Deadly as any other, especially with the poisonous slime that oozed from every surface of their bodies, but they were not quite as experienced as a haakai or a full-fledged Seraphim like Jasper, but superior to the foot soldiers of Satan, imps and hordlings.

Just then, one of the Lucies seemed to notice the winged epaulettes on his shoulders and the special signet ring he and his brothers wore, marking them as the VIK. The male mung whispered to the female. Vikar could not hear what he said, except for the word *seven*. They grinned at each other, already gloating over the prize they would be bringing home to Jasper.

Not if he could help it!

Without warning, he shot the male in each kneecap, bringing him to his broken knees, screaming with agony. A vangel bullet could injure Lucies, even "kill" them, but he needed to do more than that. Unless he cleaved its head, forehead to chin, with his sword until the body disintegrated, or pierced its heart with the specially-treated bullet or blade, the Lucie would just return to Hell to regroup. Recycling at its worst!

Meanwhile, he had the female to deal with. She swung a mace with iron spikes, striking him on one shoulder. The pain was excruciating, but he was equally skillful with a sword in either hand, and he still had six bullets in his Sig.

He dropped his cloak and turned his head, exposing his neck. "Come on, sweetling. Don't you want a little sip?"

The female Lucipire hissed and her red tongue darted in and out like a serpent. There was nothing more tempting to a Lucie than vangel blood, and one of The Seven would be especially tempting.

Unable to resist, the Lucipire lunged at him.

He turned his head quickly, and the Lucipire's teeth grazed his cheek, drawing blood, which turned the Lucipire frantic with bloodlust. That instant of distraction gave Vikar the chance to grasp her throat and squeeze until she wilted and fell to the ground. Without hesitation, he raised his sword and cut her face in half straight down between the fangs to the heart. The skin turned even brighter red, then the entire body began to slowly melt into a stinksome slime. Sulfur.

Only then did he turn to the male Lucie, intending the same fate, but the creature had managed to crawl over to the motorcycle and was already racing away. If Vikar had not been distracted and injured, he would have noticed and followed. But there were more important things for him to attend to now. Like Alex.

He shook the slime off his fingers and then walked slowly back to the SUV. It was a miracle that no one had noticed the activity at the other end of the lot, or, if they had, chalked it up to more crazy vampire wannabe shenanigans. When he got inside the vehicle, he saw instantly that Alex was in shock, shaking violently and whimpering. He wanted to comfort her but first he leaned over and opened the glove compartment, taking out a packet of holy water wipes. They were specially made by one of the vangel ceorls to remove mung slime and other Lucipire contaminants from vangel skin.

Despite still feeling unclean, he pulled her over and wrapped his arms around her. After a while, she shoved away from him and gave an embarrassed laugh. "I never thought I'd say this about an assignment, but I may be in over my head here."

That was an understatement.

"Let's go home," she suggested.

Her inadvertent use of the word *home* for his castle struck a warm note in his heart, as if it wasn't already warm enough toward her.

She was silent for most of the trip, but then she asked as he turned on the lane that led up toward the gates being guarded by Svein, "Are those creatures everywhere?"

He waited until Svein waved him through and closed the gates after them.

"Yes, there are Lucies everywhere." *Thousands and thousands, and their numbers growing like bad weeds in a manure heap with the increasingly decadent society.* "But usually only a few in any one area, and, of course, some have none at all. It's when they travel in hordes that they pose a huge problem." Now *he* was engaging in understatements by implying that one Lucipire alone was of no concern.

"So those two were probably the only ones in this area?" She gazed at him hopefully.

He considered telling her about the one he'd killed in the castle kitchen just before she arrived, or reminding her about the one that had bitten her at the B&B, or the one that had gotten away and might announce to Jasper that there was a Seven in the vicinity, but decided not to scare her any more than she already was.

Luckily, she didn't wait for an answer, or unluckily, because she was thinking too much, raising too many questions. "Why did those two come into the restaurant parking lot today? They seemed to be heading straight for . . . Oh my God! They were looking for me, weren't they?"

He hesitated for a long moment before nodding. "It's your scent that drew them."

"I smell?" she asked indignantly.

"Yes. Lucies give off an offensive sulfur odor, but mortal sinners, or those about to become mortal sinners, smell rather tart, like lemons. Not an unpleasant scent, and obvious only to vangels or Lucipires, at least in the early stages." He passed a number of contractor trucks and vans in front and in the back, too, where he parked the SUV. Turning to her, he continued, "You are lemony. Like lemon sorbet." In an effort to comfort her, he patted her hand that sat on the seat between them.

She slapped his hand away. "Those . . . those creatures could have killed you."

That surprised him, that her concern was for him. "I am already dead," he tried to appease her with his much-repeated refrain.

"You are an idiot."

"That I am." *Really, the wench needs her funny bone tweaked.*

"I don't understand. It's as if I've landed in an alternate universe. Monsters like those don't really exist. And you say I'm the one who drew them. Are there going to be more? And good Lord, the way you fought! Are you like the Hulk or something?"

"Do I look like the Hulk?"

She started to cry.

"Now, do not get upset."

"Upset?" she shrieked. "I'm freaking out here."

"Settle down, Alex. I am here to help you. In fact, we will go inside now and do another cleansing." *And if I'm lucky, I'll spill a little of that seed I mentioned earlier. Or did I just think it? Whatever.* What a wonderful word that was! *Whatever.* Too bad they hadn't had it back in his day. Whenever his mother had threatened to wallop him for pissing in her rosebush, he could have said, "Whatever!" Or when Ivak had bragged that he'd bedded six women in one night, he could have said, "Whatever!" Or whenever—

"Fuck you and your help," Alex said.

Whoa, that is certainly telling me. With his distracted mind, he had to remind himself what she was reacting so strongly to. Oh, that's right. He'd attempted to assure her that he would help with her Lucipire blood.

"If I want to sin, I'll sin. Keep all your woo-woo cleansing crap to yourself. Let me out. Right now. I'm going to D.C. where the crazies are at least human."

He flipped the door unlock mechanism, and she shot out like . . . well, a bat out of Hell. He would have smiled at his own pun, if he weren't too busy chasing after her.

They were both stopped dead in the kitchen where Armod, chomping on a hard pretzel and slurping up Fake-O, had an ominous announcement, "Mike has a message for you."

Armod spoke to him, but it was Alex who responded, "Mike, his agent?"

"Huh?" Armod said. "*No*, St. Michael the Archangel. Our boss."

Alex threw her hands up in the air and sailed out of the room, like a longship in high wind, muttering, "Demons, vampires, angels, and now the big guy himself. What next? Noah building an ark out on Colyer Lake?"

Vikar could swear he heard a distant voice say, "Oh please, God, not another ark!" But it was probably the sound of Alex shouting obscenities as she stomped up four flights of stairs to her bedroom, before slamming the door hard enough to shake a few slates off the roof.

She didn't come down at all for the rest of the day, and he let Armod bring a dinner tray up for her . . . Domino's pizza and a beer. When he pressed his face against her door, he heard her pounding away on the keyboard of her laptop. No doubt blasting him and questioning her sanity. He would have liked to do another cleansing on her, but he was not a total idiot. That could wait until the morrow.

He had been sure Mike was going to ream his arse for calling Jasper's attention to himself, or dawdling over unimportant things like furniture, or having impure thoughts, but when the angel appeared to him that night in his dreams, the message was clear: "Save her!"

Six

**How much testosterone
can one woman stand?** . . .

Have you ever seen a mung walking? I
have. They are giant, red-skinned creatures
covered with a poisonous slime. And fangs.
Long, pointed incisors designed to rip the flesh
from humans who cross their path. Especially
tasty to them are mortal sinners whom they
can add to their wicked flock.

Are they real? Or a figment of an overac-
tive imagination fueled by the vampire mania
flooding the world, or . . .

Five days later, and Alex was still at Dracula's
Castle, as she'd come to refer to her home away from
home. And she was getting grumpier and probably

more sinful by the day, thoughts of murder surely being in the mortal sin category.

Was it true, what Vikar said, that her thoughts of killing her daughter's murderers could be detected as a "sin taint" by him or other creatures of the night? And could that inclination to sin be enhanced by a demon bite? It was preposterous, of course, but it sure as hell—*and wasn't that an accidental pun?*—felt as if her anger and need for revenge were increasing.

Besides that, she still could not get over what she'd witnessed in that parking lot. There had been something evil there. It had not been a figment of her imagination.

In the meantime, three days ago she'd gotten alarming news from an assistant district attorney in D.C. regarding the trial of Pablo and Jorge Mercado, the drug cartel members who'd murdered her husband and daughter. He divulged off the record that they might get off on a technicality or receive a light sentence. Her testimony could be a deciding factor. Alex's blood boiled with hatred every time she thought about these scumbags escaping punishment. If she knew how, she'd hire a Lucipire to do the job for her, even if she risked her own life . . . or soul.

Vikar kept telling her that if she'd just let him cleanse her again, she would feel better. Well, she didn't want to feel better.

She should have gone home by now, but when she'd told Ben about wanting to testify, he urged her to stay at the castle, out of sight. It would be just like the cartel to put a hit out on her, Ben told her. So here she stayed in Wackoville, working on her story that kept changing direction the more she learned.

And, honestly, she didn't want to leave. Not yet. For reasons too close to her vulnerable heart to examine at the moment.

"Armod! That's beautiful," she said, just noticing that the boy had finished polishing the walnut sideboard and was admiring his fangs in the wavy mirror that was part of its back section. The boy was a fairly new vampire and apparently didn't have the control over their movement that Vikar and others did. He loved to pose with them extended, when he wasn't doing his Michael Jackson impressions, that was. Like teenagers everywhere, he was obsessed with his appearance, except his obsession was fangs instead of zits.

And wasn't that a marvel, that she'd somehow accepted that the fangs were real on the people here in the castle. Was there a whole subculture of paranormal creatures roaming about undetected, like that Charlaine Harris world of Sookie Stackhouse? At one time—a week ago, in fact—she would have scoffed at the idea. Now she wasn't so sure.

"This piece was easier to clean than the chairs." Armod pointed to the two armed and eighteen armless chairs that sat along the covered verandah in back where they were working on the furniture that had been delivered from the farm. There was a great deal of carving on the chair backs that Alex had forced Armod to clean with Q-tips and Murphy Oil Soap. All the seats had been pried off, and she planned to recover them herself with a handy staple gun and some fabric she'd purchased online from a design shop that she'd hired on behalf of Vikar to do window treatments and bedspreads later.

She would have liked to go into the designer's Harrisburg warehouse herself, but Mr. Bossy Viking refused to let anyone leave the castle because of the Lucipire threat, until reinforcements returned in a few days.

Right now, the bossy vampire was off doing important things, like picking the color of tile for the dungeon shower stalls, while she and Armod engaged in hard labor. Okay, that was a bit of an exaggeration. She enjoyed seeing the beauty of the old furniture emerge from its layers of dirt and mold. Jogeir was doing guard duty at the gate, while Svein had gone somewhere to feed in private off the mute blood ceorl Dagmar. Alex didn't want to think about what that might entail, but apparently it was something the young woman did willingly; it was her job, for heaven's sake.

"I notice you're not lisping so much," she said.

Armod blushed. "Vikar is helping me."

That insight into Vikar touched Alex, for some reason.

Back to the furniture. Most of the pieces were of the heavy Empire period, not to her particular taste, but suited to a stone castle where spindly Queen Anne legs would seem out of place. Plus, the mostly male vangels seemed to be of considerable size, even young Armod, who was over six feet tall and slim, but still growing.

Armod tossed his cleaning rag aside and asked, "What are we having for dinner?"

"Armod! We just got done with lunch."

He shrugged sheepishly. The boy was always hungry.

"We're having tacos," she informed him.

His eyes lit up. "And pie for dessert?"

"Yes, Armod, there will be apple pie à la mode. Your favorite. Thanks to your Aunt Sara."

"Aunt Sara Lee?" He laughed. "My favorite aunt, for a certainty."

"Let's work on the dining room table next. That shouldn't be too hard because of the large flat surface. How about you do the extension boards, while I tackle the table itself?"

While they were working, Armod said, "Why are you so mean to Lord Vikar?"

Am I that obvious? "Because he is a pig?"

Armod gasped. "M'lady! He is no such thing."

"I shouldn't have said that. It's just that he annoys me when he tells me what to do all the time, like he knows what's best for me." *All he has to do is look at me and I melt.*

"He is the best master in the world. If not for him, I would be burning in Hell."

Oh boy! What can of worms have I opened now? "What do you mean, Armod?"

"I did bad things. Very bad things. Lord Vikar petitioned on my behalf, even after St. Michael decided I was a poor candidate for the vangels."

"What? Oh, sweetheart, I cannot imagine anything—"

"I killed people. Many people."

Her heart sank.

"I was a prostitute on the streets of Reykjavik in Iceland. When I got AIDS, I knowingly, deliberately continued having unprotected sex, spreading the disease."

Her forehead furrowed with puzzlement. "I thought Iceland was supposed to be virtually crime-free."

"It is, but over the years prostitution has been legalized, off and on. Even today, selling sex isn't illegal, but buying it is."

"An odd distinction!"

Armod shrugged. "In any case, twenty men who'd been with me died, and thirty were infected before I finally succumbed myself."

She should be disgusted. She was, but more than that. "Armod, how old were you when you first started hooking?"

"Ten, but I had been taken by men since I was six. That does not excuse what I did. Not the prostitution so much, although that was bad, but the spreading of a killer disease. I did so knowingly, wanting to kill my customers."

"Are you gay, Armod?"

"I don't think so. *No.* I was a pretty child who attracted men. Pedophiles, at first. Later, when I was no longer child-like and pretty, I just offered my body where it would gain the most cash. From men. Did I mention I was a drug addict, too?"

Alex could tell that Armod struggled with his lisp as he talked. She walked over and gave him a hug. This was why the kid obsessed over Michael Jackson music. He'd never had a chance to be a real teenager when he was . . . well, alive.

Honestly, she didn't know what to think anymore. In the best of all worlds, a person's good deeds were supposed to be weighed against the bad, but when this boy was taken, he'd had no chance to repent. Ah, she realized then. The Lucipires had infected him, had influenced his willpower. This was what Vikar had been trying to explain to her.

Oh my God! Am I actually starting to believe all this crap?

"So, you see, Lord Vikar is my hero. He went out on a limb, promising to take me under his wing." Armod giggled at his own pun. "He is patient in dealing with my mistakes. And he even puts up with my Michael Jackson music, which I know he abhors."

"St. Vikar," she remarked snidely. Snideness seemed to be her pattern of late. Not very attractive, she had to admit.

"*No*, not a saint. But he is a good man. You should treat him better."

"Yes, you should treat me better," Vikar said, coming up on the tail end of the conversation and pinching her butt.

"You jerk!" She rubbed her bottom.

"That didn't hurt." He leaned closer to her ear. "Now, if I'd *bitten* your arse, that would be different."

She backed away from him. "You wouldn't dare!" Surely they didn't do cleansing that way, too, did they?

"Only if you ask." He grinned, reading her thoughts.

"What's with this constant teasing? Aren't vampires supposed to be dark and brooding?"

"There are all kinds. I can be dark and brooding if you prefer." He cast her a smoldering, half-lidded look that would set her socks afire if she were wearing any.

"We're having tacos for dinner," Armod interjected, and Vikar, bless his black heart, didn't make fun of the boy, but instead patted him on the head. "Great! My favorite! Hey, did you work on these chairs? They look like brand-new."

Armod beamed at Vikar, soaking up the older man's praise like manna. Vikar was clearly a father figure to the boy, who probably hadn't had much of one before, if any. She could almost forgive a man like that anything, even having drawn her into this weird world.

"C'mon," Vikar beckoned her then. "I want you to meet someone. You can finish up here, can't you, Armod?"

"Yes, and I will put everything away afterward."

"He thinks you're a god," Alex remarked as she followed Vikar into the castle. There were workmen throughout the house, although they were mostly done on the first floor. The whole place would need a good cleaning once they left. Even with meticulous care, there was a film of dust everywhere.

"*No*, not a god. Do not even whisper such," Vikar warned her. "Armod is just a needy boy at this stage of his transition."

"Were you needy?"

"More like broken," he murmured, but then did not elaborate even when she arched her brows at him. They passed his office and went, instead, to a large, windowless room on the other side that had once been a storage room of some sort, possibly a butler's pantry for crystal and china and such. All the shelves had been removed, and now there were two U-shaped desks that had been delivered yesterday, along with a bunch of computers, printers, monitors, and other electronic equipment too complicated for her to understand. At the moment, there were two men on their hands and knees under one of the desks attempting to maneuver a jungle of wires. All she could see was their denim-clad butts, and very nice butts they were, too.

"Hold the friggin' flashlight still, lackwit," one of them complained.

"I can't hold the flashlight and lift these cables at the same time, *lackwit*," the other countered. "Ouch! I just got shocked."

"You deserve to be shocked. How can a person with the IQ of a genius be so clumsy?"

"The same way as a person with the IQ of a penguin. What did you have for lunch, by the way? Your breath smells like garlic."

"I was kissing a waitress at an Italian restaurant in Milan."

"Kissing? Hah! You must have had your tongue down her throat to smell so strong."

"Of course."

"Good thing vampires aren't really repelled by garlic, although when it's blowing in a person's face, like your breath is—"

"Bite me!"

"Ahem!" Vikar said at her side. "We have company."

Both men on the floor went still, began to back out, then stood. Their fronts were just as attractive as their backsides, she had to admit. They were big men, like Vikar, but as different as night from day.

One of them was tall and wiry with close-clipped brown hair, piercing blue eyes, and wire-rimmed reading glasses perched midway down his nose. A Viking geek?

The other had longish black hair, a mustache, piercing blue eyes, and muscles like a bodybuilder. Put a sword in his hand, and he would be perfectly at ease on a battlefield. Or on a Hollywood set.

"These halfbrains are my brothers. I urged them to come after the Lucipire attacks. Their skills will help ensure our safety. This is Harek, who is a computer expert," Vikar said, pointing to the geek one. "And Cnut, who knows everything there is to know about security systems." Then, turning to her, he continued the introductions, "And this is Alexandra Kelly, our guest."

Both men nodded at her, suspiciously. She soon found out why.

"Vikar! She is unclean," Harek said bluntly.

"I beg your pardon," Alex said, glancing down to see if her hands or clothing were dirty. They weren't. *Ah, the lemon scent.*

"She must be cleansed at once," Cnut said.

Then the most alarming thing happened. Fangs came out on both men, and they were gazing at her like she was a yummy Krispy Kreme donut at a Weight Watchers meeting.

"I am taking care of it," a red-faced Vikar said, shoving her behind him.

"Not very well," Harek said. "The room fair reeks of lemons."

Yep, the lemon business.

"It does no good for me to set up a security system

here if you're going to wave a demon magnet like a bloody beacon," Cnut complained.

"I told you, I am taking care of it," Vikar repeated.

"We can help," Harek said.

"Yes, we will work her together," Cnut added.

Work me? Is that like "do me"? "Whoa, whoa, whoa!" She stepped out from behind Vikar's big body. "I am not engaging in any ménage à trois, not with normal men, and definitely not with bleepin' vampire angels, even if they do look like stud muffins."

The jaws of all three men dropped, further exposing fangs. Even Vikar now.

"And it's not because I'm chicken, either. I'm not afraid of you perverts."

"Ménage à trois?" Vikar sputtered. "For the love of mud!"

"Actually, that would be ménage à quatre," the geek corrected.

"A foursome," Cnut interpreted, his dour face breaking into a reluctant grin. "Now there's a thought."

"Perverts? We are not perverts," Vikar sputtered some more.

But then Harek, the brainiac, homed in on something else she'd said, "Who is she calling a stud muffin?" He, too, was grinning.

"We will see you at dinner," Vikar said to his brothers, attempting to shove her out the door.

"Tacos, not lemon chicken, will be on the table, gentlemen," Alex said, getting the last word in as she allowed Vikar to steer her away. Oddly, she wasn't frightened. Vikar would protect her. She hoped.

Once in the hall, he yanked her into his office and

closed the door. "I have given you space these past three days, but as you may have noticed in the midst of your blathering with my brothers, your situation is dire. Beginning tonight, we will exchange blood twice a day until you are pure."

"You can't make that decision for me."

"I can and I will."

"What about all that free will nonsense you keep spouting?"

He fisted his hands as if to keep from throttling her. "Once the cleansing ritual is complete, you can do whatever you want."

"Including leaving this castle?" *Why does that prospect suddenly hold no appeal for me? Is it the Stockholm syndrome, or something?*

"You can take a freight train to Hell for all I care!" He threw his hands up in frustration.

His words hurt her, for some reason. The Stockholm syndrome must work only one way. No reciprocation of sentiment. Thus, it was in a small voice that she said, "That's not true, Vikar. You do care. You care too much."

"Now you are going to psychoanalyze me?" He sighed deeply. "Why are you always fighting me? Why can't you be biddable for once?"

"Because if I stop fighting with you, I'll probably hop in the sack with you," she admitted, before she had a chance to catch herself.

The sound of the ensuing silence was deafening. At first she didn't want to look at Vikar, to see his reaction, but he took that choice out of her hands by suddenly shoving her against the closed door, his erection prodding her middle. With one hand on either side of her head, he leaned in, "M'lady, you play with fire when you make statements like that. I have not had sex for a hundred years, and I am hungry."

"I haven't had sex for a long time, either," she said, leaning up for a kiss.

He turned his face aside.

"You don't want to kiss me?"

He rested his forehead against hers. "Do not tempt me, wench. If I kiss you, I will not stop there. I will be swiving you continuously 'til your eyeballs roll back in your head and we mark every room in this castle like randy dogs."

Swiving? What a charmer? She tried to laugh, but it came out as a gurgle. Putting a hand to his cheek, she said, "Vikar, we both got aroused the other time you did that cleansing thing. You can't deny the chemistry is there. How are we ever going to exchange blood, over and over, and not have sex?"

"God help me, I do not know." He turned slightly so that he could at least kiss her palm.

Alex felt the erotic tickle all the way to her toes and some important places along the way. Fortunately, or unfortunately, the phone rang then. Stunned by the instant arousal that whipped between them, they let it go to the answering machine, and the message that came from Alex's boss was an erotic damper if there ever was one.

"Lord Vikar. This is Ben Claussen, Alex's editor. Do whatever you can to keep her there for a while. I've already told her that it's not safe for her to come back to the city at this time."

Vikar arched his brows at her for failing to deliver that news to him.

"The feds are looking for her to deliver a subpoena to testify at the cartel trial. The cartel will be watching closely to see where that delivery is made. I fear she'll become their target."

Now Vikar was shaking his head at her, as if she were a small child needing a scolding.

"I'll talk to Alex about this later, but she's one stubborn lady. And she speaks highly of you."

That comment prompted more eyebrow raising. Alex didn't recall saying anything particularly complimentary about Vikar. Had she?

After the answering machine clicked off, Vikar folded his arms and scowled at her. "You will stay," he declared firmly, "until I deem it safe for you to depart."

That's all she needed. Not only did Lucipires have her in their cross-hairs, drug dealers might be gunning for her, too, and now her boss would be in cahoots with her vampire angel host.

Could her life get any better than this?

A devil's work is never done . . .

"One of The Seven is in Transylvania? Impossible! Too much visibility there." Jasper glared at the brain-dead idiot of a mung Lucipire—*brain dead, ha, ha, ha!*—who'd come to him with that improbable announcement.

He was down in Horror reclining in his La-Z-Boy, sipping at a Bloody Mary (the real kind) and watching *Buffy* reruns on his satellite TV.

"Real vampires of any kind do not go near Count Dracula's hunting grounds," Jasper declared impatiently to his assistant Sabeam, who'd brought the battered mung into his private quarters.

"Not that Transylvania. The other Transylvania. In Pennsylvania," Sabeam explained.

"And one of The Seven was there, I tell you," the mung insisted.

He and Sabeam turned to the young male wearing leather with bullet holes in the knees, who'd not yet learned to speak only when spoken to. The mung shivered with fright. As well he should! He would be punished good and well for having lost his companion, never to return to Horror, and for failing to capture a most favored vangel, if what he claimed was true.

Sabeam was a mung, too, but he had years and much experience on this new fellow. Maybe Jasper would let Sabeam be the one to instruct him on proper discipline.

Jasper shoved Mary, an imp demon, and watched with distaste as she scuttled off like a scared crab. And he hadn't even drained her yet! "There's a Transylvania in Pennsylvania?" he inquired testily of Sabeam. "Why did no one tell me this?"

"It is a joke. I mean, the town is a joke, master." Their attention was drawn back to the young mung who was shivering so hard his teeth chattered, causing his fangs to bite repeatedly into his bottom lip. He kept swiping with the back of his hand to prevent blood from dripping onto the carpet. "The residents pretend to be vampires to draw in tourists."

"Ah! *Twilight* again! I wish that book had never been written. And *True Blood*! I swear, those Sookie Stackhouse books give vampires a bad name! I ask you, Sabeam, did you ever see a wussier vampire than Vampire Bill?"

The young mung thought he'd been addressing him and said, "Huh?"

Brain dead, brain dead, brain dead! Mulling the situation, he knew that he should send one of his haakai Lucipires or a few mungs there to investigate, but they were busy setting up the Sin Cruise on the Internet. The Sin Cruise was Jasper's ingenious plan for harvesting vast numbers of new Lucipires.

"Send Gregori and Virgana to me," he told Sabeam. "Gregori is in the training arena with new Lucipires, and Virgana is in Bermuda hiring a cruise ship. Tell Brutus and Lucretia to take over for them. If there are vangels in this Transylvania, Pennsylvania, those two will scent them out." Gregori was a haakai, once an executioner for Ivan the Terrible, and Virgana was his hordling consort. "And take this disgusting mung with you," he added.

After that, Jasper settled back and watched Angel seducing Buffy. Holy fires of Hell! He would love to have a Lucipire like Angel. *There* was a vampire with a brain! Though Jasper hated his name.

Lucifer had taken most of Jasper's collection from him by now, and the captive vangel had died without renouncing God, thus ensuring his place in Heaven, or wherever good vangels went, but all was not lost. The Sin Cruise was on the horizon, and Jasper felt certain he and his hordes would harvest hundreds, if not thousands, of lost souls in the act of sin. And there was a possibility that one of The Seven would be captured in Transylvania.

Life . . . or Unlife . . . was good!

Note to self: Order cruise wear.

Sin City on the High Seas? . . .

"Holy crap! Would you look at this?" Harek said as they finished their impromptu meeting. He pointed to the screen on his computer.

"What the hell!" he and Cnut said at the same time. While vangels avoided bad language, profanity did not seem quite as bad as sacrilegious expletives. Those they shunned like gammelost, the stinky fish hated by most Norsemen. They slipped betimes.

"Sin Cruise Planned on Internet Website," the headline read.

The AOL news article went on to say that the first ever ocean liner orgy was being planned for August off the coast of Florida, in international waters, where presumably laws against such activities would not be in effect. No children or child pornographers would be allowed, but just about everything else would be permitted.

"This is friggin' unbelievable!" Vikar said, sliding his chair closer to read. "I've never heard of such a thing."

Cnut, who sat on Harek's other side, remarked, "It was inevitable, with the way the world today is going. To Hell in a handbasket, as the saying goes."

"Sodom and Gomorrah," they all said as one.

"Look at this." Harek read the itinerary: Nude Swimming. Extreme Matchmaking. Adultery and Perversions. Nighttime Orgies. How to Engage in a Ménage à Trois. Bestiality for the Faint of Heart. Advanced S&M. Fetishes Galore. Voyeurism. Punishment as Pleasure.

"Could this possibly be something Jasper cooked up?" Vikar shook his head with wonder. Given all the evil he had seen over the centuries, he was surprised that he could still be shocked.

"Absolutely!" Harek clicked another link, then pointed the cursor at "How to Have Sex with a Vampire."

"Hah! What I want to know is how a vampire angel gets permission to have sex," Vikar said.

Harek had already moved the cursor to another topic and said aloud, "Satan Worship at Midnight."

All three of them made signs of the cross on their chests.

"Many of the things planned are illegal in this country. How can they get away with it?" Vikar wondered. "You'd think the police would be shutting them down before they start."

Harek shook his head. "Maritime laws are convoluted and hard to enforce. Territorial law, meaning the law of the adjoining land, only applies twelve miles out. From twelve to twenty-four miles, it's considered contiguous waters, where some laws apply. But beyond twenty-four miles, that's international."

"Still . . ." Vikar was finding it hard to fathom how such an event could be planned, openly, with no repercussions.

"Think about it. If a crime occurs aboard ship, what country has jurisdiction? The place where the ship is registered? The place where it started its journey? Where it docks?" Harek was still clicking away at the computer as he spoke. "Oh shit! Look where it's registered. Libya. Try to file a lawsuit there today."

They all laughed. That country had enough problems of its own.

"I can see now why all those missing persons and rape cases we hear about on cruise lines almost never get prosecuted successfully," Cnut mused.

"And most of them are never reported by the cruise lines," Harek added. "Bad publicity."

"Michael should be informed of this right away," Vikar said. "At least this activity should divert Jasper's attention away from me. That mung must not have recognized me."

"Don't be too sure of that," Cnut warned, but then Cnut was ever cautious. As he should be as one of their best soldiers.

"Where's your pretty guest?" Harek asked then.

Hiding from me, no doubt. Vikar shrugged, as if he had no idea. "I'll see you both in the morning." He rose to his feet, stretched, and yawned loudly. "I'm really tired."

Even after he closed the door and began to climb the stairs, he could hear their laughter following him. He was fooling no one. They knew exactly where he was headed.

Seven

He was bloody sex on the hoof . . . uh, fang . . .

Transylvania feature, Kelly   **Page 1**
Draft Four

What if there were angels sent to earth to save humans who are on a fast road to Hell? Not guardian angels, but fierce warrior angels who fight demons hell-bent on catching weak mortal sinners before they have a chance to repent.

What if all these angel saviors were former Vikings? No, not the football kind. The sword-wielding, plundering kind who are so good-looking, women stop in their tracks just to gape at them.

In the hills of Pennsylvania . . .

Alex had taken a bubble bath, shaved her legs and armpits, washed and blow-dried her hair, and applied Jessica McClintock body lotion from neck to toes to cover up her lemon scent. Coral Ice adorned her newly enameled finger- and toenails. She was damn well going to have sex, or someone was going to pay.

It might seem like a contradiction for her to have been resisting Vikar right and left, and now to have surrendered without any convincing on his part. Maybe that's exactly why. Her decision.

For years now, even before Brian and Linda's deaths, even before she and Brian had separated, Alex's life had been controlled by outside forces. She couldn't recall the last time she'd done something totally for herself.

She smiled to herself. *This is definitely going to be for me.*

They'd eaten dinner hours ago. Since she'd done most of the work preparing the tacos and dessert, she'd left the men to clean up. Dagmar rarely ate with them, for some reason, but Vikar claimed it was her choice.

Alex sat on her bed, legs extended and crossed at the ankles, wearing her favorite sleeping attire: jade nylon running shorts and a white tank top edged in matching green. She would have been nude if she had more nerve, or self-confidence. After all, she was thirty years old and no longer in prime physical shape, mainly because she'd been sedentary for so long. In fact, she couldn't recall the last time she'd jogged or done a sit-up. *Can anyone say sagging butt?*

Vikar knocked lightly on the door. "Are you decent?"

I hope not. "C'mon in."

He opened the door, took one look at her, and pretended like he was going to turn and go away.

But he didn't. Instead, he closed and locked the door behind him.

The only light came from the full moon, but it was enough, what with the eight windows arranged in a semicircle around the turret room.

She noticed that Vikar had taken care with his appearance, too.

Be still, my libido.

He'd obviously showered, and his wet hair was tied at his nape with a leather thong. A pure white T-shirt and black sweatpants were his only attire. He was barefoot. He hadn't shaved, but being blond, even dark blond, he had only a faint designer stubble on his face.

If eyes could speak, his would be saying, *I want you.* The fangs that were slowly emerging said it for him.

A sex goddess she'd never been before, but now . . . *I am goddess, hear me roar!* Confidence restored, Alex said, "I hope you brought condoms."

"I don't need condoms," he said, crossing his arms and yanking his shirt over his head. With his gaze holding hers, he unlaced the tie of his sweatpants and let them drop to the floor.

She could swear she heard a drumroll in her head.

After stepping out of his sweatpants, he wore only a pair of black boxer briefs that delineated a high, curved butt, narrow hips, a flat, muscle-striated belly, and a very impressive package. Plus a tourniquet around his upper arm, whose purpose she didn't want to contemplate.

"You're prettier than I am," she observed with mock chagrin.

His eyes scanned her body, slowly. "That is debatable."

"Why don't you need a condom?" She scooted her bottom over on the single-size bed to make room for him so that she was on her side with her back to the wall.

"Vangels cannot beget children."

That was so sad. Alex couldn't imagine a world without children in it, though she never intended to have any more herself.

"Besides, we are not going to have sex per se." He lay down on his side facing her and ran an appreciative fingertip from her shoulder to her wrist.

"Per se?" she choked out. *Good Lord, does he have some kind of sexual energy coming out of his fingertips, like a laser pointer?*

"Have I mentioned how much I like your freckles?"

Forget freckles, I'm still stuck back on magic fingers. She shook her head to clear it. "Per se?" she reminded him.

"We are going to have near-sex. Everything except penetration."

Sex games? Jeesh, I get turned on just hearing him say the word penetration. *Pathetic, pathetic, pathetic!* "Why? I mean, why no intercourse?"

"I am hoping that my punishment for near-sex will not be nearly as great as full-blown swiving."

He doesn't mince words, that's for sure. "You'll be punished for being with me?"

"For a certainty. Sex outside of marriage is a no-no, as compared to near-sex, which I am hoping is a venial sin." At her frown, he quickly added, "Not to worry, sweetling. I get punished for many things.

Methinks Mike is fonder of me than he pretends, and he wants to keep me around as a vangel until the Apocalypse. My original penance should have ended in 1550, but I keep having years added on, as do my brothers. Sore hard it is for a Viking to be good all the time."

"Isn't that sort of like St. Augustine, who supposedly prayed, 'Dear God, help me to be good. But not yet'?"

"Auggie gets a bad rap," he contended, then smiled at her, and, oh, his smile was a lethal weapon.

"I like the sore hard part."

"You are naughty," he said, tapping her on the chin playfully. "I like it."

I aim to please, sweetheart. "Near-sex has a certain appeal, actually. We'll be like teenagers again. Making out like crazy. Kissing. Petting. Everything but going all the way. At least that's how it was when I was a teenager. Men tend to go more wham-bam, whereas boys have to work to make it as far as third base. Of course, today teens are more advanced. Friends with benefits. Rainbow parties and all that. Oh, for the good old days!" She paused. "I'm rambling, aren't I?"

"I'm as nervous as you are."

She doubted that sincerely.

"When I was a teenager—they didn't use the term *teenager*, by the by—boys of twelve were expected to act as men. In truth, I started with 'going all the way.' Definitely wham-bam, thrust-and-peak, as an untried youthling."

She felt oddly pleased that she could stand out in some way from all the women he must have had over the centuries. Assuming she believed the time-travel-Viking-vampire-angel-demon story. "So this will be a new experience for you?"

"Yes, it will. Can we start with me counting your freckles? Harek says I need to practice my math skills."

"I hate my freckles," she said, even as she arched her back to aid in his removing her top.

Leaning on one elbow, he studied her body, and not just her breasts. He surveyed her arms and legs, as well. "I prefer to think of them as sex dust. There for my personal pleasure."

Okay, she knew that was a load of crap, but she would never look at her body again and fail to remember his words. And, really, all the experts said that a woman's biggest impediment in enjoying sex was her insecurity about her body. This guy was halfway around the bases, just by making her feel good about herself.

Was it a learned art, or was he sincere?

Right now, it didn't matter.

"Ah, I see my two favorite freckles," he said, gently flicking one nipple, then the other.

She gasped, not at his silly words, but at the sheer, exquisite pleasure of that slight touch.

His fangs were recessed now, so he appeared normal when he leaned forward and licked each of the distended "freckles." If she weren't already lying down, she might have fainted from the pleasure. But there was more to come. Way more!

Arranging himself atop her, braced on his elbows, he spread her legs with his knees, his erection prodding her inner thigh. Only then did he begin to kiss her. Long, slow, drugging kisses. Feathery and exploring. Deep and tongue-thrusting. Every time she got used to one pattern or pace, he changed. At the same time, he stroked her breasts with his coarse chest hairs by swaying from side to side.

She kissed him back and was pleased when she could draw a deep groan from low in his throat, or when he would nip her in pretend punishment. Her hands and legs could not remain still. She caressed his back and waist and buns as far as she could reach. And she used her feet to rub against the backs of his calves, occasionally wrapping her legs around him.

And he talked, too. Low, husky murmurs of appreciation and encouragement:

"Oh yes, like that."

"Open wider. Let me in."

"I have ne'er been this aroused."

"Your touch turns my blood afire."

She was already wet down below, so it was no surprise that, when he moved up slightly so that his erection touched her clitoris, she began to climax, keening her pleasure.

"Shh, not yet." He drew back and through glazed eyes she saw that his fangs were fully extended now. She should have known what was coming next, but her sex-muddled brain was on hiatus. As he began to thrust and withdraw his lower body against her, his head lunged forward and he buried his fangs in her neck.

Every nerve in her body was titillated and she began a fast climb to the most excruciatingly long climax of her life. On and on and on her inner muscles spasmed, yearned for him to be inside her. Every time the head of his penis hit the bundle of nerves in that one spot, ripples of electric shocks ran across her body. There wasn't a speck of skin or a sinew of inner muscle that wasn't affected. This was a full-body orgasm, if there ever was one. She screamed when it became too overpowering and arched her neck back and her shoulders off the bed.

She had no idea how long he sucked on her blood, or how long her orgasm lasted, but when she was finally able to lift her head, she whispered, "That was incredible."

He raised his head and kissed her lightly. She could taste her blood on his lips. She should have been repulsed, but she was oddly satisfied.

"Are we done?"

He chuckled. "We have just begun, dearling." With that, he rolled over onto his back so that she straddled him. That's when she saw that he had cut his wrist. Blood was seeping out.

"No! Oh no, I can't do that again. Let's just—"

He clasped the back of her head with one hand and forced her mouth to the cut wrist of his other hand that he held near his neck. She tried to turn aside, but he wouldn't allow that. "Drink, Alex. You must drink to become clean."

To distract her, or because he hadn't yet climaxed himself, Vikar began to undulate against her. Soon she gave herself up to sipping him, especially when he distracted her by sliding a big palm inside her shorts and cupping both buttocks, setting a pace for her moving hips. And then his long fingers reached forward between her legs, stroking her.

When she realized that he, too, was extremely aroused by her mouth at his wrist and her movements against his penis, she gave herself up to the ritual; that's how Vikar had referred to the cleansing at one point . . . a ritual. She rode him, stem to stern, sliding her now damp shorts over his briefs until he arched his hips up against her and let out a roar. She could swear she felt his semen spurting against her folds, despite the separation of two fabrics.

She hurtled into another mind-blowing orgasm.

For a long time afterward, he held her cradled against his neck, running his palms in a comforting fashion over her bare back. His heart hammered against hers, a pleasing counterpoint to hers. She could tell that he was equally stunned by what had happened.

"Is it always like this?" she asked finally.

"It is never like this," he said, kissing the top of her head, then rolling over to sit up and take off the tourniquet. Glancing down at his wet briefs and her equally wet shorts, not to mention the damp sheets, he shrugged sheepishly. "We are a mess. Should we go shower and change the linens?"

"We could," she said hesitantly, "or . . ."

"Or?"

Alex was usually not so uninhibited, but when would she ever get this kind of chance again? So she said saucily, "Or we could do it again."

Vikar laughed so hard she had to kiss him. Then she kissed him . . . just because she could.

Do angels have halos *there*? . . .

Vikar didn't need to be asked twice.

He stood and turned, lifting a surprised Alex by the waist, and set her in the middle of the room. Her small squeal of protest did not deter him in the least.

"Don't move," he ordered.

He would like to take a minute or an hour to appreciate Alex, bare from the waist up and the thighs down; he'd give special attention to her breasts . . . uptilted half globes of pure temptation. And freckles! There were freckles everywhere! But first he needed to set the stage for the next step in their near-sex lovemaking. As any warrior would tell you, it was all in the planning.

He yanked the top sheet and blanket off the bed and laid a clean towel over the center of the bed.

"I like your butt."

Whaaat? Leaning over the bed, one foot on the floor and a knee on the edge of the bed, he stopped and glanced back over his shoulder. Alex was indeed staring at his arse. He had to smile at the directness of modern women. "My front side is even better."

"Show me."

Yes, directness. "In a moment," he said, standing to lean back against the wall. "First, release your hair."

Her green eyes snapped saucily at him. Would she balk at being given orders? *No*, she would attempt to turn his order on its face, he soon realized. Holding his gaze, she reached up and unclipped a claw-like ornament that held her hair atop her head. With arms still raised, she combed her fingers through the shoulder-length strands that were wavy from her recent bath. Her posture caused her breasts to lift more. Noticing his no-doubt gaping mouth, she arched her back slightly.

The minx!

"Happy now?"

A part of my body certainly is. "Not quite."

"Really?" The wench's right eyebrow arched as

she noted the longboat straining against the cloth between his legs.

"Lose the short breeches."

"How about you?"

" 'Twould be best if I kept mine on." *Who knows what I might do when in the midst of a peaking?* "You could say these Hanes are my version of cloistered virtue, just like the short hair I told you about before that Mike forbade."

"Pfff! I don't think boxer briefs are what John Milton had in mind."

He flicked his hand toward her lower half. "Continue."

She put her hands inside the stretchy waist and lowered it to just above her nether hair, exposing all of her hips, the curve of her stomach, and a pretty indented navel. Then she tugged the waistband back up with a snap. "Oops," she said.

"Tease," he countered. *I have not had so much fun with sex in centuries. How can something that feels so right be wrong?* He shrugged. That was the problem with sin, he supposed. There was no clear-cut dividing line.

She did it again, this time shimmying so that the material, once past her hips, fell into a puddle at her feet.

He inhaled sharply. Her woman's fleece was indeed like reddish-blonde dandelion fluff. Would it be as soft to the touch? Would it smell of summer grass and sunshine? "Do it again," he choked out. "Slower this time."

At first she didn't understand. Then she did, if her soft gloating smile was any indication. She would pay for that later. Bending over so that her breasts spilled forward, she pulled the garment back up. Then, very slowly, she inched the sides down, wiggling her arse a little, before dropping the garment to the floor.

"Again. But this time face away from me."

"You're very domineering, aren't you?"

"Next time you can be domineering."

"You want me to be a dominatrix!"

"Bloody damn hell, no! Do you deliberately missay me?" Vikar had seen a porno film or two, which incidentally earned him a goodly penance, and he knew what being with a dominatrix entailed.

She grinned, having known all along what he meant.

"Keep it up, wench, and you may find out exactly what a 'master' can do in those kinds of games."

"Promises, promises," she challenged. But she turned and began the slow de-briefing again. This time he got a good look at what had to be the world's loveliest female arse. It was lush, and soft, and—*oh, my sorry self!*—covered with freckles. This would be the first time in his long history that he would willingly kiss someone's arse.

"What are you chuckling about?" She turned to face him again. "Are you laughing at my body?"

He could see the insecurity on her face. Before she attempted to cover herself, he said, "Never! I was laughing at myself and how much I want you. I am happy."

She smiled then, a glorious expression of joy that had his heart nigh melting. And was that not a flowery sentiment for a hardened Viking? His brothers would make mock of him for days if they knew.

Truly, he got such pleasure just looking at her.

Why had he never taken the time to appreciate this part of lovemaking before?

"Your turn," she said.

He pushed away from the wall and without any particular finesse dropped his shorts. Well, drop was a stretch, since his rampant enthusiasm stuck out and fought the fabric on the way down. An *enthusiasm* was the Viking male word for an erection. His erection was *very* enthusiastic.

"Oh. My!"

He glanced downward and was almost embarrassed at his vein-bulging size. Had he ever been so big? Especially after having spilled his seed once already.

"Come," he said, extending a hand to her. "Let us explore more of this near-sex. Methinks it would have been fun to be a teenager in your time. 'Making out.' Is that not what you called it?"

She let him lead her to the bed. "Believe me, sweetie, making out was never like this. Forget about getting to third base. You've gone three and a half bases and are about to slide home."

"No, no, no! No sliding home."

For what seemed like hours then, they explored each other's bodies, and, yes, he did kiss and lick and touch every one of those freckles, some in rather interesting places that she claimed to have been unaware of. In return, she oohed and aahed over every battle scar that marred his body, and she kissed, and licked, and touched them, as if to heal them more.

"What are these two long scars on each of your shoulder blades?" she asked.

"Wings."

"You have wings?"

"Not yet." *Mayhap never.* "That is where they would emerge."

"Holy cow! You really are an angel."

"Not yet," he repeated.

"There is so much I don't understand. We really do need to talk more about this . . . this 'fantasy' I've landed in."

"Yes, we will talk, but not now. In truth, no matter how much I explain, you still will not understand fully. I don't, and I have been living this 'fantasy' for nigh on one thousand, one hundred and sixty-two years." *Has it really been that long? Time flies when you're having fun,* he supposed. *Or not.* He raised a halting hand when she was about to question him more. "Later."

She nodded, but insisted on one last comment, "I never thought of angels as being . . . well, sexual."

We're not supposed to be. "I must be the exception."

But enough of that. He rolled over onto his back. "Forget about my scars. I have other body parts that need your attention."

"Oh my God! It has a halo."

He jerked to a sitting position and glanced down to his cockstand, which resembled a fat standing candle sitting in a circle of light. Breathing a sigh of relief—*you never knew what Mike was going to do to them*—he said, "That's not a halo. It's just the moon hitting off that round mirror over there and reflecting back here."

"If you say so." She was clearly unconvinced. "I think it's kind of cute, that you would have a halo around your penis."

Cute? A man does not want his cock to be cute. "It is *not* a halo."

She leaned forward to study it closer. "Let's see if you taste holy." Before he had a chance to realize what she meant, she took him into her mouth, and he about exploded. "Naaaaay!" With the sheer agony of fighting what had to be the biggest temptation of his sorry life, he lifted her off him.

"What? You don't like that?"

Are you demented? I like it too much. "Um, uh, that type of activity is too much like real sex."

"Really? Bill Clinton said oral sex isn't sex."

He snorted his opinion of that lackwit former chieftain of this country. "Our archangel mentor would beg to differ, I am sure." But there were other things he could do. And he did. Bringing her to peak three times and hurtling himself over the cliff of seemingly endless rapture. They both fell into an immediate sleep of the . . . not innocent, but deeply satisfied.

Even as he drifted off to sleep, he reminded himself that he would have to do another cleansing afore morning. So it was while the moon was still high, about three a.m., that he awakened her for more lovemaking, accompanied by his drawing on her sweet blood, and her taking his as well, this time with no protests. No doubt because she was only half conscious.

Sleep evaded him for the rest of the night as he held her cuddled up on his chest, one leg thrown over his thighs. Something strange was happening to him. It was like a soft cloud surrounded them, a nest of sorts. He watched her sleep and felt protective of her, and protected in return by her warmth. Puzzled, he was, by the myriad of feelings assailing him like pellets. Vangels worked best without emotion.

It was only when dawn began to rise on the horizon and he slipped out of bed and prepared to go downstairs for Lauds, or morning prayers, that a most outlandish idea occurred to him. It stuck with him as he showered and brushed his teeth. It stuck with him as he donned clean garments. It stuck with him as he joined his brothers and the others in the chapel to sing in the new day.

Had God sent this woman here not for him to save, but for her to save him?

Eight

A new day brought new questions . . .

Transylvania feature, Kelly   Page 1
Draft Five

Vampires are a celebrated feature in a small Pennsylvania town appropriately named Transylvania, but, unlike the common perception of vampires as fanged, undead creatures to be feared, these bloodsuckers are the good guys.

Historically, as far back as ancient Persia, there was a belief in huge creatures that could suck the blood of men. And in Babylonia, the myth deity Lilitu, or Lilith, reportedly the first wife of Adam, became the queen of demons and evil spirits.

It wasn't until Bram Stoker's *Dracula*, however, and the current *Twilight/True Blood* craze, that vampires took on a popularity that defies explanation.

According to a study by Penn State professor Lori Diamond . . .

Alex awakened to the sounds of hammers pounding, saws whirring, men's loud voices and laughter coming from all directions, outside, front and back, and inside, on various floors. She must have overslept, or at least slept past her usual early waking hour, if the workmen were already here.

Glancing at her travel alarm, she saw that it was seven-thirty. Stretching, she was reminded by aching muscles, as if she could ever forget, what she'd been doing all night long.

Which was a jarring jolt back to reality for her. What had she been thinking? Oh, she didn't regret having sex with Vikar, or near-sex. She had to smile at that distinction Vikar made so adamantly.

What bothered her was that she was an intelligent woman, and, while not a prude, casual sex repelled her. At least it had in the past. What the hell was she doing, having sex with a stranger? She giggled, she actually giggled at that. Near-sex with a near-stranger! Sounded like the title for an erotic novel.

The journalist in her reared its logical head. There were so many questions.

- Who was Vikar . . . and the rest of the people here?
- What were they planning to do with this run-down castle? No way were they planning to open a hotel!
- What was that bloodsucking business all about?
- Had she been drugged, or something, to allow that bloodsucking business to take place? And—*who was she kidding*—to enjoy it?

- What did Transylvania, the town of wannabe vampires, have to do with the loony birds up here at the castle?
- Was she being punked? Was Ashton Kutcher hiding in the bushes somewhere?
- Or scammed? Could these be criminals, setting up this heap-o'-rocks as a hideaway, or money laundering center, or something? A Viking mafia, maybe?
- Better yet, was this a promo campaign for a movie, or something? A new *Twilight*-type vampire series, or *Angels in America*, or something?
- What's with all these "or somethings"?
- And, hey, was there really such a thing as vampires? She didn't think so, despite everything she'd seen, including those weird biker demon vampires at the restaurant parking lot. *Note to self: Check local newspapers on the Net for story on death at the Blood Bath.*
- And what about angels?

For some reason, this last question bothered Alex most of all. If angels existed, then that would mean God existed, and after the cruel manner in which Brian and Linda had been taken from her, she wanted to believe there was no God. She wanted to be justified in the actions she planned to take against the Mercado brothers, if the justice system failed to punish them.

Although she'd been a lapsed Catholic, she hadn't become an atheist until the murders. What higher being would allow an innocent child to be blown into a pink mist?

She shook her head to clear it of that unwelcome image.

Alex was a woman, first and foremost, and she refused to regret last night when she'd been able to celebrate that femininity in the best way possible. That did not mean she stopped being a journalist as well. This was a new day, and she had work to do.

Vampire angels, beware. Here comes Lois Lane.

Brotherly love betimes comes with baggage . . .

Vikar was tempted to go back upstairs after Lauds and spend the day in bed with Alex, exploring all the different ways of having sex without having sex; he'd come up with several interesting ideas during morning hymns. But he was already skating on thin ice, and decided he'd best find something else to occupy his time.

After discussing the day's schedule with the contractor, he was walking past the dining room when he noticed Armod bringing in chairs to set up around the table. This was one room that had been finished.

"Master, could I speak with you for a moment?" Armod asked. He'd been helping Armod with his lisp, but he didn't think that was what the boy wanted.

The pink tint to his white cheeks should have been a clue.

Vikar walked in and sat down on one of the chairs. "What troubles you, Armod?"

Armod perched on a chair near him, and Vikar could swear his knees were knocking. "Uh, do vangels havth sex?"

Whoa! That question came at Vikar out of nowhere. Did it show on his face that he'd been engaged all night in not sex, but near-sex? "Yes, I imagine they do, although sex outside of marriage is not approved of, as you know."

Armod nodded. "But vangels do it anyhow?"

"Uh, some do." *I certainly have.* "With repercussions."

"More penance," Armod said. Inhaling sharply, as if to gain courage, he told Vikar, "I am a virgin."

Uh, I don't think so. You were a prostitute, weren't you, boy? "You'll have to explain that one, Armod."

"I have never been with a female. I am a virgin heterosexual."

Oh. Vikar wasn't sure there was such a distinction, but he wasn't about to tell Armod that.

"What's it like to have sex with a woman?"

Mike, are you listening? A little help here, please? "One of life's greatest pleasures."

"Do you think I'll ever get a chance to experience it? I asked Cnut about it, but he said the best person to ask would be Ivak, but since he is not here, I should ask you. That you know lots, too."

Lots? Thanks a bunch, brother. Remind me to thank you with a fist in your fool face. "Armod, vangels are permitted to marry other angels. Mayhap you will find a life mate." *Oh bloody hell! What a wuss answer!*

"But then we would have to stay together for the

length of the longer penance that either one has."

Vikar nodded.

"How about humans? Can we marry human women?"

"Do you have someone in mind?" he teased. Armod had been with them only a few months, and the only human women he could have come in contact with were the clerks at the supermarket.

Armod shook his head, sadly.

Vikar ruffled his hair. "It wouldn't be a desirable arrangement since the human would age and die while the vangel would live for many, many years beyond that. There have been some marriages amongst vangels with short penances, but that's all."

"Couldn't the mate be made into a vangel so they would both stay the same age until passing over?"

Vikar shrugged. "It has ne'er happened afore."

"Is that why you have never married since you became a vangel?"

Vikar really, really hated the direction of this conversation. "Exactly," he answered, though he couldn't recall any woman he'd wanted to marry, not since Vendela.

Armod's shoulder slumped with dejection.

"Armod, we serve a God of love. Did he not give us woeful sinners a second chance? You must have hope. And faith. If we do good, we will be rewarded." And that was the truth, even though Vikar had to remind himself of that on occasion.

Armod brightened.

Vikar felt like such a hypocrite, though, giving advice on a subject on which he was not clear himself.

Armod further discomfited him by standing and hugging him in thanks before rushing off to get more chairs.

Shaking his head at his sorry self, Vikar found Harek and Cnut out by the front gates, Cnut with a sketch pad in hand and Harek with a mini computer.

They glanced up at his approach, homed in on his face and neck, then grinned like shit-eating squirrels, before saying as one, "You are in suuuch trouble!"

"What?"

"You look like you've been rode hard and put away wet, cowboy," Cnut explained.

"Tell us everything," Harek said. "I haven't been laid in so long I forget what it feels like."

"We will share your bliss, vicariously," Cnut added. "Tell us everything. Every little detail. Was it good? How many times did you peak? How many times did she peak? Did you show her the Viking S-spot?"

Vikar loved his brothers, and he loved being the oldest of The Seven, but betimes, as now, he would like to knock their blockheads together. "I did not have sex. Exactly."

"Exactly? Oh, this ought to be good," Harek said to Cnut.

"It was just near-sex." Even to his own ears that sounded lame.

"I beg your pardon, brother. What did you say?" Cnut was holding a hand up to his ear.

Harek's eyes were wide with incredulity . . . and interest.

"Near-sex does not include penetration. Everything but," he admitted in a rush of words. *I can't believe I am having this discussion.*

"Are orgasms involved?" Harek wanted to know.

Vikar could feel his face heat. "Yes."

"How many?"

Harek was a persistent fellow, always had been, ever since he was a boyling, four years younger than Vikar, and wanted to know why, why, why about every blessed thing around their stead. Why do cows moo and sheep baa? What makes a longboat stay afloat? Why do women's bosoms cause men's sap to rise?

"Many," was all he would say. *Eight, to be precise. Three for me. Five for her.*

"Then it was sex," Cnut concluded.

"No, no, no," he insisted. *I want to do it again. Do not tell me it is forbidden.* "Trond told me about it."

"And you believed him?" Harek asked with disbelief. "Did you forget the time Trond told us we could fly if we jumped off the keep roof?"

"That was different." *I hope.*

"This definitely requires more investigation," Cnut told Harek. "Mayhap you could ask Mike about it?"

"Why me?" Harek stiffened his shoulders with indignation.

"You are on good terms with the archangel, ever since you introduced him to the Internet. Me"—he shrugged—"not so much since I failed to save Jeffrey Dahmer."

"No one could save Jeffrey Dahmer," Vikar said. "What are you two doing out here, anyway?"

Cnut showed him his sketches, a rough drawing of the property showing where high fences would be built all around, eventually, and where underground electrical wires needed to be laid, for now, to set up security devices. "We can do a lot of this work later, over the months even, or years, but we should have the electrical experts do their thing while they're here."

"Let's go inside and talk to J.D.," Vikar suggested.

As they started to walk toward the back door, Harek asked, "What's for breakfast?"

"Fake-O or Froot Loops, unless you're cooking," Vikar told him.

"Isn't your new girlfriend the cook?" Cnut asked.

"I do not want to be around when you ask her that question," he replied.

"She did the dinner last night," Cnut said defensively. He might or might not be jesting. They were, after all, from another era when women knew their place.

As they entered the kitchen, they saw the woman in question, sitting on a stool before the counter. Spread before her were an open laptop, legal pads filled with notes, and a Bible, of all things. Off to her right was Armod, who was indeed slurping up Froot Loops.

"Good morning, m'lady," Vikar said. He could not help the sex-huskiness of his voice.

Harek and Cnut glanced at him with amusement.

"Good morning, Vikar," she replied, and her voice was sex-husky, too. Plus she licked her kiss-swollen lips.

Harek and Cnut glanced at her, then back at him, and grinned.

"Definitely in big trouble," Harek murmured.

"What are you doing?" he asked Alex. *Are you regretting last night? Please do not be regretting. Can we do it again?*

"Taking notes for my article."

Uh-oh! Do I tell her now that there probably will be no article? Or later? Definitely later.

Cnut pinched his arm, and he snapped at him, "What?"

"The wench is talking to you," Cnut whispered behind a hand that was seemingly wiping his smirking mouth.

He turned his attention back to Alex. "You were saying?"

"I want to start interviewing for my article. You, of course, Vikar. But Harek . . . and Cnut . . . I hope you'll answer my questions, too. And Armod, of course." She gave a little smile and a wave at the boy.

Harek and Cnut said, "Uh."

Armod froze, his spoonful of Froot Loops midway to his gaping mouth.

"Did you know that there are 4.5 million links on the Internet when you Google 'fallen angels'?" Alex assumed they were all willing and was already off on another subject.

Or mayhap it was not another subject to her.

Why was she searching for information on fallen angels? "We're not fallen angels," he told her.

"Yet," Harek and Cnut added. Both of them winked at him, the friggin' Two Stooges.

"I think you should interview Harek and Cnut first," Vikar told Alex. *That will teach them to make mock of me.* "Didst know that Harek is trying to talk Mike into his own website on the Internet?"

Harek tried to elbow him, but Vikar moved quickly to the other side of the counter.

"Mike?" Alex asked tentatively, although he'd already told her who Mike was. "The archangel?"

"The very one," Vikar replied. " 'Twill be an inspirational site, will it not, Harek? An angelic Ann Landers. Life advice from the winged wonder."
Mike would smack me upside the head with a harp if he heard me talking like this.

"You're kidding," she said, even as she scribbled notes on her pad.

Harek just blushed, but shot daggers of displeasure at Vikar.

"Then there is Cnut. He can tell you about the time he told Napoleon where he could stick his sword."

Cnut said nothing, but Vikar was going to watch his back for the next hour or so. Cnut did a mean face-in-the-dirt tackle when enraged.

As for Alex reporting all this . . . he had no worry because by the time she left for home, he was fairly certain she would not remember any of what she'd witnessed here. Mike would make certain of that.

But then, she didn't believe anything he'd just said anyhow, as indicated by her laughter. She thought he was joking.

But then, all humor and teasing ended as Svein ran in and announced breathlessly, "There are Lucies in town. They're headed this way."

Then the Lucipire shit hit the fan . . .

Alex had seen many sides of Vikar thus far. Viking in appearance. With fangs as a vampire. Having the aura of angel wings at his back. As a lover. And now as a military commander.

She'd witnessed his fighting skills in the restaurant parking lot with those biker beasts, but his activity now was pure leader, and an experienced one at that.

"Svein, you take the front. Jogeir, position yourself at the back. Armod, take Alex and Dagmar up to the tower and guard their door. I'll go to the contractor and come up with some excuse that ensures all the workers are assigned jobs inside today." He turned to Harek and Cnut then. "The three of us will have to come up with a plan to divert the Lucipires away from the castle, and Transylvania itself."

"You're right," Cnut said. "That Lucie that got away from you last week must have recognized you, and Jasper is sending a horde here to investigate. We can't just erase them, because Jasper will continue to send more if he suspects we're in hiding here."

Erase? How does one erase a demon vampire? Alex wondered.

"I could give them a fly-by scent of me, then head north toward Canada," Harek offered.

A fly-by. I didn't know they could fly.

"Right," Cnut agreed. "I'll do the same, but I'll go east toward the Hudson River."

"And I'll lead the last of them south to Atlantic City. There are enough sinners there to divert their attention," Vikar said with dry humor.

I think I'm going to be sick.

"Bottom line, if at all possible, if we're going to kill them, we should try to do it away from here."

The three brothers did a three-fisted handshake for agreement.

Alex homed in on one thing in their amazing discussion. "You guys can fly?"

They turned as one to stare at her.

No one answered, but Vikar repeated his directions to Armod, "Take her to the tower room."

Alex started to protest that she wanted to stay and see what was happening. "I have a pistol. I know how to shoot." That was a stretch, since she'd had only a few lessons so far. Besides, she'd never shot a person and wasn't sure she could, even the Mercados, even whatever evil forces were approaching the castle.

Not for the first time, Alex wondered if this was all some elaborate Hollywood stunt meant to promote an upcoming movie.

"Do as you are told, Alex."

The fixed expression on Vikar's face barred any further interference from her. Where was the gentle lover? The "angel" with a sense of humor? It was as if Alex was invisible to Vikar now.

Alex continued to observe them over her shoulder, even as Armod led her away, whispering an explanation to her unanswered question. Vangels could not fly, exactly, but they could move unseen by humans through space, leave a scent for the Lucipires to follow. Sort of invisible flying.

As she left the room Alex was both alarmed and fascinated to see all the men arming up with ancient-looking swords and daggers, as well as modern guns. Each pulled on a long cape with identical winged epaulettes on the shoulders, the same as Vikar wore when he went out. The capes covered their jeans, T-shirts, and of course the weapons.

The oddest thing of all occurred then.

An aura of angel wings formed about the men's

backs, even Armod's. Like blue mists, they were, but definitely resembling angel wings. Last night, she'd thought it was her imagination, seeing an angel wing aura behind Vikar when they were making love, but this was different. And then she knew.

Angel warriors.

Nine

Honey, I'm home . . .

It was three days before Vikar returned to the castle, and he feared what he would find.

Oh, he knew from keeping in contact with Svein that Lucipires had sniffed around the perimeter, but were diverted when he and his brothers had drawn them away. Ultimately, to the far reaches of Canada where they'd battled fiercely. The scent of a Seven . . . he or any of his six brothers . . . was ten times stronger than that of all other vangels.

The contractors had continued to work and should be done with their assigned jobs in two more days, but they would not be there today because it was Sunday. Good thing because Armod had forewarned him that Alex was seriously upset. On more than one occasion, she'd attempted to leave the castle and go back to her home in Washington, despite the warning from her employer about her safety.

She was frightened; Vikar understood that. But

Vikar could not take the time to reassure her, and he had given Armod orders to hold her there, forcibly, if necessary But he could not think on that at the moment. He had more serious concerns, like his brother Harek, whom he carried in his arms. At a nod to Cnut, who was as worried as he was by Harek's wounds, the two of them closed their eyes and imagined themselves back at the castle. Within seconds, they dematerialized from where they stood atop the remote Canadian mountain and teletransported, reconstructing themselves in the kitchen. Invisible flying, but of epic speed.

For a moment, he was disoriented by the peaceful scene. Alex stood at the stove stirring something in a pot with a long wooden spoon. The kitchen was clean and shiny. A crystal vase of fresh wildflowers sat on a wide windowsill. A pyramid of oranges, apples, bananas, and grapes filled a woven basket on a sideboard, bringing more delicious normality to the room. Sunshine streamed in through the sparkling windows.

Such a homey picture after the hellish place where they had been! His heart tightened and he could scarce breathe. *Amazing how simple things like peacefulness can ease a man's soul! No doubt because it is so rare. For us.*

He shook his head to bring himself back to reality. This was not Home Sweet Home, and Alex was not the "little woman" waiting for her man. In fact, it was probably eye of newt in her cauldron and various other poisons to knock him flat on his arrogant arse.

Alex noticed their sudden appearance and screamed.

Which caused Armod, Svein, Jogeir, and Dagmar to come running.

But the man in Vikar's arms and his horrific condition caught Alex's attention. "Oh my God!" Alex slapped a hand to her mouth, her eyes wide with shock.

From forehead to toes, Harek's skin was bitten and lacerated from the Lucipire fangs and claws, not to mention at least one sword wound.

"What happened? Is he dead?" she choked out.

Well, yes, he is, but that's beside the point. "He needs help, that's all. Dagmar, are you ready?"

The mute vangel nodded and was already rolling up one of the sleeves of her long gown. Vikar laid Harek carefully on the table.

"He's loaded with Lucipire blood," he mused aloud. *More Lucipire than vangel at this point, I fear, by the reddish tint to his skin.* "We, each of us, need to feed from him, to drain the taint, before Dagmar can give him her pure blood."

Vikar went first. *Please, God, I pray, save our brother.* After making the sign of the cross, first on his own body, then on Harek's chest, Vikar bit deeply into Harek's neck where he sucked out a half cup of the most putrid fluid. When finished, he staggered to the sink in the small bathroom off the kitchen and threw up the contents of his stomach. Not enough to ease the nausea heaving his stomach, but that was all that would come up. While he was gargling with mouthwash and staring at his ravaged, unshaven face in the mirror above the sink, he realized that he would be unable to give Alex any of his blood for some time, but he would worry about that later.

Coming back into the kitchen, he saw that Cnut

and Svein were following his lead in draining Harek. Now it was Dagmar's turn to replace some of the bad blood with good. She ripped open the skin of her wrist with her own fangs and presented Harek with her open vein. While Harek took sustenance, despite his sleep-like condition, Vikar and the other males joined hands and hummed the lyrics to "Agnus Dei." Already Harek's skin color looked better, pale, but less red. Still, he remained unconscious. His wounds would heal of their own accord; it was the Lucipire blood in his system that worried them all. Later, Jogeir and Armod would drink from him, and Dagmar would feed him again, but too much at one time would harm them all.

Someday they would have equipment that would allow them to do medical transfusion procedures in emergency cases, but they were not at that stage yet. And they were unable to go to a hospital because of all the questions that would be raised.

"I made some chocolate chip cookies yesterday," Alex said. "Blood banks always encourage people to eat sugar after donating blood. Maybe it works in reverse, too."

They all looked at her, having momentarily forgotten that she watched. The procedure must be not only alarming but distasteful to her, totally different from when just the two of them were involved.

"Thank you. It cannot hurt to try," he said.

Dagmar picked up two cookies and took them with her to her room where she would rest for a while. Svein, Jogeir, and Armod mentioned going outside to secure the premises; they also took handfuls of cookies, crunching loudly as they walked away.

"I'll carry Harek up to his bed and watch over him," Cnut said, lifting up the big man with ease and grabbing a cookie as he passed by. He winked at Alex and said, "Many thanks, m'lady."

Vikar did not like that wink. Not at all.

Vikar glared at Alex, since Cnut was gone and he couldn't glare at him.

Alex glared right back. "Oh, sit down and eat a damn cookie. Maybe it will sweeten your disposition."

He sat down at the counter and took a big bite out of the cookie, finding it surprisingly good. Only after he'd eaten three of the sweet circles did he mutter, "My disposition is just fine."

She arched her brows. "What happened?"

"A battle with the Lucipires, far from here."

"Are you hurt?"

He shook his head. *Are those tears in her eyes? For me?* "Just scratches and bruises."

"Will Harek survive?"

"God willing, he will."

"Thank God!" she exclaimed, then grimaced, realizing her words belied her earlier renunciation of a Higher Power. Embarrassed, she turned away from him to stir the cauldron on the stove again.

"You could act more welcoming. In my day, a Viking man's woman welcomed him home from war in a different way. I remember the time Bad Boris's wife made love to him afore he had a chance to take his boots off. She said he made her heart go aflutter." He peered up at her hopefully through half-shuttered lids. "Is your heart fluttering, Alex?"

"You're an idiot," she said, her back still to him.

"That is true," he agreed. "Well?"

She turned. "No, my heart is not fluttering. I've been too worried about whether you would come back or whether you were roasting over some Lucipire's fire. I've been spitting mad over your orders that barred me from leaving this bizarre . . . prison. I just watched a group of hunky men hum some holy music and suck blood. And I am for damn sure not 'your woman.'"

Hunky? He smiled, he could not help himself. "You missed me."

"Pfff! In your dreams." She threw the wooden spoon at him.

With a laugh, he watched the spoon spin twice in the air before catching it by the handle. Sniffing its bowl, he asked, "What are you cooking?"

"Chicken noodle soup. My grandmother always said it was the ultimate comfort food."

He looked at the size of the cauldron. Then he looked at her, tilting his head to the side. His heart began to swell like a balloon, and his lungs burned, making him breathless. "You made me comfort food?"

"I made it for everyone, not just you." Her face was the prettiest shade of pink against the framework of her reddish-blonde hair. Freckles stood out on her nose, despite the light coating of makeup she applied every day to hide what she considered imperfections.

For the first time in his one thousand, one hundred and ninety-five years, he got a suspicion of what it must feel like to fall in love. It was so intense! Not at all wonderful, truth to tell, though mayhap the wonderfulness would come later. *Michael is going to have a field day with me on Reckoning Day.* Even that prospect couldn't slow his pounding heart.

"Why are you grinning?"

I probably look like a loopy lackwit. "Because you missed me."

"I did not," she started to say, but he stepped forward, picked her up by the waist, and before she could protest, carried her into the pantry and closed the door behind them. She squirmed out of his hold and backed up against the far wall. Shelves of canned and dry goods surrounded them on ceiling-high shelves. "Why are you doing this, Vikar?"

He closed in on her and put his elbows on either side of her head. "Why am I doing this?" *How can I not do this?* He inhaled deeply, taking in her scent, a scent embedded in his brain like one of Harek's microchips. "Because I missed you, too." *More than I can explain.*

With that, he leaned in and kissed her.

And, God help him, it felt like coming home.

Near-sex was getting nearer and nearer . . .

Alex should have shoved the arrogant lout away.

She should have demanded that he let her go, cartel danger and magazine article be damned.

She should have been repulsed by all the bloodletting and bloodsucking she'd just witnessed in the kitchen.

She should have been frightened to death by Harek's condition and what it said, without words, about the danger Vikar and his brothers had faced . . . in fact, faced every day.

She should have known the first time she'd seen Vikar that she was in big trouble.

She should have protected her weeping heart from the hurt Vikar would inevitably bring her.

Instead, she not only allowed him to kiss her, but she opened her mouth to him and whispered against his lips, "I did miss you."

"Of course you did," the conceited Viking whispered back, smiling.

A smile kiss.

She liked it.

But then he wasn't smiling anymore.

And she liked that even better.

Vikar took his kissing seriously. It was a full-body experience for him, involving not just his lips and teeth and tongue, but his hands, and hips, even his legs. What a fool she had been the other night insisting on "making out" endlessly like a teenager, as if it would be something new for this ancient warrior. Hah! He'd had a thousand and more years to perfect kissing to an art form.

Thank God for experienced men!

One hand at her nape held her face at just the right angle for his plundering kiss while the other hand reached under her behind and lifted her to tiptoes so that his already raging enthusiasm was pressed at her already raging . . . yes, enthusiasm. A good unisex word for arousal, she decided.

"Dost find humor in my kisses?" he growled against her ear, nipping the lobe.

She hadn't realized that she was returning his

smile kiss. "No. I'm just happy to see you. Can't you tell?"

"I'm not sure. I better check." On those ominous words, he kissed her deeply and at the same time stuck both big hands inside the back waistband of her jogging pants and lifted her even higher by cupping her buttocks, his long fingers extending forward between her thighs.

She squealed at the sudden movement of his wicked fingers, but did she shove the lout away? No. She wrapped her legs around his hips and tried to take over control of this love play. *Fat chance!* she soon realized when he chuckled and began a full-fledged attack on all her senses.

He kissed her voraciously, as if he could not get enough of her taste, as if he wanted to eat her up, inhale her, take her into himself. Good thing his fangs were retracted, despite his arousal, or she would be a bloody mess. As it was, she was just a mess. A melting, mewling mess of yearning, surrendering womanhood.

His hands were everywhere, caressing the bare skin of her back under her sweatshirt, rubbing her bottom, sweeping with torturous lightness over the lace of her bra. And her hands were busy, too, exploring his wide shoulders, the ridged scars on his shoulder blades, his muscled upper arms, which were adorned today with silver arm rings etched with wings, his corded neck, his beautiful hair which hung loose, except for the thin war braids on either side of his face.

Once, when she lifted her heavy eyelids, she gasped and told him, "You have angel wings. Well, not really wings. Just a blue aura of wings."

He did not seem surprised as he licked his lips. Savoring her taste? Now there was a heady thought. "'Tis just a mirage," he murmured with a sex-huskiness that was in itself arousing to Alex. "They occur when I am in high emotion."

She tilted her head to the side, licking her own lips to savor his taste. Mint, she decided. "And are you in high emotion now?"

"Can you doubt it, sweetling?"

Alex relished his odd endearments . . . *sweetling*, *dearling*, and once in the midst of their near-sex, *heartling*.

There was no time for thought then, as they both were consumed with "high emotion." If not for their clothing, they would be having sex.

Her heart was pounding hard by then, a perfect complement to Vikar's pounding heart pressed against her, chest to breast. But then she realized the pounding came in sets of seven.

"Uh-oh!" Vikar muttered, pressing his forehead against hers, attempting to regain his breath.

Another seven pounds, not of their heartbeats, but on the locked door, she slowly realized. With gentle care, Vikar released his hold on her, helping her to stand on her wobbly feet. With a quick kiss to her swollen lips, he stomped over to the door and unlocked it.

"Bloody damn frickin'—" he started to swear, then exclaimed with surprise, "What are you all doing here?"

As he stepped aside, Alex saw three large men. Three very large men, at least six-foot-four. All with long hair and war braids. All with stunning blue eyes. All wearing silver upper arm rings identical to Vikar's. All with hands on hips in an exasperated manner.

"Alex," Vikar said with a groan, "these are my little brothers. Ivak, Sigurd, and Mordr. Come to plague me, no doubt."

"Little?" the men scoffed.

"Younger," Vikar conceded.

She nodded at the men, mute with shock. Alex knew that Vikar's brothers and their entourages weren't supposed to arrive for another week or more. She hoped, for Vikar's sake, that they came alone; the castle accommodations weren't ready for large numbers yet.

Now she'd met all seven brothers. Vikar. Trond. Cnut. Harek. Ivak. Sigurd. Mordr.

"And she is . . . ?" one of the brothers demanded to know, and not politely.

"Mine," Vikar said.

When brotherly love goes too far . . .

Vikar's brothers had come to help heal Harek, and yet they were wasting their time, and his, interfering with him about Alex. As if he needed their help with a woman! Right now, since Alex had left their company, they crowded their big selves into his small office and would not leave.

"The wench has Lucie blood in her. We should kill her," said Mordr, who'd just consumed vast amounts of the food prepared for them by said wench, and in fact had filched several cookies that he munched on as he spoke. As a former berserker, Mordr ever had been bloodthirsty. *And wasn't that a perfect choice of word for a vampire angel?* Leastways, Mordr had been wrathful in his human life. Still was, though he was fighting the inclination.

"Harek has Lucie blood in him, too. Should we kill our brother?" Vikar retorted.

"That is different," Mordr contended.

Vikar just arched a brow. Then, wanting to change the subject, he gave a report on their recent deadly encounter with the Lucipires. "There were a dozen Lucipires in all sent here by Jasper. We destroyed ten of them, and badly wounded two others who escaped."

Ivak shook his head with disgust. "Not Jasper himself, I warrant."

Vikar also shook his head with disgust. "The bastard always sends others to do his dirty work."

Cnut, who had been with him on the mission, elaborated, "One of them was a haakai. He escaped along with a female hordling. Aside from the haakai, six were full demons, including two mungs, and the rest were hordlings."

In demon society, there was a social order, so to speak, just as there was with angels, or vangels. Haakai were the most powerful demons, and the highest of those were lords. Below them were full demons, or captains. The mysterious mung demons, a type of full demon, were usually large, mute, and covered with a slimy, poisonous mung. Finally, the imps and their cousins, the hordlings, were the foot soldiers of Hell.

"Did any of them talk?" Mordr asked.

Vikar nodded. "A little. The best thing is that we managed to draw them far away from here. So hopefully they are still unaware of our large numbers in this one place. Besides, it appears that Jasper is busy elsewhere, planning some big event where he will suck large numbers of lost souls into his unholy domain, all in one fell swoop. We're talking hundreds, or thousands, at one time."

"A terrorist attack?" Mordr inquired, his eyes suddenly piercing with silver fire. Mordr had been particularly agonized over his failure to prevent 9/11.

"I don't think so," Vikar said, tapping his desk thoughtfully. "In that type of event, there are as many if not more souls going to the good side as there are bad. This plan of his reeks of a harvest with the odds more in his favor."

"Before he was struck down, Harek found some disturbing information on the Internet," Cnut told them. "Remember, Vikar, that Sin Cruise?"

"Ah, *yes*, now that you mention it." He explained what Harek had shown them that day on the computer.

All the men were fascinated and horrified at the same time by the depth of depravity Jasper could get away with or that humans could be attracted to.

"Well, then, we must heal Harek as soon as possible so we can investigate this further," said Sigurd, a physician, who had already examined his wounded brother and pronounced his injuries to be grievous, but not deadly, provided his blood could be cleansed. "Harek understands computers and the Internet better than any of us."

"You can say that again. I still have trouble writing a legible letter with a quill and ink, let alone my big fingers stumbling over a keyboard," grumbled Mordr.

"Are you saying that we're safe here from another attack?" Ivak asked skeptically. "You do not think that the same scent that drew the Lucies in the first place will draw them again?"

Vikar felt his face heat before he admitted, "I believe it was Alex's sin scent that drew them initially, and they were only hordlings on a prowl, not any particular assignment."

"What is her sin?" Sigurd wanted to know.

"I'm not certain . . ."

Mordr snorted his opinion at his failure to obtain that information.

He ignored Mordr and continued, "I do know it is a contemplation of sin, not the sin itself. Yet. I believe it involves the murder of her husband and daughter. Revenge."

The others nodded their understanding, knowing full well the sins that could spin out from grief. Even Mordr.

"I sensed the second we saw you in that storeroom that the woman was dangerous to us," Mordr said, still hoping that they would opt for killing Alex, no doubt. So much for his understanding!

"But sex, Vikar? Just weeks afore Reckoning? What were you thinking? Talk about poor decisions, lackbrain!" This from Ivak, whose lust had led to more poor decisions than Vikar could count, and most involving women.

"Not sex. Near-sex," Vikar contended, though he should not be bothering to make that distinction with his thickheaded brothers. It was none of their business, really, and it would just give them more ammunition for their mockery.

"I saw what you were doing in the storeroom, Vikar. That was sex. Believe you me, if anyone knows sex, 'tis me," Ivak persisted.

Vikar's face was probably turning as red as a sun-exposed Lucipire. "*Near*-sex," he repeated.

His brothers burst out laughing, including Cnut, who felt the need to share, "He told me and Harek that selfsame story. 'Twould seem Trond gave him the idea that near-sex was not real sex."

"You do not need to speak for me, Cnut. I do have a voice."

"Trond?" They all hooted with more laughter.

"I am pleased that you find humor here whilst our brother lies dying."

They all turned sober. "You are right, Vikar," said Sigurd. "Since our blood is pure, or fairly pure . . ." None of them were perfect, and they well knew it. ". . . we three will feed Harek, whilst you, Cnut, Armod, Svein, and Jogeir take turns drinking. That way each of you will not have to drink so much of the tainted blood."

"But what of the woman?" Ivak asked.

Aaarrgh! We are back to Alex again.

He dug in his heels. "Mike sent her to me. To save. I am convinced of that."

"That may very well be, but you have not finished the cleansing, Vikar, and now that you have fed from Harek, you are infected. You cannot feed her." Ivak spoke to Vikar as if he were a new vangel and did not know the rules. "Not for days, leastways."

"'Tis obvious that it was the woman's sin scent that drew the Lucies here in the first place, even you admit that. I still say we should just kill her." Mordr folded his arms over his chest and attempted to stare down Vikar's glare.

"Alex lives," Vikar declared. "I insist and Mike will, too." He wasn't certain about the latter. Mayhap it was just hopeful thinking, but Mordr didn't need to know that.

"Then you must step back and let one of us feed her. That will leave two others to feed Harek." Sigurd folded his arms over his chest and stared at him, too, after making that pronouncement.

Vikar fought his temper, even though he wanted to say, *Hell, no!* When he was able to speak below a shout, he said, "Alex would have a screaming fit. She isn't all that happy at the intimacy of *my* feeding her. She would view another man involved in the ritual as an assault."

"Vikar, Vikar, Vikar," Ivak tsked at him. "She will be given no choice."

He curled his upper lip at Ivak, but said nothing.

"You know it is the only way," Cnut added quickly, no doubt wanting to avoid a fight. Cnut at least knew Alex better than these three newcomers to the scene and presumably had some care about her.

Reluctantly he nodded.

"Where is she now?" Mordr wanted to know.

One thing was certain. He was not letting Mordr near Alex's fair skin. If the rage came over him, he could drain her afore she knew what was happening. And he wasn't too happy about allowing Ivak with his constant raging lust near her, either. With his wenching ways, Ivak would be impaling her with more than his teeth.

"Vikar?" Mordr prodded. "Where is the wench?"

"Taking a bubble bath."

Silence reigned then as five male minds went haywire imaging the frothy scene.

When they'd been ordering towels and bed linens from the Internet, Alex had requested a supply of bath products, as well. To his chagrin, delivery had included dozens of toothbrushes and tubes of toothpaste, shampoos, conditioners, soaps, bath gels, and, yes, bubble baths. He just knew there were going to be vangels up to their fangs in bubbles come nightfall.

Sigurd summed up the situation aptly: "Have we mentioned lately that you are in big trouble?"

Ten

Bubbles, tiny bubbles! . . .

Transylvania feature, Kelly   **Page 1**
Draft Six

War is hell.

No matter if it is a family member off to battle . . . husband, wife, father, mother, brother, sister, son, or daughter . . . the pain is the same for those left behind, on both sides.

This is especially true in the Holy War going on across the world at the moment, and it's not between Muslims and Christians. It is a hidden war that threatens all souls, regardless of religion. Some would say . . .

Alex sighed, and sank lower into the lavender-scented bubbles, her one hand dangling over the side with a crystal tumbler of vodka and orange juice. Was there anything more sybaritic to a woman than a warm bath overflowing with bubbles to soothe her on the outside and a glass of wine or mixed drink to ease her on the inside?

With everything she'd seen today, her perceptions were skewed. She did not know what to believe at this point. Her famous objectivity as a reporter seemed to have faded into nothingness. How could she judge what was truth or fiction anymore?

Her life was careening out of control.

She was scared.

Setting the glass on a small metal dressing table stool she'd pulled close to the tub, she dunked under water. Time to rinse out the conditioner she'd put in her hair after shampooing. Without it, her hair went frizzy.

When she came back up, it was to see Vikar sitting on the stool, sniffing at her drink that he held cradled in his big hands.

She yelped and sank down to shoulder level. Luckily she'd put three capfuls of bubble bath in the tub, so she was covered. For now. "I locked that door. How did you get in?" She waved a hand dismissively. "Never mind. Just get out."

"I need to tell you something."

He always needs to tell me something. It is never good news. "Can't it wait until I'm done in here?"

"Well, *yes*, but since I'm already here." Shrugging, he spread his thighs to get better purchase on the small stool, causing Alex's blood to warm, even more than it already was, at the sight of those muscular quadriceps and the package in between, all too evident in tight jeans. After sniffing at the drink, he took a sip, then a long swallow that pretty much emptied the glass.

"Be careful. You'll break that stool."

"Are you saying I'm fat?"

Hardly. She pretended to consider the question.

"I wonder if two people could fit into that tub."

It was one of those old, deep, claw-footed tubs that probably *could* hold two. "Not if one of them was as big as you."

A grin twitched at his lips, telling her that he knew exactly what she thought of his bigness. He put his elbows on his knees and braced his chin on both palms, staring at the tub. "How long does it take for those bubbles to fade?"

"You'll never know," she asserted with a laugh.

He leaned forward and blew. Hard. Causing a bunch of bubbles to fly.

"Hey! Stop it! Really, what kind of angel invades a woman's privacy and—"

"We need to resume your cleansing," he said before she could say more.

Alex closed her eyes and sighed deeply. When she opened them, Vikar was still staring at her intently through eyes that were such an incredible shade of blue, like aquamarines. "Not that again! I don't think so! Honestly, Vikar, I have always prided myself on my intelligence and independence. I don't suffer fools gladly and certainly don't suffer being fooled myself. However, I have to admit that I'm in way over my head here, and I don't mean bubbles. There are too many anomalies that I don't understand."

He nodded. "I've had a thousand years to live with these *anomalies*, and I still don't understand half of them."

That was scary. If *he* didn't understand, how could she possibly stay here and blindly agree to the craziness? "The blood feeding/sucking stuff is what I find hardest to accept. That's why I've decided to leave, Vikar. Now, don't get pissed off. I'm aware of the danger. I won't rush out blindly. I'll take steps."

"Steps!" he scoffed.

She put up a hand to halt his further protests. "It alarms the hell out of me that I didn't hate what you did to me. I'm afraid I'll grow addicted to it."

If he'd smirked, she would have an excuse to swat him in the face with a soapy loofah. But instead, he took the hand that she'd raised and kissed each of her fingertips, one at a time. "I wish . . . ah, I wish . . ."

He didn't have to finish his thought. She knew what he was wishing. In fact, she shared his sentiments. *I wish we had met at a different time, under different circumstances.*

"While much that you have witnessed horrifies you, it is my reality. There is a God. There is a St. Michael the Archangel who mentors us. There are demon vampires, and there are Viking vampire angels."

She shook her head, still unable to accept his words as truth. "The only explanation I can come up with is that this must be the promotional setup for some Hollywood film. The new *Twilight*, or a Pennsylvania Dutch version of *True Blood*, or some such thing. Yes, it would be a whole lot of trouble and at times it seems so real, but what else can I believe? Any day now Stephen Spielberg or Brad Pitt will be jumping out of the woodwork."

He smiled sadly. "I would not do that to you, at this stage of our relationship."

Relationship? What relationship?

But then he added, "Dost think I resemble Brad Pitt?" He referred, of course, to Anne Rice's Creole vampire Louis de Pointe du Lac.

"No." *You're better.* "More like Eric Northman, if you must know." But, even then, he was better. Not so lean. Not so modern-looking. "I'm leaving in the morning," she told him bluntly.

He just smiled, as if to say, *Not a chance, sweetheart!*

"It's best if I leave now. If nothing else, I want to testify at the trial. I owe it to Brian and Linda. And, frankly, it's better if I go and offer, rather than have them coming here to look for me, blowing your cover."

"For me? Pfff!" He bristled at the idea she would leave for his sake. "What about your story?"

"I'll tell Ben there was no story. Not all story ideas pan out."

"You have to be cleansed. It is the reason you were sent here to me."

She rolled her eyes. "I was sent here by a magazine editor who saw a story in a bizarre town of vampire wannabes. You were just the icing on the cake."

He rolled his eyes. "I am that sweet?"

"No, you are definitely not sweet." She looked down at the bubbles that were beginning to fade, and noted that the water was cooling down. She needed to get out soon. "Vikar, you can't take away my free will. That's supposedly the principle your whole vangel society revolves around."

He shrugged.

Which infuriated her. She thought a moment,

and the most outrageous idea came to her. "I don't suppose you would kill someone for me. Two some-ones, in fact."

"Aaahhh," he said as if he finally understood. "That is the sin you are contemplating?"

She nodded hesitantly.

"Murder? *You?* Never!"

She shrugged. "Despite my anger, I might even-tually be able to accept life imprisonment for the two men who killed my husband and daughter, but it appears as if they might get off, totally, or with a lesser punishment. I can't allow that to happen. I just can't."

"What I have failed to explain to you, dearling, is we do not kill humans. If I went to those two men, I would try to save them, give them a chance to repent."

Alex felt pain like a sword through her heart. "You would betray me like that?" she choked out.

"It would be my duty, just as it is my duty to save you," he explained, his eyes pleading with her for understanding.

Not bloody likely! She did not understand. Not at all. "I think I could hate you for that."

He exhaled and said, "So be it!"

Grabbing a large bath towel, he lifted her from the tub and covered her with it. Despite her shrieks and flailing arms and legs, he managed to dry her off briskly, then wrap her tightly in a terry-cloth robe that had been hanging on the door. While she struggled and hurled insults at him, he rubbed the moisture from her hair and ran a comb through its length.

The whole time, he kept repeating, "I am sorry,

Alex, but this is how it must be. I am truly sorry."

Picking her up in his arms, he proceeded to carry her from the bathroom, heading toward his bedroom, where Sigurd waited for him, leaning lazily against a bedpost. His fangs were out.

Alex stilled, glanced at the bed, at his brother, back to Vikar, whose fangs were also extended. Then she let loose with an ear-splitting scream, *"Nooooooo!"*

Share and share alike . . .

This was the hardest thing Vikar had ever had to do, and there had been plenty of horrendously difficult tasks he'd been assigned over the years. But sharing Alex? He'd rather rip out his heart.

Hah! Given a chance, she might just do it for him.

Pounding his chest, attempting to claw his face, screeching like a banshee, she fought valiantly, but he was a Viking. Like a feather in a bear's paw she was.

"If you think I'm getting involved in some ménage à dopes, you are crazier than I thought."

"Now, sweetling, that is not what we intend." *There is no appeal in such an arrangement for me. One-on-one is the only way. Not that I am contemplating such. A man can dream, though. Can't he?*

"Here's what *I* intend." She bit his shoulder. Hard.

Even though he'd like to shake some sense into the foolish woman, he laid her in the middle of his bed and immediately came down over her, pinning her to the mattress. Holding her hands above her head and pressing his weight onto her belly and chest, he whispered against her ear, "Shh, settle down. You cannot fight what is to come."

"You bastard. You sonofabitch. You ignorant ass-hole! Don't you dare tell me to settle down. I am not having sex with you two morons."

Whoa! Even a bar of soap wouldn't clean that mouth. "You give new meaning to 'potty mouth.' Tsk, tsk, tsk! 'Tis unseemly, m'lady."

"Fuck you!"

"I wish!" *Mike is going to have a fire-breathing fit if she speaks thus to him. If she is still here. Oh please, God, let her still be here. I am not ready to let her go.*

"And, furthermore, if anyone from your dimwit gene pool lays a hand on me, I'll write an exposé on your group that will blow your cover to high Heaven . . . or Hell, for all I care."

Vikar winced, even though he knew she would not . . . could not . . . follow through on that threat.

He heard Sigurd chuckling behind him.

"Not sex, sweetling," he tried to explain. "Just—"

"What? More near-sex? I am not having that, either. And ditch the endearments. I was not your sweet anything before and I am definitely not your sweet anything now."

"Not near-sex, either." *Except mayhap a little bit before, and mayhap a lot afterward. If you are in the mood. I know I am in the mood. Bloody hell! I am always in the mood these days.*

"I'm going to sue your pants off."

"My pants off, hmm? Is that a promise?" he asked, trying to soften her mood.

But she'd somehow managed to get her knee out from under him and when he lifted himself slightly to tuck her back under, she slammed him where it hurt the most.

"Ow, ow, ow!" he yelped like a little girling, but

he managed to hold on to the wiggling woman, and it served her right that, with all that wiggling, her robe came undone and he got an up close and personal view of all her frontal assets. Despite his pain, he smiled.

Which caused her to glance downward and see what was pleasing him so. Fire practically came out of her flared nostrils now. "I swear, I am going to kill you."

"I'm already dead." Apparently, she still hadn't accepted that concept.

"Uh, do you think we could get on with this sometime soon," Sigurd said. "*Antiques Roadshow* is coming on in a half hour, and . . . whoa! No wonder you are all moon-eyed, Vikar. She is a goddess."

Vikar turned to see that Sigurd had moved to the side of the bed and was ogling Alex's bare breasts and belly. He could have spit fire himself at that moment, not wanting any other man looking on his woman. Already he could feel his eyes turning silver with fury.

"Begone!" he yelled as he laid himself over her bare skin. "I will call for you when she is ready."

"Jeesh! All I did was look," Sigurd grumbled. "Methinks you are way too jealous, my brother, and jealousy is a sin, same as envy. Tsk, tsk, tsk!"

Sigurd is preaching. At me?

"Jealousy and envy are definitely not the same thing, which you should know since envy was your deadly sin," Vikar said.

"Yoo-hoo, is everyone forgetting that I am lying here pinned to the bed by a big baboon?" Alex complained, attempting futilely to shove upward against his immovable chest.

Sigurd winked at Alex.

But Vikar couldn't be angry about that, he was too aroused by her wriggling under him.

"In any case, methinks you have found your life mate," Sigurd went on.

"Do vangels get to have life mates?" Vikar asked, when he should have just kicked Sigurd out of the bedchamber.

"I do not know. We should ask Mike when he gets here," Sigurd replied.

"Have either of you ever considered applying for entrance to the Clueless Hall of Fame?" Alex asked with exaggerated sweetness.

"Aaarrgh! We are not asking Mike about this because it does not matter. She is not my life mate. I am just saving a sinner," Vikar explained. "Now go, I'll call when she is ready."

Sigurd left with a little wave.

When Vikar turned his attention back to Alex, she was no longer squirming under him, but instead shooting icy daggers at him with her cold green eyes. Cold eyes, fiery breath . . . should be a contradiction but somehow fit her outraged demeanor. "When I'm *ready*?"

"I just meant—"

"Save it for someone who cares."

He winced. "I thought you cared."

"I might have . . . until I realized what a rat bastard you are."

"I am not a rat bastard, Alex. I am just a vangel trying to do the right thing."

"Blah, blah, blah. Now get off me, you big oaf. Forget about tomorrow morning. I'm out of here tonight."

"Your nipples are blushing."

"Huh?"

There was indeed a flush coloring her skin from her neck to . . . well, her pleasure place. No doubt due to her warm bath and his towel rubbing. Whatever the cause, he couldn't help himself. He leaned down and framed the areola of one breast with his fangs, then sucked on the nipple. She tasted like sunshine and raspberries. He hummed his appreciation against her breast, alternating laves of his tongue with nips of his teeth with rhythmic suckling.

"Do. Not. Do. This." Her moaned words were belied by her hands gripping his head and holding him fast.

By the time he moved to her other breast and used a fang to flutter the peak back and forth until it engorged and grew rosy with arousal, her legs were crossed behind his buttocks in a futile attempt to bar his escape. Futile because he had no desire to escape.

"You have to let me go, Vikar," she said, even as she arched her back for more of his ministrations.

"I know," he said, even as he moved upward, ripped off his shirt, and rubbed his chest hairs and his own erect nipples back and forth across her breasts. If he hadn't known before, he knew now that his male nipples were sensitive.

"You have to let me go," she repeated, as she used the bottoms of both feet to caress the backs of his thighs and calves.

He'd had no idea he was so sensitive there, either. Especially the backs of his knees. "I know," he said, as he licked and blew lightly into the inner whorls of her ears.

She moaned, a continuous sighing expression of erotic delight. "I want you so much," she choked out. "I have never wanted a man like this before. Never."

The pride in him reared its head, but, no, it was more than pride. It was the man to her woman that delighted in her words. "In truth, I have ne'er felt this way, either. And I have been around a lot longer than you."

He kissed her then, long, and deep, and hungry. He kept tilting his head from one side to the other, trying for the best fit, but they were all good. The wetness, the heat, the soft sounds of aroused woman were almost his undoing. He had to stop. He had to. "Alex, I must take a little blood from you. Not much because I already have too much Lucipire blood in me from Harek."

"Then don't."

"I must. Truth be told, the Lucipire taint is no doubt causing me to be more tempted than usual by your charms."

She stiffened. "Are you saying that you want me only because you have some sinful blood in you?"

"You know that is not true. I have wanted you from first I saw you standing at my front door like an angry Valkyrie. It is a fact, though, that the Lucipire taint weakens the will against sin. And that goes for you, too, sweetling. Part of your lack of resistance to me is due to the Lucipire taint."

"Oh." Clearly, she would rather be attracted to him for normal reasons. He felt the same way.

Before she could raise any objections, he sank his teeth into her neck and he almost fainted at the sheer ecstasy. There was pleasure for her, too, in the feeding. He could tell by the way her body relaxed into the mattress. And her arms went about his shoulders, caressing his hair and nape.

He soon stopped, though he could drink from her endlessly if given the chance and it were not so dangerous. For a brief, scary second he wished she had fangs and could take succor from him, too. While she gazed up at him through glazed eyes, he pulled the sides of her robe together and knotted the tie securely. Kissing her lightly, he then moved up to sit against the headboard, pulling her onto his lap. He could tell she was weak. And confused. Good. If she understood what was to come, she would be fighting him wildly again.

While he held her face against his chest and crooned Old Norse words softly into her ear, Sigurd returned, opening and closing the door softly before moving up to the bed. He chuckled when he tripped over Vikar's shirt on the floor. "Shall I take off my shirt, too?"

"Only if you want me to beat the shit out of you."

Sigurd chuckled again and asked, "Shall I present my neck? The blood from the neck is purer."

Vikar shook his head in refusal. Too intimate.

Sigurd shrugged and ripped the vein at his wrist with his own fangs. Then, hopping onto the bed beside them, he attempted to use one hand to turn Alex's head, at the same time keeping his other hand palm up to avoid blood dripping onto the bed linens.

Vikar slapped away Sigurd's hand on Alex's chin. He did not want his brother touching her. He would be the one to turn her for the feeding.

Alex's eyes shot open as she realized another person was in the bed with them. Her body went stiff with shock.

"Shh, shh, settle. It is only Sigurd."

"Only Sigurd!" she yelled. The arousal mood that had hazed her senses was fast evaporating.

"Don't worry. He's a doctor."

"I don't care if he's the pope. Get him out of here."

Thinking quickly, Vikar arranged himself so that Alex sat on his lap, frontways, her legs trapped by his. He pulled a sheet up to her shoulders to cover what he was about to do. While he kissed her neck, and whispered soothing words to calm her, she continued to struggle, but then he stuck one hand inside her robe and caressed a breast. The other hand heeled her pubic bone in a rhythmic fashion.

He saw Sigurd's eyes follow his movements with interest, and, *yes*, arousal. It was an automatic reaction, but Vikar hated it nonetheless.

Alex continued to protest and struggle futilely to get up. Turning her head to look at him pleadingly, she whispered, "Vikar. No. I don't want this."

"You will, dearling. You will." He pierced her neck again with his fangs and sipped slowly. Just little drips at a time, but enough to get her back in stasis.

When she stopped struggling, Sigurd arranged himself on a side facing them on the bed and put his wrist to her mouth, refusing to lift it when she attempted to turn away. But then her eyes drifted shut and she moaned her surrender.

As she drank from him greedily, Sigurd's gaze

connected with Vikar's. "She *is* sweet," Sigurd conceded.

"She is *my* sweet," Vikar emphasized. *Please, God.*

"How many years do you think this sweetness will cost you?"

"Some things in life are worth the pain." *Please, God*, he prayed again, though he was not sure what he was praying for, exactly, whether it was to keep her with him or for the strength to let her go.

Sigurd just laughed and rolled away.

With eyes still closed, Alex groaned her dismay over her blood supply being cut off. She had no chance to actually voice a protest, though, because Vikar had shoved Sigurd off the bed and pointed to the door.

Sigurd licked his lips and laughed at the frown on his brother's face, but then Vikar's attention was directed only on the dazed woman in his arms. She was still aroused from his earlier fondling, and he had every intention of bringing her to peak. But not in the presence of his brother.

"Out! Now!" he demanded.

"Why can't I stay and watch?" Sigurd wanted to know. "I get so few pleasures that I deserve a bit of voyeurism from time to time."

Vikar said a foul word in Old Norse.

Sigurd left, shaking his head at Vikar's possessiveness that was clearly going to cause him trouble.

Alex's eyes were opening slowly. She was disoriented and it took several moments for her to realize where she was and what had happened. She ran her tongue over her lips and tilted her head in puzzlement at the taste.

He arranged her on the bed so that he was on his side leaning over her. "Are you all right?"

With a shake of her head, she said, "No, I am not all right. I will never be all right again."

He thought a moment, then shrugged. Clueless Viking man that he was, he just blundered on, "So, do you want to have near-sex now?"

Her growl would have done a grizzly bear proud.

Eleven

Cluelessness: a manly trait
through the ages . . .

Why are vampires so popular? The dark princes of the night monopolize almost every aspect of popular culture, and yet no one seems able to pinpoint why. What happened to transform these evil monsters into heroes?

Unbelievably, some people blame it on *Sesame Street*. Could it be that the sweet-natured Count on the public TV show is responsible for this softening of the bloodsucking villain so familiar to us starting with Bram Stoker's *Dracula*? And what about Count Chocula breakfast cereal? Is it really possible that from a young age, our youth are being subconsciously influenced to view vampires as friend, not foe? If so, why?

That subject and more would be interesting topics for doctoral studies at any of our major universities. In fact . . .

"You have crossed the line this time, buster," Alex seethed, shoving Vikar on the shoulder for emphasis.

"Now, sweetling . . ."

"How could you? How could you?" She continued to shove his immovable body. Like a monument he was. Lying on his side. A monument to cluelessness.

When he flinched away from her pummeling fist, she moved herself up onto her knees and glared down at him with consternation. "Not that you haven't crossed the line before, but two men in bed with me? Unbelievable!"

"We weren't *in bed* in bed," he tried to argue.

"That doesn't even pass the giggle test."

"Does that mean you do not want to have near-sex with me?" The look of disappointment on his face was priceless.

She shook her head at him. How could a man be so infuriating and adorable at the same time? "Can you say 'clueless'? Really, men do the stupidest things and still expect women to have monkey sex with them."

"Monkey sex?" His forehead furrowed with confusion, and, yes, interest.

"Like watch ten straight hours of football, reek of cigar smoke and hot wings, and have the nerve to say, 'Hey, babe, wanna play with my balls'?"

"I do not like cigars."

"What you did was ten times worse."

"Than cigars?"

"Aaarrgh!"

"And I rarely eat hot wings. They stain my fangs."

"Aaarrgh!"

"Do not deny it, dearling, you are still aroused from our earlier love play." He smiled lazily. As if to tempt her.

She frowned. She was tempted. "No, I am not aroused," she insisted then. *Aroused would be an understatement. More like crawling the walls, I-want-you, I-want-you, I-want-you, please, please, please.*

"I can smell your ardor." He reached up a hand to caress her hair.

She slapped his hand away. "Maybe it's the lemonade I drank earlier."

"Sin scent smells like lemons. Arousal smells like woman musk." He sniffed the air and pretended to shiver with delight.

The idiot! "I swear, your IQ is dropping by the second." She drew the robe tighter around her nude body when she realized the idiot was staring up at her cleavage. "What I don't understand is how you got me to acquiesce. Am I in a cult or something? Did you spike the Kool-Aid . . . uh, lemonade?"

"Cult?" he asked hesitantly. "No, vangeldom is not a cult."

"Mind control is so not my thing. There has to be a reason why I let you do"—she waved a hand at the bed—"these things."

"There is mind control, and then there is mind control."

She rolled her eyes. "That is such a bullshit answer."

"Well, I can tell you for certain that Jim Jones is not going to jump out of the woodwork."

"Is that your idea of a joke?"

"You told me you liked my sense of humor."

"I take it back."

He sighed, no doubt because he saw prospects of sex going out the window. "When a human is bitten by a vangel . . . or a Lucipire, for that matter . . . the body goes into stasis," he explained with a blush that told her he was either lying or withholding something important. Since he was supposedly on God's team, she imagined lying was not in his repertoire.

"And . . . ?" she prodded.

With a grunt of disgust, Vikar slid off the bed and walked barefoot over to a dresser, where he opened a door that hid a compact fridge. He still wore only jeans, which rode low on his hips, drawing attention to his tight butt.

Aaarrgh! I am not looking at the moron's butt.

Taking out two bottles of water, he came back and handed one to her, which she declined, and uncapped the other, drinking deeply. Bloodsucking apparently didn't satisfy thirst totally. Personally, she intended to quench her thirst in a different way later . . . with about a quart of vodka.

Unable to avoid her questions forever, he sat down on the edge of the bed where she still sat propped against the headboard, her arms wrapped around knees she'd drawn up to her chest. When she saw the direction of his startled stare, she made a tsking sound and covered her knees with a sheet.

"I deliberately aroused you each time I took blood from you to make your stasis engage more quickly and with more intensity." His eyes—blue now, not the silver they'd been when he was aroused—held hers with an honesty she couldn't deny.

She jerked her head to the side as if he'd back-handed her and blinked her eyes rapidly to stem the tears that welled there.

Seeing her dismay, he reached out a hand to her.

But she shook her head in rejection. *It was all a ploy. He doesn't love me,* she thought, then immediately added to herself, *Of course he doesn't love me. He doesn't even know me. Just like I don't love him. Of course I don't. And I definitely don't know him.* But all that was beside the point. "You manipulated me, sexually," she accused him.

He looked as if he'd like to argue the point, but nodded instead. "I did."

His admission crushed her. No woman liked to know a man had been putting the moves on her for some ulterior purpose, not overwhelming attraction. "I've been so confused about what's happening here. I can't understand why I stay. Have you manipulated my mind, too?"

"No, not specifically, but your brain is dazed by the Lucipire taint and the cleansing rituals. So, in some ways, I may have inadvertently altered your thinking. Just a tiny bit." He held up a thumb and forefinger about an inch apart to demonstrate.

Well, that does it! The jerk has stuck his wicked fingers not just in my libido but my mind, as well. "I hate that you've done this, Vikar. I trusted you."

He finished his water and tossed the empty plastic bottle on the floor with disgust. "I never lied to you. Whatever else you may accuse me of, dishonesty was never in play."

"That's debatable," she said. "I really want to leave here, Vikar. I need to be in my regular surroundings to clear my mind."

"It isn't safe for you. Not only is your demon taint still there, though to a lesser degree, but the Mexican cartel is after you, too. Even your boss agrees with me that you should stay."

"Yeah, well, I appreciate your concern for my safety, but I'm a big girl. I got along fine before. I will in the future, too. Besides, I'll take precautions."

"Like what?" he scoffed. "How will you repel Lucipires? With a fly swatter? Or that pistol you have in your luggage? Just so you know, regular bullets are as useless as throwing rice at a Lucipire."

Really? "Aren't you being a little dramatic?"

"You know I'm not. You saw what happened in that restaurant parking lot. You saw what happened to Harek, and he is a highly skilled warrior."

She nodded. The way Harek had looked when Vikar carried him in would stay in her mind forever. One arm clearly broken since it canted at an awkward angle midway between wrist and elbow. A deep wound in his thigh exposed by the torn fabric of his jeans, possibly caused by a sword. Skin lacerations. Fang marks. Bruises. On a human, those injuries taken as a whole would prove fatal. They still might, depending on what *fatal* meant to an already dead person.

Luckily, they'd had Sigurd here, soon after their ritual blood healing. A physician, no less!

"I live in a secure high-rise, Vikar. There's a doorman, and dead bolt locks, and alarms."

"And how will you prevent a bullet from entering your heart when you leave your home?" He put a hand to his own heart. "I could not bear to have you taken by those evil creatures."

"It's not your problem."

He shook his head. "You were sent here to me." He held up a hand to halt her protests. "Hear me out, please. Mike influenced your employer to send you to Transylvania."

What? No! Never! That did not happen. "You're delusional."

"Then, the moment I saw the fang marks on your neck and smelled your scent, I had no choice but to invite you inside."

"Invite? You are definitely delusional."

"From then onward, I have done only what was required of me. No, that is not true," he conceded. "I have done more. I could not help myself."

She cocked her head to the side. "Explain yourself."

He reached over and unclenched her fingers that were still clutching her knees. Taking both hands in his, he said, "You say you are confused. Well, you are not the only one. Ever since you arrived, my emotions have been banging against the walls, and, believe you me, Vikings do not do emotion well. I do not know if this is a test Mike is tossing my way, or a punishment of some kind."

Alex tried to pull her hands away, but he held fast. "I'm a punishment, like a whipping? Or a test, like a freakin' angel SAT?"

"You missay me. It would be a punishment if you entered my life, bringing it light and joy, and then left. The dark place where you'd leave me would be the cruelest punishment."

She could feel her anger fading. *If I'm no longer*

angry, who knows what I'll do? Jump his bones, probably. I can't have that. "And the test part?"

"Mayhap you are a temptation Mike sent to test my resistance to . . . um . . . uh . . . to you."

Stutter much, baby? "What you are trying so hard to avoid saying is that you equate me with sin . . . that you need to resist sin, i.e., me."

He shook his head. "You deliberately twist my words. Why can you not understand?"

"Oh, I understand, all right. Bottom line: When are you going to let me leave?"

He stared at her bleakly, raised both her hands to his mouth, where he kissed one set of knuckles, then the other, before setting her hands back on her lap. "My first inclination is to say never, but—"

"Now see, Vikar, you say things like that so lightly. Women take such words seriously, but you toss them out like popcorn. How can you say that you might not want me to leave? What does that mean? In what capacity would I stay? As your lover? Or near-lover? Wife? Girlfriend? Friend friend? What does *never* mean to you?"

His jaw dropped at her tirade.

And Alex was mortified that she'd reacted so strongly. She was behaving like a teenager with her first crush.

"It does not matter what I want. I suspect the decision will be taken out of my hands once Mike arrives."

"And that will be when?"

"About two weeks."

"And what about my wishes? Don't I have any say in my future?"

"You do. You will."

"I just don't understand," she said for about the hundredth time.

"Trust me. Just for a little while longer," he pleaded. The mistiness in his blue eyes might have been tears.

And that was almost her undoing. "How can I? Especially after what happened here with your brother?"

"I should have notified you first."

"Now there's a left-handed apology. You aren't sorry you did it, just that you failed to inform me ahead of time."

He blushed. The big brute actually blushed.

"If I stay, and I'm not saying I will—Ben will have a heart attack if I leave without notifying him first—do you promise not to bring anyone else into the bed?"

"I promise, if you will agree to let me further cleanse you once I am pure."

She nodded hesitantly. "How much longer is this blood thing going to last? I mean, how many more times?"

"Only a few. I am being extra careful with you. Most times I can cleanse a sinner on one try."

"And then when I'm 'clean'?"

"And then I hope you will not commit that great sin you were . . . are . . . contemplating."

"Back to that again."

"We never got away from that. It has always been about the sin taint."

"There are evil people in this world, Vikar."

"You think I do not know this?"

"I'm talking about human people. Ones who deserve to die."

He shook his head sadly at her. "That is not for you to decide."

"They took everything from me. Everything. They are monstrous . . . as monstrous as the demons you kill."

"That may very well be, but vengeance is not yours, sweetling. Yes, I know it is hard to accept, but you must. You *must*!"

"If I stay, are you going to try to stop my writing a magazine article about everything I see?"

He hesitated. "You can write whatever you want. Whether you can publish it remains to be seen. The matter is not up to me entirely."

"St. Michael the Archangel again?" she scoffed.

"Exactly."

"Well, tell me this. Will I get to meet the guy?"

"Unfortunately, I think you will."

"Why unfortunately?"

"Your life will never be the same."

She started to laugh. Hysterically. "Oh, honey," she said finally, using the edge of a sheet to wipe the tears off her face. "Meeting you has already altered my life forever."

Doing the devil's work . . .

Chaos reigned down in Horror, but that was nothing new at Lucipire Central. Satan's acolytes thrived on pandemonium.

Jasper paced his cave lair with its new bank of computers set up to coordinate the Sin Cruise. What a job it had been for him to find ten geek Lucipires! The imps and hordlings claimed to be all thumbs . . .

or claws . . . when it came to typing. And the mungs kept dripping slime onto the keyboards and shorting out the hard drives, so he'd had to sacrifice full demons, taking them from their regular trolling duties. But it was worth it. This would be the biggest event for mass annihilation ever planned by Lucipires.

Even so, he could not ignore regular work. There were a dozen naked humans pinned to his life-size butterfly boards, a small start to replenishing his supply of playthings. "How's it going?" he asked Sabeam, who was putting a final two-foot pin through his latest addition, a financier who had bilked hundreds of senior citizens out of their retirement money.

Sabeam stared up at him through rheumy red eyes, fighting to control his lolling tongue that dripped drool. "This one is a fighter." Ernie Randolph, the fiftysomething man, who was hardly recognizable without his thousand-dollar suit and Italian loafers, flailed widely, screaming with outrage at his fate.

"Not for long," Jasper predicted. "In the old days before modern torture technology, it took years to 'ripen' new Lucipires, to bring them to an understanding that they should reject God and all that He preached, and accept Satan as their savior. Today, humans are weak. They have low thresholds of pain," he explained, though Sabeam should know this after four hundred years in his company, but then mungs were dull-headed betimes.

"But some of our 'recruits' never reach that point," Sabeam pointed out, "like that vangel who died from our tortures."

Jasper backhanded Sabeam for reminding him of that failure, but then he regretted his action when he had to wipe the poisonous slime off his knuckles. Drawing on his dwindling patience, he elaborated, "There is a fine line Lucipire torturers must follow, excruciating and unending, of course, but never too much at one time. Ah, well, we live and learn. Ha, ha, ha. Great cliché, that, about living."

"What's a cliché?" Sabeam wanted to know.

Jasper just rolled his red eyes.

Before departing the curing area, Sabeam patted the man's head. Not appreciating the comforting touch and too new to understand the consequences of his behavior, the fool spat a wad of mucus up at Sabeam.

"Now, now, we cannot have that," Sabeam said sweetly, then reached down and ran his sharp claws over the man's flaccid penis, causing the man to arch up on his pin, screaming with pain.

Sabeam patted the man's head again after he fell backward to the butterfly board. This time the man did not spit.

"One more thing I would show you before we leave," Sabeam said, pride ringing in his voice. "Our arrival from last week is coming along nicely. It took only three days in the killing jars for her to quiet down."

It was the female serial killer from London who had run a human trafficking ring, specializing in children. Pedophiles had a special place in Jasper's sick heart.

Not unattractive by human standards, Lily Durant had long blonde hair spread out over the back of her display board, like strands of gold. The nipples on her round breasts were pulled upward to elongate them by piercing wires strung from the ceiling. Every few days, the wires were pulled tighter. Down below, between her spread legs, a vibrating twin phallus did its work inside her body, both holes. Semen ran from her mouth from the many Lucipires who were permitted to use her at will.

The woman tried to struggle when she saw them approaching, no doubt fearing some new torture. Oh, there would be plenty of that, to be sure.

"Please . . . please . . . let me go," she pleaded.

"Foolish split-tail!" Jasper said. "Do you not know you are ours forever? Soon you will be one of us."

Her green eyes went wild with distress.

"Have you ever fucked a man with a tail, sweetheart?" he asked just before they left the chamber. "Let's make a date, shall we? Eight tonight. Wait 'til you see the places a scaly tail can go."

Her screams followed them for some time.

"Don't you just love the sound of a Lucipire-in-training?" Jasper remarked to Sabeam.

"Like choirs of angels singing," Sabeam said, then covered his head with both hands to field Jasper's blow.

Finally, they came to the killing jars that held six new victims, along with two Lucipires, Gregori Petrov and his hordling consort Virgana Dorset, the ones who had returned last night from their unsuccessful encounter on a Canadian mountain with vangels. Jasper unlocked the last two latches and motioned for the Lucipires to follow them. The female, who'd been wounded and untreated thus far, limped badly, but knew better than to disobey orders or be slow to follow them. The male, a high haakai, hissed and raised his chin with anger over his treatment, but he, too, knew enough to do as he was told by his leader.

Jasper entered his private chambers where hordlings were arranging wheeled racks of cruise wear clothing for his Lucipires to choose from for the upcoming event. He shooed them out, along with Sabeam, and walked into his office, sitting down behind a desk, not an easy task when a tail needed to be accommodated. He did not give Gregori or Virgana permission to sit, so they stood before him in the tattered, foul-smelling clothing they'd worn in battle. A faint hint of vangel blood clung to them as well, which pleased Jasper mightily.

"A report, please," he said to Gregori, but before he began, he told Virgana, "Go off and have your wounds treated. You are soiling my carpet."

Virgana ducked her head and left.

"Now, sit, Greg, and tell me everything," Jasper ordered in a more friendly fashion. The killing jar was a necessary punishment when a Lucipire failed to complete an assignment, but Gregori was a good soldier for Satan and deserved his respect. At one time, he had been a henchman for Ivan the Terrible . . . during his terrible period.

"We went to Transylvania first—"

"The vampire town in the United States?"

Gregori nodded. "Just a bunch of people pretending to be vampires as a tourist trap."

"That *Twilight* series will be the death of us yet," Jasper quipped. *What is it with me and the jokes today?*

"At first, there seemed to be a strong scent of

vangel in the area, but it proved false. Instead, we discovered a trail outside of the town leading in several different directions. A diversion. We soon tracked them to their hideout, not here in the United States but in Canada. We found not just vangels, but some of The Seven."

Jasper gasped and rubbed his hands together with relish. "This is good news. Very good news."

"Three of them, in all, along with a few other vangels. Breaking up our ranks, we managed to find them in Canada in a mountain hiding place."

"And?"

"There was a fierce battle in which ten Lucipires were lost. Only Virgana and I escaped." He bowed his head in shame.

As well he should! But Jasper already knew of their failure and they had been punished.

"But I smell vangel blood on you."

"One of The Seven was mortally wounded and was carried off by his brothers."

Jasper tapped his scaly chin thoughtfully. "That is good news, to some extent." If vangels died before their penance was completed, they did not go to Heaven, but some holding place where they would be judged later at the Final Day. On the other hand, if they'd managed to infest him totally with Lucipire blood, there was a chance they could have converted him to their ranks.

"Even better, he could live with the Lucipire taint in him. One rotten apple in the barrel type of thing," Gregori pointed out. "Plus it would be easier for us to track them down. A blood GPS, so to speak."

"This is good, this is good," Jasper said. "We must

assign some Lucipires to search that mountain area. And Transylvania, that Pennsylvania town, are we sure there is no presence there?"

"Not totally sure," Gregori conceded.

"Then send a few Lucipires there as well to investigate, but not until after the Sin Cruise. We need all our ranks working on this event if it is to succeed."

"As you wish, master," Gregori said, bowing his head.

Jasper loved when his captains gave him proper respect. As a result, he softened his regard. "Go and refresh yourself, Greg. And take one of the new Lucipires to play with, if you wish. One of them is especially . . . juicy."

Gregori smiled at him, his fangs elongating in anticipation.

What's the protocol for vampire dating? . . .

Two days later, Alex was still at the castle, in a truce with Vikar over the cleansing ritual, for the time being. Every time she passed by Sigurd, who really was a physician, of all things, she gave him a dirty look that just caused him to laugh.

"Shouldn't you be off curing cancer or something?" she'd sniped at him one time when he was watching a Michael Jackson video with Armod.

"I'm taking a break from curing cancer," he'd replied in a mocking tone.

All of Vikar's brothers, those five in residence now, thought she and Vikar's growing relationship was a great joke. Frankly, she didn't get the joke, but that didn't stop them. She could only imagine what Vikar had to put up with when she wasn't around.

"Getting lots of information for my story," she kept telling Ben whenever he called, but what she was mostly doing was helping to set up some of the completed bedrooms with linens and the bathrooms with towels and toiletries. Comfort activity.

In some odd way, these days here with Vikar felt like a vacation from her real life. Blame it on some crazy demon vampire taint in her blood, or blame it on her unresolved grief over her daughter's death, or blame it on her profound loneliness, but she was happy, and it didn't matter to her if Vikar and his clan were Vikings or vampires or angels or frickin' Hollywood actors. Maybe later it would, but for now she was riding a wave of "What the hell!" Not that she'd use that word out loud in the vampire angels' company, not anymore, after having been chastised for it innumerable times.

So it was like icing on her personal happy cake when Vikar returned to his office after talking with the contractor and said, "We should go out and celebrate."

Like a date? she wondered, but didn't have the nerve to ask as she continued to tap away at her story notes on her laptop. In the distance, she heard the trucks outside gun their motors and drive away. She saved her material and logged off. Only then did she glance up.

Lordy, lordy, the man was too good-looking, even wearing his sweaty workout clothes, a tank top and shorts and athletic shoes. Muscles rippled everywhere. Especially his broad shoulders and arms, accentuated by the silver bracelets etched with wings that ringed his upper arms. He was a magnificently proportioned thirty-three-year-old male of 2012.

"Alex! You're ogling," he said with a grin.

She shook her head to clear it, not even bothering to deny his smirking accusation. "You mentioned that we should celebrate. Celebrate what?"

"They're done. J.D. just announced that they finished their work, or as much as I contracted for. When they come back tomorrow for me to sign off, they'll take away any equipment or supplies still lying around. But, bottom line, no more pounding or cursing or screeching saws."

Vikar and his big burly brothers could use the F word or crudities like drunken sailors but they cringed like splinters under the fingernail if they heard someone use *Jesus* or *Christ* as an expletive. The workers had used lots of those.

He smiled at her, waiting for her reaction to his news, and she marveled irrelevantly at how white and even his teeth were.

"Now what?" he asked, noticing the way she stared at his mouth. "If you want to be kissed, you have only to ask."

She laughed. "I was just thinking that you must have the enamel of an elephant for your teeth to look so good after so many years, not to mention the havoc blood must wreak. If you run out of vampire angel work, you could always do Crest commercials."

"Alex, Alex, Alex," he chastised her as he sat down on the edge of the desk, way too close. Even sweaty, he was temptation on the Adidas hoof. "When you look at my mouth, you think tooth structure. When

I look at your mouth, I think long, slow, deep, soft, wet kisses that last three days."

She laughed. "You've been watching *Bull Durham* again, haven't you?"

He ducked his head sheepishly. "It's Cnut's favorite."

"Yeah, right. Blame Cnut."

"Some people claim I look like a young Kevin Costner. What say you?"

Honey, you look ten times better than Kevin Costner. Even a young Kevin Costner. "Not really."

He shrugged. "I already called Molly Maids and they'll be sending a cleaning crew in the morning," he told her. "Thanks to you."

Apparently Vikar had scared off a couple of cleaning ladies one day before she'd arrived, so he'd asked Alex to see what she could do about getting them to come back. Alex had told the local manager that Vikar was an actor and he'd been practicing a scene from a play that had a sword as one of the props.

"And the dead cow?" the woman had asked.

"The delivery guy from Peachy's Market had just left it in the kitchen when it should have been placed in the cooler."

The woman had apparently been convinced since she was sending in a crew tomorrow.

"So you want to go out and celebrate the end of construction and the beginning of cleaning?" she teased.

"That and Harek's continuing improvement. He got up and walked a bit today."

That turned Alex more serious. "What good news! I know how worried you've been." She was also aware that once Harek was well, Vikar would resume that blood cleansing thing with her. Only this morning Mordr, the crude oaf, remarked in passing that she "still smelled like bloody lemons."

"None of the vangels have ever been in such dire condition and survived." The relief in Vikar's voice was apparent.

"Vikar . . . ?" she started to ask, and wasn't sure how to word her question, ". . . if a vangel 'dies' in the course of a penance, do they go to Heaven?"

He arched his brows at her. "Do you now believe that we are vangels and that there is a Heaven and a God?"

"It was a hypothetical question. How can I believe in a God and reconcile the death of an innocent little girl? Brian was a grown man and danger was part of his work. But Linda did nothing wrong."

"There are some things beyond our understanding."

"That is a crock that religious folks feed nonbelievers."

Vikar took one of her hands in his and squeezed. "In answer to your question, very few humans go directly to Heaven; first they go to Limbo or Purgatory. There is a similar place called Tranquillity where good vangels go until the Last Judgment."

She didn't believe a word he said, she couldn't, but still she wondered where Brian and Linda would fit into that picture. *Brian was no saint, but he was not a bad man, either. How harsh of a judge would God be? Would a man like Brian be in Purgatory? But where would that place Linda? And, oh my! Does that mean Linda is alone wherever she is?*

She needed a change of subject, so she asked Vikar, "What would you like to do to celebrate?"

"We could go to town and have dinner. Maybe listen to some music."

"You mean, like a date?"

He blushed. She loved when the big guy blushed. "I have ne'er been on a date before, but, yes, I suppose it would be a date."

"I thought it was unsafe to leave the castle."

"I'll take precautions."

"It's a date then," she agreed.

I am going out on a date with a vampire, Alex crooned to herself as she went upstairs to change her clothes. She felt like a teenager invited to her first prom. She had to smile every time she said it to herself: *date with a vampire*. It could be the title of a romance novel.

But she wasn't feeling so romancey when she came down the stairs at six p.m., wearing her little black dress, the one that could be rolled up into her suitcase and shaken out wrinkle-free, along with four-inch stiletto sandals, hair in a neat French braid, makeup just perfect with her favorite Crimson Kiss lip gloss, gold chandelier earrings, and a spritz of Jessica McClintock perfume. Nope, nothing romancey about the sight she beheld waiting for her in the front hallway.

There was Vikar of course, looking gorgeous in a black silk T-shirt tucked into belted, pleated black slacks, with black loafers. Thin braids with blue aquamarine beads framed his face, with the rest of his hair hanging down to his shoulders. A hunk of a date, for sure.

But beside him stood Cnut, Mordr, Sigurd, Ivak, and Armod. Each spectacularly dressed, in his own way, whether it be designer jeans and an oxford cloth, button-down shirt, or a turtleneck and blazer. They all, including Vikar, wore identical long black cloaks with angel wing epaulettes, under which there was no doubt an arsenal of weapons fit for a Navy SEAL team. Except for Armod, who wore his Michael Jackson outfit, exposed white socks and all.

Alex felt like screaming, but instead she burst out laughing. This was going to be the date of the century.

Twelve

Dancing: modern man's foreplay . . .

What's it like to date a vampire?

Well, travel to Transylvania, Pennsylvania, and you might find out. On any summer night, couples stroll the streets of this quaint town, and most of them sport long black cloaks and fangs.

Every business has a vampire slant, one hokier than the other. But on your date, you'll want to have dinner and dancing at one of the local clubs, such as the Bloody Stake, where you can get a hamburger or filet as rare as you want, and be entertained by a band called Drac's Disciples.

Afterward, you can take a stroll down to the lake where . . .

"You look beautiful," he said to Alex as they walked down the main street of Transylvania.

And sexy, too, truth be told. Especially with those ridiculous shoes that exposed her heels and red-painted toes, their height causing her calf muscles to elongate and her bottom to arch outward. He even liked the freckles exposed on her neck and chest by the round neckline of the tight dress, as well as on her arms beyond the short sleeves, and from her knees downward. And, help! Those miles of sheer silk stockings begged a man's touch. *Not that I'm contemplating touching. Much.*

"You're drooling," Sigurd whispered in his ear.

He slammed his mouth shut, but didn't check for drool. He was fairly certain Sigurd was teasing. All his brothers had been making mock of him with great glee for days over his obsession with this woman.

"Did you hear me, sweetling?" he asked. "You look especially beautiful tonight."

Alex ignored his compliments, refusing to talk to him as she had since discovering that their date would include not just the two of them but five others as well. When her first reaction had been laughter back in the hall, he'd thought, fool that he was, that she would have no problem with a protective entourage on their date. Hah! She'd quickly let him know that she'd sooner pluck her eyebrows than get into the long black Excursion van—a vehicle she'd immediately dubbed "Testosterone Central." Had she been implying that they smelled? Did testosterone have an odor? He would have to ask someone. No, he would look it up on the Internet.

In any case, he'd convinced her to come along. Well, convince was not quite accurate. He'd picked her up and set her in the second row of seats where Armod sat on her other side. Sigurd was driving with Mordr in the passenger seat. Behind them in the third seat were Ivak and Cnut. Svein, Jogeir, and Dagmar were staying back at the castle with Harek.

And now they were in town, walking down the street, away from the parking lot where they'd left their vehicle, looking for a restaurant that would please them all. He and his brothers wanted one that served beer. Armod wanted one that played music. Alex declined to express an opinion.

"Alex, be reasonable," he said, taking her hand in his, lacing their fingers, even though she tried to clench a fist to resist his efforts. He won, of course. "I had to have at least one other vangel with us, in case there are any Lucipires still about."

She looked at him. "At least one, huh? How about the other four yayhoos?"

"Yahoo? Isn't that someplace on the Internet?"

"Yayhoo, not Yahoo."

Hmm. I cannot wait to call my brothers by that name. Later. "They asked if they could come along. Especially Armod. I could not say them nay. Must be the kind heart I am developing."

She made a very unfeminine sound of disbelief, halfway between a grunt and snort.

"Besides, Armod threatened to play Michael Jackson videos and teach my brothers how to moonwalk if left at home."

The image brought a slight smile to her kiss-me red lips, which she quickly pressed together.

"Just pretend we are alone." Even he realized how ludicrous that sounded.

"Pfff! Well, you better not be thinking any threesome, foursome, fivesome nonsense."

"Alex! It is a date, not an orgy I am planning." *If I were into planning anything of a sexual nature, it would not involve males other than myself with my very own strawberry-blonde temptress.*

"One never knows with you."

"One should know. For the love of a cloud! I may have been a great sinner in my time, but not that kind of sinner." He would have dropped her hand with disgust, except it felt too good.

"I can see the way you look at me, Vikar. Don't deny that you're thinking something sexual."

"I am a man, Alex. A Viking man. We look." *And enjoy.* "You cannot condemn me for that. Besides, you look at me the same way betimes." *And I enjoy that, too.*

She raised her haughty nose, but he could see the telling pink tint rise in her neck and cheeks. He squeezed her hand to show her that she was fooling no one, least of all him.

"What else has you in such a foul mood?"

"Do you have any idea how ridiculous we look?"

Vikar glanced around to see what she meant. Ivak and Armod walked in front of them, like the king of cool and his assistant, the prince of pop. Cnut was on Alex's other side. Mordr and Sigurd in back. An aviator sunglass–clad phalanx in matching black cloaks that kept a close eye on their surroundings, always on the alert for danger.

"You jest, m'lady," he said. "Have you looked

around this town? Have you truly looked? We are more sedate in our attire than most of these folks."

"That's debatable."

"There are cloaks being sold in the shops. Ours are just a little finer. At least we do not show our fangs, or paint our fingernails black, or have weird hairdos." Except for Armod, who had more grease on his black locks than a skinned pig.

"The problem is that you guys are just so big. Clumped together like this, I feel like I'm at a pro-wrestler event."

Now he was offended, that she would liken him to one of those steroid-ridden freaks. "Do you want to go back to the castle?"

She glanced his way and probably saw way too much. "No. Let's just find a restaurant where we can sit down and blend in. If possible."

But they were halted by the sudden stopping of Ivak and Armod, which caused him and Alex and Cnut to slam into their backs, and then Mordr and Sigurd to strike them from behind. "What in bloody hell!" Vikar exclaimed before he had a chance to catch his tongue. Mordr said something much worse. It was only by sheer strength and good balance that they caught themselves and didn't topple over like dominoes.

"Whoever has their hand on my butt better remove it at once," Alex warned.

"Oops," he apologized. "I was just making sure you didn't fall."

Five male voices snorted.

He saw now what had caught Ivak and Armod's attention. They'd taken off their dark glasses, and their gazes were locked on the glass front of an adult bookstore, a misnomer if there ever was one. It was the least bookish place he had ever seen.

In the window were displayed the covers of several pornographic videos.

"*The Story of O-Positive*," Armod said aloud. "I don't understand. Is that like HIV positive?"

"Idiot," Mordr said, slapping Armod lightly upside the head.

"Ah, but I am in the mood for good literature," Ivak said with a grin. "How about these? *A Tale of Two Vampyres. The Stakes of Wrath.* Or that one." He pointed to the left. "*Great Neckspectations.*"

"I still don't understand." Armod was frowning, although his white skin did color when he craned his head from side to side and realized what one of the pictures depicted.

"Now me, I always did like a good classic mystery movie," Sigurd added, also grinning. "*A Tomb with a View.*"

Vikar worried that they were embarrassing Alex, but then she said, "My favorite is *Vlad Really Did Impale Her.*"

His brothers glanced at him, then Alex, and burst out laughing.

"Mayhap I will not kill her after all," Mordr declared, giving Alex a wink that did not sit well with Vikar. Not one bit.

"Can we buy some?" Armod asked.

"I don't think they are the kind of thing we should have at the castle when Mike arrives," Vikar told the boy. "C'mon. Let's find someplace to eat. I'm starving."

They'd already passed restaurants and bars with

such names as Out for Blood, Suck It Up, Suckies, Addiction, and Drac's Hideout, all of which advertised with signs outside that they served red drinks resembling blood, but were either wine or fruit punch or colored beer.

They settled on a tavern called the Dark Side because it served food and alcohol. Plus a country band would be playing later. Since they were early—it was not yet seven—they were able to find several empty booths near the back, close to an exit door . . . just in case. Vikar put himself and Alex alone in one of them and let the others fend for themselves. Sigurd and Ivak sat on stools at the bar where they could keep an eye on the entire scene, while Mordr and Cnut sat in the booth in front of theirs with Armod, who was underage and forbidden from entering the bar area.

Alex ordered a steak, medium rare, with mushrooms, a baked potato with butter and sour cream, and a Caesar salad, although what that blowhard Roman had to do with green leaves was beyond Vikar. He decided to order the same, except his steak would be rare and instead of a salad he substituted stewed tomatoes with jalapeño peppers.

As soon as the waitress left, a man walked up. A badge on his white shirt read "Jack Owens, Manager." Unlike the waiters and waitresses, he was dressed in normal attire, no vampire nonsense on him. "Lord Vikar, I presume?" he inquired.

Vikar slid over and stood. "Yes, I am Vikar Sigurdsson."

All his brothers stood as well, though at a distance, watching warily.

"I'm Jack Owens, owner and manager of this

joint," the man said in a jolly fashion, extending a hand.

Vikar shook it.

"I'm also on the Labor Day committee for the Monster Mash, and I was wondering if your hotel will be open by then."

"No. I do not think so." Vikar was not about to announce to the public that there would be no hotel at all up on the mountain, but a private residence instead. Not yet, anyway.

"That's too bad. We're expecting thousands of tourists, and accommodations are in short supply." The man tilted his head to the side and gave him a speculative look. "I don't suppose you'd serve on the committee with us. We need all the fresh blood we can get."

Vikar almost choked on his tongue, and he heard Alex snicker behind him.

"Ha, ha, ha," the owner/manager added quickly. "Fresh ideas is what I meant."

Vikar smiled to show he understood. "Sorry I am to decline, but I am too busy at the moment. Mayhap in the future?"

"Definitely." Then seeing that Vikar wasn't going to continue the conversation or introduce him to Alex, even though his gaze kept shifting to her, he said, "Enjoy your meal, and come back again."

"You are too far away," he declared to Alex once the man had left and he'd signaled to his brothers that all was well. Instead of sitting on the other side of the table, as he had been before, he slid in next to her. Now they were thigh to thigh, arm to arm. "Much better."

"You shaved and put on cologne," Alex observed with an appreciative sniff. "For me?"

He nodded and considered asking her if she could smell the testosterone under the cologne, but decided to save that question for later. "I showered, too," he informed her with a waggle of his eyebrows.

"You must have been a talented seducer in your time period," she said with a laugh. "I mean, back when you were alive, or whatever you call that time."

"What? I have lost my talent?"

"You know you haven't."

"There are some things a man never forgets," he agreed with no excess of humility.

"Like riding a bicycle?"

"Or riding a woman." He grinned at her.

"Whoa! This conversation is going way too fast in a direction that could prove dangerous for us both."

That was the truth, but he'd decided to enjoy himself tonight, despite the consequences. The next few weeks would be busy with the serious business of Reckoning and Michael's arrival. He'd wanted to lighten his spirits and that of his brothers for these few short hours.

The waitress brought a bottle of beer for him and a Bloody Mary for her.

He took a long swig of his beer and remarked, "Um, cold beer tastes good. In Viking times, we drank our ale and mead warm, at room temperature. Can you imagine?"

She wrinkled her nose with distaste, then took a sip of her own drink with a straw. Her eyes widened with delight. "This is good. Potent, but good."

"Keep drinking," he urged then.

"What? You want me drunk?"

"No. Just relaxed."

"Hah! That would be the worst thing I could do. Relax around you."

He put a hand to his chest with mock innocence. "You offend me, m'lady." Then he laughed and put an arm around her shoulder, tucking her closer. After kissing the top of her head, he said, "I could get accustomed to this dating."

"They must have had courtship rituals in your time, too."

He arched a brow at her. "Either a marriage was arranged by the king or families, and a man met his wife for the first time in the marriage bed, or a man gave a woman a certain look and she met him in the bed furs that night."

"You're kidding."

He shrugged.

"And did the reverse work? Women gave men a certain look and decided whether they would make love with them or not."

"For a certainty. Especially Viking women who have minds of their own, believe you me. I remember the time Olga the Big fixed her attentions on Ivak. When he declined her favors, she tried to spear his manparts with a boat oar. Took all of Sigurd's healing talents to save his most precious parts."

"I find it hard to see Sigurd as a doctor."

"He has long been a healer. That is what we called a physician in ancient times. Of course, he was first of all a warrior when called to duty, but a healer in the off times."

"Isn't that kind of an oxymoron? Killing and healing?"

"No different than physicians serving in the military today."

"I guess so."

"Over the centuries, Sigurd has studied in medical schools. Of all of us, he has spent more time in this century. Currently, he is assigned to Johns Hopkins University Hospital where he does medical research. In truth, he is the one who invented Fake-O for us . . . he and his underlings who work with him."

Alex appeared stunned.

"What? You thought Vikings were witless men who knew naught but fighting skills or how to ride the waves on a longship?"

She blushed.

"For your information, my brothers and I, and those vangels under us . . . all of us are skilled in professions that might impress you. There is a biologist, a lawyer, an accountant, shipbuilders. Always our primary goal is to do God's work, but whenever we come upon a problem that requires a certain skill, someone is assigned to learn it."

She was staring at him as if he spoke some alien language. Then she shook her head to clear it and laughed. "I assume that until now you've had no need of architects, plumbers, electricians, and carpenters."

He laughed, too. "You have the right of it, except for carpenters. Vikings have always been skilled carpenters. We've had to be in order to construct our fine boats. And truth to tell, we were engineers and mathematicians, though we did not have those words. Even astronomers who studied the skies for direction. Building and sailing longships took expertise in all those fields."

"Well, there's a lot more work to be done on your castle. So someone better learn how to paint and plaster."

He nodded. "Actually, one of our vangels is a fine artist. Tofa will no doubt be putting murals on all the walls, if given a chance. Impish angels are her specialty. She was an assistant to Michelangelo at one time. Ah, the stories she can tell about the doings in the Sistine Chapel!

"Then there is Moddam, who was a stoneworker whom we found building the Colosseum. No doubt he can rebuild some of the outside walls whilst here. And I cannot forget Bodil, who had been a slave in Byzantium. She worked on the emperor's imperial gardens. Mayhap she will help with some of the landscaping so the castle is not so gloomy." He stopped for a moment to see Alex's reaction.

Her jaw had dropped with astonishment, but then she punched him in the arm. "You lout! You're teasing me!"

He shrugged. She would see if she stayed long enough. "You know everything about me. Tell me about you. Where do you come from? What have you been doing with your thirty years?"

"I've led a rather ordinary life. My parents were killed in a train wreck when I was a child, and I was raised by my grandparents on a small horse farm in Virginia. They died two years apart when I was in college. I inherited the farm that I later sold, giving me a comfortable cushion for living since then. I'm not rich, but I have enough to live on if I quit working."

"Ah, a wealthy heiress. If this were back in Viking

times, my parents would be arranging a marriage betwixt us." He winked at her.

"Would you protest that arrangement?" she asked.

"Not at all. Of course, at our ages . . . you being thirty and me thirty-three . . . you would no doubt be my wife number three or four. 'Twas a common practice, the *more danico*, or multiple wives."

"In your dreams, buster. I would be like one of those independent Norsewomen you mentioned. I'd wallop you over the head with your own sword before I'd share your bed."

They both paused to think about that image.

"I suspect that, for you, I would have given up any other woman, wife or concubine," he said in a voice thick with emotion.

"Damn right you would!"

His heart melted with tenderness at her vehemence, and he squeezed her close to him. "When did you wed? Tell me about this man who won your heart?"

"I met Brian in college, and we got married right after graduation. We were legally separated at the time of his death."

"Whaaat? You never mentioned that."

She shrugged. "I thought I was in love with Brian, but I think in retrospect it was just me being vulnerable after losing my grandparents. Oh, he was a good man, and I did love him. I just wasn't in love with him toward the end, especially after he'd had an affair with one of the Drug Enforcement Agency field operatives. He was a lawyer for the DEA."

He did not know what to say at that news. "So,

how is it that your child was with him at the end?"

"Visitation. He had her for a week during a school break."

"Do you blame him, as well as the men who murdered your child?"

"No. If he'd taken her somewhere dangerous, I might have, but they were in a parking lot of the Annapolis Mall. A seemingly safe place."

"Enough of this sad talk," he declared, hating the misting of tears in her eyes. "The band is going to start playing music." He pointed to the small bandstand.

"Do you dance?"

He scoffed, "Never! Real men do not flail about to seduce women. Especially not Vikings."

The tables had filled in around the tavern while they'd been eating, and the band tuned their instruments. Two men and a woman, playing piano, bass, and guitar, respectively. "Hey, folks, how 'bout we start with a little Alan Jackson?" There was much applause and whistling. Jackson . . . that sounded like a nice Viking name. Vikar sat back prepared to be entertained. The band's first song was one with a heavy rhythm called "Don't Rock the Jukebox."

"Oh, so Vikings don't dance, huh? Look at Armod. Appears as if he's about to flex his wings, so to speak. Or is that flex his fangs?" She laughed, a delightful tinkling sound, like bells to Vikar's ears.

"I should have known! I would wager this is Ivak's doing."

Several couples got up and began to dance, if you could call it that. It was more like a shaking of the buttocks and flexing of the elbows like chicken wings. Ridiculous!

But Armod was standing at the edge of the dance floor with Ivak, both of them having removed their weapons, placing them surreptitiously, wrapped in their cloaks, in the care of his brothers. Armod was eyeing a young girl sitting with her parents on the far side. The purple-haired girl, who had more rings than an Arab princess—in her ears, eyebrows, nose, lower lip, and tongue—was eyeing him back. And Ivak, the instigator, was whispering in Armod's ear. Several times Armod stepped forward, then backed up when shyness overcame him. Finally, Ivak gave Armod a look of disgust, turned to a nearby table, held out a hand in invitation to one of three women sitting there, then walked out on the dance floor with her and began to dance. Women found Ivak's neatly clipped beard and mustache a "turn-on," or so Ivak told his brothers. Repeatedly.

Vikar's eyes about popped out at what he saw next, and it wasn't the tightness of the wench's braies that must be cutting off her blood circulation from her crack forward or the size of her bosom with radish-size nipples nigh exploding from her low-cut top.

"Oh my God!" Alex exclaimed. "That boy can move." And she wasn't talking about Armod.

Ivak was indeed moving his body, and his part-ner's, in the most amazing ways. To the beat of the music, he bumped, he undulated, and he thrust, all of his movements conveying sex. If Vikar was worried about near-sex, Ivak had a thing or two to consider regarding his dance-sex, if you asked him, which nobody did. Ivak's partner didn't seem to mind at all. In fact, she laughed and mimicked all his actions and added some of her own. When she strutted away from him a short distance, then shimmied her upper body on the return dance step, every male eye in the place was glued to her jiggling breasts.

"See. Vikings do dance," Alex pointed out.

Huh? He had to think a moment to jar his mind back to the woman at his side. "I had no idea Ivak danced." *No wonder he is so successful with women. I wonder if Alex can do that shimmy thing. I wonder what she would do if I asked. I wonder if I am losing my wits.*

When Ivak glared at Armod, as if to say, *See. This is how it's done*, the boy lifted his chin with determination and walked over to the girl's table, his demeanor that of a convicted felon off to the guillotine. Surprisingly, the girl looked to her parents for permission, then got up to dance with him. Well, why not? Armod might dress weird, but he was a Viking. And everyone knew Vikings had woman-luck . . . rather, girl-luck, in his case.

And Armod was good, too. Vikar had half expected him to moon dance across the floor, but instead he took the girl's hands in his and then moved to the beat in a more subdued fashion. The whole time they talked. Thank the heavens, Armod seemed to have control of his fangs tonight. And his lisp.

"I am so happy that the girl accepted," Alex said. "He would have been devastated if she'd declined."

"Yes, 'tis the way of women to break men's hearts."

"But not a Viking's?" she teased.

"Not a Viking's," he agreed. *Not mine, leastways. Not yet.*

They watched as Ivak and Armod danced one song after another with their partners, including one where the female singer wailed out, "I'm Here

for the Party," and the crowd sang along. Vikar was
not a big fan of music. Oh, he had liked a rowdy
good time with his comrades on occasion that included ribald singing along with tuns of mead, but
more often these days, he savored silence, or soft
classical music in the background. His soul seemed
to yearn for serenity.

But then the loud band music softened in volume
and slowed down, and the bandleader announced
the next song would be last year's granny winner,
Lady Antebellum's "Need You Now."

"What's a granny winner?" he asked Alex.

"Not granny. Grammy. It's a music award. This
is a really pretty song. Very poignant. C'mon." She
nudged him with her hip to move over in the booth.

He glanced down between them and saw that her
short garment had ridden up to expose more of her
exquisite legs covered by the sheer silk hose. In fact,
the lace tops of the hose peeked out at him now.

Without thinking, he reached down to touch her
knee. He'd been right. It was like silk. Warm silk.

She slapped his hand away and nudged him
again with her hip. "C'mon. Let's dance."

"Oh no. Not me," he said, even as he stood and
took her hand to pull her to her feet beside him. "I
do not dance."

She laughed and led him to the dance floor.
"Don't worry. I'll teach you. All you have to do is
stand still. And sway."

"I do not like dancing," he insisted.

"You will."

She was right.

"Put your hands on my waist," she instructed,
then immediately added, "Not on my butt. Behind

my waist." She showed him how, as if he hadn't known what she'd meant to begin with.

He saw Mordr and Cnut, back in their booth, shaking their heads at his idiocy, no doubt. But Sigurd, still at the bar, raised a fist in the air with encouragement. There was a good-looking woman sitting next to him on the stool Ivak had vacated.

Then Alex put her arms up, idly touching the wing epaulettes on his shoulders. Alex was tall for a woman, and with her high-heeled shoes, her chin came to his neck. A nice fit. She placed her face on his chest, and showed him how to shift from side to side. Luckily, he'd secured his sword and scabbard with leather ties to his thigh so it did not clank against them as they moved.

While the female singer in the band crooned the poignant lyrics about it being a quarter after one with her being all alone and "I need you now," Vikar came to a realization that he needed something, too. Or someone. Desperately.

Ever since Alex had entered his life—*was it only two weeks ago?*—his emotions had been in turmoil. And he wasn't sure why. She was not the most beautiful woman he'd ever met. Nor the most sensual. Mayhap it was the loneliness he sensed in her that matched his own bone-deep solitary life. And, yes, he felt lonely, despite always having vangels about him.

Alex leaned back and looked up at him. She needed him, too. He could tell these things. Loneliness had a scent of its own. "See. I told you that you would like dancing."

He put his hands on her butt, despite her earlier admonition, yanked her closer, and whispered against her ear, "You ne'er told me that your kind of dancing was but a form of foresport."

"See, old man that you are, there is something you can learn from me."

"I ne'er doubted that, sweetling."

"What else have I taught you?" she asked, leaning her head back to look at him.

"How to love," he replied, before he had a chance to bridle his tongue.

But she did not even blink at his words. Instead she said, "I think I'm falling in love with you, too."

That wasn't what he'd meant.

Was it?

"Uh," he said. How dull-witted was that? Pathetic, really. He was a hardened warrior, a man seasoned by a thousand years of hard work and fighting. Always fighting. Ne'er had he avoided battle or foe, and yet he shivered like a boyling in his first bout of swordplay.

And he said nothing.

Thirteen

The path to love is often a broken road . . .

Transylvania feature, Kelly   Page 1
Draft Nine

Love is in the air in Transylvania.

Perhaps it is the popularity of vampires in books, TV, and movies, but there's something about a dark, tortured hero with incredible staying power, and not of the long life kind. The only thing sexier than a vampire today is an angel. Yes, angels are the new hot hero . . . especially fallen angels.

But what if the two were combined? Vampires and angels. Be still, beating hearts of American women, but that's just what you'll find in the sleepy town of Transylvania, Pennsylvania.

The only question is: How to catch a vampire angel? Or more important, what kind of future is there with a man who lives forever?

Maybe the answer is to . . .

Alex saw the expression of fear on Vikar's face and had to laugh. A sad laugh.

"Silly! I didn't tell you that because I expected a response." *Although it would have been nice.* "Good Lord, you look as if you swallowed a bushel of sour apples." She put a hand to his clean-shaven face and went up on tiptoes to kiss him lightly on his stunned lips.

"Silly? You call me silly," he growled and kissed her back, harder and longer. "Because I hesitate does not mean I do not share your feelings. On the contrary, my heartling."

Heartling. Hopes that Alex had thought long dead began to ignite, like embers from the ashes of her grief. She had been cold for so long.

"I am not an impulsive man, and this is all new to me."

Oh, sweetheart! Me too.

"I have never felt this way before."

Sad to say, neither have I.

"In truth, I do not understand how I am feeling, and why you have been sent to me at this time in my life, a life which truly feels godforsaken on occasion. I have nothing to offer a woman like you. A human, no less."

Hah! You think you have the patent on confusion? Bad enough that I'm falling for a vampire, but an angel, as well. She shook her head. "Not godforsaken at all, I suspect."

"What do you mean?"

"I'm not sure. Maybe all this bloodsucking business has altered my brain in some way, but I feel good. For the first time in years I'm not obsessing over my dead daughter and vengeance and how dismal my future looks." *Could it be that cleansing stuff really works?* "If there is a God, and if He did in fact send me here, then there must be a purpose to it all. What, I'm not sure. But it doesn't feel like any forsaking going on. I'm not making sense, am I?"

"More than you know."

They stood in place, just swaying in each other's arms, listening to the band morph into another slow song, this time Sheryl Crow's "The First Cut Is the Deepest."

After a while, she broke their silence, without raising her head from his shoulder. "I think we need to take what's been handed to us as a gift. Maybe a temporary gift. But let's relish it while we can." *I can't think about leaving here. Not yet. One day at a time.*

She could feel him smile against her hair. "Does that mean I get to unwrap my gift later?" he asked.

"Better than that," she said, raising her head to see his twinkling eyes. He had the most beautiful blue eyes, all the vangels did, but when he was excited, they turned silvery. "I have a really good idea for near-sex." *It's amazing what you can find on the Internet!* "You won't believe—"

"Shh," he said, putting a forefinger on her lips. "Don't tell me. Surprise me." Tucking her face back into the crook of his neck, he added, "Besides, you'll make me peak here in the middle of the dance floor. Bad enough you make my cock dance with this music foresport."

She could feel how aroused he already was and opted for teasing. "I thought that was your sword."

"It is. My mansword." They swayed from side to side for several moments, now to the music of "The Broken Road," the words of which seemed particularly meaningful to both of them. But then Vikar stiffened. "Uh-oh!"

"What?"

"Time to go home," he said, and made some kind of signal to Sigurd, who nodded.

"What? What's wrong?" she asked.

He motioned toward Armod, who was slow dancing with the girl, his chin resting on the top of her head. Even though his eyes were closed, his fangs were out. "He can't help himself," Vikar said.

Soon they were on their way back to the castle with Armod chattering away excitedly, telling them everything she said, he said, what they did, how she felt, how he felt. Alex gave the big Viking brothers kudos for listening and not making fun of the boy, although she saw Mordr and Ivak exchange amused glances.

"I will tell you one thing," Mordr said. "You will ne'er see me dancing. No matter how much I might want a woman, you would not catch me making such a fool of myself."

"It can be fun," Ivak contended.

"You looked like an idiot," Mordr said.

"I could have had the woman in the parking lot, if I wanted, after a few dance steps. How many women were lining up for your favors?" Ivak countered.

"You did not need to dance for that, Ivak," Sigurd remarked. "At least two women approached you at the bar."

"I liked the dancing," Vikar interjected. "'Twas like foresport."

Did he have to divulge that? Alex felt her face heat.

"We all noticed," Cnut hooted gleefully.

Her face heated even more.

"What you were doing was not dancing, Vikar. That was just mutual rubbing," Mordr declared.

I must have steam rising off my cheeks.

"I was referring to the jiggling and jumping that Ivak and Armod engaged in," Mordr explained.

"Whaaat?" Armod exclaimed. "I do not jiggle when I dance."

"Only my best parts jiggle," Ivak added.

They all laughed then.

Vikar took her hand in his, linking their fingers. Silence settled over the interior of the van as they drove up the lane to the castle. "I do, you know," he whispered against her ear. "I love you."

Imaginary sex was never so imaginative . . .

Two hours later, after making sure the castle was secure for the night, Vikar knelt down in his bedchamber and said a short prayer for strength. "I love her. God help me, but I love her. What should I do?"

It had to be the first time in history a man sought celestial blessing for illicit sexual activity. Oh, he wasn't asking for permission to go all the way. Even he, in his brain-fuzzy, lustsome state, was not that lackwitted. But he feared that he was on shaky ground even with near-sex.

He stood and prepared to go up to Alex's tower room.

Now would be the time for Michael to smite him down for daring to bother them with such trivial matters. Trivial for them, not him. But nothing happened.

Any other thoughts he had dissolved quicker

than a Lucipire on the way to Hell when he saw what Alex had prepared for him. The tower room was alight with a dozen different candles. She wore naught but a one-piece, thigh-length, silk garment with thin straps. On her legs were the wonderful silk hose and the high-heeled shoes. And, most ominous, she had arranged two straight-backed, armless chairs, facing each other, at least eight feet apart.

He raised his eyebrows at her.

"I have something special planned for you," she said huskily.

He loved the huskiness of her voice. It portended good things. For him. For them both. "I can see that." *Oh, my racing heart! I can see . . . and imagine.*

She shook her head. "No, you can't see what I have planned. We are going to have imaginary sex."

Like minds? "I do not like the sound of that," he said. "I have enough imaginary sex with myself."

"Trust me." At his hesitation, she added, "C'mon. You're a Viking. Be adventuresome. Put yourself in my hands."

Oh, sweetling, you are pure temptation. "I better not."

"Are you afraid?"

Afraid of how much I would like being in your hands. "Well, if you insist. What do you want me to do?"

"Take off your clothing. All of it. And sit on that chair over there."

Some men preferred virgins for bed partners, but not him. Was there anything more alluring than a woman who asserts herself in the bedsport? "You do not waste time with preliminaries, do you?"

"There is a time for that. This isn't it."

He removed his garments down to the bare skin, head to toe, and sat down, spreading his legs a bit to accommodate his already impressive thickening. "Are you going to come sit down on my lap?"

She laughed, giving his cock a sardonic study. "No."

That was blunt. "Not at all?"

She shook her head with a saucy glint in her green eyes. "No touching at all. Not on my dime."

Is she demented? "That is interesting." *I have news for you, wench. There is going to be touching. On my dime.* He waved a hand toward her. "Proceed."

She arched her brows at his peremptory gesture, then perched her pert butt on the edge of the opposite chair.

"You are not going to disrobe? Oh, I do not like that disparity. Not at all."

"In a minute. We're going to play a game."

Games, games, games! Why can women not just get on with it, like men do? "I am a great game player." He folded his arms over his chest, splayed his legs out in a relaxed pose, and inquired lazily, "What are the rules of this game?"

"We are going to make love without touching each other."

And I am to be happy about that? "Oh, that is just wonderful! My favorite kind of lovemaking!" *If you believe that, wench . . .* He sighed deeply. "Let the games begin."

"Okay, I'll start. Close your eyes. Now picture that I am touching your face. Gently. Just with my fingertips. Along your jaw, over your nose, your eyebrows, your ears, your lips."

Ho-hum.

"Now I'm going to kiss you, but first I'll use the tip of my tongue to outline their shape."

A little better.

"You have beautiful lips, did you know that?"

Do you jest? I am guilty of the sin of pride. Of course I am aware of my physical attributes.

"Your lips are full and well-defined. Perfect lips for a man."

Can we get on with the good stuff?

"Now I'm threading my fingers through your hair to hold you at the right angle, and I'm placing my lips over yours, moving gently from side to side until I get just the right fit."

Enough with the gentleness! Hard. Kiss me hard.

"I love the way you kiss me back without grabbing for me."

Ah, but I'd like to grab.

"Just your lips. You are loving me with your lips only. Part for me, darling. That's the way. Can you feel me sticking just the pointy end of my tongue inside your mouth?"

Hah! I feel it all the way to my loins.

"Oh, you rascal! You sucked me in and are drawing on me, not letting me escape. Now I'm out and in again. Over and over. You taste like minty mouthwash and your own unique flavor. Did you know you have a unique flavor, Vikar?"

Mayhap games are not so bad after all.

"Ah, you are breathing hard. Did you like my kiss?"

It's over? His eyes shot open.

She stared at him through misty green, sex-hazed eyes. Her lips were parted and moist. Was she aroused just from watching him get aroused? She was!

"Your turn," she said.

Ah, he began to understand the plan of her game . . . and its allure. He smiled and said, "Let us see what skill I have in game playing, shall we? Close your eyes, witch."

She did. Biddable, for once. *Thank you . . . Someone.*

"I have had enough of lip kisses, though I enjoyed yours overmuch. Arch your head back so I can access your sweet neck. Now, feel my whispery kissing along your stubborn jaw with a little nip at that dent in the center. Now, the arch of your neck, right there on the curve. Ummm. Delicious. Can I suck on it a little?" His fangs were out and aching. "You like my kiss there, I can tell. Your pulse is racing." In truth, his pulse was racing, too."

Her eyelids fluttered at his words.

"No, do not open your eyes. Remember the rules."

"Tyrant," she muttered.

"I'm looking lower now." *Whoa! I am definitely looking.* "I like your garment." *If Norsewomen in the ninth century had garments like that, their men would not have gone a-Viking so much.* "I like that it leaves all that creamy skin exposed and all those delicious freckles."

"What is it with you and freckles?"

"Shh! My turn to talk. You listen."

"Tyrant," she muttered again, but she had a slight smile on her lips.

"I am touching your skin with my fingertips. From your neck on one side, over the shoulder, down your arm to your wrist. I turn your arm over and trace your skin from your palm, over the inside of the wrist, the inside of the elbow, even your shaved armpits. Then I do the same on the other side. Does

your skin tingle?" *I know mine does. A tingling Viking.
What is happening to me?*

"Yes, I tingle. You *are* good at this game. You must
have played before."

"Never." *I probably would have, though, if I'd known
it could be so fun.*

"Are you done?"

"You jest." *I have just begun, sweetling. I have just
begun.* "Lower both of the straps. Slowly. And let the
garment pool at your waist."

He gasped. He could not help himself. That was
the effect her exposed breasts had on him. Another
part of his body was equally affected. If cocks could
speak, his would be singing Hallelujahs.

Her breasts were creamy globes the size of grape-
fruit halves, sprinkled with freckles. In their center
were dark rose areolae and even darker nipples. A
perfect size, not so big but giving the appearance of
being deliciously overendowed because of her slim
frame.

"Lift your breasts from underneath. Pretend I
am testing their weight to see how they would fit
in my big palms. Perfect. And now I am touching
each of the nipples to bring them to peak. Do it for
me. Pretty little buds, they are, but let's make them
bigger, shall we? Let's flick them. Harder. That is the
way. Now, shall I suckle you? Just a little?"

"Please," she choked out.

"How does that feel?"

"Wonderful," she said, then, "harder."

He chuckled. "Demanding wench! Is this better?
I have drawn your breast, areola and all, into my
mouth and am suckling hard. Very hard. Ah, but

I don't want to hurt you. So I will lave your breast, all over. And now I will do the same to the other breast."

Without being asked, she parted her legs and stiffened her legs.

Hot damn! She is peaking. Just by using wicked words. "Relax, sweetling. Let it happen. Open your legs wider. Are you wet? Do not answer. I know you are. Put your forefinger there, just for a moment, just to test."

She did and he watched as she came apart before his eyes.

He put a hand to himself to hold back his own peaking. *Think of something unsexual. Cold icy glaciers in the Norselands. Stinky lutefisk. A two-day alehead. Lucipires.*

His efforts paid off. A little. He did not ejaculate, but he was still bone-hard and throbbing.

"Are you still there? Why are you so quiet?" Her eyes opened and then went wider. "Why are you holding yourself? No fair!"

"I am only holding myself to keep from spilling my seed." He dropped his hands to his side.

"Good heavens! I don't think I've ever seen one so big outside a porn flick."

Filled with male satisfaction at what he took to be a compliment, he studied her for a long moment. Still bare from the waist up, a flush now tinted her skin all the way over her chest, her neck, up to her forehead. It was the sex flush that came after peaking. He got undue pleasure seeing her thus, as if he'd accomplished some great mission. He had. Pleasing his woman was one of a Viking's greatest fulfillments, next to riding the waves on a favorite longship, or drinking a horn of good mead after a day's hard work.

Best he rein in his pride, though. "I have seen bigger. Ketil the Horseface had one so big that maids ran when they saw him coming. And Arnstein Wartnose had one so long it hung to his knees." At the look of disgust on her face, he decided that perchance he'd shared too much.

"Close your eyes, Viking. It's my turn to spin this fantasy."

"Very well, but whilst my eyes are closed, remove your garment so that the first thing I see when I look again will be your fluffy mons. Leave your shoes and hose on. I have a hankering to see you prance about the chamber wearing those."

As he closed his eyes, he heard her make a choking sound. "I do not prance."

"Strut then."

"I do not strut, either."

"Bloody hell! Just walk then. Now, proceed. My cock is about to explode."

"Okay," she said. "I'm taking off the rest of my teddy. That's what they call this garment. Now I'm sitting back down, but you must picture me straddling your lap. You spread your knees wider to expose me more. You wretch. I need to put my hands on your shoulder to stay upright."

He smiled with appreciation of her fantasy telling.

"I love the way you smile. I melt when you smile."

"M'lady, you are obviously not aware of battle tactics. Telling a man of your vulnerabilities is comparable to handing him a bow and quiver of arrows."

"You don't want me to tell you how I feel?"

"On the contrary. I take joy in your openness. Seems to me, though, that you are already melted in certain places." He smiled some more. A woman could not do too much melting, in his opinion, despite his teasing words. With his eyes still closed, he continued with his fantasy, "Ah, I can feel your woman-dew weeping onto my chair. So much of it comes from your widespread thighs that it drips down to the wood of my chair and rolls down to coat my ballocks."

"That is so crude, and a total man fantasy," she said, but she did not sound displeased.

So, he added another crudity. "Later, I would like you to lick my balls. Dost think you could do that?"

He waited for her gasp of outrage.

There was none.

"Maybe."

He held on to the sides of his chair to prevent himself from lurching at her. *Maybe? She might actually do it? It was a jest. Not that I would refuse such ministration. I swear, I will not last to the end of this game.* But her single-word reply gave him permission to push the edge of propriety, or so he told himself. "If you do that, mayhap I will put you on all fours, like a mare, pressing your face to the floor, and kiss your arse cheeks, afore licking your woman-channel down to your pleasure bud."

"What?" she shrieked.

Ooops. I might have gone too far. "Sorry. Forget I said that."

"Are you kidding? I'll never forget *that*. Now shut your eyes and stop interrupting, or we'll be here all night."

Is that a promise? "Whate'er you say, dearling."

"I'm still straddling your lap. My hands are on your shoulders. In fact, for a moment I reach back and caress your wing bumps."

Huh? "My wing bumps?"

"Those bumps on your shoulder blades."

"Dost think you should be bringing up angel matters in the midst of sex play?"

"I don't think of what we do as dirty, or nonangelic."

"Not dirty. Sinful. Or somewhat sinful."

"I think your semantics are going to get you in big trouble."

"M'lady, I have been in big trouble from the moment we first met."

"Now, listen carefully. We're going to have real sex, sort of."

"Sort of. I am developing a whole new vocabulary. Near-sex. Sort-of sex. Fantasy sex. No-touching sex. It all smacks of celibacy to me. With that I am more than familiar, believe you me."

"Stifle."

Did the wench actually have the nerve to tell a hardened Viking warrior to stifle? Truly, she pushes the bounds.

"You have to keep your eyes shut. And no touching. Promise?"

He didn't really understand, but he nodded.

"I'm still on your lap."

"Are you still touching my bumps?"

"Forget the bumps, and stop interrupting," she snapped.

He heard the impatience in her voice and smiled.

"And stop smiling."

He pressed his lips together.

"I'm on your lap. My rump is sitting on your out-spread knees. I look down and see your erection sticking out toward my . . . okay, let's call it fluff."

He had to smile again, but quickly willed it away. "Is it red fluff?" he asked, knowing what her reaction would be.

"I do not have red hair. It is strawberry-blonde."

He tilted his head in agreement. "So, my cock-stand is waving at your strawberry fluff. Proceed."

She swore under her breath at his deliberate mis-speak. "I take you in both my hands. You're too big for one hand to enclose your girth."

Of course I am, he thought, then doused his ever-persistent pride.

"I arrange its head against my slick folds and use it to stroke myself. Can you feel how wet I am? How ready?"

He could not have spoken then if the sky was falling down on them. Which it very well might if Michael got a hint of what he was about.

"There is a drop of semen on the tip of your erection, peeking out. I use it to further lubricate myself, especially my clitoris that is unfurled and aching for your touch. Ah, that feels so good. I can't wait. Let me help you enter me. See how your mushroom head presses against my entrance. It's been a long time for me, and I'm tight. So it's with a little pop that you breach my muscles, which instantly welcome you with spasms of pure joy. Oh. Oh. Oh. You are in all the way."

Vikar leaned back so that his neck was braced on the chair back and he arched his hips upward. "Am I holding on to your buttocks now? Guiding you. Am I grasping your hips to show you the rhythm I like? In. Out. Twist a little when I fill you. That's the way."

Silence ensued then except for their heavy breathing and their one-word markings of what they were imagining.

"In!" he nigh shouted.

"Out!" she said on a long sigh.

"In!"

"Out!"

Over and over their game played until Alex let out a little choking sound and said, "I'm coming. Oh. *OH!*"

And he let out a roar of utter male satisfaction.

For several long moments, they both kept their eyes closed, panting for breath.

He was splayed out like a wet mop against his chair.

When he finally lifted his heavy lids, he saw that she was splayed as well. And he could swear he saw his man seed glistening on her strawberry fluff.

He smiled at her, and she smiled back.

"I love you," he said, and stood. Picking her up, he carried her over to the bed and laid her down. Staring down at her, he repeated, "I love you."

"Your blue wings are out," she observed drowsily.

He felt his shoulders. There was naught but air.

"I love you, too," she whispered, holding her arms out for him.

When he lay down himself and wrapped her in his embrace, he used her muddled condition as an opportunity to feed from her. It had to be done one more time. Pressing his fangs into her neck, he drank greedily but not for long. Her blood, sweeter than the finest wine, was almost totally cleansed of the taint now. Oddly, as he sipped, he could swear wings enfolded them both.

Was it a celestial blessing for their "union"?

Or a warning that he was being watched?

Either way, he could not be sorry for loving Alex.

Fourteen

**If the castle were a longship,
they could call it the Love Boat . . .**

Vikar couldn't stop smiling.

Love was in the air, and he wasn't the only one feeling the vibe.

"Son of a troll! Do you realize how goofy you look with that fangy grin?" Trond told him.

He and Trond were in Vikar's office with the door closed, sharing a cold beer and hard pretzels . . . a snack his lovely Alex had sent to them, no doubt to test the enamel on his teeth that she teased him about.

"I can't help myself," Vikar admitted. "I'm happy."

Trond just stared at him for a moment, then asked, "What's it like to be happy?"

The poignancy of Trond's question cut Vikar to the quick. He hadn't realized until now that the VIK life was not a happy one. Mostly, they were led to believe that they were undeserving of happiness. Or mayhap they'd erroneously come to that conclusion themselves. Oh, there was contentment at times, and satisfaction when they'd saved a soul or dissolved a Lucie. Even the momentary delight in some material thing, like a new Ferrari, or in Harek's case, a computer with all the latest what they called bells and whistles. The machine could do everything except drive the Ferrari.

Vikar fought for words to describe his feelings to Trond.

"It's peace and turmoil, at the same time. A wonderful, soothing rightness at being with that one special person, but roiling emotions at the intensity of your need for her."

The expression on Trond's face tore at Vikar. The life of a vangel, particularly The Seven, who had been in existence for more than a thousand years, was a lonely one. Brotherly love, even comradely love, was not the same as that between a man and woman. Ironically, Vikar, who had been wed several times before, hadn't been aware of that distinction, either. Until now.

"Where will it end, though? I mean, is there a future for you with a human?"

"That is the big puzzlement to me. By now Mike should have been hauling my arse on the carpet. Usually he does not let our transgressions go this far. Why is he letting me continue with this relationship with Alex? Why is he allowing it to build and flourish? Is it that he wants my fall to be more painful when he takes her away?"

Trond's brow was furrowed with confusion. "I agree. 'Tis not Mike's usual way of handling us."

"In any case, I decided days ago to let the future be what it may. I am taking one day at a time. If there is no future for us, and I can't see how there could be, I will at least have these memories." *And a few more, if I have my way.* Before Alex left, he intended them to have one night at least of making love, really making love, even if he spent eternity paying for the privilege.

Vikar hadn't been able to make love, or even near-love, with Alex since that one special night, but they did catch a moment alone together here and there. Enough to sustain them. For now.

In the meantime, Alex was helping Harek, who was moving about on crutches now, with a press release he wanted to send out about the castle no longer being turned into a hotel, but instead a private residence. The news had to be carefully worded so as not to raise suspicions. In addition, Alex spent a lot of time in the kitchen with Miss Borden, mostly writing up grocery lists and ordering online.

Pensively, he and Trond took bites of their hard pretzels, and chomped, loudly. It was like eating sennights-old manchet bread covered with salt, they'd long ago concluded. Not much taste, but a good way to soak up the beer. They would be meeting shortly with all the vangels who remained at the castle to make plans for their attack on the Lucies at the Sin Cruise to be held in a *week*.

Trond had returned yesterday with some of his underlings, those warriors best trained to fight Lucipires. The best of his other brothers' fighting men would be here this evening or on the morrow. Fifty in all. Specific assignments were already in the works. In fact, Sigurd and Ivak were in the computer room at the moment with a mostly healed Harek reviewing last-minute changes to Jasper's decadent event. Mordr and Cnut were in the dungeon gathering weapons to take with them.

Vikar took a long draw on his bottle of beer, then set it down on the desk. When Alex knocked lightly on the door, then entered, he was both surprised and delighted at the interruption.

She was wearing a sundress today. That's what they called a garment that exposed the shoulders and arms and half the legs of a female in the summer heat. Hers was white with big splashes of colored flowers, yellow, and green, and red.

"You look like a garden," he said, standing, and walked over to kiss her atop her hair, which she had piled on her head and secured with a clawed comb contraption. He tucked her under his arm and squeezed.

By the runes, just the feel of her against him was enough to turn his bones to butter and set his blood to a boil.

"Do I smell like a flower garden, too?" she replied flirtatiously, as she turned her head to stare up at him. When in flat shoes, as she was now, the top of her head came barely to his chin.

He sniffed in an exaggerated manner.

"Don't you dare say that I smell lemony."

"No, you are like a rose now. Or is it a lily. And, oh, look at that gloss on your lips. Dare I hope it is strawberry-flavored, like yesterday?"

"Um, do you two mind? I'm not a statue here," Trond said with a smile, calling attention to his presence.

"Did you seek me out for a reason, sweetling?" he asked.

"I did," she said. "Did you know that there are

swords and guns piled on the dining room table? Even a machine gun."

Vikar glanced at Trond, whose face hardened. Did his brother expect him to turn woman-whipped just because he was in love?

"Alex, this is what we do. We have an important . . . um, mission next week, and—"

She waved a hand dismissively. "I know all that, but do you have to put those dirty weapons on the dining room table? The wood will be scratched, and who knows what damage the oil and grime will cause?"

He and Trond burst out laughing. When would he learn to give Alex credit for being more than other women he had known?

"I'll have them removed right away, sweetling. Will that satisfy you?"

Her eyes lit up at his poor choice of words. Behind him, Vikar heard Trond choking on his pretzel.

"That's not the only reason I came looking for you," she said then with a grin that portended mischief.

"What?" he and Trond asked suspiciously, at the same time.

"You have a late arrival. A certain Olrik Jorgensson from Los Angeles."

Vikar frowned. "That is the ceorl who works under Harek. A stunt person in motion pictures, I believe. What's the problem?"

"You have to see it to believe it," she said, with a little giggle. Since giggles did not come easily to Alex, he knew he was in for another problem to solve.

"Where is he?"

"Out in the courtyard."

He and Trond exchanged puzzled glances as they followed Alex's swishing hips. A swishing she would pay for later, he vowed silently.

When they got to the open front door, they saw a small crowd surrounding Olrik, a young man he'd met innumerable times before. Except he was different now.

He was orange.

Not reddish orange, like Lucipires were betimes. Nor bronze orange like some Native Americans. No he was orange orange. Like the fruit.

"What in bloody hell happened to you?" he asked before he could curb his tongue.

"Uh, my skin was getting too light without a recent save, and I was out of Fake-O; so, instead of going to a tanning salon, I decided to try one of those spray-on tans." He shrugged with embarrassment.

Vikar and Trond clicked their gaping jaws shut, then burst out laughing. Everyone else joined in, including Harek, his master, who'd just arrived.

There were times when being a vangel wasn't all gloom and doom.

Some partings are harder than others . . .

Two nights later, Alex, wearing a demure night-shirt, slipped into Vikar's bed in the middle of the night.

"Alex! You shouldn't be here," he chastised her, even as he lifted the sheet and tucked her in beside him. "We already said our good nights earlier. I have to leave before dawn."

"I know we did, but I can't sleep. I'm worried."

He kissed the top of her head, but said nothing. The silence was telling to her, an acknowledgment that she had good reason to be worried.

"I wish I could go with you."

"Absolutely not! It's too dangerous."

"Not with you there to protect me."

"I have to focus on my assignment, sweetling. Not be distracted by you. Do not even suggest such a thing." He shook his head sharply. "You have no idea the things Jasper would do if he got you in his clutches. Depravity and torture beyond your wildest imagination."

I just have a bad feeling, she wanted to tell him, but she didn't want to jinx his trip. "Just make sure you come back."

"Of course. If nothing else, you promised me another bout of no-touching near-sex."

She smiled against his chest. "I still say, since you'll be gone for three or four days, I should use this opportunity to visit Ben, and meet with prosecutors in the Mercado case."

"I have already told you that I will go with you when I return. I do not want you leaving the castle while I am gone, not even shopping."

"But—"

"Please. It's important to me that I be assured of your safety while I am gone."

"Okay," she agreed, reluctantly.

"I've told Armod to stick to you like glue, to watch over you, but you must watch over Armod, as well. He is a child, really."

She smiled at the idea of her being asked to babysit a young vampire angel. But she wouldn't have wanted Armod to go on this trip. The day before, she'd used her laptop to Google "Sin Cruise," something she'd heard Vikar and his brothers talk about when she wasn't in the room and hush up the minute they realized she was approaching. She was appalled at what she'd read. Was there really such decadence in the world? This Jasper must be evil personified as Vikar contended. That she could accept, but that people would sign up for such perverted things . . . well, she couldn't imagine who these people were.

She couldn't think about those things now, though.

"I love you," she whispered to him.

But he was already asleep.

She didn't sleep the entire night, but pretended to be asleep when Vikar arose in the morning, while it was still dark. After dressing and going downstairs, he came back to his bedchamber. She had to laugh. She couldn't help herself.

He was wearing a wife-beater T-shirt covered with a short-sleeved, hip-length Hawaiian shirt over cargo shorts, the kind with lots of pockets. On his feet were hiking boots. The shirt probably hid weapons. The pockets probably contained ammunition, maybe even grenades, for all she knew. There were probably knives slipped into his boots.

"You find me amusing?"

"You look like you're off for a vacation at the beach."

"Are you calling me a surfer dude again, wench?" he pretended to growl.

That's what she'd called him on first arriving at the castle what seemed an eternity ago. She smiled at the memory and how far they'd come since then. "My very own surfer dude," she said softly.

"Anyhow, it's warm in Tampa, where we're going. And we have to blend in."

Alex had news for him. He and his brothers did not blend in, anywhere, but that wasn't something she needed to point out now. A tear slipped down her cheek, unexpectedly.

"Dearling," he said in soft reprimand. "Do not start again."

"I won't. Don't forget your holy water wipes."

He patted one of his shorts' pockets, then leaned down and kissed her softly. "I love you, heartling. Be good until I return."

"Be safe," she said in return.

Alex did something then that she hadn't done in a long time. She prayed. Could it be her own version of a soldier's foxhole conversion?

Fighting Saxons was a piece of cake compared to this . . .

Vikar, his brothers, and a number of the vangels were staying in a dingy hotel overlooking the harbor in Tampa where the *Lilith* was berthed. And wasn't that a perfect name for a Sin Cruise, honoring Adam's evil first wife. Lilith was the Sumerian name for a female demon.

High-powered telescopes were trained on a dozen different spots on the huge vessel, and twenty vangels had taken jobs on the ship . . . everything from mechanics to waiters, even a singer for one of the sordid musical revues.

Passengers would start boarding tomorrow morning for the cruise that was scheduled to start before noon. It would never happen, thanks to some brilliant computer hacking by Harek that was timed to take place tomorrow just as the cruise was to begin. Dynamite would have been his choice, but they couldn't destroy the whole ship and everyone on it. First of all, killing a Lucie by normal means just caused them to "die" and go back to Horror for rejuvenation; they had to be killed *and* dissolved. Then there were those sinners on board; the vangels had to attempt a save for those who might repent before dying. He and some of the others had been working the hotel lobbies and bars where early arriving passengers could be found.

All this had to be accomplished with stealth. They did not want Jasper alerted to the VIK presence. Yet. Although he had to be aware of some of his demon vampires gone missing.

Vangel missions were always complicated, Vikar thought with a sigh, this one more so because of its size and importance. Just then, he heard the key card being put in the lock and Ivak came in, looking as exhausted and bone-sad as they all were after two days in Jasper's proximity. It would be Vikar's turn to go out now.

Vikar pulled a cold beer out of the room's mini fridge that was barely working and handed it to his brother, who sank down onto one of the two beds in the room. Ivak took a sip, then frowned. "Warm beer?"

Vikar shrugged. "We are spoiled. Remember the old days? Without refrigeration, warm beer was the least of our worries. 'Tis a wonder our people did not die in great numbers from rancid meat."

Ivak cocked his head to the side. "I do not recall

that so much. Game was so plentiful that we could hunt daily. There was no need for long storage, except in the winters when it was cold enough to freeze the ballocks on a boar."

Vikar smiled and sat down next to Ivak on the bed. "Mayhap you look on the old days as rosier than they were."

"No, I know what was good and what was bad. We Vikings liked our baths, but there were some who were a bit ripe betimes. I recall being in the midst of tupping Sorcha from the Danelands and almost hurling the contents of my belly at her stink."

"Ivak! Sorcha was a goatherder. What did you expect?"

They smiled at each other.

But then Vikar turned serious. As annoying as Ivak could be, he was his brother, and whilst Vikar hardly knew him when they were alive, he'd come to love him after death. Same was true of all his brothers. "How did it go this afternoon?"

Ivak gulped several times from his beer. "I wiped out three Lucies, and I saved a woman at the Marquis Hotel pool. She is on her way home to Memphis. Seems her husband has been talking her into some perversions of late. She wasn't aware of what would be expected of her on this cruise."

Good work for an afternoon, but minor when considering there had to be a hundred Lucies in the area, mayhap even two hundred, and God only knew how many sin-tainted humans about to go to Hell unless the vangels were able to save them.

"Mordr wants us all to meet at five at the warehouse," Ivak told him. They'd rented a large room, more like a giant storage locker, where they'd secured all their weapons and had set up tables with computers and recording devices. All the vangels wore ear buds, connected to Harek's central communication system, even though they could usually telepath thoughts, to some extent.

Vikar glanced at the watch on his wrist and said, "Why don't you shower and sleep for a while. I'll wake you in an hour and a half. I'm going out to study the situation up close. Holy heavens, but I would like to run into Jasper. Bringing him down would give me immense personal satisfaction, wiping the world of evil personified."

"And you'd score extra brownie points from Mike," Ivak noted with a wry grin.

"There is that."

Moments later, Ivak was in the shower and Vikar was gearing up with pistols, knife, and holy water. No place to hide a sword under his loose shirt and shorts. In this hot climate, cloaks would be as out of place as a bikini on a polar bear. The specially made bullets that he loaded into his pockets contained bits of the True Cross, or slivers specially blessed by He who had hung there. The knives had been quenched in the symbolic blood of Christ, based on an ancient method of warfare in which knives and swords were heated to white hotness, then doused to hardness, not in cold water but in the blood of their enemies.

Vikar stood in an alleyway close to the ship, watching the activity to and fro along the boardwalk and the gangplank. Some of the workers he recognized as his own vangels. Svein, for example, was pushing a metal contraption on wheels that contained boxes stacked one atop the other. It might be food supplies, but Vikar suspected they were sex toys. Yes, he could see better now. One of the boxes read: "Whip It Up: Fantasy Fun." Jogeir, who was working as a cook, said that one room on the ship contained hooks on the ceilings with hanging chains. Wrist and ankle cuffs were attached to the walls at strategic places so that a body would be spread-eagled whilst still upright. Torture 101 was Vikar's guess.

Lucipires were humanoids in that they could take on any form they wanted, to hide their usual grotesque demon characteristics. As a result, many handsome men and beautiful women manned the cruise ship.

If only Vikar knew which one was Jasper! What a coup that would be to take down the Lucie prince! It was hard to guess, though, whether Jasper would be strolling the decks or barricaded in some luxury suite.

Lucipires could mask their scent, as vangels could, too, but the mask was short-lived and not always strong enough. Speaking of scents, Vikar went stiff. A gorgeous female was strolling toward him.

If she was a hooker, she was high-class. With big blonde hair, flawless skin, a thigh-length, strapless red dress, and what appeared to be five-inch red high-heeled shoes. She smiled as she got closer and Vikar grabbed the first thing that came to hand. A small vial of holy water. He tossed it at the woman, cringing at her scream as her skin began to melt off. He must move quickly before they drew attention. Although this was a seedy section of town where people tended to ignore what was happening, he could take no chances.

The fangs came out on the Lucie, along with scales on her slimy skin. She was no longer the beauty she'd been a few moments ago. With a hiss of outrage, she lunged for him, but he ducked back. They were both in the alley now, and he was fighting off her clawing hands. What he couldn't allow was for the Lucie's fangs to get into him. He could very well end up in the same condition Harek had been for weeks. Not the way he wanted to return to his Alex.

The Lucipire's skin sizzled as it melted off. Of course, it would eventually grow back if she escaped, something he could not allow. Pulling out the knife hidden in his high-topped hiking boots, he rushed forward, thrusting the knife into her evil heart. With a gasp, the Lucie began to dissolve before his very eyes until nothing was left but a puddle of sulfur-smelling slime. One less demon vampire to haunt the world!

Panting for breath, Vikar wiped his knife on a patch of grass and headed back toward the hotel. Along the way, though, he saw three young women . . . well, thirty to thirty-five years of age . . . standing on his side of the street, staring across the road at the cruise ship.

"I don't know, Crystal, it's one thing to go on one of those online bondage websites, but five days trapped on a ship with a bunch of perverts? Some of those women we saw signing up at the hotel registration looked liked whores. Even, well, depraved, especially the one with all the body piercings." The woman speaking looked more like a librarian than a bimbo. She wore shorts and a shirt with straps, but they were loose. Modest by Florida beach standards.

"Oh, Bonnie, you are such a prude!" The woman

named Crystal licked her crimson lips. She had red hair of an odd, garish shade, short and spiked. Her tall, too-slim frame was clearly outlined by a skin-tight body suit. Were there really nipples that large on a woman? Maybe she'd had nipple enhancement surgery, just like some women had breast enhancements. Was there such a thing? "Bonnie, honey, did you see the guy from Jasper, Inc. at the welcome breakfast? Yummm!"

Crystal, honey, I saw the man, too. If you only knew what he really looks like! Red eyes, lolling tongue, a tail.

Crystal was still raving about the Lucie. "Man, he could be master to this slave girl any day. I swear, he looked just like Brad Pitt."

Ha, ha, ha! Brad Pitt with drool, maybe.

"And that other guy from Jasper, the one trying to get us to sign up for the nude pole dancing contest, he could be a young Kevin Sorbo from that old *Hercules* TV series."

Crystal, you are in for a rude awakening if you step on that boat. Very rude!

"Oh, Crystal, you always say things like that! I don't think you do half the stuff you claim to. You wouldn't really pole dance, naked, in front of men, would you?" Bonnie giggled nervously as she addressed her friend. Then she turned to the third woman. "What do you think, Trish?"

"I know we only met online, but I feel as if we're friends," Trish said carefully. "We don't have to do anything we don't want to. I say, let's go on the cruise. We can pick and choose what activities we're comfortable with." Trish was attractive in an unobtrusive way. Brown hair, straight down to her shoulders. A beige silk blouse tucked into camel-colored slacks. Her eyes gave her away. Even with contact lens the red showed through, giving the blue color a purplish tint. She was a Lucipire.

Vikar followed them into a casual restaurant down the street. Sitting at the counter, he ordered a cup of coffee, a beverage he hated, although the caffeine would be welcome after so little sleep. The three women were sitting in a booth, chattering away over their lunches.

When Bonnie, the one most likely to be saved, went to the ladies' room, he followed discreetly behind. When she came out, he put a hand over her mouth and dragged her out a side door. "Do not be frightened, Bonnie. I mean you no harm. Do you understand? Nod your head."

She nodded, clearly terrified.

"You must get away from here as soon as possible. Do not get onto that ship. Let me tell you what Jasper and his 'shipmates' plan for you." He then detailed all that would happen to her, in graphic detail, and the ultimate outcome. Death. He wasn't sure if she believed him, but her eyes had gotten wider and wider as he'd talked. He removed his hand from her mouth and asked, "Didn't you look at the agenda on the Sin Cruise website?"

She shook her head. "Crystal took care of all the details. She told me it was like a singles cruise with perks."

"Pfff!" he said. Then, "Do you want to go back inside, or would you prefer to go back to your hotel, alone, and leave?"

"Shouldn't I talk to Crystal first?"

He gave her a skeptical look.

"Right. She would probably talk me into staying."

Vikar put his hand on her head then and closed his eyes, letting her feel his "angelic" energy. While he had her in stasis, he leaned forward and bit her neck, taking in a small amount . . . no more than a half cup, of her sweet blood. When he opened his eyes, she was unaware of what he had done to him, but sensed something important had happened. She was staring at him. "*Who* are you?"

"Your guardian angel?"

She laughed. "Yeah, right."

"You better hurry," he advised.

"Thank you," she said, leaning up to kiss his cheek. Then she ran in the opposite direction.

Vikar had no chance to pat himself on the back when he reentered the restaurant and noticed one of the other women coming toward him. The Lucie. His stars must be aligned today.

She hesitated in the hallway, looking over his shoulder to see where her friend . . . rather, potential victim . . . had gone. Then she looked directly at him.

He crooked his finger at her, then smiled, showing her his fangs. Before she could register whom she was facing, he took a quick, whooshing step, grabbing her by the neck, and hauled her out the side door and then into the back, trash-bin section of the restaurant. This Lucipire wasn't as strong as the other had been, even though she was actually a he. Lucies could take on either of the sexes, at will. Within moments, he was staring at a pile of slime at his feet.

"Two points, our side," he said, pumping his fist in the air, then immediately teletransported himself back to the hotel where Ivak was sleeping like a baby. A big, six-foot-four, naked baby with a sleep hard-on big enough to impress Goliath's sister, if Goliath had a sister.

"Jeesh!" he muttered, the things an older brother had to do! He knocked on the wall, to wake his brother up.

To Ivak's credit, he awakened, immediately alert, a necessity in a world where demon vampires flourished. With no embarrassment whatsoever for his condition, he stood, stretched, and yawned loudly before walking over and grabbing a pair of boxer briefs from his carry bag. He put a hand over his cockstand to ease the tighties over his still engorged thickening.

"Don't you have to do something about *that* before we leave?" Vikar asked.

"No! If I had to 'take care' of tweaking the Twinkie"—he glanced downward at the huge bulge in his underwear—"every time it popped up, I'd have permanent tendonitis in my right hand."

Twinkie? Way more information than Vikar needed to have imprinted in his brain.

"Pee-you!" Ivak exclaimed. "You smell like rotten eggs."

"Two Lucies," Vikar preened, "and one save."

"All in one hour? I'm impressed," Ivak said. "Are you going to shower before the meeting?"

Vikar shook his head. He was hoping there would be more "kills" before the night was through. "You do know that masturbation is a sin, don't you?" he remarked to Ivak as they left their room.

"A venial sin," Ivak emphasized. "It better be."

"Are you sure about that?"

"If I were you, I would worry more about what

kind of sin 'near-sex' is going to be, instead of a little ol' jacking off."

Ivak was right about that.

"What are you two arguing about?" Trond asked, coming out of a door down the hall from their room.

"Vikar has suddenly become the expert on sex sins. What think you of tweaking your Twinkie?"

"What?" Trond frowned with puzzlement. "Do you mean—"

"A hand job," Ivak explained.

Vikar put his face in his hands. Then he said, "Please! Trond is the one who told me about near-sex to begin with. What do I care what he thinks of . . . self-pleasuring?"

His brothers laughed then, and he couldn't help but join in. Betimes a man just had to laugh at himself. Or cry.

They were the last to arrive at the warehouse where the other brothers had already gathered, along with about twenty vangels. Other vangels were on board, but they would be informed via their ear buds later of any changes in plans.

Vikar noticed something interesting then. He and most of the other vangels in the room had golden, suntanned-looking skin. Saving a human, even the small amount of blood taken, was like heavenly Vitamin C to a vangel. Lack of a saved's blood over time turned the skin white and then transparent. But feeding thus was pure health.

After each of the vangels gave a report, Harek summed up the results. "Thirty Lucie kills thus far, including two mungs and one haakai. Plus, eighteen saves. Under normal circumstances, that would be great work for a two-day period, but there are a lot of Lucies here. More than I have ever seen in one place in the past five hundred years."

"In our defense, we've been trying to scatter our kills so they're not all in one place or one time. The saves won't be detected by the Lucies until folks who signed up for the cruise fail to show up," Cnut said. "We've been trying not to call attention to our presence until the last minute."

"They must know we're here by now," Sigurd contended. "When I talked to Svein a few minutes ago, he mentioned a lot of hush-hush talk about the ship. Small groups here and there. You can bet they'll be on guard now, more than usual."

"Has anyone seen Jasper?" Ivak asked.

They all shook their heads. No one knew what disguise the Lucipire master would be in.

"Come over to the tables," Mordr said then. He was in charge of this operation, being the most skilled in military tactics. "Here is the plan."

Despite the danger of being recognized, all of The Seven, except Harek, would be slipping onto the ship and killing as many Lucies as they could find. Most important, they wanted to find Jasper and eliminate him for good. In addition, they would be herding any employees or passengers on the cruise into a locked room where they could attempt to save them. Timing would be everything if this was to work. Sabotaging the cruise wouldn't preclude it ever happening in the future, but they would worry about that later.

Harek showed them the computer setup and what he would do to disable the ship, but it was like speaking a foreign language to Vikar. And Vikar was proficient in fourteen languages. Geek speak, that's what it was. He could tell that Mordr felt the same way because his blue eyes were starting to glaze over.

At the end of the meeting, when they'd all been given assignments, they knelt down to pray, as they did before all important missions. "Dear Lord, please lead us in this battle. Dear St. Michael, have your wings at our backs."

Fifteen

**It was the biggest longship
he'd ever been on . . .**

The time had arrived.

Vikar stood guard in the corridor outside the engineering center of the cruise ship. The *Lilith* was small by cruise ship standards, only five decks and a passenger capacity of fifteen hundred, but its brochures promised the luxury of a *QE2* in a smaller, more intimate setting. *Intimate* being the key word for the types of activities planned. The boat was registered in Libya, so many of the technical crew did not speak English, an asset when all the Lucipires on board were discussing their evil intents.

Vikar and all the vangels were arranged in strategic places around the ship and on the shore, including the warehouse where Harek's important role in this mission was about to take place. One by one, the vangels reported to one another via the ear buds and hidden mics on their shoulders. Wherever possible, they'd made contact with the cruise line employees, those who were not Jasper's vassals, and with passengers already on board, herding out those who could be saved. They were all in a separate locked stateroom on the ship and would disembark eventually, if all went according to plan.

Unfortunately, some sinners had already been taken by the overanxious Lucies; those fallen were already on their way to Hell, or Horror. Vikar had no idea at this point how many were lost, and he might not know for weeks when the authorities would start reporting missing people. He and the vangels would be long gone by then.

An additional fifteen Lucies had been dissolved since he and his five brothers had come on board, but mostly they were lower-level imps and hordlings, the foot soldiers in Jasper's army. The goal of the operation today was to prevent the cruise from taking off into international waters, and to wipe out as many Lucies as possible in the process. If they could save some humans who'd not yet crossed the line into unredeemable mortal sin, that would be good; the sinners would have time to repent when released, if they so chose.

Passengers had begun boarding at eight, and they were set to launch by eleven . . . only forty-five minutes from now. Vikar had been on the ship for the past seven hours, since four a.m., and he'd seen plenty. The *Lilith* could only be described as a moving bordello, except it was way worse than that.

Vikar had seen some sinfully amazing things in his time, but the things Jasper intended as entertainment for his "prisoners" on this cruise amazed him. Some of the sex toys could be better described as sex torture instruments. And, yes, that's what the passengers would be, prisoners, before being killed, thus ensuring a quick chute to Hell, or being taken back to Horror if they showed potential for being turned into Lucipires.

The ship abounded with seemingly handsome men and beautiful women in scant attire just dying to get it on with the passengers, no matter what they looked like, their age, or their experience. Meat, that's all the passengers were to the Lucies. New meat for Hell's fires or Horror's chamber of . . . well, horrors. The public address system played constant music with a sensual beat, setting the stage for what was to come. Various Lucies were already cajoling the newcomers to come partake of some titillating activity.

Vikar liked to think that he would not have been attracted by such a scene when he'd been alive, but who could know for sure what temptation, even the most disgusting type, would do to a weak man? And weren't all men, and women, weak in some areas of their lives? It made Vikar wonder if the sexual orgies that had occurred in ancient Rome weren't Jasper's doing, as well.

"Well, well, well. Vikar Sigurdsson," a smooth, accented voice drawled.

Vikar swiveled, fully expecting to confront Jasper, but instead it was one of Jasper's haakai captains, Gregori Petrov.

The Russian's fangs were out, and although he was still in humanoid form, wearing a cruise line uniform, he was slowly changing over as his bloodlust overtook him. The eyes were turning red, and he appeared to be growing taller.

There was no time to wait. Vikar raised his Sig and fired, but Gregori lunged at the same time, and the bullet missed his shoulder by a hairsbreadth. Vikar's weapon had a silencer on it, so no ship personnel were alerted. Yet.

A fight to the "death" ensued then, and Gregori more than matched him in strength and skill. By sheer luck, Gregori slipped on his own slime, and Vikar was able to get off another shot from his pistol, directly between the Russian's two red eyes, then another into his heart.

Vikar felt no overwhelming triumph in defeating this once great Russian general, but a relief that he was gone, forever, and a sadness that great men could be brought so low.

Just then, a woman screamed behind him.

Vikar swiveled, weapons at hand.

A female Lucie gaped at the body dissolving at Vikar's feet. He remembered her being at Gregori's side on that Canadian mountaintop. He could almost believe there was love on the hordling's face for her fallen lover, but then she straightened, hissed her outrage, and flew at him.

He was prepared, a knife at the ready. Her heart, which presumably was already breaking, broke indeed now, under his special blade, and her slime soon mixed with Gregori's.

Vikar's attention was immediately diverted by the sense of movement underfoot. The cruise ship had launched. Already? The engines had been turned on over an hour ago, but departure wasn't set for another half hour.

Into his mic, he yelled, "Harek? What's going on?"

"Cool your jets, bro. I want them out in the water a bit before I shut them down."

"You want, you want . . ." he sputtered. "You're going to screw around and ruin the whole mission."

Another voice interrupted in his ear, "He knows what he's doing, Vikar. He got orders from Above." It was Mordr. "You've got more to worry about. I fully expect Jasper to show up there once the engines stop. Be prepared. I'm a bit . . . occupied at the moment." In the background he could hear the scream of a Lucie, then Mordr muttered, "Damn, damn, damn! I hate slime."

Vikar's attention was drawn to the closed door of the engineering room now where he heard a commotion. Chairs being moved, voices raised. There were no Lucies in there, only professional cruise members working. Luckily, these spoke English, although Vikar spoke Arabic in various dialects and could have understood their words if they'd been Libyans.

"What the hell . . . ?" one man inside shouted. "My settings are going wacko."

Another said, "We aren't supposed to move yet. Who the hell gave the launch order?"

Still another man said, "I liked it better in the old days when engines were fired by coal and we didn't have to depend on friggin' computers."

"Miguel, you were around when they rowed the boats."

"Ha, ha, ha!" the Hispanic-sounding Miguel countered. "Even cars are ruled by computers today. My Toyota truck went haywire, and the regular

shop wouldn't even look at it. Had to take it back to
the dealer where they have a specialist."

"Whoa! Did you feel that? We're already a mile
out from port. And, sonofabitch, look at those dials.
They're spinning numbers so fast I can't keep up."

"Me too. In fact, my monitor just went dead.
Should we call a Mayday?"

"You're an idiot, Miguel. Maydays are for when
the ship is sinking. We aren't sinking. We're . . . oh
my God! We're already three miles out, and we're
doing . . . what the hell . . . are we doing figure eights
in the water?"

"Impossible!"

"Somebody better alert the captain that we need
help here," Miguel said. "And somebody better call
that creepy character, Jasper, who's running this
freak parade. He's gonna have a shit fit."

While one of the men was presumably calling,
one of the others remarked, "Man, I knew this particular cruise sounded too good to be true. Here I
was planning on having a little fun on this trip, for
a change."

"Me too," Miguel whined. "A blonde in housekeeping asked me to meet her tonight in the dungeon, whatever that is. Some new club, I guess."

Vikar stepped back into a hidden alcove and
watched and waited. People came and went, including a ranting chief officer of the cruise ship. Vikar
managed to kill two more Lucies, but he was waiting for a bigger fish. Jasper.

Throughout the ship, he could hear via his ear
buds all the other vangels hard at work. Sounded
to Vikar like there would be a lot fewer Lucies by

nightfall. And pandemonium seemed to reign on the open decks as passengers realized the ship was probably going nowhere other than in wide loops, at least for the time being. If Harek did his work as planned, the ship would be disabled for more than a few hours, more like days, or weeks. By then, Jasper and his crew should be gone. Maybe for good.

Just then the air seemed to crackle and all of Vikar's senses went on full alert. If evil had an odor, it was approaching. Both vangels and Lucipires had heightened senses, including smell. Jasper had a distinct scent, when up close, as did The Seven. Into his mic, Vikar whispered, "J, on the way."

"Ten-four," Mordr said. "Be there in a sec. I have to . . . oomph! Correction. I have a little problem to take care of here. Come here, you friggin' creep. Time to go home to Papa Lucifer."

Okay, Vikar was on his own, unless one of his brothers managed to show up. He pulled out his Sig, which was a bit bulky with the silencer, a knife, and even some specially treated throwing stars. The floor of the corridor almost seemed to shake as the figure approached. Vikar's heart raced with anticipation. He made a sign of the cross over his chest reflexively.

He'd seen Jasper before. Of course he had. Over a thousand-year period, they had to have the occasional run-in, but the head Lucie was always in disguise. Today was no different.

In fact, it would be laughable if it wasn't so pathetic.

Vikar was about to duke it out with Clark Gable. Good ol' Rhett, complete with mustache, in a white plantation-style suit with a red shirt and white silk tie, all designer quality, no doubt. But from his stateroom above, or wherever he'd been holed up, storming down here in a rage, he was already transforming. His eyes gradually turned from brown to crimson, matching his shirt, and his fangs inched out until they almost touched his jaw.

When Jasper saw him, and recognized him as one of The Seven, the Supreme Lucipire reared up, almost like a dragon about to breathe fire at him, and roared. He actually roared.

The door of the communications room opened a crack, three faces peering out, then immediately slammed shut when they saw the two of them. Vikar spun a star at Jasper's neck, but it just glanced off. Jasper must have the hide of a rhino.

Before Vikar had a chance to aim his Sig or get a firmer grasp on his knife, Jasper tackled him to the floor and tried to bite his neck. Fortunately, Vikar was able to shift quickly enough that his skin was only grazed, but already he could feel the burn of the Lucie's poison. Over and over, they rolled, each striking blows. Finally, Vikar had control. Jasper was on his back. And Vikar had his knife raised high.

Without warning, Vikar felt a blow across his head, knocking him off Jasper and against the wall. But the blow hadn't come from a weapon. No, it was an enormous paw of a hand, which now reached out and lifted its master from the floor. Vikar recognized the seven-foot-tall mung assistant who hefted the severely injured Jasper up and over his shoulder.

When Vikar tried to attack, the mung shoved him aside like he was a bothersome fly and began to stomp away.

"Attack, Sabeam! Attack!" Jasper was yelling as

he struggled to get out of Sabeam's fireman's carry.

By now, Jasper was in full Lucie mode, complete with tail, which kept slapping at Sabeam's face. Jasper was screaming obscenities at his assistant, who paused, confused as to what he should do.

Vikar managed to get two shots off, one between the shoulder blades and another into the back of Sabeam's thigh.

The injuries didn't slow down the mung, who'd resumed lumbering away. The wounds would be fatal to him later, though. The effect of vangel bullets in a Lucipire could not be reversed.

Of course, Vikar had lost Jasper, which was more important.

Trond arrived then to help him up off the floor where he'd sunk down, trying to stop the flow of blood from his head wound. Sabeam's hand was sharp with scales, not to mention heavy. Before he had a chance to speak, Trond was turning Vikar's face this way and that, examining his neck, and then he was searching his arms. He even lifted his T-shirt, to see if he had any bites there.

"If you dare to pull down my shorts, I swear you will be sorry," Vikar said, scrambling to his feet. "It's only my pride that's injured." Well, that wasn't quite true. He was bruised and scratched, just not bitten.

"I lost him," Vikar told Trond. "I had Jasper in my grasp, and I lost him."

"Win some, lose some," Trond replied.

Vikar arched his brows.

"Okay, some losses are bigger than others."

"Mike is going to be livid."

"Mike is always livid. Anyhow, you have to come up on deck and see what's happening."

"Good or bad?"

"Just amazing."

Before they left, Vikar knocked on the communications center door and said, "Hey, guys, you can come out now."

The door opened a little once again, and one fellow peeked out. Seeing that Jasper was gone, he opened the door wider. Seeing him and Trond, who looked relatively normal with their fangs retracted, the guy asked, "What the hell is going on?"

"Beats me," Trond replied. "I think there was some kind of break in the electrical circuits."

Vikar gave his brother a glance, impressed with his quick thinking.

Trond winked at Vikar.

When they got up to the deck, the ship came to a lurching stop. Passengers and crew members alike were scurrying around like chickens with their heads cut off. Unable to disembark from the vessel since it was a short distance from shore, people were shrieking, crying, screaming, talking animatedly. Some even questioned whether it was part of the Sin Cruise's launch agenda.

The Lucipires seemed to have disappeared. Now that the element of surprise was gone, the vangels would leave, too.

"This is what you wanted to show me?"

Trond shook his head. "Look out there. You thought the boat was moving in a figure eight. But look closely at that design left by the bilge water."

It wasn't a figure eight he saw, and forget bilge water. The design in the water was a set of shimmery silver wings.

"Michael!" he and Trond said at the same time.

The archangel always had to get in the last "word."

There were news helicopters overhead, and police sirens could be heard in their open mic to Harek onshore. He and the other vangels would have to teletransport out of here ASAP.

They were all back in the warehouse two hours later, packing up their supplies, laughing and teasing each other about the roles they'd played that day. It felt surreal after all they'd just experienced. Was the mission a success or a failure? Hard to say, although Vikar personally felt like a failure.

Besides, five vangels had been lost in the melee that had occurred while Vikar had been below fighting Gregori, and then Jasper and Sabeam. Fortunately, those vangels had been killed and were now hopefully in Tranquillity. The worst possible outcome would have been for any one of them to be captured. Despite those losses, fifty-five Lucies were gone and an equal number of souls saved.

But there were so many demon vampires still out there, and so many humans to be saved. Sometimes Vikar was just weary of it all. The VIK mission seemed endless.

Well, they would find out soon enough whether they'd succeeded or failed. The Reckoning would be held in less than a week, and Mike was not shy about expressing his opinions. Vikar would have much to reckon for.

But then his mood lightened.

Before the Reckoning, he still had time to be with Alex.

When he glanced at Trond, his brother shook his head at him with amusement. Vikar suspected he had a goofy grin on his face . . . again.

When all else fails,
bring out the Krispy Kremes . . .

Alex sat in the backyard on a kitchen chair she'd dragged outside. She was letting the sunshine dry her newly shampooed hair that she'd combed back off her face and tucked behind her ears.

But she was a born multitasker, never able to just sit still. So, with her bare feet resting on a low stool, her knees were raised, helping to hold in place the laptop that she was tapping on energetically in yet another attempt to draw an article out of her stay here in Transylvania. The problem was that the story kept changing, or maybe the real story was just being elusive and she hadn't discovered it yet.

Who was she kidding? She was worried sick about Vikar, who had been gone four days now, and the words she was typing out could very well be gibberish.

She had a glass of diet lemonade and two Krispy Kreme donuts sitting on a tray on the ground. If Vikar didn't get back soon, she was going to gain ten pounds. Krispy Kremes had become her comfort food of choice, especially the glazed ones that oozed white cream icing.

The wet lick on her shoulder was her first clue that she wasn't alone, but the familiar nip of fanged teeth told her loud and clear that Vikar was back. "Vikar!" she cried as she closed her laptop and set it on the ground.

At the same time, Vikar reached and lifted her by the waist up into a tight embrace. It was hard to tell who squeezed tighter then. Alex with her arms

wrapped around Vikar's shoulders, her face burrowed into his neck? Or Vikar with his muscled
arms a vise around her lower back?

She was weeping with relief.

He was shh-ing her in assurance.

By the time she began kissing him all over his
beautiful face . . . his forehead, his mouth, his eyelids, his mouth, his cheeks, his mouth, his jaw . . . he
was laughing joyfully. In between kisses, they murmured their pent-up emotions.

"I was so afraid," she said.

"I missed you so much," he said.

"What a brute you are for not calling me!"

"If I called you once, I would have called a hundred times."

"Armod taught me to moonwalk."

"Show me later. Naked."

"Don't ever leave me again."

"Alex, sweetling, you know I can't promise that."

"Let's go have near-sex."

He laughed. "This close to the Reckoning? I'm not
that brave."

She pulled back, and Vikar reluctantly set her on
her feet. It was then that she got her first good look
at her returning hero.

He wore a muscle shirt—a sweatshirt with the
sleeves and neckline cut off—over running shorts
with athletic shoes. In contrast to that modern attire,
he had Viking arm rings on both upper arms . . . the
same ones his brothers wore, too. Etched wings in a
Celtic design on solid silver. Most important, every
bit of skin exposed was a golden suntan.

"You jerk!" She smacked his chest.

"What? What is amiss?"

"Don't you 'amiss' me." She smacked his chest again.

"Dearling." He took both of her hands in his and laughed.

Oooh, that was a big mistake! "Think I'm funny, do you?" She kicked out at him, forgetting she wore no shoes, and her bare foot just brushed his . . . erection? She raised her eyes to his.

He shrugged. "I told you I missed you. A lot. Why are you suddenly such a fierce kitten?"

Kitten? Oooh, them was fighting words. "Because I've been alternately crying and eating Krispy Kreme donuts every minute you've been gone." She pointed to the tray on the ground. "And, you . . . you've been lying on the beach sunning yourself, no doubt ogling all the beach bunnies in bikinis."

"Ah," he said as if suddenly understanding. Sitting down on the chair, he pulled her onto his lap. "The color of a vangel's skin changes when they save human sinners. Wait until you see Svein and Jogeir. None of my saves wore bikinis, I assure you. As for the female Lucies, well, if you think I am attracted by red eyes and slime, you do not know me well. Unless they are your red eyes and slime." He waggled his eyebrows at her.

She smacked him again on his chest, but only lightly. Not that hitting him harder had done much against his immovable chest. "Everything went well then?"

He shrugged. "Overall, it was a success, but I had Jasper in my hands and lost him."

She sensed the guilt that was swamping him. "Do your brothers and the rest of the vangels consider you a failure for Jasper's escape?"

"No, but—"

"No buts. I suspect you're being too hard on yourself."

"Or mayhap I am not being hard enough."

"Let your precious Michael make that judgment. And speaking of him, do you have any idea how many people have already arrived? Two dozen!"

"Sweetling! Do you have any idea how many will be here by next Sunday when the Reckoning starts? Two hundred and fifty."

Her jaw dropped before she burst out laughing. "I think I need to get some more Krispy Kreme donuts."

When they were walking back toward the house, his arm over her shoulders, her arm wrapped under his arms and across his waist, she told him, "I have a really good idea. You should put a gazebo back here. With climbing roses. Think of the privacy."

Rolling his eyes, he told her, "I have a really good idea of what we could do with a Krispy Kreme donut. In a private place."

Sixteen

Asylum of the dead, for sure . . .

Transylvania, Pennsylvania, is a story for the ages. All ages of people, that is.

Kids love it here because of the woo-woo atmosphere. A carnival horror house but better. Where else can you walk down the street and be scared over and over by the hiss and fangs of vampires? Or blood dripping off an exposed neck?

Teenage girls who brought the Cullen family of *Twilight* to popularity are here in abundance. There's always the possibility they will find their very own Edward right around the corner. And where the girls are, teenage boys are, too.

Adults like the campy stores where you can buy anything from cloaks to vampire porn.

Restaurants and bars give a new twist to "a
night on the town." You could call it dating
with an edge.

　　And behind it all is the story of how this
depressed community decided . . .

One day before the Reckoning, and Vikar was
living in a madhouse. He'd even taken to eating
Krispy Kreme donuts for stress.

Although it would be for only a few days, the resi-
dency of the castle was now up to two hundred and
fifty, as he'd predicted, and growing. Aside from The
Seven, innumerable jarls, karls, ceorls, and thralls
had arrived for tomorrow's Big Event. So many that
some slept outside in tents. Vikar had given up his
own bedchamber for Dagmar and ten other blood
ceorls, who were kept busy feeding those of the
masses who'd been unable to sustain themselves
with recent saved humans or Fake-O.

Excitement was in the air.

Everywhere Vikar turned, there seemed to be a
new disaster. A washing machine overflowing with
suds. Music playing too loud. One young ceorl arguing with another over whether to watch NASCAR
or baseball on the TV. A dent in the newly painted
woodwork during swordplay, which was forbidden
indoors after the chapel statue debacle, which Vikar
did not want to think about. Someone getting mud
on Miss Borden's newly washed kitchen floor. A
new vangel trying to kill a mosquito with a lance.

Not to mention a lot of drinking going on, and
not of blood. No, these were Vikings. Beer was their
beverage of choice.

As he'd predicted, Tofa had arrived with her painting supplies and had already half completed a mural in the entrance hall depicting St. Michael the Archangel ridding the heavens of Lucifer and his fallen angels.

"Tofa ever was a suck-up," Mordr had remarked on first seeing her work of art.

"I don't know," Sigurd had replied, "she's made Michael look a bit like Pee Wee Herman, if you ask me."

Then there was Bodil, who was doing as Vikar had predicted, as well. Here only two days with her apprentices, and she had the exterior of the castle looking like a landscaper's dream. In fact, Bodil and Alex had drawn up plans for a rose garden in the back complete with trellises and, yes, a gazebo. A gazebo, for thunder's sake! Who ever heard of a Viking in a gazebo?

The fact that Vikar could smile in the midst of all this chaos was a miracle, some would say. He gave credit to Alex and her effect on him. *That* was a miracle.

"Is everything ready for Mike's arrival?" Trond asked as the two of them patrolled the property, checking over the security fences that had been erected as temporary measures until more permanent barriers could be put in place.

"As ready as we can be."

"Does Mike come alone?"

"No. Gabe and Rafe are coming with him. The Reckoning of so many of us will take two days as it is, even with three of them working one-on-ones. Last time, in 1912, there were only a hundred of us.

Now, two hundred and sixty-seven, with a dozen more recently saved humans being considered to join our ranks."

Trond nodded. "I heard one of them is a military hero. Any more details on that one?"

Vikar shook his head slowly. "Mike is being mysterious about this man who's still in Afghanistan, not even dead yet."

"Holy fjord!"

"You got that right. Announcing a new vangel before the person is even dead! That's a new one for us."

"Will the three of them stay here tomorrow night?"

Vikar shook his head, then grinned. "I can't imagine how we would entertain those dour angels during the evening hours."

"Oh, I don't know," Trond said. "Hymns? Prayer? *The 700 Club*. A DVD of Charlton Heston as Moses? Biblical Trivial Pursuit? Or that old TV show *Touched by an Angel*."

"Next time I will name you entertainment director."

Trond bowed as if he'd paid him a great compliment. "So they'll be leaving here by nightfall tomorrow, I presume."

"Right," Vikar concurred. "They'll be off to the Vatican to plague the pope. All that priest pedophilia has God up in arms."

"As He should be!" Trond said with disgust.

"But they'll be back here during the day until the job is complete." Vikar reached into the paper sack he carried with him and asked Trond, "Care for a Krispy Kreme donut?"

Angel flying too close to the ground . . .

The sound of hundreds of birds flying overhead awakened Alex the next morning. Well, she assumed it was birds since it resembled the sound she recognized from the days back at her Barnegat cottage when the geese would fly south for the winter.

Except that had been in the fall, and this was only August. And there was no honking.

Her eyes shot open to the bright sunshine of a new day. Sunshine that was suddenly cut off, as if by a cloud . . . or a large flock of birds.

The sound of the birds died, and the sun shone again, accompanied by a wonderful, indefinable scent. Like cloves. Or incense. And the air seemed to shimmer, as if it had currents of energy in it. She breathed deeply and felt the oddest sense of . . . serenity.

The silence was odd, too, now that the bird fluttering had ended. With all the people in the castle, even this early, there should have been the sound of activity.

But wait. Suddenly there emerged the sound of one single male voice. "Ho-san-nah!" Each syllable was drawn out with musical perfection. And then a full chorus of voices burst out with the most joyous hymn. Many, many voices.

Goose bumps rose over every inch of her skin at the sheer beauty she was hearing.

The archangels had arrived.

Vikar had warned her to stay up here in the tower room, unless she was invited downstairs, but there was no way she was going to miss this. Whatever this was!

So she dressed quickly in a short-sleeved white shirt tucked into camel-colored, pleated slacks with a brown leather belt. On her feet were white sandals. After quickly brushing her teeth, she pulled her hair back with a claw barrette. No time for makeup.

She walked slowly down the stairs, though, because she found she was suddenly shaking. Literally shaking, and she felt light-headed, as well. Probably all the sugar she'd been eating lately. Well, of course, she was nervous. Frightened, really. If she found downstairs what Vikar had been telling her was coming . . . rather *who* was coming . . . her life would be changed forever. Not that it hadn't been already.

If there was a St. Michael the Archangel in the parlor, then there had to be a God up above. And that would mean . . . She couldn't even imagine what that meant. At the least she would be taken back to her childhood and the blind belief in things unseen. Except there would be no blindness after today.

And what about Linda? *Oh please, God, let me find out about my little girl*, she found herself praying.

When she got to the wide staircase leading to the first floor, she saw all the vangels kneeling shoulder to shoulder everywhere, even in the halls and in the open doorway leading outside. She sank down onto a step near the top giving her a narrow view into the parlor where three men sat in high-backed, armed chairs that had been brought there last night from the dining room. Oddly, they now appeared to be like thrones. All the furniture had been pressed against the wall.

The three men were tall. And beautiful. Not just handsome, or attractive, they were beautiful beyond description from long hair to perfectly sculpted features. Although they wore modern attire, what appeared to be designer suits with crisp white shirts and striped power ties, they had wings coming out of their backs. Massive white wings. With hysterical irrelevance, she wondered if they had special holes cut in the backs of their jackets so the wings could emerge or retract.

Most important, an incandescent light outlined each of the figures. Not a halo, unless it was a full-body halo.

Kneeling in a half circle, about six feet away from the archangels—*what else could they be but archangels?*—were Vikar and five of his brothers. Harek, whose leg was still injured, leaned against a nearby wall with his crutches. There were a small number of female vangels present, about two dozen, compared to the two hundred and fifty or so legion.

Alex's heart thumped so hard that it was a while before she was able to pick up the words being spoken by the archangel in the middle. Michael?

The dark-haired man . . . angel . . . raised a hand in front of him and made the sign of the cross, blessing all those before him. "Vikings, I come to you with a message from on high. We are pleased."

A sigh of relief swept over the crowd. Alex saw two young men at the bottom of the stairs, big men with soldier bodies, weeping joyfully.

Despite the positive note of his message, Michael's expression remained somber. "Many changes are coming to the VIK and all vangels," Michael said.

"Thou will no longer travel through time to do your work. Instead you will stay in this year and the future to curb the tsunami of sin that washes over the land."

Interesting that the archangel would use the word *tsumani*, Alex thought. She considered it a modern word, but then she supposed angels were timeless.

"Vikings! Jasper must be stopped!" Michael yelled in a thunderous voice, pounding a fist on the arm of his chair. "Your most recent efforts, though commendable, were a mere dent in the stone walls of his depravity. Thou must rid the world of his evil." He pounded the chair again.

Alex could swear the walls shook.

Everyone in the crowd bowed their heads, as if in shame for failing to do their jobs.

"Thou have done well," Michael added in a softer voice, "but thou must do better. This is war we wage. Satan must not win! Jasper must be stopped."

Murmurs of assent rippled through the crowd, like a wave.

"Henceforth, headquarters for the VIK will be here in this castle in this small town. Later, other satellite headquarters will be established around the world. I will increase your ranks ten-fold in this century. By the time I return here in one hundred years, Jasper and his unholy flock will be no more, or, let it be known, there will be no more vangels. That is God's will."

An ultimatum? Alex's heart wept for Vikar, who would be put under such pressure.

Silence pervaded the castle as Michael waited for the implications of his pronouncement to sink in. But then she realized that the silence was continuing way too long. When she looked up, she noticed Michael staring straight at her through piercing blue eyes.

She gasped.

"There is one here who does not belong," Michael said.

All eyes turned toward her as the vangels noticed the direction of Michael's stare.

"Who dares to intrude?" Michael's question was directed at Vikar, who had stood.

Vikar raised his chin, as if prepared for a blow, and said, "She is . . ."

Alex felt tears well in her eyes at the agony she saw on Vikar's face. Oh, how she hated to have put him in this predicament!

But then Vikar cemented her fate when he said, with no hesitation now, "She is my beloved."

Viking, what were you thinking? . . .

Vikar sat in his office waiting for Mike, and his personal Reckoning meeting. He felt like a prisoner on death row.

Gabe and Rafe were using the dining room and a side parlor for their one-on-ones with the vangels, starting with the lowest level upward. Blood ceorls were excluded. They were always pure.

He'd already seen some horrified vangel faces following interviews, meaning huge additional penances, but he'd also seen some joyous ones, which meant either an end to their vangel life, or short penances left.

Mike had conducted a few of his meetings already, but was in the computer room at the moment with Harek discussing ideas for an angel website. To everyone's surprise, Mike had been receptive to the idea of doing God's work on the Internet superhighway. "Silly Vikings!" Mike had chastised them when they'd broached the idea so tentatively, "The Lord has always been willing to go after sinners. If He waited for them to make the first step, Heaven would be a lonely place."

In the old days, being called a "silly Viking" would have been insult enough to prompt a war, or at the least, a lopped-off head. Turning the other cheek came sore hard for a Norseman.

Tomorrow morning the three archangels would meet with The Seven to discuss what had happened on Jasper's Sin Cruise. "This is worse than Sodom and Gomorrah," Mike had grumbled when given a brief preliminary report. "You must prevent its happening ever again."

Easy to say. But how?

Vikar tried to tidy up his desk as he awaited his hearing. Alex was up in the tower room where Mike had ordered her to go until he "addressed her situation." Whatever that meant. The worst that could happen, in Vikar's opinion, would be her exile from the castle. That would be the worst thing that could happen to Vikar, too. He planned to intercede on her behalf.

Just then, the door opened and Mike walked in, carrying a folder, which Vikar knew held his fate. "Viking," he said, his only greeting.

Vikar would have liked to rudely say, "Archangel," in reply, but he was no dummy. Instead, Vikar nodded his head in acknowledgment and rose from his chair, moving to the front of the desk where two chairs faced each other.

Mike had removed his suit jacket and tie and rolled up the sleeves of his shirt. No wings at the moment. His human form was not much taller than Vikar, but appeared larger. Certainly more intimidating.

Sitting down opposite Vikar, Mike opened the folder and examined a printout from Harek's software program. He frowned in a couple of places and nodded in others. "Overall, you have done well, Vikar. Not perfect, of course, but He does not expect you to be."

"I failed with Jasper," Vikar confessed. "I had him in my hands and allowed him to escape."

"It was not Jasper's time."

Just like that, Vikar was absolved of that particular guilt.

Back to perusing his folder, Mike remarked, "Mostly, I am seeing venial sins. We are especially pleased with your mentoring of Armod. If it had not been for your most recent activity, I might even have said you could take a hundred years off your penance."

Uh-oh! He suspected what "recent activity" Mike referred to. Best not to volunteer any sins, though, just in case it was some other "recent activity."

Mike stared at Vikar then.

Being stared at by St. Michael the Archangel was enough to cow the hardest warrior, but he prided himself on his brave demeanor. *Oops, that pride thing again!*

Finally, Mike let out an exasperated exhale, and said, "What were you thinking?"

"Um. What exactly are you referring to?"

"Near-sex?"

Vikar could feel himself blush. "I didn't go all the way."

Mike laughed. The archangel actually laughed. Vikar hadn't known he had it in him. "There is that, I suppose. But tell me, why? Why would you risk everything for a mere woman?"

Mere woman? Has he never heard of equality of the sexes? It's the twenty-first century!

"It was an expression, Viking."

Vikar hated it when the archangel read his thoughts.

"I repeat, why would you risk everything for *this* woman?"

Vikar bristled. "Because I love her. Yes, I know that vangels are not permitted that luxury, but I cannot help myself. I love her."

"Vikar, Vikar, Vikar. Have you learned nothing?"

Huh?

"Why do you think you are here on earth?"

"Punishment?"

"Fool Viking!"

"Fool Viking" was as much an insult to a Norseman as "silly Viking." Vikar gritted his teeth before offering, "To do good?"

"And how do you accomplish that?"

"By killing Lucipires?"

Mike shrugged. "All these things are means to an end. Do you not understand what God is all about? Why humans were ever put on earth?"

All the fine hairs rose on Vikar's body as he began to understand where Mike was going with this conversation. Could it really be as easy as that?

"Love. God wants all his people to love," Mike elaborated.

"*That* kind of love?" Hope turned some men into pitiful creatures. For a certainty, Vikar felt pitiful at the moment.

"All kinds of love. First, love of your Maker. But then love of family, friend, neighbor, enemy, and even that of man for his mate."

"Are you saying . . . ?"

"No, Viking, I am not giving you permission to have carnal knowledge of a woman outside of marriage. And for what you have done thus far, consider twenty years of extra penance."

Only twenty years? Vikar nodded, but he was totally confused.

"Let me ask you this, Viking . . . if I, on behalf of God, asked you to give up this woman, would you do so?"

"I would," Vikar answered without hesitation, "and, truth to tell, I would be thankful for the days I had with her. That does not mean I want to send her away. A sword to the heart it would be for me."

"Would you die for her? Would you give your life to save her?"

"In a heartbeat."

Mike smiled then, and the smile of an archangel was a most wondrous thing. Rare and splendorous. Like warm velvet to a cold human heart.

What did it mean?

"Your most grievous of the seven deadly sins is pride. A prideful man is often a narcissist. You were, for a certainty. Everything you did revolved around yourself and self-aggrandizement. True love means putting yourself aside and thinking of others first."

Vikar had never thought of his pride in such a way before. He *had* been a self-important man, now that he thought on it. His life, from his first wife Vendela onward, had been about pleasing himself.

Mike leaned back in his chair and studied him. "Would you marry her?"

Now that was an unexpected question.

Vikar frowned, considering. "I know that some vangels wed, even with humans, but they have been ones with short penances left. No, much as I would want to marry Alex, I could not watch her grow old and die whilst I stay the same age."

"What if there were other options?"

If Vikar weren't sitting down, he might have fallen over at the sensation of blood draining from his head. He felt faint. "Dost mean turning her into a vangel?" He shook his head sadly. "She would have to die and undergo the agonizing change for that to happen and I would not inflict that on her."

"Maybe that should be her choice."

"Do not offer it to her," Vikar ordered.

He could tell that Mike was not happy with his dictating terms, but then the archangel said, "There is one other option. If you wed her, she could stay her same age and live as long as you do, but when you pass to the Other World, she would have to go, too."

"What? *What?* Do you mean . . . I don't know . . . what if . . . how?" he stuttered. Then, "Was this always on the table as an option for us vangels?"

"No. I just thought of it now."

"I need to think about it."

Mike flashed him a disgusted look for not jumping at the offer, but then shrugged as if to say, *Dumb Viking!*

Vikar had no chance to react to that latest insult because his head was swirling with everything that Mike had said, but then he could not think at all because Mike made his final pronouncement.

"Send the woman to me."

Seventeen

The angel gave her a gift most precious . . .

Cynics beware! You aren't going to believe what is happening in Transylvania.

Angels arrived today in this small Pennsylvania town. Yes, that was angels, as in plural. In fact, three angels. And not just any angels. No, these were the crème de la crème of angels. Archangels.

Numerous sightings were called into the 911 Center, as well as the local newspaper. Huge winged creatures with human bodies.

All over the area, people claimed to witness miracles. Small miracles, but miracles nonetheless. A bank official suddenly approving a portfolio of loans for folks previously deemed poor risks. The long-broken bells of St. Vladimir's Church bursting forth with tolling mu-

sic. A child with leukemia suddenly cured;
well, doctors claimed it had been an unfortu-
nate misdiagnosis. Several couples halfway on
the road to divorce decided to reconcile.

Most obvious were the smiles. A sense of
well-being pervaded the air. And people were
"paying it forward" right and left without being asked. The waitress given a huge tip donat-
ed the extra money to the local animal shelter,
which was able to rescue a litter of puppies
left on the roadside, which led to a boy with no
birthday presents . . .

Alex had been weeping softly for the past two
hours, and she wasn't sure why.

It was monumental, what she'd seen downstairs.
Angels. Honest-to-God angels! There was no deny-
ing their existence now.

For weeks, she had been on the fence about the
vangels, one day refusing to believe they could possibly be what they claimed to be, and the other accepting that life sometimes contained things that
were miraculous, for lack of a better word. This was
more than that. Actual, visual proof that celestial
beings were here among us.

Seeing and believing was one thing, but its effect
was still staggering, and that's why she wept. This
changed everything for her. Life as she'd understood it was all wrong.

She hadn't been offended when ordered back to
her room. She'd needed time to assimilate everything. By the time she'd gotten her emotions somewhat under control and gone into the adjoining
bathroom to wash her face and apply a tinted mois-

turizer to hide her reddened nose and eyes, Vikar was in the bedroom waiting for her.

The first thing she noticed was the worry on his face.

"What?"

"Mike wants to talk with you."

"Is that a bad thing?"

"Not necessarily."

"You're scaring me."

He walked over and took her into his arms, pressing her face against his beating heart. *The beating heart of a dead man,* she had to remind herself.

"What happened in your meeting? Are you being punished for being with me? I'm not going to let that happen. I'll talk to Michael. Tell him to punish me instead of you."

He stepped away from her and gave her a look of dismay. "You can't tell Mike what to do."

She shrugged. "I can try."

"Besides, my punishment is small. We can discuss it later. No, it is something else."

"What?"

"I'm not sure." Thus the anxious expression on his face.

So it was with trepidation on both their parts that Alex approached the office a short time later. To her dismay, Vikar told her outside in the hallway that Michael wanted to talk with her alone.

When she walked in, the archangel was standing near the window, staring pensively into the distance. What was he seeing? The mountain? The sky? Heaven?

Despite being dressed in modern attire, this man was clearly more than human. Even without the wings she'd seen earlier, he was angelic. A sort of radiance emanated from him. Not a halo. And not actual light. Not even an aura, precisely. Maybe there was no word for it.

In any case, she knew she was in the presence of someone of heavenly importance. Should she bow, or get down on her knees?

He turned and smiled at her, gently.

Alex whimpered. It was as if he'd reached out and wrapped her in the comfort of his wings. As if he not only could read her mind, but read her needs as well.

"You have a question you wish to ask, my child?"

Alex knew exactly what he meant. She sank down into a chair, fearing that her rubbery legs would give out on her. Without her realizing it, tears were streaming down her face. "My daughter?" she choked out.

"Close your eyes," he said.

Without question, Alex did as told. Suddenly, into her mind came an image. A cloudy place, at first. Then a garden. Sitting on a bench was a woman. A woman of such beauty and serenity Alex had never seen. The Madonna. Then the Blessed Mother opened her arms to someone or something in the distance. And Linda, her daughter, as Alex had seen her last, came running forward, launching herself at the Madonna. Close on Linda's heels was the aged German shepherd Tillie, who had died when Linda was only three. Sitting on the Blessed Mother's lap, Linda appeared to be chattering away, and the woman was smiling gently as she caressed her soft hair. Gradually, the image faded, and Alex opened her eyes.

She sobbed now, with joy and relief. "Thank you," she whispered.

The archangel nodded, then sat down across from her, handing her a white handkerchief. "Now, what are we going to do about Vikar?"

That stopped her sobbing and brought her up short. "What do you mean?"

"Do you love him?"

"With all my heart."

"Would you give up your former life to be with him?"

Alex wasn't sure what he meant by that, but if he meant, would she stay here at the castle, there was no question. "Yes."

"Would you die for him? If asked, would you give your life for his?" It wasn't a question she'd ever considered before, but again the answer came quickly. "Yes. Of course."

"So be it!" Michael pronounced, whatever that meant. Then, in a normal tone of voice, which couldn't possibly be heard outside this room, he said, "Vikar, come here."

Within moments, Vikar knocked on the door and entered. His worried glance went from her tear-streaked face to the archangel.

"I believe you have a question to ask your lady, do you not?" St. Michael prodded Vikar. Her lovely Viking might not be aware of it, but the archangel loved him, Alex could tell.

With an expression of sudden understanding, Vikar went down on one knee before Alex, took her hand in his, and said, "Alexandra Kelly, will you marry me?"

"What? Oh my heavens! Get up off your knees.

You're embarrassing me." Then she noticed the serious expression on his face. "You're serious?"

Almost immediately, Vikar added, "Never mind. I shouldn't have blurted it out like that. I take it back."

"You can't take back a marriage proposal," she told him.

The archangel was shaking his head at Vikar's hopelessness. "Vikings!" he muttered under his breath, and walked out of the room, motioning with a wave of his hand that they should continue without him.

Vikar looked puzzled. "I haven't told you about the conditions Mike has set. If we marry, your life would be tied to mine forevermore, or as long as I live. If I am a vangel for another hundred years, you would live another hundred years. If I die tomorrow, you would die, too."

Now Alex was the one with her brow furrowed with puzzlement.

"Let me see if I understand. You've been given permission to marry me, and I'll become immortal, sort of, but it would be as if I were an appendage to you, sort of. Is that right?"

"Sort of," he said. "So, will you marry me?"

"That is the lamest marriage proposal I have ever heard."

"Is that a no, then?" His shoulders slumped with dejection. He was still kneeling on the floor.

"That's a hell, yes. Not to the appendage business, but we can discuss terms later. *My* terms."

"I knew you would say yes," Vikar said then, after standing and drawing her up into his embrace.

"Yeah, right," she said. "Hey, what woman

wouldn't jump at the chance for her own personal fountain of youth?"

His shoulders slumped again. "That is why you agreed? Not because you love me?"

"I didn't hear *you* say anything about love, Vikar," she pointed out.

He frowned. "I didn't say that I love you? I must have. I asked you to wed with me. Of course I love you."

"Then, yes, yes, yes."

Sometimes the bumps on the road to happiness are BIG ones . . .

Alex was blissfully happy for the next few weeks.

She and Vikar discussed ad nauseam all the implications of her marrying him.

"I like the idea of being with you for a long time," she told him, "as long as you don't make me into a vampire."

"You won't be a vampire, but you have to understand that I could die tomorrow."

"If you really must know, there was a time when I contemplated suicide. Oh, don't worry, it was just a blip of an idea when I was at my lowest point. I'm willing to chance it."

"It's a risk I don't like putting on you. Besides, long life gets boring after the first hundred years."

"I would never get bored with you," she said, and ran a fingertip up his bare arm, from wrist to the edge of his T-shirt.

"There is that," he said, winking at her.

She melted when he winked at her.

And he knew it, she could tell by the twinkle in his blue eyes.

"Besides, you will be extra careful when you have me to come home to."

"There is that, too," he agreed, and ran his fingertip up her bare arm, and in her case up to her shoulder since she was wearing a tank top in the excessive heat. He smiled when he noticed the goose bumps he'd created. "I love your goose bumps almost as much as your freckles."

In the end, she'd made him propose again. And she accepted again. They were waiting for a few weeks, just in case Michael would be able to return for the ceremony.

The three archangels had returned for the second day of Reckoning and stayed until nightfall when all their work was done. For now. How they'd gotten to Rome and returned so fast defied human explanation. Alex wasn't even trying.

She and Vikar had decided not to engage in any sex, near or otherwise, until the wedding. No sense taking a chance that Michael might change his mind.

Now she and Vikar were alone at the castle, or as alone as they could be with twenty-seven others. All the brothers had left with their numerous vangels, off on various "saving humans" or "destroying Lucies" assignments. Vikar could be given a mission on a moment's notice, as well. So Alex bided her time and tried not to worry. Too much. She also tried her best to hide her fears from Vikar, not wanting to spoil this short engagement period.

She'd told Ben about her engagement, and he'd been apoplectic at first, wanting to come immediately and "rescue" her. But when she assured him how much she and Vikar loved each other and how happy she was, he gave his blessings, with reservations.

As much as she would have liked him and Gloria to come to the wedding, she knew that was impossible, and she made excuses for why he couldn't come. Even so, the Mercado trial was coming up soon, and Vikar was coming with her to D.C. They planned to have a short honeymoon in the capital, with a quick trip to the Jersey shore, as well. She promised Ben that he would get to meet her husband then.

But then there was a change of plans.

A few days after her phone call to Ben, her editor called, all excited, telling her to turn on the TV. The two Mercado brothers had been murdered outright as they walked from the prison van into the courthouse for a preliminary trial meeting. The assassin or assassins hadn't been caught yet. Speculation abounded that their own drug cartel had killed them to avoid any possibility of a plea deal. Alex had other ideas.

"Did you have something to do with this?" she demanded of Vikar once she'd located him in the dungeon where he was training some new vangels in weaponry. They had a real gun range in the basement.

Once he understood what she was talking about, Vikar denied any involvement. "But I cannot be unhappy about this turn of events," he said. "Now it is done. You can truly put the past behind you."

Alex wasn't so sure about that, although plans for revenge had been out of her mind for some time now. Whether that was due to the cleansing of her blood, or her happiness with Vikar, Alex couldn't be sure. All she knew was that the fate of her child's murderers was in other hands now.

"That means we won't be going to Washington to visit Ben, doesn't it?" Vikar had put down his pistol and pulled her into an embrace. How was it that he could sense when she needed a hug?

"I'll have to go sometime, though," she said. "I can't just let my condo sit empty forever. I should probably sell it."

He nodded. "But methinks you should hold off on selling your cottage on the bay. I have a yearning to go asailing with you one day."

"We could do that." She reached up and kissed him on the cheek. "Have I told you lately that I love you?"

He glanced at his wristwatch. "Not in the past hour."

They smiled at each other. This love between them was so new they couldn't stop touching each other. And smiling.

"I better go up and call Ben back."

"I'll be up soon. I need to shower. Wouldst care to wash my back?" He waggled his eyebrows at her.

The change in Vikar's demeanor of late, so light-hearted and happy, warmed her heart. Especially when she considered that she was responsible, at least in part, for the change. She waggled her eyebrows back at him. "Only if you'll reciprocate."

A short time later, she was on the phone with Ben.

"Awful as it is to say, I'm glad the Mercado brothers are dead," she told Ben.

"Me too. I was afraid you were going to do something crazy."

I might have. "Anyhow, I'd still like to work for *World Gazette*. Freelance, if that's possible."

"Of course. I'll pass along any assignments that might interest you. *Will* there be a story there in Transylvania? God, I can't say that name without grinning."

"Same here." She considered a moment, then said, "There's definitely a story here, Ben. Stories, actually. The town would be an easy, light feature, of course. An upbeat tale of a depressed town turning itself around. Plus humor. Did you get the shirt I sent you?"

"Yes, and Gloria thanks you for the blood jam."

Alex smiled to herself. Amazing the products this enterprising town produced. Not just the jams. But specially bottled drinks, like Blood-Aid, Blood Rush, Blood Bull, Drac's Brew. And vampire's blood sausage. Ground Chuck, Bill, and Ed. Fang candy. "Anyhow, the castle could be a feature in itself. People love renovation stories, and a castle in the middle of Pennsylvania, even more."

"Send me pictures, Alex."

"I will. Plus I told you about that Amish farmer who stored all this furniture for fifty years. I know the Amish have been overdone, but everywhere you turn, there is a new angle."

"Like the Amish casket maker you told me about?"

"Right."

"What about your fiancé's family. He's a Lord something or other, isn't he?"

Alex hesitated, in shaky water now. "I'm not so sure about doing a story on Vikar's 'family.' Not that they aren't interesting"—*more like unbelievable*—"but they like their privacy."

"Objectivity, Alex," he reminded her.

"Objectivity versus privacy," she countered. "My privacy, as well as Vikar's."

"I still think I should come out there and see exactly what's going on."

"Maybe later, Ben. Not yet. Wait until we're done with the renovations."

Those renovations might be ongoing for years and years. But then, she could conceivably be around for ages, literally. She didn't like to think of that aspect of her new life. One day at a time was her new motto.

Unfortunately, that day came way too soon.

The next morning, about five a.m., Svein knocked lightly on the door and came into their bedroom. She and Vikar slept together, without sex. Vikar said he was earning his wings the hard way.

Vikar was instantly awake, asking, "What is it?" He stood and pulled on a pair of sweatpants even before he got his answer.

"It's Armod," Svein said.

Alex clicked on the bedside lamp, and the expression on Svein's face terrified her.

"What?" Vikar demanded.

"The boy snuck out last night. To meet that cashier down at the Uni-Mart. They went to a Michael Jackson revue over at the university."

Alex knew that big-name concerts came to the Bryce Jordan Center at Penn State, and she'd been aware of the revue being planned for this weekend, a mixture of old video clips and Michael Jackson impersonators. But Armod had been denied permission to attend when he'd asked Vikar. He was still too new a vangel to control himself, Vikar had told him.

"What happened?" Vikar prodded.

"The girl came back alone, battered and bruised. Fang marks on her neck. And"—Svein gulped—"she had a note. One of those 'To Whom It May Concern' things."

"Tell me." Alex could tell by Vikar's stony expression that he already suspected what had happened.

"Jasper has him."

Greater love hath no man . . .

Vikar was in the chapel, praying. For Armod. For himself. And for Alex, whose life would once more be devastated by the loss of a loved one.

Vikar had to exchange himself for Armod. After all, Vikar had been responsible for Armod during this training period. He should have been aware of his doings. And now . . .

Vikar had done all the talking and brainstorming and arguing with his brothers that he was going to do. In fact, he'd ordered them not to come back to Transylvania under any circumstances.

No one knew precisely where Jasper's headquarters were hidden. If Michael knew, he wasn't telling them, and, in fact, there was only one time in their history when the archangel had intervened on their behalf. It had been a particularly egregious act of Jasper's involving a nunnery. After that, Michael had sworn he would never enter that devil's domain again.

So, not knowing where Jasper had taken Armod, the only other alternative was to draw him or his minions out, as they'd done on the Canadian mountain. Even with Jasper's troops vastly diminished after the Sin Cruise, the head Lucipire would undoubtedly have some of his soldiers patrolling that area.

But what would such a fight accomplish? More deaths, possibly including some of their own vangels? And still no news of Jasper's hideout, unless they managed to capture one of the Lucies and torture the information out of the beast. How long would that take? By then, Armod would have been subjected to days, maybe even weeks, of unspeakable acts.

No, Vikar had to offer himself in Armod's place. He would go to the Canadian mountaintop where he would spread his scent about, and wait. He would let it be known that he was prepared to destroy every last one of them in battle, or he would lay down his arms for Armod's return.

Thankfully, he had not yet married Alex. Much as he would miss having the long life with her that he'd anticipated, at least she would not die on his death.

In the meantime, he'd locked himself in the chapel by himself for the past hour so that Svein and Jogeir and the others could not harangue him anymore. He would leave his parting with Alex for last. Her weeping was a knife to the heart that he could not bear at the moment.

What he was about to do would require all the strength, physically and mentally and spiritually, that he could garner. He feared he would be too weak.

Even now, with less than twenty hours in the hands of Jasper's beasts, Armod would have suffered unimaginable torture. He might never recover, even if released today.

Once Vikar entered Horror, and Armod left, Vikar knew that he would never return to the castle. Not that he had any hopes that his end would come soon. Jasper would want to torture him endlessly until he renounced God and became one with the Lucipires.

Alex did not know the full extent of Jasper's depravities. There was that to be thankful for.

Michael was surprisingly silent in the face of this disaster. Was Vikar to take his silence as approval for what he was about to do? Or disapproval?

Vikar made the sign of the cross and left the chapel. He shook hands with some of the vangels, was surprised to see a distraught Miss Borden, who kept swiping at her eyes with her apron, and gave quick hugs to Svein and Jogeir. The latter two, he'd instructed to take over his duties until Michael assigned one of his brothers to the castle headquarters. And now for Alex.

Grabbing his cloak, he walked outside and found her in the gazebo. He was well-armed under the cloak in case the Lucies chose to fight, rather than barter.

"Alex, heartling," he said, drawing her up into his arms.

"I won't say good-bye to you. I won't!" she declared.

He shrugged.

Her refusal to say the words was a moot gesture. "I am so sorry to put you through this, my love, but I cannot be sorry for the time we have had together."

"I love you. I will always love you. Maybe we'll

meet again . . . on the other side. No, no, no! I am not going to think like that. You *will* come back."

"Don't do this to yourself." He kissed her wet cheeks, stroking damp strands of hair off her face. "This is the end. There is something you must do for me, though. When Armod comes back, reassure him that this was not his fault. It was meant to be."

"Bullshit! It was not meant to be! Oh, don't worry. I won't make Armod feel bad, but you putting yourself in that monster's claws is not predestined. Dammit! I don't want—"

"Shh! I must go now." He kissed her one last time.

"I'll pray for you," she said, even as he was disappearing.

And then he was gone, to that mountaintop in Canada to await his entry into Hell . . . or Horror. Same thing.

Eighteen

**Where's heavenly intervention
when you need it? . . .**

St. Michael the Archangel was getting royally pissed. Or was that heavenly pissed? Regardless, he was mightily annoyed.

Why were all these people bothering him? Vangels to the right of him. Vangels to the left of him. And one particular human female who had just called him a vulgar word. He wasn't even sure if he had one of those anymore.

Did they think he had nothing to do but cater to their every whim? Pray, pray, pray! But did they ever pray to thank him for all the things he'd done for them? No! Just complain, complain, complain.

In a whoosh of feathery wings, he shot himself down to earth and that castle in the Pennsylvania hills. "Well?" he shouted.

Two dozen vangels came running, along with the woman of the foul mouth. Their jaws dropped open, except the foolish female, who put her hands on her hips and raged, "It's about time!"

"What would you have me do?"

"Save him!" twenty-eight voices yelled as one, including the cook, who was waving a cleaver in the air.

"Send me back in his place," demanded Armod, which was a ridiculous notion. Even after a week, the boy could barely walk.

"No, me," Svein and Jogeir said. The last straw . . . rather, feather . . . was when the woman said, "Either send me to help him . . ."

He arched one brow, wondering what help she thought she could be.

". . . or kill us both."

He arched both brows now.

"Please," the woman begged. "The Bible says, Ask and you shall receive."

"That phrase is open to interpretation." And much overused by people seeking favors, in his opinion.

"Grant this favor, and I'll go back to church. I'll pray every day. I'll—"

"Enough!" He raised a halting hand. There was nothing worse than a human trying to bribe an angel. "I'll see what I can do."

Michael had sworn never to enter Horror again after that last time eight hundred years ago when he'd gone to give Jasper a warning from God about his stalking a nunnery in Switzerland. Not that Jasper had heeded the message.

"Thank you, thank you, thank you," the woman wept, dropping to her knees with relief.

"I did not say I would save him," he was quick to add. After a week in Jasper's clutches, he doubted there would be much of Vikar to save, anyhow.

Moments later, he stood outside Jasper's unholy cave and inhaled deeply to prepare himself for what he would see. Then he let out a loud bellow that nigh shook the earth. "JASPER! Come forth and speak to God's messenger."

And he got an unholy response, "Go to Hell!"

Michael was annoyed before, now he was feather-flying, thunderbolt-throwing, sword-wielding furious. He went in swinging.

Hell hath no fury like an archangel scorned . . .

Vikar had been in Horror for only a week, but it felt like a century. Every minute of the days had been filled with the most abominable torture. All 10,080 of them.

He'd thought that having every bone in his body broken was bad enough, but the disgusting things they did to his phallus and anus, the things they stuck in his mouth . . . they defied torture. An abomination, that's what they were.

And the poor victims he saw about him drew his pity, even if these had been dreadful sinners before arriving here. In particular, he was repelled by what was being done to the woman placed in a glass vat of snakes. Hundreds of them. She had been taken out after several hours, on to other tortures, but then she was placed in the snake "pit" again. Over and over, this agony was repeated until now the woman's eyes were permanently frozen wide open with insanity.

But even that had not been the worst. Today they brought out a giant cross and crucified Vikar, with his hands and feet nailed to the wood. No sword through the heart, though, and no draining of all blood from his body. No, that might have killed him, and they did not want that.

Until Vikar renounced God and agreed to join them, this torture would continue. He prayed he could stay strong until the end. The only thing that kept him going was thoughts of Alex. In his mind, he replayed every contact he'd had with her, from the day she knocked fiercely on his front door to his final farewell. Every word exchanged. The kisses. The near-sex. The smiles and laughter. He could swear he had the scent of her in his nostrils to bar the evil smells around him.

Jasper was especially incensed because Vikar had destroyed his longtime assistant, the giant mung Sabeam. Apparently, one of his bullets had nicked the demon's heart.

Just then, the walls of the cave shook and he heard a familiar voice call out "JASPER!"

Michael?

"Lucipires! Your end is near! How dare you, Jasper? How dare you?" The voice seemed to come from a distance, outside the cave, but still the stone walls reverberated with its echo.

Michael was here? Why? What did it mean? Michael had sworn long ago that he would never again enter this particular devil's domain. *Am I dead?*

Vikar wondered. *Have I passed over and not realized I am gone from this world? Is Tranquillity just around the corner? When will this agonizing pain end?*

The evil leader of the Lucipires came running out of his office. "Did you hear that?" he shouted to his new assistant, Eglan, a hordling who quivered every time Jasper came near. "Get that damn VIK off the cross. And gather our new demon vampires. Hurry. We must leave."

"But . . . but . . . will we not fight this person who shouts outside the cave?" Eglan asked. "It is only one man."

Jasper swatted the hordling with an arm. "Are you daft? That is not a man. That is Michael. An archangel."

Putting a hand to his face where Jasper had hit it, Eglan persisted. Hordlings were known to have small brains and little sense. "There are fifty or more of us. Why can't we—"

"It would take a hundred and fifty of us to fight Michael, you blithering idiot." Jasper was stuffing gold bars and various weapons into a leather satchel while his other Lucies were scurrying about, opening locked killing jars and restraints on torture tables to grab victims to take with them.

Eglan was struggling with a pair of huge pliers, trying to remove the spikes from Vikar's feet.

Vikar had not thought his pain could be any more excruciating. He'd been wrong. For a moment, he blacked out.

By the time he awakened to the sound of screams at the cave entrance, about a hundred yards away, Eglan had managed to remove only one nail.

"Hurry up!" Jasper yelled when he saw how little progress his assistant had made.

For a long, shocking moment, Vikar saw Jasper considering whether he should chop off his hands with the sword at his side, to get him quickly off the cross. But Vikar was up too high for Jasper's sword to reach.

"Thank you, God!" Vikar prayed. He'd done a lot of that, praying, the past week.

Frustrated at the possibility of losing a captive VIK, and muttering something about "Not enough time," Jasper then took a long pole and slammed it against Vikar, breaking his nose once again and cracking his cheekbone. "We will meet again, you irritating sonofabitch."

By the time thunder crashed and lightning hit the earth above the cave, causing a massive crevice to open in front of Vikar, there was not a single Lucie or Lucie victim left in the cave. Except for Vikar. And dozens of writhing snakes that came crawling from the open vat.

Vikar could barely see out of eyes that were swollen almost totally shut. Blinking several times, he finally managed to make out the giant angel who stood before him, wings widespread, a sword in one arm and a lance in the other. Anger had turned his face into a granite mask.

Was it Jasper who drew the archangel's fury, or Vikar for taking matters into his own hands by exchanging himself for Armod. But then Vikar noticed the oddest thing. Tears streamed down the angel's face.

For me? Vikar tilted his head in confusion, and even that slight movement had his head nigh exploding.

"Who else, Viking?" Michael answered his unspoken question.

Vikar felt tears burn in his own bruised eyes.

Michael dropped his lance to the ground and raised his broadsword high.

Vikar braced himself for the blow that was about to come. Now he understood the angel's tears. Vikar's life as a vangel was about to end.

The sword was swung in a wide arc, but not at Vikar's body. Instead, it cleaved the cross near its base. In a flash of movement, Michael caught the cross on its way down, laying it gently on the dirt floor. Staring down at Vikar, the archangel said, "You are no longer pretty, I fear."

"You, on the other hand, are a sight for these sore eyes," Vikar commented. Just that amount of speaking caused his cracked lips to open and bleed once again. He could not care about that. Michael had come for him, and was kneeling over his tortured body, removing the big nails from his hands. Eglan had already taken the one out of his crossed feet. "You will have scars," he remarked idly.

Vikar was confused. Why would it matter what scars he had on the Other Side? Just then, another thought occurred to him.

"Do not be any more of a fool than you already are," Michael said as he picked him up gently and began to carry him from the cave.

As careful as Michael was, the pressure of his body against the archangel's embrace caused Vikar such unbearable pain that he lost consciousness, again. But only for a short time.

When he drifted awake, he found himself standing on the edge of the cliff outside the cave. He swayed on his feet, the bottoms of which had been flailed raw. As awful as he felt, he could feel the broken bones in his body beginning to heal.

"We will have to fly, but I think you are too heavy for me to carry," Michael said, an odd tone in his voice.

Vikar tilted his heavy head to the side, but then almost fell over as he stumbled. The bumps on his shoulder blades were afire. And, holy clouds! There were wings, big freakin' wings with at least an eight-foot span, growing out from his back.

Michael took his hand then and they both rose from the ground, wings fluttering in the gentle breeze. Soon they were soaring high above.

"Shall we go home now, Viking?" Michael asked.

Vikar nodded, but he wasn't exactly sure which home Michael meant. A few moments later, when he recognized the land below and the castle on the hill in Transylvania, Vikar's heart began to beat wildly. He turned in question to his sky partner.

"Your work is not yet done here, Viking."

Look homeward, angel . . .

They were all crammed into the chapel, and had been for the past two hours, ever since Michael had left them. Praying silently. Many of them weeping, but not Alex, who was convinced that the archangel would come through for her.

Where did this faith come from? When did I start to trust in a higher being?

She was not surprised, therefore, when there

was the sound of wings overhead. She smiled as she followed the crowd through the house, across the kitchen, out to the backyard. Her smile died quickly when she saw the two figures that had landed.

Landed!

There were two angels there. Michael, and another angel, a naked one, who landed on his feet, then stumbled and fell forward on his face.

"He's not used to his wings yet," Michael explained with an amused wink.

Did an archangel just wink at me?

"You should have seen him almost miss the top of that evergreen at the bottom of the lane. Talk about brush burns!" Michael rolled his eyes.

First winks, now rolling eyes. What next?

The other angel's wings started to retract and Michael rolled him gently onto his back.

Alex put a hand to her mouth to stifle her cry. This poor creature had been beaten and cut badly. The whole face was a swollen blob. The Pillsbury Doughboy, but worse. There wasn't an inch of skin, head to toe, that wasn't bloody, broken, or bruised. Alex hurt just looking at the poor man . . . or angel . . . or whatever he was.

Where is Vikar?

Alex felt awful thinking of herself when this man had been hurt so badly, but she couldn't help herself. As the others helped the man to his feet . . . in fact, Svein and Jogeir lifted him so his arms straddled their shoulders and his feet were off the ground . . . she walked up to Michael and tugged on the sleeve of his white belted gown. "Please? Is there any news of Vikar?"

He arched his brows at her. "No foul names for me now?"

"I'm sorry for that. But I've been so worried. I *am* so worried. Did you . . . did you find him?"

"Child," Michael chided her, then turned to glance at the poor man/angel who was staring at her through the bare slits of his eyes. His cracked lips were working as if he wanted to speak, but couldn't.

"Oh. My. God!" she whimpered. It was Vikar. She reached out for him, but was afraid to touch him for fear of increasing his pain.

"Ugly . . . now," Vikar gasped out.

"Oh, you foolish man!" she said. "Your beauty is from the inside."

He tried to laugh, but it came out as a gurgle.

"I told you so, Viking. Pride ever was your downfall, and all for naught," Michael pronounced, and he was gone before Alex even had a chance to thank him.

Later, they had Vikar in his bed, washed and medicated. She'd fed him some of her own blood to help rejuvenate him. It wasn't nearly enough, so each of his brothers, who'd arrived posthaste, gave him some, as well. Sigurd said it would probably take weeks for his body to heal. Even then he would probably have scars and possibly a crooked nose. Maybe even a limp. None of that mattered to her. He was back, that was the most important thing.

"Sit with me," he urged as he was drifting off to sleep.

She sat down on the edge of the bed, touching only the tips of her fingers to his hand, still careful of hurting his battered body. Before he fell asleep, she had one question to ask: "Are you a real angel now?"

He smiled, a grotesque, adorable lift of his lips on one side, and said, "Your angel. Only yours."

How do you say "I do" in Old Norse? . . .

It took two months for Vikar to heal, and his body would never be quite what it had been before. Alex didn't care. He was alive.

Besides, maybe being a mite less gorgeous would be a good thing. That never-ending pride weakness of Vikar's.

Besides, Alex thought the bump on his nose gave him character, and his brothers claimed to envy the scars on his hands and feet, surely signs that he was marked as special. Otherwise, he had regained most of his strength, and his skin color was more than healthy with all the blood Alex had been giving him on a regular basis.

As for the wings . . . Vikar told her that he wasn't ready to be an *angel* angel. Viking vampire angel was enough for him. And flying? Whoa! That had been scary for him, to say the least, and not just because of that close call with a tree. He loved retelling the story over and over to his brothers, each time with a little extra embellishment.

During this time of recovery, because of his weakened state, or so he tried to claim, Vikar agreed to marry her soon. Alex had worked her wiles on him mercilessly. *Who knew I even had wiles before this?*

She didn't care what he said about the risks. To her, the bigger risk was not having him as her husband, even if for a short time.

So here she was on her wedding day, waiting for the ceremony to begin, and she couldn't be happier. She had no idea if the wedding would be legal by modern standards, but it had to be the only wedding in history performed by an archangel. Michael had come back specially for them.

"Why are you smiling?" Vikar asked. They were standing on the back verandah, waiting for the call to come forward to the gazebo that had been transformed into an altar.

At least a hundred vangels were standing outside, not wanting to miss this momentous event. It wasn't often that vangels married, and it had never happened with one of The Seven.

"I'm happy," she replied to his question, and her happiness wasn't just because they were marrying. When Michael had shown her the image of her daughter, it was as if a shutter had come down on the horror of her past. She was only looking forward now. A long ways, she hoped.

And no way could she think of the archangel as Mike, as the vangels did. It was too irreverent. When she'd voiced that opinion to Vikar, he'd replied that Vikings were known for their irreverence. He said it as if that was a good thing.

"Are you sure about this?" he asked now, taking her hand and kissing her knuckles.

"Absolutely."

"But if I die, you will, too."

"That's all right."

"But it could happen tomorrow. There is no guarantee that we will share a long life."

"Stop worrying," she said, squeezing his hand.

"There will be no children," he reminded her.

"Stop it, will you? We've discussed all this. You and all your vangels will be my family. It is enough."

"Do not deny that you would have liked babies."

She tilted her head in concession. "I had already decided not to have any more children, after Linda, but, with you, I would have liked to make a baby." She shook her head to rid it of the sweet possibilities: a little blond boy with her green eyes, or a pretty strawberry-blonde-haired girl with his rascally blue eyes. "Honestly, sweetie, the compromise I'm making is worth it. Please, let's not discuss this ever again."

He was the one tilting his head in concession now.

"You look very handsome today," she said.

He winked at her, as if to say, *Of course.* He wore a navy-blue suit with a pale blue shirt that brought out the brightness in his eyes. His tie was a special purchase of hers, blue angel wings on a white background, that she'd found on her quick trip to town, where she'd bought the perfect wedding dress. A cream-colored lace cocktail dress, tight to the waist, then flowing out in increasingly bigger flounces, one covering the other, down to her calves, with matching shoes. In her hair, she wore a garland of flowers that Armod had found at a farmers' market, miniature pink roses and baby's breath.

"You are the most beautiful bride I have ever seen," he countered. At the look of adoration on his face, she could almost believe it was true.

And then it was time.

Michael wore a long white garment with a rope belt. Very plain. About his neck hung a heavy gold crucifix. And his wings were out, fully. On either side of Michael stood Vikar's six brothers and Armod, who looked gorgeous in formal suits. Even Armod, who had put aside his Michael Jackson attire for the day. Ever since his capture and release, Armod idolized Vikar in a way that Vikar found exasperating, but Alex found amusing. The boy would grow out of it eventually.

Ivak gave a low whistle at her when they got closer, and Vikar scowled at him in return. It was adorable that he could be jealous. Michael also scowled at Ivak, which caused Ivak to duck his head sheepishly, but not with any significant remorse.

The wedding ritual that followed was a conservative one, even a bit sexist in the love, honor, and obey vein, but Alex couldn't mind. She and Vikar knew what they were promising each other. At one point, Vikar slipped a gold signet ring onto her finger, a smaller replica of the one he and his brothers wore with the winged emblem. Afterward Michael gave them his blessing and left in a poof of feathers.

If they'd had more time, Vikar would have liked to incorporate more Norse elements into their wedding. Not the pagan rituals, but some of the traditional things, he said. Alex was happy the way it turned out, though. Simplicity had its own charm.

To the cheers of his fellow angels, Vikar kissed his bride and led her toward the verandah where Lizzie had prepared a sumptuous wedding breakfast to be held outdoors on folding tables that were already being set up. A small band of vangels was prepared to entertain them later. Who knew? Viking vampire angel rockers.

"You know what happens next, don't you?" Vikar whispered in her ear.

"The *brudr-hlaup*," she said with a yelp, running toward the castle in the bride running, a Viking practice Vikar had told her about.

The lout arrived at the doorway before her, though, unencumbered by high heels as he was. He stood leaning against the door with his sword drawn. Holding her eyes, he laid the weapon across the threshold and said with a twinkle in his dancing blue eyes, "Once you cross this sword, you are mine to do with as I will."

"Is that so? Maybe I'll start a new tradition. When I step over this threshold, you are mine to do with as I will."

"Works for me," he said, smacking her on the rump lightly with the flat side of his sword after she jumped the threshold.

What followed was a rip-roaring Viking feast. Nothing vampiric or angelic about the vast amounts of beer; roast Angus beef (no boar being available); hard rock, country, and even some Michael Jackson music; and dancing. With the dearth of women, some men had to dance together, and wasn't that a sight to behold? Big hulking Norsemen trying to follow Ivak's steps in learning to line dance.

Midway through the feast, when it was only three p.m., Vikar yawned widely and winked at his wife. "Methinks it is time for the real celebration to begin."

His brothers, no fools, hooted with laughter.

She wasn't fooled, either. "Oh? More beer?"

He winked at her. "No, foolish wench, I am about to show you the famous Viking S-spot."

**A hard-on is a hard-on,
even when a century-old one . . .**

Vikar had an "enthusiasm" that had been building for, oh, a hundred years. The "thickening" might very well drag on the floor if he were not so tall, he thought with a Viking bridegroom's right to overexaggeration on his wedding night.

The skalds could no doubt write a saga about it.

Or not.

"You're laughing," Alex said against his ear, then stuck the tip of her tongue into the whorls, just to tease him.

"Witch!" He almost stumbled as he continued to carry her up the stairway to his bedchamber.

After he set her down on her feet and gave her a quick kiss, they both burst out laughing. Who said Vikings weren't romantic?

About the bedchamber his vangels had arranged numerous candles and vases of cut flowers. Armod must have been especially busy at that flower mart. He hoped that's where he'd gotten them. Bodil would have a flying fit if the boy had cut any of the precious roses he'd planted outside. In addition, a bottle of champagne cooled in an ice bucket. He would have preferred a hearty mead, but the sentiment was appreciated. In addition, someone . . . he assumed Lizzie . . . had laid out a tray of food, what modern folks called finger foods. Cheese, crackers, and such. The appetite he intended to work up would hardly be appeased by such meager fare, but again he appreciated the sentiment.

"I bought a special negligee," Alex said as she walked about the room, sniffing the various bouquets.

When would women realize that the greatest aphrodisiac for a man is skin? "Save it for another day. My hunger for you is too great. I would no doubt rip it off."

She laughed. "Promises, promises."

"Dost not know yet, wench, to never challenge a Viking?"

"Oh, really?" She started to walk on her deliciously high heels across the room away from him, giving her hips a little jiggle that caused the flounces of her garment to . . . flounce? It was like a flag afore a raging bull. He planned to make her do that sexy, rump-wagging walk again later. Naked.

Then she had the nerve to tell him, with a saucy glance over her shoulder, "By the way, did I tell you I'm not wearing any underwear?"

That did it! With a laugh, he made his way to her with a whoosh . . . one of the advantages of being a vangel . . . picked her up by the waist, and had her back up against the wall, feet dangling, afore she could blink.

Did she cower then? Or acquiesce? No, she put her arms around his shoulders and straddled his hips, pressing her mons up against his thickening.

His knees almost gave way.

Lifting the hem of her dress, he ran his hands up the sides of her bare legs to her buttocks, which were indeed uncovered. Then he checked the waistline. Betimes modern women fooled men by wearing those thong garments, but no, his new wife was totally unclothed down below.

He grinned and nipped at her chin. "You exchanged vows bare-arse naked in front of an archangel?"

She grinned back. "I took my panties and stockings off when we were back in the house. Ivak gave me the idea."

"Ivak? I'll kill him. Well, not kill him, of course, but I will hurt him. Make him less comely to women."

"Why? You don't like me to be ready for you?"

"Ah, sweetling, I love that you are ready for me, but I do not relish my brother making such a suggestion."

"I was kidding," she said. Then, "The question is: Are you ready for me?"

"Do you doubt it?" With a modicum of effort, his thickening was free and raised between them, thanks to that wonderful modern invention, the zipper.

Alex glanced down and raised a brow. "A blue steeler? For me?"

"Who else?" But wait. If this woman thought she was running this show, he had a fjord to sell her in the Arab lands. Tucking himself back inside his braies, carefully, the zipper being both a convenience and a possible enthusiasm killer, he set her back on her high-heeled feet. At the confusion on her face, he said, "I want this night to be special. I've waited too long to have it end with one thrust."

"You sweet talker, you!" she remarked with a smile, then sat down in a wingback chair near the window and crossed her legs, giving him an ample view of her thigh up to what Armod's favorite singer called Neverland. "Something special, huh? Okay, baby, show me everything special in your repertoire."

Repertoire. He would show her repertoire. "I love you, Alex," he said then.

"Back at you, sweetheart. A hundredfold." She was rocking the foot of her upper leg backward and forward, the shoe dangling from her toes. Did she do it deliberately, or was she as aroused as he was? The latter, he suspected.

He walked over to the dresser and pressed the button on a music player someone had left there. Immediately, a raw male voice began crooning something about "Let's Get It On."

"Marvin Gaye?" she hooted.

He shrugged. "I would not know one singer from another. 'Tis my brothers' doing." He reached out to turn it off.

"Don't you dare," she ordered.

He arched a brow at her.

"That is quintessential make-out music. More panties have been dropped to that song than you could imagine."

"That could very well be, but Vikings have other methods."

"Like raping and pillaging?"

"I have decided that you will owe me a bounty every time you make that ridiculous accusation in future." And he had some very graphic ideas of what those bounties would entail.

She didn't look at all daunted by that threat. In fact, she grinned.

He took off his jacket and laid it over the dresser behind him. He loosened the constricting tie at his neck, only then noticing her lips part as she watched him closely. Hmm. Slowly, very slowly, he undid the buttons on his shirt, then eased it off his shoulders, letting it drop to the floor.

Her pink tongue peeked out, and she licked her lips. It was an unconscious movement, not deliberately designed to entice.

But he was enticed nonetheless. Any more enticed and he would be embarrassing himself like an untried youthling.

Still leaning back against the dresser, he toed off one black loafer, then another.

"You're not wearing any socks," she pointed out.

"I forgot. When I was getting ready for our wedding, I was a bit excited. Mordr had to remind me to put on a tie."

"Mordr?"

He understood her surprise. Mordr was not usually concerned about fashion.

"I love your feet," she said.

"Huh?" he glanced downward, not about to tell her that Mordr had also said he needed a pedicure, which Dagmar had luckily offered to provide. Until then, he hadn't even known what a pumice stone was.

"Your feet are lovely. Long and narrow with high arches. Manly."

Of course they are manly. What else would they be? Dainty little toes and heels to support my big frame? "Thank you." Then he quickly added, "You have nice feet, too. Especially do I like your colored toenails."

She laughed at his lame counter-compliment.

"I am offended, though. Here I stand, bare-chested, exposing all my impressive muscles, and you admire my feet. Something is wrong with me?"

"You know there isn't. I'm trying to regulate my excitement. If I look at certain places on your body, like your chest . . . or elsewhere"—she glanced downward—"I might just jump your bones."

"Oh please, do not regulate your excitement. Please, jump my bones."

"I thought you wanted to slow things down."

"I've changed my mind. Come here, wife."

Biddable, for once, she stood and walked toward him. There were tears in her eyes.

"What? Why do you weep?" He opened his arms to her and pulled her close.

"I love you so much. We can tease each other 'til the cows come home, but I just want to make love with you and show you how much I appreciate the gift that you are."

"I was just playing, Alex. Sorry I am if that made you feel unloved."

"Silly husband! I like to play, too. But later."

He was still stuck on the cows coming home, whatever that meant, but then he realized that Alex was just saying what he felt, soul-deep. There was a time for games, and a time for the serious business of love. This was the latter. "You are my soul mate, and I am yours. It only took a thousand years for me to find you."

"Exactly, my love. Exactly."

Nineteen

Just WOW!...

Alex was lying on Vikar's big bed, totally naked. *Who knew a Viking could disrobe a woman so fast?* She watched her new husband approach, also totally naked. *Who knew I could disrobe a man so fast?*

And *wow*! It was a woman's romance novel cliché to say her man was huge, and a man's fantasy cliché to say he was well-hung, but, well, just, *wow*! Forget blue steeler. They should have a new name for ones like this. A big boy! Or hot doggy! Or a wowzer! Yeah, that's what she would call it. A wowzer!

"I am afraid to ask what that smirk on your face means, Alex."

"I'll tell you later," she said, opening her arms to him.

He arranged himself gently atop her, his wowzer nestled between her already spread thighs. Leaning down to kiss her, he was extra careful not to

·

scrape her with his fangs, a fact of vangel life when aroused.

They kissed. And kissed. And kissed some more. In between they whispered endearments, or love words, or just murmurs of sweet pleasure. The kisses were wonderful, slow-building prods to an already high arousal. She squirmed beneath him, wanting more, but acquiescing when he whispered, "Let me." That was all. "Let me." Two simple words. But to her, they were sex personified.

Vikar adored her then, with his mouth. With his calloused fingertips. With his hairy chest. With his knees and, yes, even his toes. She adored him, too. Combing her fingers through his long hair that had side braids for his wedding intertwined with green beads. To match her eyes, he had told her. Who said Vikings didn't know how to use flowery words! She traced the muscles of his upper arms, taking delight in the arm rings he wore almost all the time, three-inch silver bands etched with angel wings. She kissed his fingers, one at a time, and then his palms.

They rolled, over, and over, and over again. When she was on top, she rubbed her slick woman's folds over his erection. When he was on top, he sucked her breasts until she climaxed.

When she was on top again, she punished him for making her come before entering her by using her tongue in his mouth, like a simulated penis. When he was on top again, he pressed her knees wide apart, braced himself on extended arms, and entered her in one long thrust.

He was too big!

He couldn't fit all the way!

Alex's eyes went wide and she gasped. It wasn't painful. It was just not enough.

But then Vikar reached between her legs from behind and did something inside her body that she could swear caused her vagina to twitch and her uterus to shift. He was in her to the hilt now.

"What . . . what did you do?"

"Shh. Later," he said, an expression of fierce concentration on his face.

Alex was filled, totally, now. Even so, her inner walls kept shifting and spasming to accommodate his size.

"Am I hurting you?" he asked in an agonized whisper.

"A little. A good hurt, though."

He smiled, or tried to smile. Lifting her legs, he set her heels on his shoulder and began the exceedingly long thrusts and withdrawals where her grasping channel provided a delicious friction, trying to hold him in. His head was arched back, his fangs extended over his tightened lips as he tried to prolong the slow journey of their mating, but he was unable to last for very long, especially when she had a second orgasm, and came around him in a gush of wetness.

"You feel like hot honey around my cock," he gasped out. "Do you taste as sweet?"

"I don't know, but if you dare to pull out I'm going to kick you where it hurts."

"Have I told you lately how much I love your fierceness?"

"Have I told you lately that you talk too much?"

He laughed and began the short, hard, pummel-

ing strokes that shoved her up against the headboard and presaged his own approaching climax.
When it came, it was with a roar of triumphant pleasure, after which he released her legs and fell on her,
almost unconscious with satiety. She did not mind
his weight that pressed her to the mattress. In fact,
she caressed his sweat-dampened shoulders, especially his angel bumps that almost seemed to throb,
like heartbeats.

Finally, he raised his head and said, with wonder,
"That was worth a hundred-year wait."

Vikings who doo-wop? . . .

Three hours later, Vikar lay stunned. He was all
fucked out. Literally.

He was a Viking. Norsemen thought they knew
everything there was to know about sex. Hah!

He'd had no idea he could make a woman ejaculate. He'd had no idea he could move a woman's
uterus with his cock. He'd had no idea he could come
to rock-hard "life" so many times, after peaking.

Thinking he would show his saucy wife a thing
or two about the lovemaking arts, he'd initiated her
into the famous Viking S-spot on her body. But, not
to be undone, she'd shown him his G-spot. Holy
clouds! Vikar had not known that men had G-spots.
Wait until he told his brothers *that*. On the other
hand, they would be wanting Alex to show them,
and he couldn't have that.

Alex slept beside him, tucked up against his
side with her face on his chest and a knee pressing

against his finally flaccid cock. He could feel her breaths against his heated skin and he could hear the pounding of her heartbeat.

But, no, the pounding he heard was coming from outside. Footsteps on grass, he guessed. Could it be Lucies?

Quickly, he jumped from the bed and grabbed for his sword. Going over to the open window, he peered outside carefully.

"Oh, good heavens!" Alex said, having come up beside him.

Outside stood his brothers and about a dozen other vangels. All of them obviously *drukkinn*, because they swayed as they tried to stand in a straight line, then burst out in song.

"Um, wah, um wah, um wah . . ." They kept chanting the odd sounds at the same time they danced two steps to the right, two steps to the left, pumping their elbows at the same time. Except Mordr kept tripping over his big feet, and Trond kept pinching some female vangel's behind . . . Regina, he was pretty sure. He'd best be careful. Regina could wield a witchly curse faster than a Lucie on speed. Suddenly, they burst out in song, "Why do fools fall in love?"

"Aren't they adorable?" Alex said.

"Huh?"

She was clapping her hands together with glee. Fortunately, she had a sheet wrapped around her body or she would be giving his vangels more than applause for appreciation.

The serenaders resumed their odd "Um, wah . . ." singing.

"What are those grunting noises they're making?"

"Don't you know anything about rock 'n' roll?"

Apparently not.

"That's classic doo-wop music. What they're singing is a famous Frankie Lymon and the Teenagers song from the 1950s."

Dwop? Teenagers? And she's pleased? "Um. That's nice," he said. Then, "How do we make them go away?"

"Don't be such a grouch."

"Kiss, kiss, kiss!" the crowd shouted when the song ended.

Gladly, he kissed Alex, but only a short kiss. He wanted his "family" gone.

When it appeared as if they were about to burst into another song, he leaned out the window.

"Hey, Vikar," Regina yelled in a shriekish voice that could peel rust off a lance. "You forgot your pants."

"Hey, Regina," he yelled back. "You forgot your broom."

But he was not about to get in a shouting match with the woman, especially when she had the power to put a curse on one of his favorite body parts. Not what a man wanted on his wedding night.

"Trond!" he shouted out. "Did I tell you there is a barrel of honeyed mead direct from the Norselands hidden in the dungeon behind those boxes of toilet paper?"

Before Vikar could finish his sentence, there was a mad scramble of all the vangels for the castle back door.

A short time later, he and Alex sat in bed drinking champagne and eating cheese atop crackers.

There would be crumbs on the sheets, but he could not care about such small discomforts. Alex had just asked him a question that stunned him.

"If I give you my blood periodically, will that be enough to sustain you?"

He nodded, slowly. "We vangels need the blood of saved humans every so often. You qualify. The Fake-O and the blood ceorls' supply, even the tanning beds, help, but they do not have sufficient nutrients to keep us from going white-skinned and eventually transparent-skinned. In the old days, it was a huge problem. We had to stay in hiding during those periods, until we were given a new assignment. Otherwise, there were vampire hunters after us, not distinguishing between good and bad vampires. I cannot tell you how many times we vangels have had stakes through our hearts, which of course did not really kill us, little did the hunters know. Still, it was inconvenient. And disgusting, truth to tell."

She was staring at him as if he'd grown two heads.

"What?"

"You've been staked?"

"Only once, but Ivak was staked a half-dozen times afore he learned to run faster."

"I really have landed in bizarroland."

He felt his heart tighten in his chest. "You have regrets?"

"Oh, Vikar, how can you ask such a question?" With a speed and efficiency he could admire, she swept the tray with their drinks and small meal aside, not caring that it bounced onto the floor and created a mess. Then she climbed atop him. Bless a woman who knew how to climb atop a man and impale herself all in one fell swoop. He had not even known he was erect. Hah! Who was he fooling? He'd been erect nonstop since he'd met her.

Wiggling her butt on his thighs, she asked, "Does it feel like I have any regrets?"

It didn't.

And at the end, when she let him feed on her neck while he peaked down below into her clutching folds, he almost wept with joy. Before the Reckoning, he'd thought his future held only bleakness. If this was the reward for a life lived well, then he truly should be spreading the word.

"I love you," he choked out.

"I love you more," she said. "And by the way, your blue wings are beautiful."

Mission not so impossible this time . . .

The following months were sheer heaven to Vikar, or as close as a vangel could get to that blissful place. Marriage agreed with him.

He was insatiable. Alex told him so repeatedly, but she was usually smiling like the cat living in a milk house when she said it. And she did let him feed on her on a regular basis, as promised. His skin had never looked so good since he became a vangel. Fanging and fucking were the most erotic combination, though Michael would cringe to hear him use such words.

Speaking of that, while the others continued to refer to the archangel as Mike, Vikar could only think of him as Michael now. Perchance in another hundred years or so of being annoyed by his celestial mentor, he would come back to that rude nickname. For now, he was only profoundly thankful.

But there was something important he had to do now, and he was not looking forward to it. "Alex, dearling," he said, coming up behind her in his office where she was trying once again to write the article for her magazine. "There is something I must tell you."

She turned abruptly, no doubt alerted by the tone of his voice. "What? No! Don't tell me. You're not going out again. Oh please, don't—"

"No! You will not interfere with my work. Just as I do not interfere with yours." He'd conceded weeks ago that he would not stand in the way of her writing. He trusted that she would do nothing to endanger the vangels in her articles.

To soften the impact of his words, though, words that had to be said, he took her hand and pulled her to her feet, giving her a quick kiss. "A short trip, Alex. No danger," he said, although truthfully he wasn't sure about that. Even though Jasper had gone underground, so to speak, and it should take a long time for him to recoup, there were no guarantees. Plus, his orders from Michael had been ambiguous to say the least: *Go to the National Naval Medical Center in Bethesda.*

She sighed, then let her stiffened shoulders slump with resignation. "I suppose I have to let you go, don't I?"

He nodded. "While I am gone, you and Dagmar can watch all those sad chicken movies on the TV."

"Chick flicks," she corrected him with a grin.

He'd known precisely what they were called. He'd just wanted to lighten her mood. In truth, it broke his heart to watch some of these movies with her, especially ones that involved children. Despite her resignation to a life with no babies or toddlers or children of any kind in evidence, he knew she felt the loss. She said having him was enough. Well, it would have to be.

"Don't take any bubble baths while I am gone, though," he advised. "You know how much I like to share."

She smiled. "When do you have to leave?"

"An hour ago."

She nodded. "Be safe, my love."

"I'll be back in time for your birthday," he said. Until Alex arrived, the vangels had little knowledge about birthing day celebrations. In fact, he and his brothers had no clue exactly when they'd been born. Now there was a big calendar in the kitchen with birthdays marked for himself and all twenty-seven of the vangels here at the castle, as well as his six brothers. If they didn't know the date, Alex gave them one.

"You better be. Lizzie promised to make a special cake for me."

"I can't wait." In truth, he was more enthused about the present he'd bought for her. It should have arrived by then. "I think you're going to like my gift for you."

"A wowzer?"

He laughed. In fact, he laughed every time he heard Alex use that ridiculous name for his cock when it was in a high enthusiasm. "That, too." What he'd meant was the fancy spa tub he'd ordered for the bathing room, one that should make her bubble baths even bubblier. And big enough for two.

"I don't need presents. Just you."

"You have me."

The Lord taketh away, and the Lord giveth . . .

Vikar entered the military hospital in Bethesda, Maryland, and bypassed the receptionist, heading straight for the elevators. He had no clue where he was going and why. Just following instincts and that annoying voice in his head that kept prodding, "Hurry!"

Alone in the elevators, he didn't bother pressing any buttons and was not surprised when the elevators stopped on a particular patient floor and the doors opened. He turned right and began to walk down a corridor, scanning open doors of patients' rooms on either side of him. Critically injured patients, by the looks of them. Finally, he stopped at one particular room. The card insert by the hospital door read: "Major Magnus Eric Sigurdsson."

Vikar's heart began to thump wildly.

"Are you family?" a passing nurse asked.

"Apparently."

When Vikar went in and saw the condition of the man lying on the bed, he knew he was not long for this life. Both legs had been amputated. Bandages covered his chest where there was presumably a wound. Bruises and cuts marred all the skin Vikar could see above the light blanket. So many machines and tubes sustained him that it was almost obscene. And, thank God, there was no lemon scent. This was a man headed for a better place. Oh, not Heaven, but Purgatory, he would guess.

A quick glance around the room showed him a uniform hanging in the closet, its drab brown color brightened by myriad bars and stripes and shiny metals. On a dresser in the room was an open case displaying a Purple Heart.

He walked closer to the bed, and the man's eyes lifted slowly. Blue . . . a very recognizable blue. Hard to tell what color his hair was since it was cut so short. The man had to be more than thirty, possibly thirty-five. He must be an army lifer to have such rank at this age.

"Jesus Christ!" the man murmured.

"I am not Him," Vikar said, trying for a note of levity in face of the unacceptable expletive.

"Hey, man, do you know that you have wings? Blue wings. Sort of wings." The man licked his cracked lips. "Holy crap! Now they're white. And huge." All those words seemed to have depleted his strength, and he sagged even more into his bed.

The blasted wings! Ever since Michael had graced him with wings, they burst out without warning. Embarrassing, really. Luckily, not everyone could see them. Otherwise, he'd be locked in a zoo somewhere. The Celestial Aviary House.

Vikar picked up a glass with a straw sitting on a bedside table. He wasn't sure if he should be giving the dying man water, but at this stage, what could it hurt? Putting a hand behind the man's neck, he lifted him slightly, and put the straw to his mouth.

He drank thirstily, then sank back with a sigh. He appeared more alert now. "Are you an angel?"

"Sort of," he repeated the man's words back at him. "In truth, I believe I am your grandfather." Of sorts.

The man tried to laugh and it came out as a cough. "Not old enough," he choked out.

"I age well, Magnus," Vikar said with a shrug.

"Call me Mag."

Vikar nodded. "I am Vikar Sigurdsson. I have no short name."

"Huh? My wife . . . my late wife. . . . Cindy . . . died last month . . . drunk driver . . . she did a genealogy. One . . . my ancestors . . . some Viking dude . . . named Vikar . . . Sigurdsson."

"That would be me."

"Am I dead?"

"Not yet." He put a hand on the man's chest and let him feel his energy. At the look of fear that flashed on the boy's face, he tried to reassure him, "You are going to a better place, Magnus. Believe me when I tell you that you have naught to worry about."

The soldier shook his head, then winced at the pain just that movement caused. "I have . . . much . . . to worry . . . about." He tried to sit up as something seemed to occur to him. His frantic movements set off an alarm, and a nurse ran into the room. "Major Sigurdsson, you must sit down."

Thankfully, his wings had retracted.

Ignoring the nurse, Magnus told Vikar, panting for breath, "Get . . . folder . . . over there . . . first drawer. And a pen."

While the nurse fiddled with the tubes and made

clucking sounds of reprimand, the soldier signed a number of different papers. Then he ordered the nurse to witness his signatures. Afterward he handed the folder to Vikar and told him to give them to a lawyer whose card was inside.

Huh? Since when did he become some stranger's messenger boy. *Not a stranger*, he reprimanded himself right away. *A descendant of my blood.*

Lying back against his pillow, exhausted by these small efforts, he said in a voice so low Vikar scarcely heard, "I prayed for help. You came. You are the answer to my prayer."

Vikar would have liked to hoot with laughter at the idea of his being the answer to anyone's prayer, but all the machines started going crazy, and Vikar was busy with the work of last rites, praying over the boy's body, helping his journey from this world to the other.

It was only later, after he'd left the hospital, that he glanced inside the folder and saw that the boy had left him a bequest. No, two bequests.

Who says miracles don't happen? . . .

Three days later, Vikar and his six brothers stood at a gravesite in Arlington National Cemetery where a military funeral fit for a hero was being conducted for one of their own. There was no family present, and only a few military comrades who spoke of his valor in the field.

When the bugle played taps, there was not a dry eye among them. The Seven all wished they'd known this brave boy.

As they walked away from the gravesite, Harek held him back. "So, are you going to accept your bequest?"

"I have no choice but to accept. You know that better than any. Still, I *am* stunned."

Harek, with his trusty laptop, had checked and found no living relatives of Major Sigurdsson, other than Vikar, assuming Vikar could really be considered blood kin. *Do thousand-year-old ties really count?* Harek had also affirmed Vikar's legal rights in accepting the bequest.

It was a happenstance Vikar had never expected when he'd left the castle three days ago on a routine mission. In the old days, he would have said the Norse jester god Loki must be playing a twisted joke on him. Today, he suspected another celestial being.

"How will Alex feel about this?"

"She'll be ecstatic." *I hope.* "Not the birthday gift I had planned, that is for sure." *Definitely no bubbles involved in this, unless they are of the blowing kind.*

That evening, still reeling with shock, Vikar arrived back at the castle, carrying his bequest. Bequests, actually, as in plural. Blessed gifts from a dying man. For a certainty, he was now convinced that Mike had to have had a hand in this. Why, Vikar couldn't imagine. Mayhap the gift was for Alex and not him.

Since his arms were full, he used an elbow to press on the doorbell. Not once. Or twice. But seven times.

Almost immediately, the double doors swung open and Alex stood there with a welcoming smile on her face. Which immediately disappeared as her jaw dropped open and her eyes went wide.

Into the stunned silence, he gave her his most winsome smile and winked. "Honey, I'm home."

She did not smile at his jest, nor did she appear to be melting at his wink, as she was wont to do.

So he tried again, nodding at first one, then the other of the now squirming bundles nestled in the crook of each arm, one of which was drooling gobs of spit onto his neck, the other reeking like a privy in high summer. "Happy birthday!"

"Wha-what?" she stuttered.

Uh-oh. Backtrack here, Vikar. Start from the beginning, you dolt, he advised himself. "Alex, I would like you to meet Gunnar and Gunnora Sigurdsson."

She put a hand on each hip and tapped a foot impatiently. Behind her, he could see his band of vangels gathering with curiosity.

"Who do they belong to?"

"You?" he offered hopefully.

Her brow furrowed with confusion.

"Us?" he amended as a concession.

Still no enthusiasm as far as he could see. In fact, she said, "Have you gone crazy?"

"I've been there for some time, as you well know," he joked.

More foot tapping. Apparently, she wasn't in a joking mood. "Where did you get them?"

"A dying soldier gave them to me."

"Vikar Sigurdsson! You really are crazy. People can't just give you babies."

Looking from one to the other of the ten-month-old mites, one of which was gnawing on Vikar's earlobe, the other sucking wildly on a tiny thumb embedded in its mouth, he shrugged. "Apparently, they can."

"The police will be on your doorstep."

"No. They will not." *Fortunately. Or is that unfortunately?* "These children are mine." *Believe it or not. Even I have trouble believing it.* "Do you not think they are sweet?" *Except for the stink.* "These are my grandchildren many, *many* times removed," he told her.

"Of course they're sweet," she exclaimed, waving a hand in front of her face to compose herself.

Which drew the attention of Gun and Nora, as he'd come to call them on the endless trip back to Pennsylvania in a sleeping car on the slowest moving train in creation. He'd urged his brothers to accompany him, but they'd just laughed and said he was on his own.

The little blue eyes of the babies blinked at Alex. Then they broke into toothless grins, recognizing a kindred spirit, he assumed. Or leastways, a motherly spirit, he hoped.

"Aaaahh!" she moaned.

He recognized a moan of surrender when he heard one, and breathed a silent sigh of relief.

Tears began to well in her eyes and overflow.

Mayhap not surrender after all. "I thought you wanted children."

"I do," she said, and opened her arms wide, not to him, but to the children.

He could not care. Not being a fool, he handed her the stinksome one. Also, not being a fool, he put his free arm around Alex's shoulder and kissed the top of her head. "I love you, sweetling," he said.

"I love you, too," she replied, even as the babe in her arms reached out a hand and caught a tiny feather floating down from above.

He and Alex glanced at each other in wonder, then burst out laughing. What else could they do?

Babies are said to be an affirmation that God still has faith in man . . .

Transylvania feature, Kelly   **Page 1**
Final Draft

A Lesson in Life

When I first arrived in Transylvania, Pennsylvania, I expected it would be a waste of time. A town with a vampire theme? Puh-leeze! How hokey can you get! [See sidebar titled "Transylvania: Not Your Usual Drac Hideout."]

But I soon recognized that cynicism is a cloak many modern folks wear like armor, myself included. Forget about the depressed community that has managed to survive, and even thrive, in these hard economic times. The more important lesson is one of faith . . . the willingness to believe despite all odds.

If we cannot see, or touch, it must not exist. Doesn't matter if it's vampires, or angels, or God. Even demons.

I have learned in this small Pennsylvania town a lesson that can be learned anywhere. If we open ourselves to all possibilities, miracles can happen.

They did for me.

Keep reading for
an excerpt from

KISS OF SURRENDER

The next book in
Sandra Hill's
Deadly Angels series

Coming in October 2012
from Avon Books

Prologue

In the beginning . . .

In the year 850, in the cold darkness of the Norselands, Trond Sigurdsson snuffled and snored and burrowed deeper into his bed furs. He was a man who held a deep appreciation . . . some might say an unnatural appreciation . . . for his creature comforts, and that included rest. Lots of rest.

In truth, he would not mind sleeping the winter away like a graybeard, which he was not at only twenty and nine, but a shiver passed over his body as he noticed that even the hair on his head felt frozen. Despite his druthers, he started to twitch and awaken. Which was a shame because, as jarl of these estates, there was naught he *had* to do.

So why bother rising? This time of year, the gods graced them with only an hour or more of sunlight, and he was not about to go out to the barns or stables and engage in menial labor. For all he knew, or cared, the teats had already frozen into icicles on his milch cows. Who needed milk anyhow?

Of course, there had been those pleas from the villagers yestereve—and the day before, truth to tell—begging him to come rescue them from an impending Saxon assault. Or was it the Huns? How ridiculous! Surely, even Saxons were not so demented as to engage in slaughter on a cold, dark, winter's day. And Huns were more like to attack the keep itself. Still, he should go check, or send a hird of his soldiers to check. Trond might be lazy in many regards, but he was a far-famed warrior when the mood favored him, and he did have responsibilities as jarl of this region.

With a sigh, he contemplated his choices. He would have to rise, clothe himself, rouse his soldiers who were no doubt suffering the alehead, break his fast on cold fare, have horses readied, and ride through the blistering wind through withers-high snow for a half hour and more. All for foolish, no doubt unfounded fears.

Mayhap later.

Trond stretched out one bare toe to the left, and found naught but cold linens. And to the right. More cold linens. He understood now why he was freezing; 'twas the lack of body heat. Frida and Signy must have slipped out to their own bed closets off the great hall during the night. No swiving to while away the waking hours, he concluded with a jaw-cracking yawn. Then immediately recoiled at his own stale mead-breath. No wonder his concubines had left his presence. No doubt he had let loose ale farts in his sleep, as well, as was his habit, or so some maids had dared to complain. Should he get up and rinse his mouth with the mint water he favored? And wash the night sweat from his odorsome body? Nay. Best he stay abed and rest.

And so he drifted off to sleep, once again.

When he awakened next, the room was alight with the brightest sunshine. How could that be? At this time of the year? Sitting up, he let the furs fall down his naked body and blinked against the blinding light. Only then did he notice the stranger standing in the corner.

He jumped off the mattress and stood on the far side of the bedstead, broadsword in hand. A tall man stood there, arms folded over his chest in a pose of impatience. He wore a long white gown, tightened at the waist with a rope belt, like a woman's gunna or a robe worn by Arabs he'd met in his travels. Despite the loose garment, Trond could see that he had a warrior's body. And he was a beautiful man, Trond observed, though he was not wont to notice such things about other men, being uncommonly handsome himself. In this case, it was hard not to admire the perfect features and long black hair hanging down to his shoulders. Or the strange light shimmering about his form.

"Ah, at last the slugabed rises," the man observed.

Trond had felled men for such disrespect, but that would require more energy than he was ready to exert. "How did you get in here? Where are my guards? Who are you?" Trond demanded.

"It is not a question of how I got here, Viking, but why." He said Viking as if it were a foul word. "Do not concern yourself with who I am but what I will be . . . the thorn in your backside. Forevermore."

"What? You speak in riddles. Are you a god?"

"Hardly," the man scoffed.

"Did Odin send you? Or Thor?"

"Do not blaspheme, Viking. There is only one God."

Trond nodded his understanding. Actually, he practiced both the Norse and Christian religions, an expediency many Norsemen followed.

"I am St. Michael the Archangel," the man informed him.

And I am King David. "Is that so?" he replied skeptically. "An angel, huh? Where are your wings?"

To Trond's amazement, a set of massive wings unfurled out of the man's back, so large that the snowy white tips touched the walls on two opposing sides of his bedchamber, and feathers fluttered to the rush-covered floor. "Convinced, Viking?"

Trond just gaped. Was he in the midst of some *drukkinn* madness? A dream, perchance?

"You have offended God mightily with your sloth," the angel pronounced. "You and your brothers have committed the Seven Deadly Sins in a most heinous manner." He shook his head as if with disbelief. "Seven brothers . . . seven different sins . . . what did you do, divvy them up? Or did you draw straws?"

Trond assumed that was some attempt at warped angel humor. He did not laugh. Instead, he glanced at the doorway and asked, "My brothers? They are here?" Last he'd heard, his six brothers were scattered throughout the Norselands on their own estates, hunkered down until springtime when they could go a-Viking once again. When the angel declined to respond, Trond went on, "What's so wrong with a little sloth, anyhow?"

The angel's upper lip curled with disgust at his question, but then he pointed a finger into the air betwixt them where a hazy picture appeared. 'Twas like looking into a cloud or a puff of swirling smoke, and what Trond saw caused him to gasp with dismay.

"Because you were too lazy to get up off your sorry arse, this is what happened today," the angel told him.

It was the nearby village being beseiged by marauding soldiers. Saxon or Hun, 'twas hard to tell. They were covered with furs and leather helmets. More important, his people were being slain right and left, heads lopped off, limbs hacked away, blood turning the snowy ground red. Women and children were not being spared, either. It was a massacre. One soldier even impaled a still wriggling infant onto a pike and raised it high above his shoulders.

Gagging, Trond turned aside and upheaved the contents of his stomach into a slop bucket.

"And that is not all," the angel said. "Look what pain your indifference has caused, over and over in your pitiful life."

Now the cloud showed Trond as a youthling watching indifferently as other Viking males beat Skarp the Goatman almost to death. Skarp had been a fine archer at one time, but later became the object of ridicule due to a head blow in battle that had rendered him halfwitted.

Then there was a view of himself not much older, fifteen at best, though already a soldier, observing his comrades-in-arms raping a novice nun in a Frankland convent following a short bout of pillaging, short because it had been a poor convent with little of value to pillage. Although he had not engaged in the sexual assault, he'd done naught to intervene, despite the blood that covered the girl's widespread thighs. Odd how he could recall so vividly the red splotches on her white skin! And the screams. Now that he thought on it, there had been much female screaming. And male laughter.

"Was that the beginning, when you first began to hide behind your shield of apathy? For surely, you followed a path of indolence thereafter. Like a slug you are, slow to move, except for your own wants and needs."

One image after another flickered through the mist. Him ignoring a fourteen-year-old dairymaid who claimed to be carrying his child. Later, he'd heard that her father had turned her out, and she'd died of some fever or other.

Then there was his mother seeking a boon from him, which had been inconvenient at the time. The expression of hurt on her face showed clearly, as did the coldness in his. Had that favor been so important to his mother? Why had he not bothered to find out? She'd died soon after of a wasting disease whilst he'd been off a-Viking.

Trond felt sickened when he saw himself and all his sins. What was wrong with him? Why didn't he care? About anything or anyone? It was selfishness, of course, but more than that. To his surprise, he felt tears wet his bearded face.

"I suppose you have come to take me to your Christian hell in payment for my sins," Trond said with resignation.

"Not exactly," the angel replied. "God has other plans for you."

Trond arched his brows in question.

"Satan has put together an evil band of demon vampires to roam the earth harvesting human souls before their destined time. Lucipires, they are called. Our Father has charged me with formation of a different type of band to fight those evil legions. Vikings, to my eternal regret."

Trond's brow furrowed with confusion. "*You* are going to lead Viking warriors in battle against some demon vampires?"

"Not exactly."

Trond didn't like the sound of that. "What exactly?"

"Viking vampire angels," St. Michael explained. "Vangels."

Trond started to laugh. "You are going to turn Vikings into angels? You would have better luck turning rocks into gold."

The archangel was not amused by his laughter. "Viking *vampire* angels," he emphasized. "For seven hundred years, you and your brothers will lead the fight against the Lucipires."

"With your magical powers," Trond said, waving a hand at the cloud picture and at the shimmery light that surrounded the angel, "why don't you just annihilate the demon vampires yourself?"

"That is not the way God works."

Trond mulled over everything that the angel had told him. "Seven hundred years is a long time."

"It is. Or you can spend eternity in Satan's fire."

Death by fire was ne'er a pleasant prospect. He'd seen Olaf the Bitter consumed by fire from a pitch-lit arrow. Yeech! And *eternal* fire? "Not much of a choice there."

St. Michael shrugged. "Do you agree?"

Trond was no fool. He could tell that the archangel would just as well see him on a quick slide to hell. "I agree." But then he asked, "What exactly is a vampire?"

The archangel smiled at him, and it was not a nice smile. Before he had a chance to ponder that fact, Trond's body was thrown onto the rushes where pain wracked every bone and muscle in his flailing body, especially his bleeding mouth and shoulder blades where it felt as if an axe was hacking away at the bones.

"It is done," the archangel said after what seemed like hours, but was only minutes, and disappeared in a fading light.

Done? What is done? Trond felt himself rise above the floor, viewing his dead body, which lay on its one side, curled in a fetal position. Fangs stuck out of his mouth, like a wolf, and there were strange bumps on his shoulder blades.

But then in a whoosh of movement Trond was back in his body, and he was flying through the air, out of the keep, into the skies. Where he would land, he had no idea. He was fairly certain Heaven was not his destination. Nor Valhalla.

One

You could say he was a beach bunny . . . uh, beach duck . . .

*I*f it looks like a duck, and walks, like a duck . . . hey, Easy, can you give us a quack? Ha, ha, ha!"

Trond Sigurdsson, best known here in Navy SEAL land as Easy, gritted his teeth and attempted to ignore the taunts military passers-by hurled his way, especially when he noticed that the bane of his current life, Ensign Nicole Tasso, was standing there, along with Lt. Justin LeFontaine, or Cage, who'd been the one teasing him this time. Cage was LeFontaine's SEAL nickname, appropriate considering his Cajun roots. Cajuns were folks who lived in the southern United States—Louisiana to be precise—and were known to eat lots of spicy foods, drink beer, play loud rowdy music, and were generally wild. A little bit like Vikings, if you asked Trond, which no one did.

He didn't mind the teasing all that much, but no red-blooded male—and, yes, his blood was still red, and, yes, he was still a man—wanted a good looking woman—even one Trond absolutely positively did not desire or even like—witnessing him down on his haunches, walking around like a friggin' duck, making an absolute ass of himself. A duck's ass!

"You're working Gig Squad? Again!" Nicole just had to remark.

As if it is any of her business! But then Nicole was a nosy, bossy, suspicious woman who'd made it her goal in life to uncover Trond's secrets, or improve him, or both. *As if!*

Gig Squad was a SEAL punishment that took place every evening in front of the Coronado, California, officers quarters where Navy personnel leaving the chow hall could witness the humiliation of the punished trainees. Squats. Push-ups. And, yes, duck walks.

His infraction? Jeesh! All he'd done was hitch a ride on a dune buggy when told to jog this morning in heavy boondocker boots for five lackwitted miles along the sandy shore. What was wrong with the ingenuity of taking the easy way to a goal? "Work smarter, not harder," that was his motto. The SEAL commander Ian MacLean apparently did not appreciate ingenuity. Not this time, and not when he'd slept through an indoctrination session, or yawned widely when a visiting Admiral came to observe their exercises, or complained constantly about the futility of climbing up and over the sky-high, swaying cargo net when it was easier to just walk around the blasted thing.

Truth to tell, he was not nearly as slothful as he'd once been now that he was a vangel . . . a Viking vampire angel. Nigh a saint, he was now. Leastways, no great sinner. But Mike—as he and his fellows vangels rudely referred to St. Michael, their heavenly mentor—kept hammering away at him that sloth embodied many sins, not just laziness or indifference. Supposedly, Trond was emotionally dead, as well. Insensitive. Ofttimes apathetic and melanchcly. "You have no fire in you," Mike had accused him on more than one occasion, as if that were a trait to be desired. "Your foolery and lightheartedness mask a darkness of spirit. You are sleepwalking through life, Viking. A dreamer, that is what you are."

So here he was, more than a thousand years later, still a fixed twenty-nine years old, still trying to get it right. Before vangels were locked into modern times, a recent happenstance, their assignments had bounced them here and there, from antiquity to the twenty-first century and in-between, back and forth. He'd been a gladiator, a cowboy, a Regency gentleman, a farmer, a pilot, a ditch digger, a garbage man, even a sheik. A sheik without a harem, which was a shame, if you asked him, which no one did.

And now a Navy SEAL, even as he continued to be a VIK, the name given to he and his six brothers as head of the vangels. He understood the VIK mission and how it applied here, as it did with all assignments . . . killing demon vampires or Lucipires and saving almost-lost human souls. Still, many of the SEAL training exercises were foolish in the extreme, if you asked Trond, which no one did. Walking around like a duck . . . was that any way for a thousand-plus-year-old vampire angel to behave? And a Viking at that!

It was demeaning, that's what it was. And PITAs

like the always bubbly, always on-the-go, always mistrustful "Sassy Tassy" didn't help matters at all. By PITA, he didn't mean a pet lover, either. More like a Pain In The Ass. He tried ignoring her presence now, but it was hard when Cage added to his embarrassment and Nicole's amusement by further taunting in that lazy Southern drawl he was noted for, "Why dontcha fluff yer feathers fer us, Easy?" He was referring to the exercise where a detainee not only waddled around like a duck but flapped his elbows at the same time. Twice the pain and twice the humiliation. To Nicole, Cage added with a shake of his head, "That Easy, bless his heart, is the laziest duck I ever saw."

The final insult was Nicole's smirk at Cage's remark. Oooh, he did not like it when women, especially Nicole, smirked at him. Then she added further insult by telling Cage, loud enough for Trond to hear, "Maybe he should just ring out and save us all a lot of trouble."

SEAL trainees could "volunteer out" at any time by ringing the bell on the grinder, the asphalt training ground at the compound. Actually, huge numbers of those who started out in SEAL training dropped out. Quitting was not an option for Trond.

Once Trond managed to control his temper and the huffing of his breath . . . it was hard work, waddling was . . . he duck-walked toward the woman whose back was to him as she continued talking, in a lower voice now, to Cage, who idly waved a hand behind his back for dismissal of the Gig exercise. At the same time she was standing in conversation, she bounced impatiently on the balls of her boots, as if raring to get off to something more important. The blasted woman had the energy of a *drukkinn* rabbit.

Meanwhile, the SEAL charmer was smiling down at Nicole, and she was smiling back, even while she bounced. Nicole had never smiled at him, but then he'd never tried to charm her, either.

Trond noticed that Cage's eyes were making a concerted effort not to home in on her breasts that were prominent in a snug white razorback running bra with the WEALS insignia dead center between Paradise East and Paradise West. Leastways, they looked like Paradise to a man who hadn't had hot-slamdown-thrust-like-crazy-gottahaveyougotta-haveyou sex in a really long time. Or any other *real* sex, for that matter. Near-sex, now that was a different matter. He was the king of near-sex. *Not that I'm planning any trips to Paradise, near or otherwise. Nosiree, I'm an angel. Celibacy-is-Us. Pfff!* In any case, WEALS—Women on Earth, Air, Land, and Sea— was the name given to the female equivalent of SEALs, which stood for Sea, Air, and Land. A female warrior, of all things!

He shook his head like a shaggy dog . . . or a wet duck . . . to rid himself of all these irrelevant thoughts.

"Are you sure about that, darlin'?" Cage was saying to Nicole.

Trond had no idea what they were talking about, but one thing was for damn . . . uh, darn . . . sure, if he'd ever called Nicole darlin', she would have smacked him up one side of his fool head and down the other.

Trond was still down in his duck position while the other poor saps had risen, their punishment over for now. Without thinking . . . Trond's usual M.O., unfortunately . . . he leaned over and took a nip at Nicole's right, bouncing buttock, which was covered nicely by red nylon shorts. Luckily, he'd been a vampire angel long enough that he could control his fangs; otherwise, he would have torn the fabric.

With a yelp of shock, Nicole slapped a hand on her back side and swiveled on her boot-clad heels. SEALs and WEALS were required to wear the heavy boots to build up leg muscles. Hers were built up very nicely, he noted with more irrelevance, although the shape of a woman's body was never irrelevant to a virile man. And Vikings were virile, that was for sure.

All this exercise must be turning me into a brain-rambling dimwit. Or is it the celibacy?

"What? How dare you?" she screeched.

I dare because I can, my dear screechling. Rising painfully on screaming knees, he stood, reaching for a towel and wiping sweat with purposeful slowness off his face and neck. His drab green t-shirt with the Navy SEAL logo clung wetly to his chest and back. "Oops!" he said, finally.

At Avon Books, we know your passion for romance—once you finish one of our novels, you find yourself wanting more.

May we tempt you with . . .

- **Excerpts** from our upcoming releases.

- Entertaining **extras**, including authors' personal photo albums and book lists.

- Behind-the-scenes **scoop** on your favorite characters and series.

- **Sweepstakes** for the chance to win free books, romantic getaways, and other fun prizes.

- Writing **tips** from our authors and editors.

- **Blog** with our authors and find out why they love to write romance.

- **Exclusive content** that's not contained within the pages of our novels.

Join us at
www.avonbooks.com

AVON
An Imprint of HarperCollins*Publishers*
www.avonromance.com

Available wherever books are sold or please call 1-800-331-3761 to order.

FTH 1111